"I ne

T

"If you haven't already discovered the romances of Anne Gracie, search for them. You'll be so glad you did. She's a treasure."
—*Fresh Fiction*

"A powerfully emotional, steal-your-heart story . . . This magical romance not only warms your heart, it raises your temperature, too. Brava!"
—*Romantic Times* (top pick, 4½ stars)

"Have you ever found an author who makes you happy? Puts a smile on your face as soon as you enter her story world? Anne Gracie has done that for me ever since I read *Gallant Waif* and through every book thereafter."
—*Romance Reviews Today*

"One of the best romances I have read in a long time . . . *The Perfect Waltz* is the book to share with a friend who has never read a romance novel—consider adding it to your conversion kit."
—*All About Romance*

"It's rare to find a novel that's so moving and entertaining at the same time. I'd give a ten to the whole series if that were possible."
—*Romance Reviews Today*

"One of those books that needs to be read from beginning to end in one sitting. Honestly, I couldn't put it down!"
—*Romance Reader at Heart*

"Romance at its best . . . I was captivated by this story . . . Rush out and pick up this book—you won't be disappointed."
—*Romance Junkies*

His Captive Lady

Anne Gracie

BERKLEY SENSATION, NEW YORK

THE BERKLEY PUBLISHING GROUP
Published by the Penguin Group
Penguin Group (USA) Inc.
375 Hudson Street, New York, New York 10014, USA

Penguin Group (Canada), 90 Eglinton Avenue East, Suite 700, Toronto, Ontario M4P 2Y3, Canada
(a division of Pearson Penguin Canada Inc.)
Penguin Books Ltd., 80 Strand, London WC2R 0RL, England
Penguin Group Ireland, 25 St. Stephen's Green, Dublin 2, Ireland (a division of Penguin Books Ltd.)
Penguin Group (Australia), 250 Camberwell Road, Camberwell, Victoria 3124, Australia
(a division of Pearson Australia Group Pty. Ltd.)
Penguin Books India Pvt. Ltd., 11 Community Centre, Panchsheel Park, New Delhi—110 017, India
Penguin Group (NZ), 67 Apollo Drive, Rosedale, North Shore 0632, New Zealand
(a division of Pearson New Zealand Ltd.)
Penguin Books (South Africa) (Pty.) Ltd., 24 Sturdee Avenue, Rosebank, Johannesburg 2196,
South Africa

Penguin Books Ltd., Registered Offices: 80 Strand, London WC2R 0RL, England

This is a work of fiction. Names, characters, places, and incidents either are the product of the author's imagination or are used fictitiously, and any resemblance to actual persons, living or dead, business establishments, events, or locales is entirely coincidental. The publisher does not have any control over and does not assume any responsibility for author or third-party websites or their content.

HIS CAPTIVE LADY

A Berkley Sensation Book / published by arrangement with the author

PRINTING HISTORY
Berkley Sensation mass-market edition / September 2008

Copyright © 2008 by Anne Gracie.
Cover art by Voth /Barrall.
Cover design by George Long.
Hand lettering by Ron Zinn.
Interior text design by Laura K. Corless.

ISBN: 978-0-425-22324-6

BERKLEY® SENSATION
Berkley Sensation Books are published by The Berkley Publishing Group,
a division of Penguin Group (USA) Inc.,
375 Hudson Street, New York, New York 10014.
BERKLEY SENSATION and the "B" design are trademarks belonging to Penguin Group (USA) Inc.

PRINTED IN THE UNITED STATES OF AMERICA

10 9 8 7 6 5 4 3 2 1

Acknowledgments

Writing is in some ways a lonely occupation but for me it has brought a whole new world of friends.

Thank you to Barbara Schenck and Linda Brumley for unfailing encouragement and critical support, and to the Maytoners—a very special bunch of brilliant women who bring new meaning to the word friendship.

Finally thank you to all my readers: you make it all possible.

One

She looked like a drowning madonna. Harry Morant couldn't help but stare. Her face was turned up to the sky, drenched, her skin accepting the misty drizzle the way a flower accepts the rain. Dark hair clung in soaking tendrils around her face, hung in damp ropes down her back, mingling with the dark oilskin draped around her shoulders. Her complexion, pure and creamy, glowed like a pearl in the wet forest gloom. It was shimmering, pale, almost unnaturally so.

Harry slowed his horse, Sabre, and rode closer to the heavy dray grinding its slow way through the New Forest. He kept Sabre to the edge of the road, avoiding the churned-up mud made by carts and carriages.

His companion, Ethan Delaney, gave him a surprised look and slowed his horse also. Harry took no notice. He only had eyes for the woman.

Her face was fine-boned and narrow, with high cheekbones. Her nose was long and straight but her mouth was lush, soft, and vulnerable. Harry stared at her mouth and swallowed.

She sat on the back of the cart, wedged between barrels and packing crates, squashed in like a last-minute piece of baggage. Her feet dangled above the road. Her shoes and the hem of her skirts were covered in mud. Beside her was a small carpetbag.

A slight movement caught his eye. Half hidden by the canvas, pressed up against her skirts, lay a mud-covered spaniel. It watched Harry warily but made no sound.

The woman showed little awareness of the road unfolding beneath her as the four great cart horses churned doggedly through the mud, straining against the load. Her body adjusted without thought to the lurching of the vehicle. She didn't appear to hear the constant stream of obscenities that flowed from the driver's mouth. Occasionally she flinched at the sound of the whip he used so freely.

She didn't take her eyes off the sky. Not once.

A milkmaid, perhaps, on her way to a hiring fair, or some young servant woman traveling to take up a new position. Maybe the carter's daughter. No, he decided, not that—she was not well enough cared for for that. Unless the carter was a brute.

She looked exhausted. Her eyes were huge, dark-ringed, and weary against the pallor of her skin. Her bare, ringless hands clutched the edges of the oilskin, holding them together, keeping the worst of the rain off.

Harry slowed Sabre until he and the woman on the cart were traveling at the same speed. Beside him Ethan made a resigned sound, then urged his horse ahead.

Sabre stepped delicately through the rutted mud of the track, bringing Harry almost within touching distance of the girl. Not a girl, he realized. A woman. Five-and-twenty, perhaps?

Their faces were almost on a level when her gaze dropped and their eyes met.

Harry couldn't drag his eyes away. Her eyes were a deep sherry color. Steady and clear, like gazing into a deep forest pool, pure, but dark with the tannin of fallen leaves.

His gaze devoured her face, her skin, moon pale and glistening with mist. Pale, soft lips, cold from the rain, parted slightly as she looked back at him. Now he was close enough to see each individual droplet of mist clinging to her long dark lashes. He had a mad urge to taste one. He was close enough to touch her. What would she do if he simply reached out and gathered the moisture from her lashes with his fingers, but even as the thought occurred to him, she blinked and the possibility was lost.

Just as well. It was a crazy notion.

The rain had darkened her hair. He wondered what color it would be, what it would look like in the sun. Damp tendrils framed the thin face, clinging to her forehead, her temples, her cheekbones.

Harry's fingers itched to reach out and rearrange a curl that hung almost in her eyes, in danger of tangling itself in her long lashes. Would it curl around his finger if he did? Like a living thing?

Lord, but she was wet! Her gaze hadn't shifted, and suddenly Harry felt a wave of heat surge through him. To cover his sudden confusion he lifted his hat, as if in greeting. Instead he found himself reaching out and placing it gently over her sodden curls.

It sat low on her forehead hiding most of her face. She didn't say a word, just tipped back her head and, from under the brim of his hat, gave him a long, thoughtful look.

"You should climb under cover." He nodded toward the heavy canvas that had been tied over the cart's contents. It would be close and dark in the small space between the boxes and she wouldn't be able to see out, but surely it would be better to be dry in a dark enclosure than to sit open to the sky, exposed to the rain.

She followed his glance, then gently shook her head. He couldn't see her eyes properly anymore, but her mouth moved, and his eyes fastened on the soft curve of her lips. Another wave of heat passed through him.

Sabre sidestepped restlessly under the involuntary clenching of Harry's buttocks and thighs and for a moment he was blessedly occupied with controlling his mount, seizing the distraction to try to get his own body under control.

He should move on. Ethan was no doubt waiting impatiently ahead and Harry was expected in Bath for dinner.

Besides, this woman was some kind of milkmaid or servant girl. Nothing could come of it. And Aunt Maude was already making arrangements.

But somehow . . . His gaze devoured her.

He hadn't felt like this in . . . years.

The forest thinned. Harry glanced ahead. They were coming to a fork in the road. One continued on toward Shaftesbury, and thence to Bath, while the narrower road branched away to the right. He would let fate decide whether he pursued an acquaintance with this woman or not.

He walked Sabre along beside the cart, saying nothing until they reached the turnoff. The cart turned to the right.

So be it, Harry thought. Fate had spoken.

He prepared to ride off, but found himself staring at those small, cold-roughened hands clinging to the side of the cart. Without thought he pulled off his leather gloves and tossed them into her lap.

She caught them and, from under the deep brim of his hat, gave him a puzzled look.

"Put 'em on," he muttered. "Your hands look frozen."

For a moment she didn't move, then she slid first one hand into his glove, then the other. They slipped in easily; the gloves were far too big.

And then she tilted the hat back and gave Harry a smile.

Harry stared, gave her a jerky nod, and urged Sabre to the west.

Much later it occurred to him that he hadn't actually heard her say "thank you." He remembered seeing her lips shaping the words. He'd nodded stupidly and ridden forward, passing the cumbrous dray without noticing, oblivious of everything except that smile.

"Well, that's a turn-up for the books," Ethan said as Harry joined him. "Givin' away hats now, is it? I thought that was your favorite." His gaze dropped to Harry's bare hands. "And, no—tell me not your gloves, your Polish fur-lined gloves. I've envied you those gloves for years."

Harry shrugged. "She was cold. And wet." He wasn't quite sure what had got into him, either.

Ethan snorted. "I'm cold and wet, dammit. Colder and wetter because of the snail's pace you adopted beside that blasted dray. I've been practically frozen many a time since I've known you *and* I'm supposed to be your friend. If you'd wanted to give away those gloves, you could have given them to me."

Harry said nothing. He wasn't going to add to Ethan's enjoyment of the situation by trying to explain the unexplainable.

Ethan persisted, an irritatingly knowing smile on his battered face, "Harry Morant, we've traveled the length and breadth of the peninsular for years, in ice and snow, through battles and burning heat and I've never known you to give away a good pair of gloves, or your favorite hat."

"That was different. I needed them then."

Ethan gave him an incredulous look. "And you don't need them now? Man, it's pissing down if you haven't noticed."

Harry had noticed. He pulled his collar higher and rode on. "So," Ethan said after a moment. "What's her name?"

Harry shrugged.

"She wouldn't tell you?"

Harry shook his head. "I didn't ask."

"Well, where does she live?"

"She didn't say."

"What *did* she say?"

"Nothing."

"Nothing?"

"Nothing."

"God give me strength. And what did you say—no, don't tell me, nothing, or as good as."

"Not everybody is as garrulous as yourself, Delaney."

"No, but, Harry, lad, even stumps have to talk if they're to find themselves a woman."

Harry said stiffly, "My aunt is finding me a wife as we speak." He wasn't "finding himself a woman." The girl on the cart looked pathetic, that was all. And he just . . . gave away his hat.

"Your aunt," Ethan said in deep disgust. "What kind of man gets his aunt to find him a bride?"

"A prudent one."

Ethan made a rude sound. "And you with that pretty face of yours—why, the women line up for you, man!"

Harry snorted.

"I saw 'em at that ball for your brother's weddin', hangin' around you like Spanish flies hang around meat. Now if it was me, with my ugly mug, I'd understand bringin' in an aunt, but you . . ." He shook his head.

"They were about as welcome as Spanish flies," Harry told him.

Ethan exploded with laughter. "Pull the other one, boyo. I heard you creepin' in around dawn every other morning, smellin' of some lovely's perfume—and a different perfume every time."

"That was the trouble," Harry muttered.

"Lord grant me such trouble."

"They didn't want *me*," Harry said.

"Could have fooled—"

"They weren't even interested in talking to me." They'd made Harry feel like a—what was the word the Italians had for it?—*gigolo*. Called to my lady's bed at my lady's whim, but never invited for dinner, never a ride in the park. And of course, never a dance, for with his bad leg he looked a sight on the dance floor.

"Talking?" Ethan's jaw dropped. "Oh, aye, you're famed for your conversation, aren't you?"

Harry gave him a look. Ethan laughed and patted Harry's cheek. "As silver-tongued as the black stump you are, me lad, but at least the ladies appreciated your other qualities."

Harry shrugged. "It was just bed sport." They might have been ladies, but they'd never treated him as an equal, as a gentleman. Just a gentleman's by-blow.

Ethan gave a deep sigh. "Just bed sport, eh? A terrible thing to endure."

Harry couldn't help but smile. "No, but it was harder than you think."

Ethan glanced at Harry's crotch and said, "Well, it would have to be, the amount of use it got."

They both laughed. They rode in silence for a short while, then Harry said, "Every single one of them was married."

"Well, that's only reasonable, isn't it? You wouldn't want to be ruinin' a virgin, now, would you? I'm sure those fine London ladies had done their duty by their husbands and produced an heir or two, so what's the harm in them havin' a little fun with a good-lookin' young feller like yourself?"

Harry thought about it. "They'd made vows, Ethan."

"Aye, but they'd probably no choice in the matter. You know how it is with the aristocracy—they arrange these things. It's only lucky peasants like meself who get the luxury of marryin' for love."

Harry seized the opportunity to turn the conversation away from himself. "If it's so wonderful, Ethan, why have you never married?"

"Too busy up till now, fightin' wars for poor, mad Farmer George. But don't you worry, I've got me eye on a little filly. I'll be married before the year's out, count on it."

"You? Who?" Harry was surprised. He couldn't think of anyone, any girl or woman who Ethan had been seeing lately. "Anyone I know?"

"Ah, well, that would be tellin', and I won't be tellin' until the lass herself agrees." He gave Harry a rueful grin. "She's not an easy lass like yon London ladies—takin' a great deal of difficult wooin', my girl is."

"Difficult wooing?" Harry couldn't believe Ethan was serious. If Ethan was walking out with a woman, surely he'd have noticed.

"Aye, no doubt it's a foreign concept for you, boyo, with that face of yours, but we lesser mortals are obliged to woo our intended. I'm gettin' quite practiced at it—want me to give you a few pointers so you can woo a fine aristocratic lady of your own?"

Harry sniffed. "I've no time for lengthy wooing, and I have no intention of marrying a fine aristocratic lady who'll happily make a cuckold of me in a few years. I've asked my aunt to find me a bride from the middle classes—they're more moral than the aristocracy. Respectability is a passion in the middle classes."

"But you'll still be after makin' an arranged marriage?"

"I suppose so."

Ethan pursed his lips thoughtfully. "I'm just bog Irish, so what I know about the aristocracy or the middle classes you could fit on the head of a pin, but it strikes me that any lass that's been pushed into a marriage of convenience would be more likely to develop a wanderin' eye a few years down the track than a lass that married for love."

"I'm not marrying for love. It's all rubbish, anyway."

Ethan gave him a considering look. "Ah yes, I remember hearing something about that. Lady Andrea or Anthea—some name like that, wasn't it?"

"I was a foolish boy then," Harry said curtly. "I'm done with all that nonsense. I'm a practical man now."

"Oh aye, of course you are," Ethan agreed. "That's why your hair is sopping wet and your hands are frozen."

Harry gave him a sharp look, but before he could think of a word to say, Ethan was saying, "And here we are at the turnoff, so I'll be biddin' you good-bye. Good luck in Bath with your aunt and your respectable middle-class girls. I'll be checkin' on that horse, and I'll let you know if I come across any likely properties for purchase on the way." And with a wave, Ethan cantered away.

Nell Freymore tilted the man's hat back and watched the handsome stranger ride off to join his friend.

What sort of man gave his own hat and gloves to an unknown female riding on the back of a cart? A bedraggled female at that.

He was a horseman, she could tell that from his horse, a magnificent, proud-stepping black Thoroughbred. And from the way he rode with an easy grace that could never be taught, as if he were born on horseback. Papa had ridden like that, before.

She'd noticed him well before he'd got close enough to see his face. She'd been watching his horse. She always noticed horses, couldn't help it. And both his horse and that of his companion were exceptional animals; the black strong and with a long, graceful gait, and the roan ugly, but very powerful. Both horses looked to be very fast.

She wanted one of those horses. Quite desperately. They ate up the miles with such easy speed. It was agonizing being in the heavy dray, traveling at such a frustrating snail's pace. All that could be said for it was that it was as fast as she herself could walk, and easier, because she'd been so very tired when the carter had offered her a ride. She was grateful for it, but oh, to be on a fast horse.

She watched the men, half hoping one of them would

vanish and the spare horse would be left wandering, for
Nell to catch and ride away on. She lived on such fantasies
these days, dreaming her life was different. It was foolish
she knew, but sometimes fantasy kept hopes alive.

She needed that more than anything.

As the horsemen came closer, she'd found herself
dwelling on the taller one. There was something about him.
His friend talked and smiled as they traveled, but he rode
quietly, as if lost in his own thoughts. Self-contained.

She wasn't sure what made her realize he was watching
her. He was still quite a distance away when she knew. She
felt it.

She'd pretended not to notice, had looked away, hadn't
wanted to met his eyes. She wasn't as comfortable around
men these days. She'd gazed up into the canopy, looking
for a chink of blue sky.

It was always a hopeful sign, that glimpse of blue, but
today the sky was as it had been for weeks. Gray. Cold,
pitiless gray.

She'd intended to ignore him—them—as they passed,
as if they weren't there. His friend passed at a smooth, easy
pace: a wink to her and cheery greeting to the carter up front
and then he was gone.

But *he* had lingered, slowing, moving his horse closer and
closer until he was so close she could smell his horse and the
damp wool of his greatcoat. She couldn't pretend any more
that he wasn't there.

Unwillingly, almost without volition, she'd dropped her
gaze.

His eyes were as gray and somber as the sky, his gaze as
intense as hard frost, burning into her. Scorching.

And then he'd given her his hat.

And then she'd really looked at him. At the hard masculine face sculpted by a master, the straight, arrogant nose,
the thin, beautiful, chiseled lips. Masculine beauty incar-
nate.

It was one of those moments when time just slowed, seemingly endless, and yet afterward was over in a flash.

The whole exchange had lasted perhaps five minutes. He'd uttered a few words, she hadn't even spoken. For once in her life her nimble, too-ready tongue had failed her; she had no idea why. And at the junction he'd given her one last burning look and cantered away.

She wasn't sure what had passed between them, other than a hat, gloves, and a scant handful of words. But she'd never forget that face or those curious, cold gray eyes that burned.

Her frozen fingers tingled as slowly the feeling in them returned. The gloves were warm—warm from their fur lining and from the heat of his big, strong hands. They warmed her frozen fingers.

They warmed her bruised spirit even more. The kindness of a stranger. Unexpected. Incalculably touching.

Nell clung to the side of the lurching dray and impatiently watched the countryside slowly slipping by. It became more familiar with every mile. She needed to be home. She needed to be doing. All this slow traveling gave her too much time to think, brood, grieve.

She lifted her gaze to the dark tracery of the almost-denuded trees against the gray sky. Winter was coming. The world was dying around her.

No. No, it wasn't. Nothing, nobody was dying. Only Papa had died. Only Papa. She had to believe it.

She was going home. She would be all right then. She'd get some money together and return to London. And this time she'd find her, find Torie . . .

Where there was life there was hope, they said.

Leaves, crimson and gold, drifted to the ground and lay buried in mud. And the questions, as always, churned unanswered in her mind.

Why, Papa, why? Why not tell me what you intended? Why pretend to believe me and then act in secret?

Evasions, lies, and secrets, always, all her life. And now when it was so important, when she needed to know more than life itself, it was too late. The knowledge gone with Papa to the grave, and only questions remaining.

Why, Papa, why?

The misty rain turned to a soft drizzle and dripped off the brim of the hat. Her face stayed dry. She was all out of tears anyway.

When she'd left home last, summer was bursting forth and the world was green and bursting with life. Now she was returning home, summer's flowers had withered away, winter was returning, and the world was dying around her.

Nell ached with emptiness. It would be better when she was home. She could think more clearly there, work out what to do next.

She might even be able to sleep . . .

Oh God, if only she hadn't fallen asleep that night. She could have, would have been able to stop him. But she'd slept and, sleeping, had lost everything.

She'd barely slept since. She was so tired.

She forced herself to sit up straighter. "We're nearly home and then I'll have money again, and with money anything is possible, isn't it, Freckles?"

A tail thumped and the dog sat up and licked Nell's nose.

"Thanks for the vote of confidence." Nell gave Freckles a hug. What would she have done without Freckles? She'd been such a comfort and a staunch friend.

Freckles brightened at the attention and snuffed interestedly at the man's gloves. She gave Nell such a hopeful look that Nell felt like laughing. "No," she said. "These gloves are not for you."

A pair of mournful brown eyes darted from the glove to Nell and back, demonstrating Unutterable Longing, alternating with Wistful Reproach.

This time Nell did laugh aloud. "Yes, I'm sure they smell very interesting but gloves are *not* for dogs. And look, there is the steeple of St. John's. In another twenty minutes we'll be home."

*T*o Nell's surprise, the main gates of her home were closed. As far as she could remember they'd never been closed before. A chain had been passed through the bars and a padlock fastened it tight.

Puzzled, she walked along the fence line to where she knew there was a gap where the stones had fallen down. Freckles bounded through and Nell followed.

She walked down the drive. The rain had stopped, but she could see nobody around. It didn't feel right.

The closer she got to the house, the stronger the feeling grew. She mounted the front steps and pulled on the door-bell. She heard it jangling away inside but nobody hurried to answer.

She would go in the back way. The kitchen door, at least, was never locked.

"Yes? Can I help you?"

The voice startled her and she swung around. The question had come from a man she'd never seen before. He was a small man of about thirty, neatly, almost finickily dressed in black trousers and a coat with a nipped-in waist and heavily padded shoulders. His thinning hair was brushed forward in an unfortunate attempt at the Brutus style and he carried a briefcase.

"Who are you?" she responded. He looked like a lawyer.

"I am Mr. Pedlington." He looked her up and down as if she were an insect, then sniffed. "There is no work to be had here."

Nell supposed she did look rather bedraggled. She'd walked so far and then there was the rain, and all that mud.

"I'm not after work," she told him pleasantly. "I live here. I'm Nell Freymore."

His eyes popped. "Freymore?" he exclaimed. "You don't mean—Not the late—"

"Yes, I'm his daughter."

Pedlington looked uncomfortable. "I represent the firm of Fraser and Shaw." He paused, as if she should recognize the name.

She didn't. She waited for him to explain.

He cleared his throat. "Has nobody told you?"

"Told me what?"

"Oh dear." He ran his finger around his tight cravat.

His manner was making her nervous. "What is it I'm supposed to know?"

"Er, the house. The property."

"Yes?"

"This house—" He gestured.

"I know which house. It's my home, after all."

He swallowed. "It's not. Not anymore. My firm has been commissioned to sell it."

"Sell it? You can't sell it—it's mine." He didn't seem to take it in, so she added. "It belongs to me."

"No. I'm afraid . . . your father—" Pedlington hesitated. "He lost it in a card game."

"He couldn't have," Nell said. She saw the lawyer was about to explain and added, "I mean I know he loses things in card games—he's always done it. He's lost just about everything he's ever owned. But he cannot lose this house because it doesn't belong to him. He signed it over to me years ago . . ." Her voice trailed off. Pedlington was shaking his head.

"It was all perfectly legal," he explained. "I've seen the documents myself. The deed of both house and land is in the possession of our client. Solely."

Nell stared at him for a long moment, then her knees gave way. She plonked down on the top step, her thoughts in turmoil. "You mean this house has gone, too?" Papa had lost her home, along with everything else? He'd sworn the deeds were in her name.

Lies, always lies.

"Yes."

"Then where am I to go?"

"I don't know. I'm sorry." He cleared his throat and said with a mix of sympathy and officiousness, "But you cannot stay here. You must leave."

Two

Firmin Court, Wiltshire
Ten days later

"The house, I must confess, is a little shabby," Pedlington, the agent, said in an apologetic voice, "but a little refurbishment—"

"It's extremely shabby; in fact the whole estate reeks of neglect," Harry Morant said with a pointed glance at ancient velvet curtains hanging in shreds.

Pedlington grimaced. "I fear the late earl was rather negligent in the fulfillment of his duties . . ."

Harry snorted. Duties be hanged. The way he'd heard it, the late earl had neglected everything except the gaming tables. But his neglect would be Harry's gain.

Pedlington continued, "This property is not part of the overall estate. It came to him through his late wife, so it's not entailed."

They walked from dusty room to dusty room, down corridors hung with faded paper dotted with darker patches to show where paintings had once hung and furniture once stood. If this place wasn't entailed, Harry wondered, why hadn't the earl sold it? He'd sold everything else he could lay his hands on.

The fourth Earl of Denton had brought a large and prosperous estate to ruin. He'd mortgaged it to the hilt, sold everything that could be sold, and even then it hadn't been enough to cover his debts. At last, facing debtor's prison, he'd had a heart attack and died. In the middle of the road, Harry heard.

Then the scavengers had moved in; the bailiffs and those the earl had owed money to, picking over the leftovers of the once-great estate, wringing from it every penny that could be wrung. Pedlington had been appointed by the London firm whose task it was to salvage whatever could be retrieved from the mess.

Harry had heard all about it in Bath. He'd cut his social engagements short, much to his aunt's annoyance. There was no point anyway. The middle-class fathers of the girls his aunt had collected had made it clear to him that they aspired higher for their daughters.

So Harry had ridden down here to inspect the property. Before the late earl had acquired Firmin Court, the estate had been renowned for its horses.

"I don't imagine the fifth earl is relishing the task ahead of him," Harry said. Poor bastard.

Pedlington shook his head. "No, indeed. He's the late earl's second cousin—lives in Ireland—and had no idea of how things stood. The poor fellow got quite a shock when he heard the full sum of it. Fainted, I'm told. What use is a title when it comes with an estate that's mostly entailed and crippled with debt?" He gave Harry a hopeful glance. "At least this property can be sold."

Harry ignored it. This house had been stripped bare, and not recently. The rooms smelled of disuse and dust, but there was no odor of damp or decay. They passed from room to room, Harry insisting on being shown everything, though the house mattered least to him.

"What the—" the agent muttered. One of the bedchambers was locked. The agent tried key after key with increasing annoyance. "It's just a bedchamber, sir, of no interest. It is in the same condition as the rest of the house."

Harry raised an eyebrow. "And you have no key?"

"No, but I assure you I shall obtain it forthwith," Pedlington said in a tight voice.

Harry, uninterested in a missing key, strolled back along the hallway. "Is that all you have to show me?"

"Would you have any interest in viewing the kitchen regions? Or the attics and servant's quarters?" Pedlington's tone said he did not expect it.

Harry made a dismissive gesture. "I'm not sure if there's much point. The neglect is appalling, as is the dust." He added as if in afterthought, "But perhaps the kitchen, though I expect it'll be hopelessly inadequate. And since I've come all this way I might as well look at the outbuildings."

Pedlington, by now sure his trip had been made in vain, sighed. "Yes, sir. We can reach the outbuildings through the kitchen door." They retraced their steps, their footsteps echoing on the bare wooden floor. A good, solid floor, Harry noted, with no sign of woodworm.

Harry repressed a faint smile at the agent's dejection. In the ragged, empty fields that surrounded the house, the grass grew thick and lush. If the stables were as solid as the house, he'd make an offer.

All this place needed was a little money, a lot of hard work, and good management. His legacy from Great-aunt Gert would provide the money; Harry could provide the rest.

The stable doors were ajar. Pedlington frowned. "I'm sure I locked this the last time I was here."

As they approached, a dog stuck its head out of the door. It growled as they approached.

Pedlington stopped dead and eyed the dog nervously. "Shoo, shoo, dog," he called, flapping his hands. "Go away."

The dog stood in the doorway, curling its lip in a low

growl. She was a beautiful animal, a springer spaniel, white, with dappled brown markings.

Harry addressed the dog sternly. "What do you mean, madam, growling at us in that ill-mannered tone? Behave yourself." The dog, recognizing an authoritative voice, gave him a sheepish look, and the tip of her long, feathered tail wagged a little.

"Just as I thought, you're all bluff, aren't you, sweetheart?" Harry squatted down and clicked his finger at the dog. "Come on, introduce yourself."

Squirming in a coquettish manner, the dog edged closer and sniffed Harry's fingers. Her tail wagged harder, she licked his fingers, then rolled onto her back.

"That's better," Harry said as he scratched her stomach. The dog writhed in bliss. Harry straightened and the dog leapt to her feet, her tail swaying gently as she watched him.

Pedlington looked at the animal with dislike. "That animal is not supposed to be here. There is no dog on the inventory. It's a stray."

"Yes, but quite harmless, as you can see. So, let us look at the stables."

Pedlington didn't move. The man was too nervous of the dog.

"I can inspect the stables by myself," Harry told him. "These doors got opened somehow. You go and check the other exterior locks."

Pedlington eyed the dog, then nodded. "I will then, if you don't mind, sir. It wouldn't do if vagrants got in."

Harry stepped inside. The dog followed him and headed straight for a scarf and what might be gloves lying just inside on the cobbled floor. Harry frowned. The items looked too good to be lying on the cobbles but the dog flopped down, placed her paws on either side of the pile, then lay her muzzle possessively on top of it. She had no intention of moving.

"Very well," Harry told her. "You guard that stuff and I'll

look at the stables." Her tail thumped twice, but she didn't move.

Harry looked around him and exhaled slowly. It was exactly what he'd been looking for; stalls for forty horses at least, and the stable buildings looked as solid as a rock—in better condition than the house, in fact. The cobbled floor was clean and well swept, the air inside smelled of fresh hay and—Harry sniffed—horse. *Fresh* horse.

An oilskin cloak hung from a peg and a hat. Harry frowned. It looked like—a sound caught his attention. What the devil? It was a horse in distress. The sound was followed by a low murmur.

He ran down the central aisle of the stables, checking each stall as he passed. Empty—all but the last. The lower door was shut, but the top part was open. He looked over.

A mare lay on her side on the hay-strewn floor, straining to give birth, her bony flanks wet with sweat. She was in clear distress, rolling from side to side. It was not a good sign. A young woman crouched beside the mare, in perilous proximity to the flailing hooves. Harry couldn't see her face.

He shrugged off his coat. "How long since she went into labor?"

"Nearly fifteen minutes since her waters broke." The woman's voice was grim. She didn't even turn her head. She poured what looked like oil from a small bottle into her palm.

"That's too long." Harry hung his coat on a hook.

"I know." She corked the bottle and set it aside. "The foal is presented wrongly."

Harry could see. The mare's tail had been wrapped in a cloth and her distended entrance was visible. He could see the bubble of the amniotic sac protruding, and within it, the shape of a single tiny hoof.

There should have been two little hooves, followed soon afterward by a nose. "The foal needs to be turned in the womb," he said, rolling his shirtsleeves up.

She finished slathering her hand and right forearm with oil. "I know. I'm about to try."

"I'll help." Harry unlatched the stable door.

"No! Don't come in—you'll upset her!" The woman turned an urgent face toward him.

It was her. The young woman from the cart. He caught only the slightest glimpse of her, a blur of pale skin and worried eyes, but he was certain.

"Stay back! She's nervous of men."

Harry ignored her. "Do you *want* to be kicked in the head? You can't help her when she's in this state."

As he stepped into the stall the mare's head jerked and her eyes rolled back, showing the whites. Her ears flattened, her lip curled and she made an agitated move as if to stand.

The woman swore and tossed Harry a bright glare as if to say, "You see?"

Harry did see, but it wasn't going to stop him. She needed help and he knew a lot about nervous mares.

She turned to soothe the mare, using her hands and a low, melodic, rhythmical flow of words. It was mesmerizing, he thought. Any creature would be spellbound. He moved quietly closer and joined in.

"Hush now, my lady," he crooned to the horse, "You don't know me but I'm not going to hurt you. You're in a bad way, and frightened, I know, but we'll soon fix that." He took the mare's halter in his hand, patting and soothing her with voice and touch.

The mare's eyes flickered, but after some more eye-rolling, she seemed to accept his presence and calmed a little.

"Thank you," the woman said over her shoulder, and still in that mesmerizing tone. "I have to say I'm surprised. Toffee is usually very nervous around men."

No doubt Toffee had good reason, Harry thought grimly, eyeing the faint scars on the mare's thin flanks. At some stage someone had beaten the mare unmercifully.

But all he said was, "I've spent my whole life around horses. Now, do you want me to try to turn the foal?"

"No, I'll do it" the woman said. "It's supposed to be easier with a small hand."

She was right, and she seemed to know what she was doing, so Harry positioned himself in a way to protect the woman from any flailing hooves and said, "Whenever you're ready."

It was amazing. For the past two weeks he hadn't been able to get her out of his mind and now, here she was, not two feet away from him. What was she doing at Firmin Court, on her own in a deserted stable, assisting a mare giving birth?

He watched as she waited for a contraction to finish, took a deep breath, then broke the sac with her fingers. Fluid gushed over her hand as she took the little hoof firmly in her hand and pushed it steadily back, slipping first her hand, then her whole forearm into the mare's entrance.

"Is the foal alive?" he asked.

There was a silence, then, "Yes." She frowned and felt around. "One foot is tucked under him. I'm going to try— ahhh—" She broke off on a gasp as another contraction rippled through the big animal, clamping down on her arm.

Harry winced in sympathy. He'd experienced it himself. It was damned painful. He would have expected a woman to cry out, but she didn't make a sound.

She waited until the contraction was over, then pushed and groped, straining with the mare, as she fought to turn the foal's leg around. It was a delicate process. Forcing it could badly injure the foal or the mare.

She grunted, gave a soft sound, then carefully began to pull back. In a slow, steady movement she drew first her arm, then her hand from the mare. She opened her fingers and Harry saw two tiny, dark forelegs emerge, followed an instant later by a nose.

"You did it!" Harry breathed.

She gave no sign that she'd heard him. She sat back on her heels, a second contraction came and the whole foal came slithering out in a messy gush of fluids.

The mare lifted her head and stared at the wet, dark bundle still partially encased in the sac. She sniffed it carefully, then began to lick her baby clean, starting with the head.

The woman didn't move, so Harry slipped a hand under her elbow to help her to rise. She started at his touch and rose unaided in a swift, graceful movement. "She needs to be alone with her colt," she told him and ushered him out of the stall.

She leaned on the stall half door, wiping her hands on a cloth. She didn't take her eyes off the mare and foal.

Harry didn't take his eyes off the woman.

He could see her properly now she wasn't shrouded in rain and canvas. She was medium height, with a thin, intense face. Her skin, now dry and in the gloom of the stables, was still moonlight pale, soft and pure. He'd imagined her hair would be lighter once it dried, and it was, caramel-colored and streaked with gold. Today she wore it caught back on her nape in a loose knot from which tendrils escaped.

She wore an old brown riding habit, well worn and out-of-date. A hand-me-down, he decided: good quality cloth, but too loose in the chest and too tight in the waist.

She turned abruptly and sank to the cobbles. "Oh God, oh God." She crossed her arms, hugging herself with hands that shook. "I didn't think I could do it. I thought she'd— they'd both—" She broke off and took several deep, jagged breaths. "When I felt that foal inside—" Her head dropped to her knees. "Thank God."

"Had you never done that before?"

A few more deep breaths and she looked up. She shook her head. "No." A tear rolled down her cheek.

Harry wanted to taste it. Instead he passed her his handkerchief.

She jumped when his hand touched her arm, as if she'd

forgotten he was there. She stared at the handkerchief. "What's that for?"

"You're weeping."

"No, I'm not," she said quickly. She scrubbed at her cheeks with her hand. "I never weep. There's no point."

Harry raised his brows, but before he could say anything she scrambled to her feet again and turned away to stare at the mare.

She was very thin. And she looked even more exhausted than the last time he'd seen her. He felt a spurt of anger. Someone ought to be taking better care of her.

Who was she? A groom's daughter? A farmer's? Did she live close by?

He couldn't believe his luck finding her again. Fate, giving him a second chance. Harry was not one to waste a second chance; they came rarely enough in this life. But he wasn't going to rush his fences, either. She was tense; he could read it in every line of her body.

"I remember Toffee herself being born," she said after a while.

"She's a beautiful animal. Her Arabian heritage shows. My guess is she's a beautiful mover."

She gave him a thoughtful glance. "Yes, she's fast, too."

Close up, he could see tiny gold flecks in the wide, sherry-colored eyes. Under his gaze they turned wary and self-conscious. She turned back to the stall. "I suppose that's why she's still here. She's impossible to catch."

"You seem to have managed." Harry itched to bury his fingers in those tendrils at her nape, to stroke the tender skin beneath.

"Yes, but she trusts me."

"I'm not surprised. Is she yours?"

"No, no, she's not." She opened her mouth as if to say something else, but closed it again.

Harry said, "From the look of her coat, she hasn't been paid much attention in recent months."

"No."

"Unusual treatment for a valuable animal in foal."

"Indeed."

"On a par with the rest of this estate," Harry said. "The whole place has been neglected for years. Only the stables are fit to be used."

She sighed. "I know."

He tilted his head to look at her. "Not one to run off at the mouth, are you?"

She shrugged.

Harry's mouth quirked. And people called him a stump. He caught a faint whiff of her scent, then sniffed again, trying to place it. Lye soap? Not what a young woman usually smelled of. She'd used it for the birth, he supposed.

They stood side by side at the stall door and watched the mare washing her colt, freeing him of the remains of the amniotic sac and the fluid, learning him with long sweeps of her tongue. It was a sight Harry never tired of.

He glanced at the woman's profile and saw another tear slide down her cheek as she watched the first precious bonding of mother and babe. Her soft, vulnerable mouth trembled. She bit it and dashed the tear aside almost angrily.

I never weep. There's no point.

"Do you live around here?" he asked quietly.

She was silent a moment, then said, "In the olden days they thought animals really did lick their young into shape."

Harry noted her evasion. Fair enough. She knew nothing about him, but that could be rectified.

"I'm Harry Morant, by the way." He held out his hand.

She hesitated, then shook it. "Nell, I'm—just Nell."

"How do you do, Just Nell," he said. Her handshake was firm. Her skin was soft enough but there were old calluses there; at one time she had been used to hard physical work.

She wore no ring. Her clothes were ill-fitting and out-of-date, but the cloth was good quality and the garments well made.

She'd spoken very little, but from what he could make out, her accent was unmarred by any regional burr.

So who was she?

She hesitated, then said, "I suppose you've come for your hat and gloves."

"No, I—"

The stable door creaked open a little wider. "Mr. Morant," Pedlington called. His voice echoed. "Is that anim—oh, there it is. I shall wait for you out here."

Harry grinned. "He's scared of your dog," he told Nell.

"She wouldn't hurt anyone."

"I know. Come on, let us put Pedlington out of his misery."

"Oh, but—"

"Toffee doesn't need you now. She needs to be alone with her colt." Harry took her arm and after a brief hesitation, Nell allowed him to escort her down the length of the stables, toward the door.

After a dozen steps she gave him a sidelong glance. "Does your leg hurt?"

It was as good a way as any of asking about his limp. Everyone did, sooner or later.

Harry surprised himself with his answer. "No, it's been that way as long as I can remember." He usually implied it was a war wound. People were so much more comfortable with the idea of a gallantly wounded soldier than the truth: that he was a lifelong cripple.

As they reached the entrance, her dog bounded forward. "Good girl, Freckles." Nell picked up the scarf and gloves and dusted them off, saying, "She follows me unless I give her something to guard, and I didn't want her near Toffee while she was foaling." She took down the coat and hat from the peg and handed him the hat and the gloves. "Thank you for the loan of these. They warmed me more than you'll know."

Harry took them awkwardly. He didn't know what to

say. Part of him wanted to tell her to keep them, and that was stupid. She had no need of them now, and they were too big, anyway.

She took a thin strip of leather and looped it around the dog's neck, then stepped through the stable door into the bright light.

"Everything is securely lock—" Pedlington stopped dead, staring at the woman.

"This is—" Harry began.

"Lady Helen Freymore, I know," the agent said, sounding none too pleased about it.

Lady Helen Freymore? Harry blinked. Freymore was the family name of the earls of Denton. He'd seen it on all the estate documents. He stared at her.

"Just Nell" was *Lady Helen Freymore?*

The woman who'd traveled in the rain with her muddy feet dangling off the edge of a rough cart, the woman who'd expertly assisted a mare through a difficult birth was *an earl's daughter?* There must be some mistake.

"Lady Helen, you *know* you're not supposed to be here," Pedlington said in a voice that expressed both pity and exasperation. "I explained it all to you before." He darted an embarrassed glance at Harry, then continued in a low tone, "You cannot stay here. The house has sat empty for months, and my instructions are to sell it vacant possession." He stressed the word "vacant."

"I do understand, Mr. Pedlington," she said calmly. "And I have made other arrangements, but the mare was in distress."

"Mare?"

"Yes, she's rather old to be foaling again, and as it happened the foal presented in the wrong position. Both dam and colt would have died had I not been here to turn the foal in the womb."

"Lady Helen, please!" the agent expostulated, turning puce with embarrassment. "You should not even *know* of such things."

She gave him a thoughtful look. "Yes, but I do. I've never understood why females should be kept ignorant of a process that, after all, is their—"

"Lady *Helen*!" The agent cast Harry a mortified glance.

She sighed, but spared the man's lacerated sensibilities further. "The mare used to be mine, so her welfare matters to me."

"Well, she's not yours anymore," the agent said in exasperation, adding, "I was assured you had somewhere to go, Lady Helen."

"I have, of course," she said with dignity. "I was to leave this morning, in fact, but—"

"Then please do so. The animals are none of your business. They will be sold to whoever wants them."

Her pale skin suddenly flushed with color. "You mustn't move her! She's just given birth, and the weather is becoming more bitter by the day. The foal should be—"

"They're not your concer—"

"I'll buy them both," Harry interrupted.

They both turned to stare. "You?" she said.

He nodded. "And I'll take good care of them. My word on it." He held out his hand.

She took it. Her handshake was firm for a lady. He could smell her, the scent of soap, and horse, and fresh hay, and warm, sweet woman. One tug and he could pull her into his arms, taste those soft lips . . .

What was he doing? Harry tamped down on his eager body. He didn't even know her.

But he surely wanted to, lady or not.

"Thank you." She smiled at him, that piercing, radiant smile that had dazzled him in the forest.

And his body thickened.

And his brains scrambled.

And not a single word remained in his head.

"Mr. Morant, I cannot be responsible for any animal left here," Pedlington's voice broke through his reverie. "It must be removed from these premises. Mr. Morant? Lady Helen? I really must insist."

The man sounded distinctly peeved. Harry wanted to swat him like a Portuguese mosquito.

"And Lady Helen, I must also insist that you leave Firmin Court. I did inform you more than a week ago that it no longer belonged to your family, and you have wantonly disregarded my instructions. Indeed, I will go so far to say that technically you are trespass—"

She ripped her hand from Harry's grip and turned on the agent. "How dare you say so! My mother's family have owned Firmin Court for hundreds of years and I have a duty to the estate that"—she made a scornful gesture—"lawyer's papers do not account for. But my bag is packed and my travel arrangements made, and now that my mare is safely taken care of, I'll be gone before the day is out."

"You said that before," the agent said sulkily. "And yet—"

"And you're worried that I'll hang around like a tinker's dog to embarrass the new owners," she flashed angrily. "You need not—"

"What rubbish," Harry interrupted savagely. He turned on the agent. "Address one more disrespectful word to Lady Helen and I'll shove your words so far down your throat you won't speak for a year."

Pedlington's eyes popped, but he clamped his mouth shut.

Harry turned back to Nell, who regarded him with wide, surprised eyes. "I apologize on Pedlington's behalf, Lady Helen. I'm the new owner and you're welcome to stay here as long as you like." *Forever, if you like,* he caught himself adding silently. And where the hell had that come from?

She stared at him and moistened her lips. Harry swallowed.

The agent made a strangled sound in his throat and said with cautious hope. "The new own—you mean—?"

Harry said severely, "I mean I'm prepared to make you

an offer, though I doubt it will delight your masters. However, with the state this place is in . . ." He shrugged.

"Oh, but—"

"Gentlemen, I shall leave you to your business," Lady Helen interrupted. "Mr. Morant, Mr. Pedlington, good day to you both."

Harry caught her by her arm. "You're not leaving." He was filled with an urgent need not to let her disappear.

She glanced at his hand holding her tight and gave him a puzzled look. "No," she said after a moment. "I'll be back to make sure the afterbirth comes away cleanly and the foal is able to walk and drink from his mother first."

Pedlington blushed.

Harry forced his fingers to unwrap from around her arm. "Don't leave," he instructed her.

She gave him a cool look, and he realized he'd barked an order at her in the same tone as used on men in the army. And he'd hauled Pedlington over the coals for disrespect.

He said awkwardly, "We have the matter of a hat and gloves to discuss." It was all he could think of.

Her face softened and a faint smile lightened her eyes. "Yes, of course. Weighty matters."

His body ached as she left. She moved gracefully, unhurriedly. Her figure was not at all fashionable, but his body was hard and aching and he wanted her with a fierce longing he'd never experienced before.

In the forest he'd imagined her as a lost Madonna—madonna of the forest. *Ma donna*—Italian for *my lady*. Nell Freymore. Lady Helen Freymore. His lost lady of the forest.

And this time he wasn't going to let her go.

Even if she was a lady born.

Harry had been courted and flattered by some of the most beautiful ladies in the *ton*. He'd learned full well and to his cost what elegant ladies wanted from Harry Morant: a lusty tumble and that was it.

The young Harry Morant hadn't understood . . . hadn't realized that he was welcome between the thighs of a high-born lady, but that her hand could never be his . . .

He'd learned his lesson at the tender age of three-and-twenty, young, naive, and head over heels in love for the first and only time in his life.

Harry hadn't been naive for years now. And he knew exactly what to expect from highborn ladies.

At the kitchen door she paused and turned to glance back.

He felt a sharp stab of longing. She was neither beautiful, nor voluptuously built, and she certainly employed no arts to attract. But he couldn't take his eyes off her. And his body hardened possessively whenever she was close. A milkmaid or a farmer's daughter, he hadn't cared.

But an earl's daughter. Now that was an unexpected irony.

Three

Nell filled a large pitcher with water and carried it carefully upstairs. She set it on a side table and pulled a key from her pocket. Even in her own house with all the exterior doors securely locked, she still needed her own door to be locked. She turned the key and entered her room for what was probably the last time.

The last time.

She plumped down on her bed at the realization. There was no reason to stay a moment longer. She had to leave Firmin Court. The only home she'd ever known.

She'd dreamed of bringing Torie back here . . .

Torie . . . She couldn't think about her yet.

She looked around her bedchamber, the place in which she'd dreamed her girlish dreams; the room where her girlhood and her dreams had come to an abrupt end.

She'd expected to spend her life here. It was her one security, the knowledge that the deed was in her name and that even in the grip of his gambling fever, Papa could not touch it.

How wrong she'd been. He'd probably intended to transfer the deed—he always meant well, poor Papa, but somehow he never could own up.

Lies, always lies. Even though he'd loved her dearly— she had no doubt of that—he still lied even about the most important things, always feeling he had to protect her from reality, always hoping against all logic that somehow, he'd be able to turn things around, pull the rabbit out of the hat and make everything all right—no, better than all right. Papa always expected to make it wonderful.

Only he never could, and it only ever got worse, until finally here she was, penniless and without a home.

And with Torie lost somewhere . . .

She'd be in London soon, she reminded herself. The vicar had spotted the notice in the newspaper and she'd applied for the position and got it. Companion to a widowed lady who wished to make her first visit to London.

In the midst of her despair, it had seemed like a sign.

She briskly stripped off her clothes. There was nothing like cold water and a good scrub with soap and flannel to get the blood moving. She washed herself as thoroughly as she could—she didn't have time to heat water for a bath— and turned to select something suitably companionish to wear.

Since her come out five years before, she'd always preferred plain, dark-colored clothing. She didn't like to draw attention to herself. She chose a moss green, high-waisted woolen dress with a green and gray pelisse with pewter buttons.

How amazing that the man with the burning gray eyes was here. And that he'd bought her home. And her horse. They would both be in good hands, she felt certain.

She packed the last of her clothes and glanced at the shelf that had housed her doll collection for as long as she could remember. There were a dozen, at least, mostly beautiful dolls in perfect condition. Whenever Papa won at

cards, he'd brought her a doll from London. They sat in a
row, looking perfect, smiling, clean, and angelic. At the end
one doll sagged lopsidedly; Ella, the oldest, the most battered, the most beloved of Nell's dolls.

Mama had made Ella with her own hands. Ella was short
for Cinderella and she was a happy-sad doll. You held Ella
up one way and she was dressed in a ragged, gray dress
with an apron over the top, and her face was sad. But you
turned Ella upside down and her ragged dress fell over her
face and there she was, happy and smiling, dressed in a
beautiful, shiny red ball dress.

Nell had never played with dolls much—she'd always
preferred dogs and horses—but when Mama had died, she
took to taking Ella to bed with her. Ella wasn't just made
by Mama's hands, her clothes were made from scraps of
Mama's own clothes. Nell remembered seeing Mama in
that beautiful red ball gown.

Poor Ella looked very much the worse for wear now,
with one button eye missing, half her hair chewed off by
some dog, and the red dress quite faded. There was no room
in the portmanteau, but Nell could not possibly leave Ella
behind, to be tossed on the rubbish heap.

Nell hesitated, then took out a pair of slippers that
pinched her and laid Ella in their place. It was ridiculous for
a grown woman to want to keep a doll, but she couldn't help
herself. Tossing Ella away would be like tossing Mama
away.

If ever she needed Mama's happy-sad doll, it was now.

She closed the catch, took a last look around her room,
picked up her bag, and left. She did not go immediately
downstairs, but went to the estate office. She wrote a list of
names on a sheet of paper and tucked it in her sleeve, then
picked up her portmanteau and headed downstairs.

Angry voices were coming from the kitchen; the normally dry, precise tones of the agent now sounding pee-
vish and almost shrill, overshadowed by a loud, blunt,

vulgar voice that Nell had known and loved her whole life.

If that agent was being horrid to Aggie again . . . Nell hurried toward the kitchen.

"No, Mr. Finicky-pants, I won't take myself off—" Aggie was saying in a belligerent voice.

"You are trespassing, madam, and—"

"Don't you *madam* me, you little worm! Trespassing?" Aggie snorted loudly. "Who do you think you're talking to? I'm Aggie Deane and I've lived here more years than you've had hot dinners! And while Miss Nell's here, I'm here. It's not right for an earl's daughter to be on her own."

"She should not be here, either. Both of you are trespa—"

Aggie made a loud, very rude noise. "Oh, bite your bum. I'm here to make Miss Nell's dinner and you can bleat rules at me till you're blue in the face, but I'm not budging."

Nell paused outside the kitchen door and listened, a smile on her lips. She should have known no London lawyer would get the better of Aggie.

"Madam, I can have you arres—"

"Pedlington," a deep, masculine voice cut across the quarrel. "Not another word. Take yourself off to the White Hart at once and draw up those papers. I'll meet you there this evening to sign them and to give you a draft on my bank."

"But this old woman—"

"I'll 'old woman' you!" Aggie snapped. "If anyone in this room is an old woman, it's you, carrying on as if—"

"That's enough, Mrs. Deane. I said immediately, Pedlington." Mr. Morant's voice was soft, but it had all the effect of a whip crack.

There was a sudden silence, then Pedlington said in a sulky voice, "Very well, sir, but I take no responsibil—"

"Go!"

Nell listened and heard the kitchen door open and close.

"Well, now, sir," Aggie said approvingly. "I come all

prepared to dislike you on account of you taking Miss Nell's home from her, but anyone who can get rid of that worm-ridden, prating little windbag with so little fuss—well, sir, I have to say—"

"Is that the kettle boiling?" Mr. Morant cut off the speech as Nell entered the room.

"Heavens, yes, and here's Miss Nell, and me without the tea made." Aggie bustled to the stove.

Mr. Morant's eyes ran over her. "That green suits you," he said and Nell felt suddenly self-conscious. She resisted the urge to smooth down her skirts and check her hair. She'd always been almost invisible to men; her one and only season had been a disaster. Half the time she didn't even get a dance unless one of Papa's friends took pity on her.

And yet this man—by far the most attractive man she'd ever met in her life—seemed to give her his complete attention. And said green suited her.

She swallowed. If only she'd met him when she made her come out . . . when life was so much simpler . . .

It was too late now.

"I checked on the mare and they're both splendid. I've dealt with the afterbirth," he told her. He noticed her surprise and said with a quirk of his mouth, "Well, she is mine now, remember."

Yes, Nell thought, but she wouldn't have expected him to deal with a messy job when she'd said she'd do it. It was . . . gallant.

Aggie had laid a place at the kitchen table with a cloth and cutlery. Mr. Morant pulled out a chair for Nell to be seated. He must wonder at her, sitting at the kitchen table, instead of having Aggie bring it through to the dining room.

As a child Nell had loved the warmth of the kitchen. And of late years, as more rooms in the house were closed off and Nell took to minding the pennies, she had found herself gravitating there more and more often. Recently, of course, it was the only practical choice.

"Will you be having a spot of luncheon, too, sir?" Aggie asked. "It's nothing grand—just soup and toast and a bit of something sweet to follow."

Mr. Morant hesitated.

"There's plenty," Aggie assured him.

"Please do," Nell told him. "Aggie will have brought enough for several meals and since I'm leaving in an hour . . ." She felt quite ill at the prospect and wasn't the slightest bit hungry, but Aggie would fret if Nell didn't eat.

"An hour?" Aggie exclaimed in dismay.

Nell nodded. "You knew it would come, Aggie."

"I know, dearie, but so soon . . ." With a sigh, Aggie brought a cloth and swiftly laid a place opposite her for Mr. Morant. "Now sit yourself down, sir, and I'll bring the soup directly."

Mr. Morant sat and Nell immediately wished Aggie hadn't put him opposite her. Those intense, gray, grave eyes burned into her like a physical touch.

"Where are you going?" he asked.

She straightened her cutlery and avoided his gaze. "To London. You will remember to give Toffee a good hot mash each morning, won't you? Her condition is rather poor and—"

"The mare and colt will be well cared for. What will you be doing in London?"

It wasn't his business. Just because he'd bought her home didn't mean she had to tell him anything. She'd had enough people pity her. "A bran mash with boiled linseed—"

"I know how to mix a mash," he said as Aggie placed bowls of soup in front of each of them. "I'm a horseman. I bought this place for the stables. She'll have the best of care. So"—he fixed his gaze on her—"I presume you're going to relatives."

"No," Nell said and addressed herself to her soup with great concentration. At first it was hard to swallow with him watching her, but then his gaze dropped and she spooned the thick, savory liquid up quickly. It was delicious, she was sure, but she tasted nothing.

He sat there, looking big and somber and handsome, his eyes full of questions. Two could play at that. "So, Mr. Morant, what are your plans for Firmin Court?"

He gave her a slow smile, acknowledging her attempt to distract him. Nell swallowed and hoped she wasn't blushing. He probably smiled like that at every female he met. There would be a trail of hearts from here to London, she had no doubt.

"I'm going to breed horses," he told her. "Thoroughbreds. Racehorses."

Nell was silent for a moment, her throat thick with envy. Breeding Thoroughbreds was—had been until recently—her own dream. To bring back Firmin Court to the glory it once had. "My mother's family—this was her childhood home, you know—used to breed horses, too. Firmin Court used to be renowned for its horses."

He nodded. "I know. I heard about it when I was in Bath recently. That's why I came here in the first place. I saw at a glance it's perfect for what I want."

She nodded and tried to be glad that the estate would be cared for now, if not by herself. "Have you been in the horse-breeding business long?" she asked.

He swallowed a mouthful of soup and said, "No, I've been at war for most of the last eight years. But my partner and I have been planning this for years." He made a self-deprecating grimace and added, "Soldiers are always full of plans for afterward, but this time a legacy from my great-aunt helped make the dream a reality."

He finished his soup and made a halfhearted attempt to refuse a second helping. "It's excellent soup," he told Aggie, making her splutter with insincere denial as she plied him with additional helpings.

He might be quiet, but he had more charm than any man had a right to.

Nell asked him more about his plans, and as he explained about his ambition to breed, race, and sell Thoroughbreds, he polished off several thick slices of toast, crunching through it with white, even teeth. Aggie, who loved to feed any man, and couldn't resist the big, good-looking ones, kept the toast coming thick and hot and even added a pot of her best damson jelly.

He gave the old woman a lopsided, boyish smile in thanks and Nell added Aggie to the lists of his female conquests. The elderly woman bridled with delight as he slathered on the jelly. It seemed he had a sweet tooth. And he was quite, impossibly handsome.

Nell finished her meal as quickly as she could, ate half a slice of toast, then rose.

"I'll just go and check on—"

"Sit down and I'll pour your tea," Aggie told her.

"Oh, but—"

"You're not leaving this house without a good cup of tea in you and that's final," Aggie declared. "And I made jam tartlets this morning and you'll eat one, my lady, or I'll want to know the reason why." She placed a plate of small jam tarts in front of Nell much as she'd lay down a gauntlet.

Recognizing from the "my lady" that her old nurse was seriously distressed by her impending departure, Nell obediently sat and began to nibble on a tart. Aggie sniffed and poured the tea.

Mr. Morant devoured a tartlet, then gave Nell an expectant look. "Now, about your future—"

"I'm going to London," she told him before he could ask again. She reached into her pocket and pulled out a paper, which she handed to him. "This list might help you to get started. All highly recommended."

She drank her tea in three large gulps and stood. "I'll just check on Toffee and her colt if you don't mind," she said. Taking a steaming kettle with her, she let herself out of the building.

Harry watched her go, frowning. She seemed very brittle.

"Brought that mare into the world, she did," Aggie told Harry. "Its mam died, see, and it was very weak. Miss Nell fretted over the little one as though it were human. 'Is lordship wanted to put the filly down, but she fought 'im for it and won. Just a little lass she was, eight, or thereabouts, but she stood up to him right proud until 'e gave in. Raised it herself and trained it—the talent runs in the blood—her mam was the same. All that family were mad for 'orses. Miss Nell near broke her heart when her pa sold it for a mighty sum to be raced by other folks."

She shook her head as she wiped the table down. "The new owners treated her cruel hard, nearly killed the poor beast. So Miss Nell scraped together the money to buy her back—she'd stopped winning by then, was a mess of nerves, poor thing." She rinsed the dishcloth and sighed. "Break her heart to say good-bye to that 'orse again, it will."

"What will your mistress be doing?"

Aggie's mouth tightened. "Can't say, sir."

Harry frowned. "Will you be accompanying her?"

"No, she's found me a place as housekeeper to the vicar, so *I'll* be all right," the old woman said with emphasis. "Well, the poor man needs it. Getting old, he is, and forgetful. And he's going to take that dog of hers, too. She'll miss her Freckles something shocking, poor lass, but she can't take a dog, not where she's going."

So she was going alone. Harry didn't like the sound of that. The vision of Nell sitting drenched on that cart haunted him. "Is she not going to some family member?"

Aggie snorted. "The Irish cousins? Not them! Anyway,

if she's to run and fetch for folk—" She broke off guiltily. "Look at me, runnin' on about nothin'. I'll be off and get the last of my things."

Harry nodded absently. He was reading the list she'd given him. On it was a list of names.

"Mrs. Deane," he said to Aggie. "Perhaps you could enlighten me as to the meaning of this. Your name is here, too."

He showed Aggie the paper. She squinted at it vaguely. "Sorry, sir, never was much of a hand with reading."

He started to read it to her.

"It's so unfair," Aggie burst out before he was halfway through. "Near worked herself into the ground, she did, keeping this place goin' when her pa was busy dragging it into the gutter. Miss Nell ran herself ragged, squeezing out every penny she could to make sure nobody on the estate starved. Just about knocked her endways, it did, when she come back and found out all her scrimping and saving had been for naught and that her pa had gambled it all away."

He held up the paper. "And this list?"

"It's everyone who worked here in the last year, sir, them who stayed on after the money ran out, stayed on for Miss Nell. After she got taken away by her pa last Easter, they all got turned off without so much as a penny or a promise. She never knew until last week." Aggie wiped her eyes with her apron. "I dunno where she went. Come back a shred of her former self, she did, and with such sad eyes."

"So these people need jobs?"

Aggie looked up, her old eyes lighting with hope. "With you, sir? They would. Oh, sir, and if you tell Miss Nell, it'd take a load off her mind, it would. Worries about everyone, that girl."

Harry nodded and shoved the paper in his pocket. "I'll be back in a week, all going to plan, and I'll follow these people up then. I value loyalty. No one who worked for Miss N—Lady Helen will go wanting this coming winter." Last winter, he knew, had been exceptionally hard.

"Oh sir," Aggie said, her voice cracking. "I take back every bad thing I ever thought about you."

Harry headed for the stables. He found Nell standing at the stall half-door, watching the scene with a dreamy, oddly wistful expression on her face.

He peered over her shoulder. The colt was on its feet and drinking from its mother. All that could be seen were four long, splayed, spindly legs, a small dark rump, and an excited, waggling tail. Harry smiled. He never tired of the sight. And it was a good omen—the first foal born in his stables.

"He looks a strong little fellow," he commented.

"Yes, he's lovely."

"That note you gave me with the list of names, I'll take most of them on. Aggie told me they're all loyal workers."

There was a long silence, then she said, "Thank you," in a choked voice. Tears glittered on her lashes. She turned away so that he would not see, saying, "It *shames* me that they have been so ill-used. Some day I hope to pay them all what they are owed, but in the meantime . . . Thank you."

He caught a glimpse then of the rage and utter humiliation she felt at her father's careless, spendthrift ways.

She pulled out a handkerchief, blew her nose fiercely, and began to mix a hot mash for her mare. Harry watched. She knew her way around horses; he could not have bettered the mix.

"What will become of you?" he asked her after a few moments.

"Me?" she repeated. "I'm going to London."

He said nothing and didn't shift his gaze. It always worked and this time was no exception.

"If you must know, I have found a position, a job—a very good one."

"As?"

"As a companion to a widowed lady. And there's no need to look at me like that," she added in a crisp voice. "It is what we ladies come down in the world do. I'll probably spend my time reading to the old dear, taking tea with her, and visiting the sights of London—it will be a most agreeable life, I'm sure."

True enough, he supposed. It was the kind of things ladies did. It'd bore him rigid. "No family?"

She shrugged. "Some distant cousins in Ireland that I've never met. And since they've already been burdened with Papa's debts, I have no intention of adding myself to their problems. There is no shame in working for one's living."

He said nothing for a few moments, then, "You could work for me."

She frowned. "As?"

He shrugged. "I'm not sure of the term. You could work with the horses, training them as you've done here. Aggie told me you're born to it. Doing what you did before, only for me, not your father."

Nell stared at him. To stay here and continue working with her beloved horses. Did he have any idea of what he'd just offered her? Her dream on a dish. She closed her eyes for a moment, imagining it. But it was impossible.

She had to find Torie.

She shook her head. "I'm sorry. It's a fine offer, but it's not possible." She had no intention of explaining the real reason; luckily there was no shortage of others.

"Why not?"

"There would be a great deal of talk. Bad enough for you to take on an unmarried woman of gentle birth to work in your stables, but to have an earl's daughter as one of your trainers—it would be a scandal."

"You've already survived the scandal of your father's bankruptcy," he pointed out bluntly.

"Yes, but this would ruin us both. I am an earl's daughter, and you are—you are . . ." She faltered, not knowing what to say.

"I am the natural son of an English earl and a maidservant," he finished for her.

She looked at him in surprise. "Are you?" she said. "I didn't know. I just thought you were not of the *ton*. But if you are what you said, then, yes, that would make it worse. They would gossip about me, of course, but they would hold it against you. They'd resent it that someone they considered an upstart could employ a lady in a menial position."

He snorted. "I don't care what they think."

She laid her hand on his arm and said earnestly, "No, but you must. You seem to be an ambitious man."

She paused and he gave an offhand nod, confirming her impression.

"Well, if your plan is to breed and train Thoroughbred racehorses, it is the gentlemen of the *ton* you must deal with—they are the ones who rule racing, who purchase the horses. If you employed me, those same gentlemen would see it as an insult to their class. They'd *hate* you for it. They'd refuse to do business with you and you'd be politely and invisibly blackballed."

He shrugged. "They wouldn't if you married me."

Shocked, Nell let go of his arm and took two steps backward. "Married you?" She couldn't believe her ears.

"Why not?"

She stared at him dumfounded for a moment. *Why not?* "I've only just met you. You can't want to marry me."

He just looked at her as if to say, why not?

She felt her face heating. Her first ever proposal— probably the only one she'd ever get—and it was delivered with as much emotion as a grocery delivery. She had no idea how to respond.

"Y-you can't possibly l-love me." She flushed as she

heard what she'd said. How gauche! How stupid! Ladies of her class rarely married for love. It was all position and money and land. Not that she had any of that.

He gave her a bemused look, as if she'd said something foolish. "I've only just met you," he reminded her.

"I k-know. Which is why you can't possibly mean what you just said."

"I meant it."

She stared at him, at the big, quiet, self-assured man. A man of few words. But those few had the power to rock her. He'd marry her? The handsomest man she'd ever met in her life would marry her, poor, plain Nell Freymore, the gambler's daughter?

"Why?"

"I think we'd do well together."

"Do you know how old I am?" she asked him. She'd been on the shelf for years.

"I thought about five-and-twenty," he said.

"I am *seven*-and-twenty."

He shrugged. "I am nine-and-twenty. Does it matter?"

She stared at him. He didn't seem to understand. For a moment she considered it. Skinny, plain Nell Freymore, who'd been on the shelf for years, marrying this beautiful man, this tall young lion with the deep voice and the steady gray eyes.

Oh God, but the temptation, just for a moment, was appalling. She could just leave her past, her problems behind, stepping into a secure, comfortable future. It was exactly what Papa had planned for her.

But she would have to choose between this handsome stranger and Torie and she couldn't. There was no choice.

His face was impassive, his gray gaze unreadable. Was he already regretting his impulsive offer? She could never regret it. To know that someone had asked her, at least. Even if the very idea was impossible.

"No, no, thank you. It's very kind of you, but I'm afraid it's impossible," she said softly.

"I'm not being kind," he said, still in that calm, deep voice.

"I'd better leave now," she murmured. "The coach will be passing the church in an hour or so."

He said nothing, nothing about the coach and nothing about his amazing offer. It was as if he'd never spoken.

Nell took three more steps, then stopped and slowly turned, the woman in her unable to leave it alone. "I have to know," she said finally. "I have a question for you. Will you tell me the truth?"

His eyes narrowed, but he said, "I will."

She examined his face intently and then gave a little nod. "Is it because of my title? The reason you asked me, I mean."

"I suppose that's part of it," he admitted. "It would do a man no harm to have a titled wife."

She nodded. "And my skill with horses would be useful, too, I expect."

"It would. I don't deny it."

"I see. I thought as much. Thank you for your honesty." She turned to leave again.

He cleared his throat. "But they are only part of the reason I asked you to be my wife."

She turned back. "What else could there be?"

He swallowed and looked uncomfortable.

Stupid Nell, she thought. What was she doing? Angling for compliments now? Pathetic.

His face darkened and he cleared his throat.

"No, don't worry—" she began. "I didn't mean it." She turned proudly away.

He cleared his throat. "The thing is, I am—" He swallowed again. "You're lovely and I'm very attracted to y—"

"Stop it. Please." She held up her hand. "I don't want to listen." She didn't want, couldn't bear labored, insincere compliments for the sake of misguided male gallantry.

He stared at her. "You did ask. And I thought women wanted to hear such things."

"Not when they're not true. And we both know they're not."

His brows snapped together. "Are you calling me a liar?"

She gave a miserable shrug and mumbled something about if the cap fits.

"Well, it damned well doesn't." He stepped up to her, so close she could smell him, the faint scents of leather and horses and expensive cologne and man.

She forced herself to stand her ground. She'd asked for this, so she must face the consequences.

His cold gray eyes blazed with emotion as he said in a low, vehement voice, "I am not a man of words. I have been likened, in fact, to a stump. My attraction to you is not an easy thing to admit to, especially since you've turned me down, but I promised you honesty. And that's what I gave you—every word of it."

Nell could not meet his eyes. She wanted to believe him—what woman wouldn't? But she was under no illusions about her own looks. She'd had her nose rubbed in them all her life.

He'd been kind again, thinking she wanted compliments—even false ones—and then she'd shamed him, exposing the lie. She wanted to sink into the ground.

There was a long silence, then he added quietly, "If any man called me a liar as you have done, I would knock him to the ground."

She flinched and braced herself.

He said softly, "You may think me a bastard, but I've never harmed a woman yet, and I don't intend to start. But since you refuse to take my word, and since I refuse to let you believe me a cozening, insincere liar, I must resort to the most basic way of convincing you that I do indeed find you most attractive."

She looked up, puzzled.

"Lady Helen," he said. "Forgive me, but—"

To Nell's shock, he kissed her. With complete assurance, he seized her by the waist and planted his mouth very firmly over hers. She'd never experienced such a thing in her life. Her mouth had been open with surprise and the hot male taste of him coursed through her body like a red-hot poker sizzling in a jug of spiced wine.

She made no attempt to struggle, had no thought of it. She was too shocked, too . . . amazed by the sensations surging through her. One hand waved ineffectually, then settled lightly on his shoulder. Her other hand was caught between their bodies and gradually she became aware of what the back of her hand was pressed against: his male parts. His very hard, very aroused male parts.

She should have pushed him away, struggled, something, anything, but her body seemed to have no will of its own. The taste and heat and power of him poured into her; she was helpless to resist. And all the time she could feel him, there against her fingers, hard and hot and growing larger and harder by the minute. Like a big human stallion, throbbing and urgent against her flesh.

It did not last long—less than a minute, she thought later, though at the time it felt like forever, and then he released her and stood back.

They were both breathing heavily.

She tried to speak but there were no words.

"Forgive me," he said stiffly. "I should not have kissed you, I know; not on such short acquaintance. But I wanted you to know that what I said was no lie. None of it. I realize my suit is unwelcome . . . but I wanted you to know." He gave a jerky bow.

Know? Her whole body throbbed with knowledge.

He did find her attractive. She blinked. Very attractive, he'd said, and his body had demonstrated . . .

No man had ever found her very attractive. The only time she'd ever attracted the attention of a man had been for quite other reasons . . .

He'd made her no false promises—God, as if she believed in promises anymore. But Harry Morant had given her evidence. Hard evidence.

Her fingers still tingled. Very hard.

But no matter how tempted she was, a marriage between them was just not possible. She could not make the choice he would demand of her once he knew. She felt like weeping, but she had no tears left.

There was no question of what—who—she would choose. But it was so hard. The most beautiful man she'd ever met in her life and he *wanted* her.

Every part of her body throbbed with the knowledge of that wanting. Her blood was afire with it.

She managed to acknowledge his bow with a nod. "Thank you," she said in a choked voice, "but my answer stands." Head held high by some miracle of training, Nell managed to walk away from him with some semblance of dignity.

She felt him watching her leave. A woman could burn forever in the banked passion of those cold gray eyes. That was another part of the problem.

She'd endured much in her life and she knew she was strong. She mightn't have beauty, but she had strength. Nothing and no one could break her spirit—not even this man.

But he could easily break her heart. And he would, when he found out what she'd done—birthed an illegitimate daughter whom she loved more than life itself.

When Harry Morant, who'd spent his life living down his own birth, discovered that, he would turn away from her. And that would break her heart.

If it wasn't already broken . . .

Until now, Nell hadn't ever thought of herself as a

coward, but as she marched away from Harry Morant, her head held high so he wouldn't imagine she cared the snap of a finger for what had just happened, she had to admit it: she was a coward through and through.

Four

Nell sat squashed between a large man who smelled
of cloves and another, even larger, who reeked of
onions. She felt a little queasy. It wasn't their combined
smell though; it was that she was leaving her home forever.

Her home, and all her girlhood dreams.

They weren't anything special, her dreams; just a man
to love and horses to breed. And babies . . .

Torie . . .

She faced the back of the coach. Through the window of
the coach she could see the village getting smaller and
smaller, until at last she could only see the church spire.
Then, finally it was gone.

The stagecoach lumbered along the muddy road, swaying and jolting. It was marginally faster than the dray she'd
arrived in and a great deal warmer and drier.

Her two neighbors had spread themselves comfortably,
knees planted wide apart and arms relaxed comfortably,
while she was wedged in tightly. Two couples sat opposite,
the men taking up twice the space of their wives, even

though both women were comfortably built and one of the men was positively skinny. Why was it that men always took up more than their fair share of space? At least they kept her warm, she told herself, albeit in a clovey, oniony way.

And she was on her way to London, not directly, but soon. The arrangement was to meet her new employer in Bristol, then she and Mrs. Beasley would travel to London.

And then . . . then she would resume her search, her search for her daughter. For Torie.

She ached at the thought. Her breasts throbbed. She should have removed the bandages that bound them before she left. Her milk was long gone.

But, oh, how she ached for her baby, for her precious, tiny daughter. She'd kept the bandages on, reluctant to lose even that, a frail, tangible link, to the child that was . . . somewhere.

Lost. Stolen away.

Victoria Elizabeth . . . Torie, after Nell's mother.

Nell folded her arms across her breasts. She ached with unanswerable questions. Who was feeding her little Torie now? Was anyone? Oh God, let her be alive, she prayed.

That torment was always with her, like a coal burning through her consciousness, day and night, the fear that like everyone else in her family, Torie might be—no! She couldn't think like that.

Papa was misguided, but he wasn't evil.

But he'd had no right to take her baby from her, no right to steal her away in the night. If only she'd divined his intentions . . . but he hadn't breathed a word. If she'd known, she would have fought tooth and nail for her daughter.

Guilt wracked her. She should never have let herself fall asleep. Only, after the birth she'd had a touch of fever and she was so tired, so tired . . .

What had Papa done with her daughter? Where had he taken her?

They'd found him dead at the crossroads, on the way

back from London. Dead, and the whereabouts of her baby gone with him.

Dead men tell no tales.

She knew why he'd done it. He'd told her when he first came to see her after locking her away for nearly six months. For her own good. To save her reputation. So she wouldn't have to suffer for his bad judgment . . .

But she'd told him no. That she wanted to keep her child. That she loved Torie.

He'd assured her she wouldn't have to live with the results of his mistakes. That she could make a new life, put it all behind her, forget . . .

As if Nell could ever forget the baby she'd carried beneath her heart all these long months. In Nell's mind and heart, her little Torie had no connection with the events that had started it all, for which Papa blamed himself so deeply.

It was true that when she'd first discovered she was pregnant, she'd started off despising "it," hating "it," wishing "it" had never been conceived, but then . . . the first time she'd felt that tiny flutter of life in her womb . . .

She'd never felt anything like it.

She remembered placing her palm over the spot, and waiting, breathless, until she felt it again. And then, suddenly, she didn't have a "thing" in her belly, she had a baby. A tiny, innocent baby.

A child that had nothing to do with anyone else, that had nothing to do with the ugliness that had preceded it. There was just Nell and her baby.

And in the long, lonely months in the strange house where Papa had taken her, shut away with strangers—kind strangers, but strangers, just the same—she'd fallen more and more in love with the tiny helpless creature growing inside her, moving, kicking, wrapping herself around her mother's heartstrings with every movement.

Nell's baby, Nell's child. Nobody else's.

She would sit for hours in the chair beside the window—they wouldn't let her outside for fear she might be seen—with Freckles snoozing beside her. Freckles was the only friend from home Papa had permitted. He didn't even trust Aggie not to gossip. Nell was to be hidden away with strangers, under a false name. Papa wasn't going to let her suffer for his mistake . . .

As if locking her away from everything she knew and loved—except her dog—wasn't making her suffer. Typical Papa, always locking the stable door after the horses had escaped.

So she sat with Freckles, growing a baby under her heart, dreaming of how it would be and making plans. She would take the baby home to Firmin Court, to where Mama was born, and Nell would teach her everything Mama taught Nell—and more, because Mama had gone and died when Nell was seven.

Her. She'd somehow never thought it would be a boy. But she wouldn't have cared if it was. She only knew that she loved it.

And then the long, lonely labor through the night, as pain after pain shafted through her until she thought she might die of it, as Mama had. And finally at dawn, as the clear, gray, gold light spilled over the horizon, she had her baby.

Her daughter. Her precious, beautiful Torie . . . a tiny, fiercely wailing creature with a red face and gold fuzz and a mouth that was pure, furious rosebud, and tiny little fists with fingers coiled like exquisite, budding ferns.

And when the midwife had put the tiny creature to Nell's breast, and the angry wails cut off in mid-scream and the little mouth suckled, a fierce love swelled up inside Nell until she felt she would burst with love and joy and pride. She had a daughter.

She'd hugged Torie to her and whispered in her miraculous, delicate ear that she'd love her forever and wouldn't ever leave her . . .

But two weeks later Papa came, his first visit since he'd left her there all those months ago, and the next morning he and her baby were gone.

She blamed herself. She should have known, should have thought, should have suspected . . .

But she'd *told* him she loved her baby. She showed him her beautiful daughter and told him with such pride that she was naming her Torie—Victoria Elizabeth—after Mama.

And Papa had wept and said Nell was his good, brave girl and that Papa would make everything all right.

She hadn't realized what he meant. As far as Nell was concerned, everything *was* all right. Her childbed fever was passing and she was awash with love for her daughter and for the world. Her baby was strong and healthy and she didn't care about anything else. She didn't care about not being married. She didn't care about people finding out. She only cared about her daughter.

Besides, Papa was always making vague and futile promises to make everything all right. He never kept them, so she'd thought nothing more of it.

And oh, what a mistake that had been.

As usual Papa only saw what he wanted to see. And he could only see Nell's baby as a child of shame, a mistake— a mistake for which he blamed himself.

And so while she'd slept, he'd sneaked into her room at night and removed the mistake, leaving a letter that instructed her to forget all about it . . .

It, not her.

As if she could. As if anyone could, even if they wanted to. And Nell didn't want to. She wanted her baby, her precious, daughter, her Torie.

"Do you mind, miss?" One of the men in the coach— the clove one—addressed her, a little embarrassed.

Nell looked up startled. She'd forgotten where she was. Everyone in the coach was staring at her.

One of the women opposite leaned forward and patted

her knee. "You was rocking, miss, back and forth, like you was trying to put a babe to sleep. Only there weren't no baby. It made the gentlemen uncomfortable-like."

Nell looked down. "I'm sorry," she said in a choked voice. "It won't happen again."

W hat on earth had he been thinking? Making an offer to a girl he'd known a few hours—and an earl's daughter at that.

Mounted on Sabre, his favorite horse, Harry rode slowly, leading a string of horses. Behind him rode Ethan, and several grooms, each of them leading horses. Harry was moving most of his stable from the Grange, his brother's property on the coast, to his own place.

The negotiations for Firmin Court had left Pedlington wrung out and disappointed and Harry quietly elated. Harry had brought the estate books from the house and had pored over them for several hours with a grim expression while Pedlington watched, getting more and more glum.

And he asked questions that intimidated the agent; savage questions like, "How many local families have starved since your firm took possession of the property?"

In the end, Harry had been so ruthless in pointing out the many severe defects in the property that the agent even expressed surprise that Harry would even take on such an apparently unsatisfactory property.

But Pedlington was a townsman, for whom peeling, faded wallpaper was a defect. He didn't see the property the way a countryman did. Firmin Court had been badly run down, but fundamentally it was everything Harry had ever wanted.

And now it belonged to him. A home of his own.

It was the first part of his dream come true; he should have been ecstatic. He was ecstatic, he reminded himself. It was just that he couldn't get that unnerving moment of madness out of his mind. What ever had possessed him?

You could always marry me.

Fool! He hadn't been thinking, that was the trouble. Or at least, not with his brain.

It had been too long since he'd lain with a woman. That's why he'd acted so uncharacteristically, so impetuously.

It was the only explanation he could think of.

His brain had been so scrambled with desire for Lady Helen Freymore that he'd spoken without thought.

Thank God she'd turned him down.

Of course she had. She was an earl's daughter, a lady. Ladies of the upper crust were out of bounds for the likes of Harry Morant. She might be down on her luck now, but all those born-to-rule instincts were deep within her—look at the way she'd pokered up when Pedlington became too pushy; that graceful spine had stiffened and those soft eyes had spat fire and ice and she'd coolly put the man in his place.

Harry had become more aroused than ever, dammit.

No, he knew the sort of girl he wanted; a quiet, well-dowered, middle-class girl who'd respect him and not make a fool of him. She'd dutifully allow him access to her bed and that would be his problem sorted.

And her eyes and mouth wouldn't turn a man's brains to mush. Or make him blurt out things he didn't mean to say.

"There's a village down there in the valley." Ethan interrupted Harry's reverie. "Will we stop for some lunch?"

They'd set out with a large basket stuffed with food—compliments of Harry's foster mother, Mrs. Barrow, but they'd made it a slow journey and her food was finished.

"No," Harry decided. "Send one of the men down to buy some pies or some bread and cheese and ale. We'll be at Firmin Court before sundown." He'd deliberately chosen the back roads so as not to draw attention to the fact that he was moving so many valuable animals.

It would have been safer to move them quickly, but he'd kept to an easy pace. He was hoping to race several of the horses in the next few months and he didn't want them to lose condition.

From his vantage point on the hill, he watched the villagers moving about their business. Behind the church, a pair of lovers were making a secret tryst; a stocky young man and a young girl, lissome and pretty. Harry watched them for a moment, touching, kissing, murmuring sweet nothings, then he turned his face away.

Young fool. Letting himself get entangled by love.

He hoped the boy survived it.

Y-you can't possibly l-love me. And that damned lower lip of hers had trembled, sending a jolt of raw passion through him. His body stirred at just the memory.

Of course he couldn't love her—he'd only just met her, and he didn't believe in love at all—especially not the at-first-sight sort of nonsense.

What he felt was desire, lust, whatever you cared to name it. His whole body was racked with it every time she was close. And you didn't marry for desire; you took a mistress.

Harry gazed down at the thatched roofs of the village. He needed to make a visit to the city—and soon, if that's where abstinence got him.

Not London. Lady Helen would be in London by now. Being a lady's companion. Stupid job.

He rode on, brooding. A lady's companion should be the same as a man's—a dog. It wasn't a job for a grown woman. She should be married, with a brood of children keeping her busy, not attempting to entertain some rich, bored old lady.

No, he wouldn't go to London. He'd write to his aunt again and remind her she still hadn't found him a likely wife. He needed to be settled, getting on with his life. He needed relief from the tension that kept him like a taut bowstring. Traveling to the city took up too much valuable time, and taking a mistress in the country simply wasn't an option.

The country wasn't like London, where bored married

ladies of the aristocracy played musical beds and everyone turned a blind eye. In London a man could keep a mistress in a discreet house that nobody knew about and visit her whenever he wished.

In the country everyone found out about everything. And blind eyes were for beggars.

It wasn't respectability that bothered him. He couldn't care less what people thought of him, and in any case, few people ever blamed the man.

The woman, on the other hand . . .

He had few memories of his real mother; she'd died when he was a little boy. But he'd learned the word "whore" as a toddler, from hearing people fling it at her in the street, over and over, some to her face, and others behind her back. The earl's whore and her little bastard . . . That was Harry.

He wasn't a bastard at all, not legally. His natural father had bestowed a handsome dowry on his pregnant maidservant and the village smith, Alfred Morant, had married her well before Harry was born.

People still called Harry a bastard.

And when the blacksmith—Harry never used his name—when the blacksmith drank too much, which was often, he'd call his pretty blonde wife a bloody damned whore as well, and thump into her soft flesh with his huge, meaty fists.

The moment the man started drinking, his mother locked little Harry away so he'd escape the broken bones and bruises she suffered. A vicious kick had broken Harry's hip as a toddler. He carried the limp to this day. After that his mother took the beatings for him.

It was because Alfred loved her, Mam would explain to Harry afterward, weeping. Alfred had always loved her and wanted her, and he was just angry that the earl had had her first . . . But what could she do? He was the earl.

Mam had died when Harry was five or six. One blow too many and an unborn child died with her. "Whose child is this one, whore?" the smith had bellowed, even though Mam had never looked at another man. She never even left the house anymore—she couldn't face the village eyes assessing her bruises, the eyes that said she deserved every one.

After his mother's death, Harry's life had become much harder. The smith had kicked him out and he'd lived like a stray dog, on scraps from the other villagers.

Then one day Barrow, a groom for a great lady, had brought in a horse to be shod and found Harry bruised, half-starved, and shivering out the back. He'd brought him home as a gift to Mrs. Barrow, a childless, motherly woman, who'd taken one look at him and taken him into her warm heart.

The Barrows worked for Lady Gertrude Freymore, the earl's dragonlike spinster aunt. That austere lady had taken one look at Harry and realized the blood connection. Along with his half brother, Gabe, she'd raised him as a gentleman and when she died, she'd left him a legacy.

But Harry never forgot his beginnings . . .

He would never take a countrywoman as mistress. Marriage was his only option. He would write to his aunt as soon as he got home.

The thought warmed him. He had a home of his own for the first time in his life. And soon he would have a wife to warm it. And settle his . . . brains.

"*T*is a grand place you've got here, Harry, lad," Ethan exclaimed enthusiastically. As soon as they'd settled the horses into the stables, checked on the work that had been done in Harry's absence, and informed the new cook that there would be eight men to feed, Harry had taken Ethan on a tour.

"Those stables are magnificent. There's everything a man could want—even the remnants of a training track, if my eye doesn't deceive me."

"It doesn't," Harry said, grinning. "Lady Helen's ma-

ternal grandparents—this was their estate, you know—
were famous for breeding Thoroughbreds. They bred and
trained a number of winners in their day."

Ethan quirked his eyebrow. "Lady Helen, eh? And I gather
she's a fine, pretty lass, this Lady Helen."

Harry blinked. "What makes you say that?"

Ethan shrugged. "You've only mentioned her about a
dozen times in the last few days."

Harry scowled. "That's only natural—it's her home I've
bought."

Ethan nodded solemnly. "Natural, yes, the very word I'd
have used."

"Those fences will need to be renewed before winter
sets in." Harry ignored the knowing amusement in Ethan's
eyes and pointed at the offending fences. "Some of them are
so rotted they'll splinter if a horse rubs against them."

"Indeed they will," Ethan agreed, sobering. "First thing
in the morning I'll get a couple of the lads to go over all the
fences and make an estimate of what we'll need."

"I've already done it," Harry told him. "The lumber
should arrive tomorrow."

Ethan whistled. "You wasted no time, did you?"

Harry made an offhand gesture. "I want to get as much
done as I can before winter sets in." The truth was he was
burning up with unfulfilled desire and tramping around in
the cold, muddy fields was just the thing to dampen any
lingering . . . energy.

"What's that place?" Ethan pointed to a cottage on the
edge of the estate, close to the village. "It looks deserted."

There was obviously nobody in residence; it was a chilly
day and every other house in the village had smoke coming
from the chimney. The garden in front of it was unkempt
and ivy straggled up into the thatch.

Harry called one of the local men over. The day he'd
signed the papers to purchase the estate, he'd returned and
with the help of the vicar and Aggie had found half a dozen

men to start work on the most urgent of the repairs. "What's that house?" he asked the man. "Who owns it?"

"You do, sir," the man said. "Used to be the estate manager's house, but when the money run out, 'e didn't stay on. Well, 'e wasn't from around here—a foreigner, 'e was, from up Leicester way, I do b'lieve. Nobody lives there now, 'cept spiders, I reckon."

Harry thanked him and the man went back to work. Ethan stared at the cottage with narrowed eyes. "Mind if I have a look at it, Harry?"

"Of course not. Though I don't see why you're so interested."

Ethan didn't answer. He was halfway to the cottage. Curious, Harry followed him. There was a wooden gate that groaned as they pushed it open, and weeds in the front garden, knee-deep.

Ethan prowled around it, peering into the diamond-paned windows, squinting up into the deep eaves, and stripping ivy off the walls to examine the surface beneath. "Do you have a key?" he asked Harry.

"I'm not sure." Harry pulled a bunch of keys from his pocket and examined the front door lock to see if any of them might fit.

"No need," Ethan said suddenly. He'd tried the door and it just opened; it was on a latch. The two men went inside. It was dusty and there were cobwebs, but otherwise the air was sweet, with no smell of mildew or damp. The stairs creaked a little under the two men's weight, but there was no sign of rot.

"It's exactly what I need," Ethan said, as he inspected the last of the three bedrooms. Like the main house, the cottage was solid and only in need of superficial repairs. "Will you sell it to me?"

"Of course, if that's what you want," said Harry, surprised. "But why do you want to buy a cottage? It's not as if you need a house of your own."

"Ah, but I will," Ethan said, picking at some flaking whitewash with his thumbnail.

"I assumed you'd bunk down in the big house, as we did at the Grange. What's the point of a house with ten bedrooms otherwise?"

"I don't mind where I lay me head, as you well know," Ethan said. "But a wife expects to be mistress of her own home. If I had a snug wee cottage all ready, it might tip the decision in me favor."

"A wife? You don't have a wife."

"Aye, but I told you I was doin' some serious courtin'," Ethan reminded him. "And since you're talkin' about getting a lass of your own, I'll need me own place. Two wives under the one roof? Not on your life, boyo."

"No, I take your point—but who is this mystery woman, Ethan?"

Ethan winked. "Wait and see. Don't you worry about my love life—you go off and do some serious courtin' of your own. What about this Lady Helen of yours?"

"What about her?" Harry said, instantly defensive. "I told you I only met her for a few hours. It's nonsense to assume she means anything to me. Why should she? I hardly know her. I merely mention her from time to time because she has left her imprint on this place. From what people have told me, she single-handedly kept half a dozen families from starvation last year when the crops failed so disastrously, so it's hardly surprising if her name keeps coming up. Anyway she'll be in London by now, showing some old lady the sights and reading to her, and taking *tea*." His vehemence surprised him and he cleared his throat and looked out of the window.

Ethan gave him a long look. "Aye, I can see you haven't given the lass any thought at all. Not a bit."

"That's right. Now, I'll just go and see how those men are doing," Harry mumbled and marched out of the cottage, leaving Ethan and his annoyingly smug expression behind.

Ethan just didn't understand. His frustrating courtship was causing him to imagine everyone else was in the same state.

Harry had no time to think of women; he had an estate to get back into shape. And when he had time, he would pop up to Bath where Aunt Maude would have found him a suitable bride. No trouble at all.

*F*or the next two weeks Harry and Ethan raced to get as much outdoor work done as they could before the first snows arrived. They mended fences, repaired outbuildings, and replaced broken slates on the roof. Inside the house a team of local women and men scoured the house from top to bottom, leaving it bare and clean.

Harry and Ethan worked like demons, snapping out orders as though they were back in the army. The estate workers soon found no one could slip shoddy or slapdash work past them. Harry and Ethan were hard taskmasters but since they worked the hardest of anyone, nobody minded. The failure of the harvests the previous year and the closing down of the big house meant most of them had faced the prospect of a very bleak Christmas. And possible starvation.

Now, with employment, and solid currency in their pocket at the end of every week, there was a feeling of renewed hope in the air as they settled into a routine of hard, satisfying work.

At the end of the third week Harry received his first visitors. He had no idea they were coming; one minute he and Ethan and the head groom, Jackson, were at the front of the house discussing whether an impending bank of clouds betokened snow, and the next minute two sporting curricles hurtled through the front gate, not slowing for a second as they negotiated the narrow entrance, one hot on the heels of the other.

Once inside, the second vehicle, a black and yellow curricle pulled by a pair of matched bays, swung out and tried to pass the other. They traveled at breakneck speed, jostling for first place, sending the freshly raked gravel of the drive flying.

"God a'mighty," Ethan declared. "He's never going to pass him. He'll overturn—"

"Lay you a pony he wins," Harry said.

"Done," said Ethan, staring as the bays strained and the curricle pulled forward, grazing the wheels of its rival. The light, high-sprung vehicle bounced and swayed perilously. The driver laughed and urged his team faster. "He's mad."

"It's Luke," Harry said. "You know he doesn't care if he lives or dies. And Rafe knows all his tricks. They've been racing each other for years."

Rafe Ramsey and Luke Ripton were his two closest friends after his brother, Gabe. They'd all gone to school together, they'd joined the army together, and together, somehow, they'd survived eight years at war.

"They're both mad," Ethan declared.

"Magnificent, just magnificent," Jackson murmured in a reverential tone. "Such beautiful movers. I ain't seen such high-blooded lovelies bowling up the drive of Firmin Court since Miss Nell's mam were alive. It does my old heart good to see them, it does."

"Those bays are particularly fine, aren't they?" Harry agreed. "Though I think the blacks might have the edge in stamina."

"Aye, very powerful shoulders," Jackson agreed.

"They're still stark, starin' mad," Ethan repeated. "They'll break both their fool necks."

Harry squinted. "Is that a new curricle Rafe's driving, Ethan? Very nice, don't you think?"

Ethan glanced at him. "You're still mad, as well."

Harry grinned. It wasn't the first time he'd been called mad; they all had. He, Gabe, Luke, Rafe, and their friend

Michael had been called the Duke's Angels, for their names and because they rode dispatches for Wellington.

After Michael's death, their nickname had changed to the Devil Riders, possibly because of Wellington's habit of exhorting them to "ride like the devil" or because after they'd lost Michael there was a new edge to their willingness to take risks. At that time none of them particularly cared whether they lived or died.

The two curricles sped along, neck and neck, heading toward the front of the house.

"Holy Mother of God, that lunatic's going to put them up the front steps," Ethan gasped and leapt to the side. Jackson muttered an oath and hurried after him. Harry folded his arms and waited. He'd seen this particular maneuver of Luke's before.

As expected, at the very last moment, Luke hauled his horses back and they snorted and plunged to a stop, steam coming from them in clouds, a bare six inches from the steps. The second curricle pulled up beside it three seconds later.

There was a sudden silence, broken only by the horses stamping and blowing for air. Several grooms who'd come to watch the race hurried forward to take the reins. The two drivers, both in elegantly cut, many-caped driving coats and high, curly-brimmed beavers descended their vehicles in a leisurely fashion.

Luke affected a start when he saw the second. "Rafe, my dear boy—you've arrived, at last!" He yawned. "I thought you'd never get here."

Rafe, six foot tall, whipcord lean and elegant to the fingertips, pulled off his driving gloves and unknotted his white silk scarf with leisurely movements. "Dreary timing, I know. I was held up on the road by a most tedious fellow in a black and yellow curricle, a positive slug—as slow as a wet week he was, I promise you." He pulled out a quizzing glass and leveled it in ostentatious surprise at Luke's black and yellow curricle. "By Jove, I do believe the slug was you, Luke. What sort of cattle are you driving these days?"

Chuckling, Harry went to greet them. Ethan, too, came forward with a wide grin, saying, "As hey-go-mad as ever, I see. Peacetime life too tame for you, then?"

Rafe Ramsey raised a sardonic eyebrow. "Hey-go-mad? I? You are mistaken, my dear Ethan. It is my friend who is mad; I merely indulge him. My only problem is that I'm near faint with thirst." He gave Harry a meaning look.

"Oh indeed," Harry chuckled. "You poor feeble creature, come inside and I'll pour you a reviving draught."

"In that case, I feel a faint coming on, too," Ethan declared.

"And me, for I won," Luke reminded them.

"I know, I just won twenty-five pounds on you," Harry told him.

Luke's jaw dropped. "A *pony*? You only bet a pony on me?" He gave a disgusted snort. "At least Rafe wagered a monkey."

"Ethan, you're a man of fine judgment." Rafe stared down his long nose at Harry. "And you bet against me, Harry, my old friend? I'm wounded, deeply wounded."

Harry grinned, unaffected by his friend's nonsense. "As soon as I saw you had a new curricle, I knew it would take the edge off. You might risk your fool neck but a new curricle? Not likely!" Chuckling, the friends entered the house while Jackson supervised the grooms ushering the magnificent beasts into his tender care.

They were just inside when Rafe turned to Luke. "Did you forget the basket from Mrs. Barrow?"

Luke cursed and ran lightly back down the steps to fetch a large wicker basket from the curricle.

"From Mrs. Barrow?" Harry asked, puzzled. "My Mrs. Barrow?"

"Yes, that good lady has sent you an enormous basket of foodstuffs. Apparently you're living in the direst conditions in some foreign county and like to fade away to a shadow."

Harry grinned. That was Mrs. Barrow, all right. "But how—where did you see her?"

"At the Grange, of course, where else?" Luke said, dumping the basket on a nearby table.

"What were you doing there?"

Rafe rolled his eyes. "I know your penmanship is atrocious, dear boy, but if you'd written to inform us you'd moved, it would have saved us the trip."

"Not that we minded," Luke interjected. "She cooks like a dream—none of this French nonsense everyone's so mad about, but real food for real men. Frankly, Harry, I was all for staying on there. I'll wager you won't feed us nearly as well."

"I won't," Harry confirmed as he poured the drinks. "And I'll make you work."

"Work? Heavens, *quel horreur*," declared Rafe. "I remember work. I don't like it. It makes you dirty." He flicked at his immaculate buckskins with fastidious fingers and tried to keep the twinkle out of his eye.

"Doing it too brown, Rafe," Harry said with a grin. "There's not one of us who've forgotten the way you jumped into the rubble of that bombed Spanish church. You dug for twelve hours straight and were yellow mud from head to toe."

Rafe shrugged. "That was different—there were children trapped there. And I never did get the wretched mud out of my clothes. Ethan, you're a man of fashion, you'll appreciate my position."

Ethan nodded earnestly. "Oh I do, sir, I do. In fact I well remember a time when there weren't any children trapped in the ruins of a certain monastery, nor any monks neither but—" He frowned thoughtfully. "That wasn't you, was it,

sir, heavin' a pick with the best of them under the hot Spanish sun?" He winked.

Rafe grinned. "Ah, but I'm sure I knew we were going to
find that wine." He sighed. "Superb stuff it was, too, remember? Wish we had some now. I'm going to need it if you're
going to turn me into a slave—oh!" He felt in his pocket and
drew out two letters. "I almost forgot. Mrs. Barrow gave me
these to give to you." He passed them to Harry.

Harry broke the seal and read the first one. "It's from my
brother, Gabe," he told them. "He's coming to England next
month. Apparently Callie insists on it—I can't imagine
why."

"Wives do that," Rafe said gloomily. "Insist." He shuddered and drank deeply.

Harry poured his friend another glass of wine. Rafe's
older brother, Lord Axebridge, was hounding him to make
a marriage with an heiress. Rafe's brother was happily
married, but his wife had been unable to bear children, so it
was Rafe's duty, as his brother's heir, to provide the heirs
of the next generation. And replenish the family coffers.

Poor Rafe had been trying to avoid the inevitable ever
since he'd emerged from the war relatively unscathed. He
didn't relish the role of sacrificial lamb—not when it involved marriage.

"Is anyone else comin' with them?" Ethan asked diffidently. "The boys, mebbe?"

Harry consulted the letter. "Yes, the boys and several of
the Royal Zindarian Guard—oh and Callie's friend, Miss
Tibby. She and Callie are going shopping."

"That explains it," Luke said. "Ladies always like to
shop. No shops in Zindaria—not like London. When're they
coming?"

"December," Harry told him. "They're staying for Christmas."

He broke open the second letter, read it, and swallowed.
He took a large drink of wine.

"Who's it from?" Ethan asked curiously.

"My aunt Gosforth," Harry said. "She says she's found me several very eligible bridal possibilities. I'm to come to Bath next week and meet them."

Five

"Come now, Harry," Aunt Maude said, "don't make a fuss—I just need a strong arm to lean on if I'm to negotiate that dreadfully steep hill."

"It's downhill, but I'll fetch you a sedan chair, shall I?" Harry knew perfectly well what his aunt wanted of him, and a strong arm was the least of it. She wanted his company in the Pump Room.

Harry loathed the Pump Room, with its rituals, its gossip, the vile tasting waters, and worst of all, the community of genteel spinsters who eyed the arrival of a young man in their midst with all the excitement of a fox come into the henhouse. Only Harry didn't feel like a fox; he felt, under their avid gaze, like a tasty ear of wheat.

And Aunt Maude knew it, too, curse her. She found the whole thing enormously entertaining.

"You wouldn't begrudge a frail old woman your help, would you?" she said in a plaintive voice.

"Frail, is it, Aunt Maudie? And who was it danced every

dance at the ball last night?" Harry arched his brows. "Must have been some other frail old woman."

"It was because I danced every dance that I am feeling so delicate this morning," his aunt responded with dignity.

"Oh, it was the dancing, was it? I thought it was the champagne. How many glasses was it?" her unrepentant nephew responded.

Maude, Lady Gosforth, clutched her head and said with asperity, "A gentleman would not count."

"I didn't," Harry said. "I *lost* count."

"Well, if you must be so vulgar as to refer to it," his aunt declared, "you will understand why I am in need of the restorative powers of the waters at the pump room. And since the only reason I went to the ball last night was to assist you in this search for a wife, the least you can do is escort me."

It was a barefaced lie. Wild horses couldn't keep Aunt Maude from a party, but Harry was aware she'd gone to a lot of trouble for him. He sighed and presented his arm. "All right, but only to the door."

"Nonsense." His triumphant aunt tried not to smirk. "You are clearly liverish and out of sorts. You need to take the waters."

"I don't," he snapped. "It's filthy stuff and I can't bear those rooms, full of old tabbies and—" He broke off and said in a firm voice, "I'll escort you there, but that's my limit."

He was in a foul mood. For the past three days he'd done everything Aunt Maude had asked him to do: dressed up like a tailor's dummy, sat and walked and made painstaking conversation with daughters and their fathers and mothers. He'd been as agreeable as he could possibly be to a bunch of people he never wanted to see again.

It had all been a complete waste of time. He was no closer to finding a suitable wife than he had been the last time he'd come to Bath. Worse, in fact, because then he wasn't comparing every blasted girl he met with *her*.

Nell, Lady Helen Freymore, with her creamy, pure complexion and her honey-dark voice. No girl he'd met had such a clear direct gaze, such quiet self-possession. And none could create such . . . fire in him.

But Nell hadn't wanted him. She preferred to be off in London pouring tea for some rich, no doubt indulgent old lady. Nell preferred to run errands rather than be married to Harry. And Harry was miles away in Bath looking for a substitute who wouldn't stir him up as she did.

So why was he all stirred up?

Aunt Maude wasn't in the sweetest of tempers, herself. She continued, "But you must. I've put myself out searching high and low for eligible middle-class girls, but you're so liverish you won't even give them a chance!"

"I did give them a chance," he told her. "It's not my fault if they weren't what I asked for."

She smacked him lightly on the hand. "Pish, tush! I find you three of the most ravishing girls and you say they're stupid—"

"They are stupid."

She rolled her eyes at him. "Pretty girls don't have to be clever, you irritating boy!" She took a deep breath and continued, "But being a loving aunt, I find you two more intelligent, lively, and still remarkably attractive girls and you say they're dull."

"They were."

"How would you know? You hardly exchanged a word with either of them."

"I did. The black-haired one liked cats, hated dogs, and was frightened of horses. And the yellow-haired one talked about poetry and went on and on about that Byron fellow." He snorted.

His aunt smacked his arm again. "Every female in England is in love with Byron, you savage! It is the fashion! The fault is not with the girls but with you. Anyone would think you didn't want to get married, but since that's obviously not true, the only explanation is that you are liverish. And a course of the waters will cure that."

Harry scowled and stumped unevenly along beside her. "I'll escort you inside, but I won't swallow any of that stuff," Harry growled, "so cease and desist, or else walk the rest of the way down this street on the very strong arm of your extremely capable footman." He gestured to the liveried servant walking quietly behind them.

His aunt sniffed, but said no more.

Their entrance caused a discernible stir of interest in the population of the Pump Room. Harry didn't feel the slightest bit flattered—he was the only male in the room under the age of seventy. He fixed his gaze on the benches set aside for peeresses and marched his aunt across the room, intending to seat her and be gone.

It took him longer than he planned, as his aunt stopped every few feet to greet acquaintances, but eventually he had her settled with one of her cronies and with a glass of the vile water in her hand.

He was about to take his leave when he heard a voice behind him say, "Lady Helen! What a clumsy creature you are!"

Lady Helen? Harry's head jerked around and he stared across the room. It was her, Nell. What the hell was she doing here? She was supposed to be in London.

A richly dressed, tightly corseted woman with a florid face was speaking to her in a loud voice, as if she were a half-wit, saying, "Well, don't stand there, girl, pick it up at once."

He watched as Nell bent with her usual grace and picked up a shawl from the floor. His mouth dried. She looked just the same. Beautiful. Thinner, perhaps. She shook out the shawl, examined it, and made to pass it to the woman.

She didn't look at Harry, didn't so much as glance his way, but he was sure she knew he was there. She couldn't have missed the entrance his aunt had made.

"No, no, you stupid girl!" The woman recoiled in a stagey manner. "It's soiled. I can't be expected to wear a soiled shawl." The woman cast a long-suffering glance around the room, clearly playing to the audience.

Nell stood in profile to him, her head held high in a lovely cameo, receiving the reprimand with an expression of quiet indifference.

How dare she be indifferent! How dare that woman speak to her like that. He wanted to strangle the red-faced cow.

He wanted to march across the room and pick Nell up and take her back to Firmin Court, ride with her through the forest . . .

Nell said something quiet to the florid woman.

"No, it's not perfectly clean at all, Lady Helen," the woman declared in scornful, ringing tones. "I'm surprised you have such low standards. Run home and fetch me another. Off you go. It shouldn't take you long." She flapped her hands at Nell as though she were a child or a dog, saying, "Don't just stand there. Hurry along, Lady Helen. I'm already feeling rather chilled."

Harry gritted his teeth as Nell quietly folded the shawl and hurried out into the street. He made to follow her.

His aunt gripped his sleeve tightly. "You can't leave yet. It's too fascinating. That's the atrocious mushroom I was telling you about the other day. Remember?"

Nell would be back, Harry reminded himself. She was just fetching another shawl for the cow. He would speak to her then, when he was calmer. For a second he'd wanted to strangle that woman. Talking to Nell like that. He allowed his aunt to pull him down beside her.

The florid woman smoothed her skirts with a satisfied expression and looked complacently round the room. She glanced at Harry and her expression sharpened. Without taking her eyes off him, she ran a finger around the neckline of her dress, which framed a deep bosom, in the cleft of which a large glittering jewel rested.

His aunt made a rude sound under her breath. "The airs that woman gives herself! She's forty if she's a day. Don't you remember the tale?"

Harry vaguely recalled her telling some story about some vastly irritating woman but a great many things offended his aunt. Aunt Maude talked a great deal: the story had washed over him. Now he wished he'd listened.

"Remind me," he said, his eyes on the door.

"She calls herself Mrs. Beasley. She is a rich widow—the rumor is her late husband was a sausage manufacturer, but she keeps her vulgar origins secret—or tries to. As if she doesn't give herself away with every word she speaks." Aunt Maude snorted.

"And the one who dropped the shawl?" Harry asked casually. He felt his aunt turn her head to stare at him. He pretended not to notice.

"She didn't drop it at all." Aunt Maude's friend Lady Lattimer leaned forward. "I saw the whole thing. That Woman threw it on the floor deliberately to put Lady Helen in the wrong."

Harry clenched his fists and forced himself to say in a mildly curious tone, "Lady Helen?"

His aunt gave him a thoughtful look. "Her paid companion. She's Lady Helen Freymore, the daughter of the disgraced Earl of Denton—he gambled away his estate and killed himself. The girl is too poor and too plain to get a husband, never mind the scandal her father made."

His aunt cast the florid woman a contemptuous look. "Nasty, vulgar creature! She simply loves having the daughter of an earl at her beck and call, and she doesn't allow the poor girl a moment of peace."

"How does she stand it?" Harry muttered.

Aunt Maude gave him another piercing look, but said in a mild voice. "None of us has spoken to her—La Beasley doesn't allow it, but the girl seems to take it in her stride."

"She must be a simple creature," Lady Lattimer said. "Mrs. Beasley belittles her with every word, yet Lady Helen never turns a hair. She just smiles, and the humiliations roll off her like water off a duck's back." She shook her head. "No woman of spirit would stand to be spoken to like that by her social inferior."

"She's not simple at all," Harry found himself saying, then aware of his aunt's beady gaze on him, added, "At least she doesn't seem so . . . er, from what I saw just now . . ."

His aunt fixed him with a baleful look and said in a goaded voice, "No, well, she wouldn't, of course. From what you saw just now."

Ignoring his aunt's gimlet stare, Harry scanned the room. He needed somewhere he could talk to Nell on her own, without all these watching eyes.

"I believe she's desperately poor," continued Lady Lattimer, unaware of the undercurrents. "Quite literally doesn't have a penny to her name, poor girl."

Harry spotted two doors down the back of the room. He rose, saying, "Excuse me, Aunt Maude, Lady Lattimer, I must just . . ." and strode off to investigate.

When he returned, Lady Lattimer was dozing and his aunt was watching him with an annoyed expression.

"To think of all that time I wasted on all those other girls," Aunt Maude muttered, thumping Harry on the arm as he sat down.

It was becoming a pattern. He moved his arm out of reach. "I don't know what you're talking about."

Aunt Maude snorted. Harry passed her his handkerchief. She stared coldly at it down her long, Roman nose. "What's that for?"

"From the sounds you've been making, you're coming down with a cold," he told her.

She glared at him and gave a loud, contemptuous sniff. He smiled faintly and put his handkerchief away.

She glanced at her friend, who was gently snoring, then said in a low voice, "So, how long have you known Lady Helen?" she asked him.

"How did you know?"

She gave him a withering look through her lorgnette. "Oh, spare me—I've known you since you were child. Besides, it was obvious. I throw nearly a dozen girls at your head and you take not the slightest notice, and now, suddenly, you're asking oh-so-casually about somebody's paid companion, a plain and unprepossessing girl whom you cannot take your eyes off. And you expect me to believe you've only just laid eyes on her?"

He shrugged. "I've seen her around."

There was a short silence, then his aunt said, "It's more than a passing curiosity, isn't it?"

"Perhaps." Harry admitted after a moment.

It wasn't perhaps, at all, he suddenly realized. It had hit him with the force of a thunderclap just now, when he'd seen her across the room.

There was no "suitable bride" for Harry; there was only Nell. He didn't know how it had happened, he didn't know why; he only knew it was so.

"You told me you wanted a girl from a thoroughly respectable background; a pretty, quiet, moral, and middle-class girl, preferably well dowered."

"That's right."

His aunt made a frustrated noise. "Apart from being plain as a pikestaff, this girl's got no money, no connections, and is tainted by scandal. Her father gambled everything away, then died at a crossroads! Right out in the open where anyone could find him. Appalling *ton*."

"Yes, he should have chosen a more fashionable death," he said ironically. "And she's not plain as a pikestaff," he said irritably. It was her clothes, he supposed. Aunt Maude set great store by how people dressed. He ran his finger around his tight collar. "If you look past those drab clothes, I think you will find she's lovely."

She stared at him in silence for a long moment, then arched her well-plucked eyebrows knowingly. "Well, well, well, and I never thought to see it."

"See what?" He eyed the door impatiently. Where the hell was she? She'd been gone far too long.

She patted his cheek. "Smitten, that's what you are, my boy."

Smitten? He stared at his aunt. "Nonsense," he mumbled. "I'm just . . . concerned for her welfare." He was, too. Nell looked exhausted, as if she were being worked too hard. There were still those shadows beneath her eyes. And she was thinner.

He found himself clenching his fists in frustration. How dare that cow sit there so smug and comfortable, sending Nell running around the town on made-up errands.

"How did you meet her?"

"The estate I bought was one of her father's minor estates," he told her. "She was there when I inspected it." He kept his eyes on the door. "Where the devil is she? She's been gone for ages."

"It's a ten-minute walk each way to that woman's lodgings. Have patience."

He scowled and folded his arms.

"Just look at the state of you!" Aunt Maude shook her head. "It would have saved me a great deal of bother if you'd told me about her in the first place, Harry."

"I didn't know she was here," he confessed. "She said she was going to London."

"Then why didn't you go to London instead of wasting my time?" Aunt Maude said with asperity.

He hesitated then said in a low tone, "Because she'd already turned me down."

Aunt Maude dropped her lorgnette. "What? That girl—

that plain little spinster with not a penny to her name or a friend in the world—turned you down? And chose life with La Beasley instead?"

Harry gritted his teeth. He wasn't exactly flattered, either, especially not when he could see what she'd turned him down for. He recalled what she'd said about taking tea and reading aloud to a sweet old lady and tried to stifle a surge of ignoble satisfaction. How wrong she'd been. She should have chosen him.

"What did you do to her?"

Harry clamped his mouth shut. Wild horses wouldn't drag that tale out of him, not to a living soul. He felt his face warm as he recalled the way he'd hauled an earl's daughter into his arms and ravished her mouth till they both could barely stand.

"Nothing. I was perfectly polite," he said stiffly. "I made her a perfectly correct offer."

"And she turned you down." His aunt chuckled. "I must meet this girl," she declared. "There's more to Lady Helen Freymore than meets the eye."

Nell clutched the shawl to her and raced up the steep, cobbled street, ignoring the startled looks of the passers-by. The shawl wasn't the slightest bit soiled, of course, it was just an excuse Mrs. Beasley had made to draw attention to herself, but oh, how glad Nell was of it. An escape.

She was shaking.

What was Harry Morant doing in Bath? In the Pump Room, of all places? He surely couldn't have known she was here.

Bath had been a last-minute detour. Mrs. Beasley had been feeling run down and her physician had recommended that on her way to London she stop off at Bath and take the waters. They'd been here a week now, and this morning

Mrs. Beasley had announced that on Monday they would depart for London.

Two more days.

But Harry Morant had seen her and she could tell by his face that he wasn't going to ignore her. She'd watched him out of the corner of her eye the whole time, from the moment he'd stepped through the doorway with his aunt.

A frisson of feminine excitement had rippled through the room. Who could blame the ladies, she thought; he was such a handsome man, so tall and broad-shouldered and so . . . manly.

She could still not believe that he had offered for her.

She'd almost been tempted—what woman wouldn't be? But it was just for a moment; there was really no choice. She had to find Torie.

And finding Torie would remove whatever slender chance of marriage Nell had.

No gentleman would take on a wife with an illegitimate daughter, especially if that wife had neither fortune nor looks.

Harry Morant was ambitious, a man who was determined to move up in the world. More important, he was a man trying to put his own irregular birth behind him.

So she wasn't—she couldn't be—interested.

She was certain Torie was somewhere in London. Papa had died the day after he'd stolen her baby away, and he'd died on the London road, so he must have been coming back from there.

She'd buried him in the village where he'd died. She'd sold his horse to pay for the funeral; she didn't have the money to pay for him to be taken home. She tried to learn as much as she could about the circumstances of his death, and where he had been before, but nobody could tell her anything.

She then traveled as far as she could toward London,

questioning everyone she encountered on the way. Several people had seen him coming back from London. Not one of them had seen him with a baby in a basket lined with white satin.

She'd searched and questioned people all along the London road until her money ran out and she'd sold her own horse. She kept going, certain that news of her daughter would be at the next house, or the next. Finally, destitute and reeling with hunger and cold, she realized if she was not careful, she could die in a ditch, or at a crossroads, like Papa.

And then what would become of Torie?

So, refusing to despair, she'd turned around and dragged herself home, back to Firmin Court. She had to get home and prepare herself properly for this search.

So her baby must be in London—somewhere. Nell was determined. No stone would remain unturned. She would search till she dropped.

She reached Mrs. Beasley's lodgings and hurried upstairs to fetch another shawl. She would have to go back inside the pump room, face those smoking gray eyes.

She hoped he would stay away, but she didn't feel very optimistic. He was going to cause trouble, she knew it in her bones. She'd seen the way he'd stiffened in outrage at the way Mrs. Beasley had scolded Nell about the shawl. He was going to get all gallant on her.

And if he did, there would be hell to pay.

Mrs. Beasley liked to be the center of attention. She'd lived her life until now as a virtuous wife: now she was ready to become a dashing widow. Her nastiness didn't bother Nell in the least. There were compensations. She kept Nell at her beck and call every waking moment, but since the woman never rose before midday, Nell's mornings were totally free.

In London, Nell would be able to use those precious

morning hours to search for Torie. Few positions would allow her that much freedom. She needed—quite desperately—to keep this job, and not have it threatened by a well-meaning man who had no idea of how things really stood.

*E*very one of Harry's senses sharpened the moment Nell slipped quietly back into the Pump Room. She was a little flushed and her chest rose and fell rapidly; she'd been running. He frowned at her chest. She'd seemed quite flat in that region before. How had he missed those delicious curves?

He felt his body stirring and hastily forced it to behave. He was in the Pump Room, for heaven's sake, with his aunt beside him.

"Here, dear boy, drink some water." A glass was pressed into his hand and without thinking, he lifted it to his lips and drank deeply. "Faugh!" He just managed not to spit out the foul-tasting spa water. "That's disgusting."

With a smug smile Aunt Maude removed the glass from his hand. "Yes, I know, and you deserved every last drop, dear boy, for putting me through all those dreary cits. I am inclined to forgive you, though—"

"Oh, are you indeed?"

"Yes, for this promises to be extremely entertaining, whatever the outcome. Do you know she hasn't glanced even once in this direction? It's most unnatural. Do you think she's making a point?" She smiled at Harry guilelessly.

He glowered back, a bitter taste in his mouth. "It won't do her any good. I have every intention of speaking to her."

"And I suppose you think you'll just walk over and start talking to her. As if that harpy isn't going to interfere?"

He gave her a cool look. "Naturally I have a plan."

"Have you indeed?"

"Yes, it's a simple matter of strategy. You and your friend Lady Lattimer will engage the enemy in conversation."

"Will we? How delightful. And what shall we talk about?"

"I don't know. Some sort of private feminine matter."

"What would you know about private feminine matters?"

"Very little, thank God, but it will give you an excuse for banishing Nell—"

"Nell?"

"Lady Helen." He tried to ignore the smile playing about his aunt's lips. She was enjoying this, damn her. "The point is, you must make it clear to the woman that you wish for private conversation with her and only her, and to that end you will send Lady Helen and myself to another part of the room. Leave the rest to me."

She patted him on the cheek a second time. "Excellent, dear boy. I can see why you made such an excellent soldier. Just one thing."

"Yes?" he said, impatient to get started.

"Be careful. La Beasley has a fancy for you; she has been watching you like a cat watching a mouse hole for the last fifteen minutes. If she sees your interest in Lady Helen, she will turn on the poor girl like a snake. So be discreet, my boy."

"I am always discreet," Harry informed her coldly.

Harry's aunt rose and shook her friend awake. "Come along, Lizzie, we're going to talk to La Beastley."

Lady Lattimer spluttered to consciousness. "What? But I don't want to speak to—"

"Nonsense. It will be an adventure," declared her friend. "We are going to rescue Lady Helen from the gorgon's clutches."

"Oh, in that case . . ." Lady Lattimer rose and straightened her lace cap. The two ladies swept across the room toward Mrs. Beasley much like two ships of the Spanish

Armada bearing down on a small fishing boat. Heads in the
pump room swiveled. Conversation buzzed, then died to an
avid silence.

Mrs. Beasley watched their approach with frozen fascination as it dawned on her that two titled ladies had finally
noticed her. She rose from her seat, smiling.

"Mrs. Um . . . ?" Lady Gosforth inquired, as if she did
not know very well who the woman was. She did not even
look at Nell.

The woman curtsied. "I am Mrs. Beasley, ma'am, and
you are Lady Gosforth."

"I know," said Lady Gosforth, inclining her head gra-
ciously.

Mrs. Beasley tittered. "And of course, I've seen Lady
Lattimer here before. A real regular, she is."

Lady Lattimer raised one aristocratic eyebrow at such a
person's presumption in daring to notice her regularity or
otherwise. "Indeed," she said in a quelling voice.

Nell stood quietly to one side. Mrs. Beasley made no attempt to introduce her. She glanced past the two ladies, to
where Harry stood a short distance away, examining a print
on the wall.

"And will your gentleman friend be joining us?" Mrs.
Beasley asked.

"No," Lady Gosforth declared. "We wish to have private conversation with you—of a feminine nature. A gentleman would not wish to be present."

"I see." Mrs. Beasley looked vaguely alarmed.

There were four ladies present, counting Nell, and only
two seats. Lady Gosforth gestured for Mrs. Beasley and
Lady Lattimer to sit down, turned to her nephew and said,
"Harry, a chair, if you please."

Harry brought a chair for her, and seeing Nell was still
standing awkwardly by, was about to fetch her one when
his aunt said, "No, we wish to have private conversation

with this lady—please find another seat for her companion, Miss Er . . ."

"Lady Helen—" began Mrs. Beasley.

Lady Gosforth cut across her. "Find Miss Er a seat over there somewhere, Harry, and then take yourself off, there's a good boy." She waved him away and turned back to Mrs. Beasley, saying sweetly. "My nephew, you know, and therefore too young to be of any interest to ladies of our age."

Since Mrs. Beasley was a well-preserved forty and the two aristocratic ladies well into their sixties, Mrs. Beasley tried not to look affronted by this suggestion. She managed a strangled smile and watched, frustrated, as one of the most magnificent men she'd ever seen offered his arm to her drab little companion and escorted her to a distant corner.

"My dear friend Lady Lattimer has been admiring your jewelry," announced Lady Gosforth, kicking her dear friend on the ankle.

"Ow—er, yes, your jewelry," Lady Lattimer said with an indignant look at her dear friend. She pulled out a quizzing glass and peered at the vulgar array of jewels displayed on various parts of Mrs. Beasley's person. "There's quite a lot of it, isn't there?" she mumbled. "And it's very, er, sparkly."

Feeble as the attempt was, Mrs. Beasley responded with a smug preen. "Yes, Mr. Beasley, my late husband, delighted in purchasing trinkets for me." She fingered a large ruby brooch, surrounded by diamonds, that rested in the vee of her cleavage. "Mr. Beasley used to say jewels only enhanced my beauty."

"Fascinating. Tell us the history of each piece," Lady Gosforth instructed her.

"Go away," Nell whispered to Harry as they crossed the room. She was very aware of the eyes observing their progress. "Leave now and do not talk to me."

Harry tucked her hand under his arm. "I thought you were going to London."

"I was; I still am. We leave in two days," she hissed. "Please, just go away. If she sees us talking—"

"Yes, she, your employer—the very picture of a delightful little old lady . . . of the vulture clan."

"She doesn't bother me."

"She annoys the hell out of me," Harry said. "How the devil do you stand the way she talks to you?"

Nell attempted to withdrew her hand from his grip, failed, and said pointedly, "At least she doesn't swear at me."

"No, she talks to you like a dog—worse than a dog. You miss Freckles, I suppose."

The abrupt change of subject caught her unawares. "You've seen Freckles?"

He nodded. "She comes over to the house almost every day, from the vicarage, looking for you. She misses you."

She bit her lip. "I miss her, too. I'm sorry she's a problem."

"She's no problem. Aggie uses her as an excuse to pop over every now and then, just to keep an eye on us. In any case, my partner, Ethan, is happy to take the dog home. Personally I wouldn't mind if Freckles moved in permanently."

She gave him a warm smile. "She is a lovely dog, isn't she?"

His grip on her hand tightened. He stopped dead and stared down at her for a long moment.

She gave him an uneasy look and glanced around. His behavior was drawing unwanted attention to them.

He seemed to realize it, for he moved on as if nothing had happened, saying, "If I'd known I was going to see you here, I could have brought her to Bath for a visit."

She shook her head. "No, she'll soon settle down and stop missing m—where are you taking me?" A young boy in an apron held open a brown baize-covered door leading from the main area of the Pump Room.

Without a word of explanation, Harry steered her through it. He pressed a coin into the waiting palm of the boy, saying, "Make sure we're not disturbed."

Nell found herself in what seemed like a small storage room. "What do you mean, not disturbed? I'm not staying in here with you!" She tried to push against him.

"You were worried your employer would see you talking with me," Harry said as he closed the door and leaned against it. "Now she won't."

There was a window that led into a back courtyard of sorts. Nell eyed it, but abandoned the thought of climbing out. It would be ridiculous, and besides, she had no fear of Harry Morant. She looked at his tall, powerful body and his broad shoulders. His big fists were clenched.

She folded her arms and glared at him. "You've clearly gone to a lot of trouble to set this meeting up, so what is it you have to say to me? Say it and let me out. I don't appreciate being shut in small rooms against my will."

Harry frowned. "Say to you?"

"Yes." She waited.

"I shouldn't have done it," he said finally. "Forcing that . . . kiss on you as I did. I apologize. I meant no disrespect, but that's no excuse. I treated you like a wanton."

She blushed, remembering the scene in the stable. He was not simply referring to the kiss, she saw. It was clear he'd realized where her hand had been, trapped between them.

But that had been unintentional. He'd treated her like a woman, not a wanton. She'd relived that kiss over and over in her mind ever since.

"I didn't m—" She stopped. If she said she didn't mind, he'd think her immodest, even a bit trollopy. She groped for an appropriate expression. "I forgive you" sounded too saintly. "It's all right," she said. "I won't hold it against you."

His expression abruptly went blank and she suddenly realized what she'd said, remembering how her hand had inadvertently pressed against his aroused flesh. Holding it against him . . .

"I didn't mean that literal—" she gasped. She pressed her hands over her hot cheeks. "Oh dear."

She glanced at him again and his face was so rigid she couldn't help but giggle. "I was trying so hard for sophisticated indifference," she confessed. "I've made a mull of that, haven't I?"

He relaxed, rueful amusement in his eyes. "I think we both did."

A short silence fell. "Well, if that's all," Nell began. She was well aware of the time passing. She did not want to get into trouble.

"No, that's not why I brought you in here at all," he said. "I didn't even think of it until just now when you asked me what I had to say to you, and I recalled that I owed you an apology."

"Then what was it? I don't have much time, you know."

He stared at her for a long moment, his eyes scanning her face in a way than made her prickle with awareness. "You're not getting enough sleep," he said finally.

She blinked. "You brought me in here to tell me that?"

His hand came up and cupped her cheek, tilting her head gently to the light. "You have lilac shadows beneath your eyes," he said softly. "They're beautiful but they shouldn't be there." His big thumb stroked gently along her cheekbones. "And you're thinner. There are hollows here that weren't there before." His thumb caressed the hollows.

Nell swallowed, her mind suddenly blank. She was braced for an argument, for bullying even, but not for this . . . for this tender . . . concern. She had no defenses ready against that.

She stared into his smoky gray eyes. She could smell him, smell the clean, fresh scent of his shaving cologne, of clean linen and the faint scent of coffee.

"You need taking care of," he said and his soft, deep voice shivered through her. "And I'm the man to do it."

His big, warm palm held her, and she wanted to lean into it, to press herself against his big, hard body, so strong, so sure, to let him just take over and do with her what he wanted. It would all be so easy, so much easier, and he was so very strong and appealing. And beautiful. That mouth of his . . . so tender and so dangerous . . .

There was some reason she shouldn't give in to him, some reason she had to keep fighting herself, as well as him . . . only just now she couldn't think what it was.

Slowly, slowly his head bent toward her. She knew she should push him away, or turn her cheek . . .

But her cheek rested in his palm and she couldn't bring herself to pull back, and those gray eyes wove a spell so that she could not move a muscle.

And she was tired, so tired . . . tired of battling against the world, of being alone, always alone, tired of resisting him, and tired of fighting herself. A kiss would do no harm, surely? One kiss, just for comfort . . . for the cold nights ahead . . . His lips touched hers, lightly at first, a warm whisper of sensation and she softened.

Both hands cupped her jaw and she felt like something precious, cradled in his palms. He bent his head to lavish her mouth with tiny feather kisses. She hadn't really been kissed before—certainly nothing like this: she'd half braced herself for an assault on her mouth, but the sweet, unex-pectedness of these soft, fleeting caresses had her melting against him.

His gaze burned into her and she closed her eyes against

the intensity. She could still feel it through her lids, the way you felt the sun through closed eyes.

He ran his tongue along the seam of her lips. With her eyes closed, she felt each touch more intensely than ever. He did it again, and again, and she clutched at his shoulders, shivering helplessly at the warm, delicious sensations that quivered through her. Her lips parted and he kissed her with his whole mouth, and she shivered again at the heady taste of coffee and Harry Morant on her tongue.

She pulled him closer, loving the hard, solid feel of him against her. She could almost feel the whole length of him against her body; hard, leashed power, pressing against her, into her.

She kissed him back as he had kissed her, tentatively at first, then more confidently, tasting him with her mouth and tongue the way he had tasted her.

She pushed her fingers up through his thick dark hair, loving the feel of the hard, beautiful bones beneath, and as his tongue plunged into her, she arched against him and fisted a handful of hair, pulling him closer.

He groaned and pulled her hard against him.

"Come home with me," he said. "Come home to Firmin Court and marry me. You don't belong in this sort of life. And you'll hate London."

Shocked, she pulled out of his embrace. She staggered back against the wall. The feeling of the rough, cold brick against her palms braced her. "What did you say?"

"I asked you to marry me." He frowned. "It can't be that much of a surprise. I did ask you once before."

"Yes, but you didn't mean it."

"I meant it." He lifted her hand and kissed the hollow of her palm. "Don't you remember?"

Her fingers curled with memory. Her cheeks burned. She snatched her hand away. Of course she remembered. She wouldn't, couldn't forget. "You've only met me twice."

He shook his head. "It was three times—there was the forest, remember? But twice was all it took."

She couldn't take it in. "You know nothing about me and yet you want to marry me?"

"Yes." There was no hesitation.

She stared at him, dazed. She had a clear choice; she could marry Harry Morant—the most beautiful man she'd ever met in her life. He wanted her. He'd made that more than clear; the imprint of his wanting still burned sometimes against her palm.

And she wanted him; her knees went weak at the sight of him.

He wanted her and he meant to look after her. He would, too, she knew it. It was more than she'd ever been offered in her life.

But she couldn't go back to Firmin Court, not without Torie. It was incredible enough that this dark, intense stranger wanted Nell on such short acquaintance. But Torie, too? Hardly.

Even Torie's own grandfather hadn't wanted her.

She took a deep breath and said quietly, "Mr. Morant, I'm deeply honored by your offer—more than I can say—but I must refuse. I'm sorry. I can't return to Firmin Court. It's just not possible."

"Why not?" he asked bluntly.

"I don't have to explain," she told him. "No should be enough for any gentleman."

He folded his arms and leaned against the door. "Perhaps, but I'm not a gentleman."

She tried to think of how to explain it. She couldn't tell him about Torie, not after Papa had gone to so much trouble to shelter Nell from the scandal of her pregnancy. No. The more people who knew, the more likely the secret would get out. Her daughter would *not* be labeled a child of shame.

Nell had it all planned out. As soon as she found Torie,

she was going to take her to some remote part of the country where nobody knew her and pose as a widow with a child. Torie would never know the circumstances surrounding her birth. Only three people knew, and one of them was dead.

"Believe me, Mr. Morant," she said, "you're better off without me."

"I'll be the judge of that."

"Not the sole judge, I'm afraid. The choice lies with me, and I'm going to London with Mrs. Beasley. Nothing you can say or do will change my mind."

He frowned. "Does she have some hold over you?"

"No, of course not. But the employment she gives me is very convenient."

"Convenient?" he said savagely. "Two weeks in her company and you're thinner than ever. Your eyes are haunted and you can't tell me she doesn't bully you. She treats you like a skivvy or an imbecile in front of your social inferiors. Convenient? To be sent running thither and yon at the behest of a harpy?" He reached out and cupped her chin and his voice deepened. "To be looking so damned exhausted when you should be blooming?"

A lump formed in her throat at his words, but she pulled back. She had to resist him. For Torie's sake. "It doesn't bother me."

"Well, it damn well bothers me."

"But it isn't up to you, is it?" she said quietly. "Now will you let me out or must I scream?"

Recognizing the steel in her voice, he reluctantly stepped aside.

"Yes, Harry, that was wonderfully discreet, I agree," Aunt Maude said as he walked beside her sedan chair on the way back up the hill. "I particularly admire the way after dragging her across the room, you stopped for a ten-second pause in which you stared down at the girl like a half-starved cannibal about to pounce—just in case there was a person in the room who had not already noticed—and then towed her through that back door out of sight. I wonder you never thought of joining the diplomatic corps, like your brother, Nash."

"Half brother," growled Harry stumping along beside the chair. "And all right, perhaps I was not as discreet as I'd planned to be, but that girl . . . rattles me." It was hardly the word, but there was no word for what Nell Freymore did to him.

"Really? I would never have noticed," his aunt said dryly.

Despite his frustration, Harry's lips twitched.

"That's better," she said. "Now instead of you stomping along like a bear, I suggest you put a little more thought into what you want from this girl, and why. Are you sure it's not just because she's refused you that you're so determined to pursue her? I imagine you haven't had many knock backs before this."

"Just the one," Harry said, "if we're talking marriage."

"Oh yes, the Lady Anthea incident."

Harry gritted his teeth. "Nell is nothing like her."

"Not in looks, no—Lady Anthea might be a witch at heart, but she was and still is a stunning beauty. Whereas this girl is a plain little thing, though sweet when she smiles, and with pretty eyes, as you said. She could do with dressing, in my opinion."

"This has nothing to do with Anthea," Harry snapped, annoyed at the implication. "And Nell isn't plain at all: as you say, it's just her clothes."

"Whatever their difference in looks, the fact remains that they are both the daughters of earls," his aunt said, forthright as ever. "Except this girl's father isn't alive, nor does she have brothers to give you a public horse-whipping."

Harry clenched his teeth at the blunt way his aunt referred to the biggest humiliation of his life.

His aunt reached through the curtains of the sedan chair and caught his arm. "Be sure, Harry, before you make a fool of yourself, that your pursuit of Lady Helen is not some deep-seated desire to prove to yourself and all the world that you *can* marry the daughter of an earl."

He looked at her in shock. "It's not," he said automatically, but to tell the truth he wasn't sure. Nell had asked him the same, only not quite in the same way. And he'd admitted it; part of her attraction as a wife was because of her title. He'd just never associated it with what his aunt called the "Lady Anthea incident."

They reached his aunt's house and Harry helped her from the sedan chair and paid the chairmen.

In the hallway, Aunt Maude said, "So you're sure in your mind about your motives for wanting Lady Helen?"

"It's nothing to do with that business." Anthea was ancient history.

"You're in love with her then."

"In love? No!" He added firmly, "Good God, no," in case she got any peculiar ideas. He'd been in love once, and it wasn't like that, thank God.

She stopped and arched an eyebrow.

"It's convenient, that's all," he explained.

"Convenient to pursue a destitute girl whose father left her with nothing but the scandal of his passing, a girl who has refused you twice in preference to employment with a harpy—*convenient*?"

For a moment, Harry didn't know what to say. He could hardly tell his middle-aged, widowed aunt that he was motivated as much by lust as anything else. But his aunt was waiting and seeing as he'd involved her, he owed her some kind of explanation.

"She needs looking after," he said.

"Agreed, but so does half the population of England. And in case you haven't noticed, she's employed, which half the population isn't."

That was true. But he didn't know half the population, and it angered him, seeing those lilac shadows beneath Nell's eyes. But somehow he couldn't explain those feelings to his aunt.

The feelings he had for Nell, he couldn't explain, or name them. All he knew was they weren't love.

He knew about love. He was never going to let himself fall into its toils again.

"She's good with horses," he offered finally.

Aunt Maude stared for a moment, then made a half-stifled noise. "G-good with horses, of course." A choke of laughter escaped her. "Why didn't I think of that? Good with horses. Just what a man wants in a wife." She pulled a wisp of lace from somewhere. "Oh, Harry, dear boy, life was such a bore before you came to visit." She swept away, wiping tears from her eyes, chuckles floating back in her wake.

"I'm going out for a ride," Harry called after her. "I'm not sure when I'll be back." He was coiled tight as a spring. He needed to work off some energy.

She paused on the stairs and looked back. "Will you be staying until Saturday after all, do you think? Only you were invited to dinner at the Anstruthers, and I refused on your behalf because you said you had to be back at Firmin Court by Saturday."

Harry wrinkled his brow. "Did I?" He remembered perfectly well. He'd told her that when he was feeling suffocated by potential brides. Before he knew that Nell was in Bath.

"Yes, you said you couldn't leave all the work for Mr. Delaney."

"There's a limit one can do at this time of year," he prevaricated. "So I'll stay on here a few more days." At least until Nell left for London. "But leave the Anstruthers invitation as is, thanks."

"And what of Mr. Delaney?"

"Oh, Ethan will manage. He's very capable. There's nothing he can't do."

Six

*E*than Delaney sat sweating over a sheet of paper covered with blots and scratchings out. He muttered curses under his breath as he wrestled with the pen. It was so much trickier now that he was living at Firmin Court. At the Grange he'd been able to consult with Mrs. Barrow over this word or that.

Somehow, he didn't mind women knowing. Mrs. Barrow was a talker, but she'd never breathed a word of his little problem to another soul.

Trouble was, there was nobody he could ask here.

He tried again. No. It was wrong, he was sure of it. He threw down the pen in disgust. "Ye're a fool, Ethan, and ye'll never be any different."

Beside him went a thump-thump-thump of a dog's tail. He glanced at the dog. "Aye, Freckles, 'tis all very well for you, life's easy for you. Two houses to live in and your pick of scraps from two kitchens. And they call it a dog's life."

He folded the paper and tucked it in his breast pocket. He never left his attempts lying around for anyone to see.

"Come on, dog, night's falling. I'll take you back to the vicara—" He broke off. The vicarage . . . A vicar was like a priest, wasn't he?

A man could only ask . . .

He whistled for the dog and set off for the vicarage at a brisk pace.

Aggie greeted him warmly at the door. "A nice cup of tea, Mr. Delaney?" she offered, already reaching for the tea caddy. It had become a bit of a ritual; Ethan brought Freckles back for the night, had a cup of tea with the old woman, exchanged the news of the day, then walked home.

"Er, not right now, Aggie, thanks," Ethan said, feeling a little uncomfortable. "Would it be possible for me to see the vicar?"

"The vicar?" Aggie said, surprised. He'd never asked to see the vicar before. "Of course, sir, I'll go and ask."

She returned in a moment, saying, "Go through, Mr. Delaney. He'll see you now."

She ushered him into a shabby but comfortable study where a fire crackled brightly. Books were everywhere, lining the walls, scattered about on tables and stacked beside the vicar's chair. There was also a fine chessboard with intricately carved chess pieces in ebony and ivory. Ethan didn't mind a game of chess.

The vicar rose from a worn, leather armchair as Ethan entered. "Welcome, Mr. Delaney," he said in a mellow, priestly voice.

He was a thin, stooped man in his seventies, with a fringe of pure white hair. According to Aggie he'd been married once but lost his wife to childbirth and had never had the heart to remarry.

Ethan shook the man's hand. There couldn't be a greater contrast, he thought, between his own big, scarred, rough-skinned paw and this man's frail, elegant white hand.

The vicar waved him to a seat and when they were both seated, said, "Now, Mr. Delaney, how can I help you?"

"I'm not Church of England," he blurted. "I was born Catholic, though I'm not religious." He looked at the priest. "Does that matter?"

The old man smiled. "Not to me. I am here for all God's children."

Ethan pulled a wry face. "I'm not so sure I'd call meself one of God's children, Father. I've done a hel—er, plenty of bad things in me life. Years in the army."

"You're still a child of God," the old man said gently.

"Mebbe." Ethan shifted uncomfortably. "The thing is, I know Catholic priests are not supposed to tell what they've been told in confidence. I'm not so knowledgeable about Protestant priests, I mean—"

The old man leaned forward. His eyes were deeply set and faded blue, in the way of men who have looked on the world for many years. "Are you here to confess, Mr. Delaney?"

Ethan looked at him in horror. "Good God, no!"

The old man laughed and sat back in his chair. "Then what is it? I promise to keep your confidence, as long as you haven't broken the law."

"No, it's nothing like that." He glanced around the room. "Would I be right in thinking you're an educated man, Father?"

"Call me vicar, or Mr. Pigeon. And yes, I was at one time something of a scholar, though not for many years now."

Ethan took a deep breath. "Well, I'm not, Vicar—educated, I mean. Not at all. Never went to school, never learned to read or write, until I asked a lady to teach me last year."

"Good for you. It's never too late."

"I hope not," Ethan said fervently. "My problem is, though, she's gone to live in another country, and though I seem to have picked up reading just fine, me writing's atrocious and me spelling's worse."

The old man nodded. "I see. And what is it you want of me?"

Ethan ran a finger around his collar. "I'm wondering, Vicar, if you'd mind very much helpin' me out from time to time with me spelling." He gave the man a straight look. "I don't want anyone else to know about me little problem, see?"

The old man said nothing.

"I'll pay," Ethan told him. "I was born poor bog Irish—and not ashamed of it—but I'm hopin' to move up in the world and don't wish to look like a fool among educated men."

"Being denied education is nothing to be ashamed of, Mr. Delaney," the vicar said, "and my guess is you're far from a fool." He steepled his fingers and gazed thoughtfully at them for a moment, then said, "I noticed you looking at my chess set when you came in. Do you play?"

Ethan nodded. "A bit."

"Would you give me a game, Mr. Delaney?"

The old man was turning him down gently, Ethan decided, by changing the subject. "Aye, I'll give you a game, sir," he said heavily. He'd been mistaken, thinking the vicar an enlightened man. He was obviously of the class who believed a man should not be educated above his station. Ethan had come across many of that sort in his life, especially in the army.

He fetched the heavy chessboard while the vicar cleared a small table and placed it between them.

"You first," the vicar said, and with a shrug, Ethan made his first move. There was a small knot of anger inside him at the smooth rejection and he resolved to thrash this old man with his soft white hands that had probably never done a hard day's work in his life.

It was not so easy. The vicar had a wily mind, and for all his quiet ways he played a cutthroat game, managing to surprise Ethan more than once. Slowly Ethan's anger drained away as he got more and more caught up in the game. Two hours later the match ended in a stalemate.

The vicar sat back in his chair with a long, satisfied sigh. "That's the best game I've had in years, my boy. That settles the fee."

Ethan looked up. "The fee?"

"For your lessons. You said you were willing to pay."

"Yes, but I thought—"

"You're right, of course, I would normally do it for nothing. It's been a long time since I've done anything as useful, and I do enjoy having pupils, but now that I've seen how well you can play, I can't resist. For every lesson, I want a game of chess."

Ethan gave him a slow grin. "Well, in that case, sir, you owe me a lesson." He pulled the sheet of paper from his pocket. "So would ye mind showin' me the errors I've made in that?"

The vicar pulled out a pair of pince-nez and scanned the paper quickly. He peered over the top of his spectacles. "A letter to a lady?"

Ethan felt his face warm. "Yes, sir. To the lady who taught me my letters in the first place."

The old man smiled. "And you'd like her to be proud of her pupil. Excellent." He read a bit more and paused. "And would she be an elderly lady?"

"No, sir."

The old man's eyes twinkled. "Pretty, is she?"

"She would say not, but then she's never seen herself when she looks into a man's eyes and gives him that smile of hers. She has her own sort o' beauty and has loyal and lovin' ways." He added defiantly, "She's a fine-bred lady, and way above me in station, but I'm by way of courting her." People wouldn't approve of that, either, Ethan thought, but he didn't care.

The vicar's snowy brows rose. He glanced at the address on the back of the paper. "The Principality of Zindaria? That's a long way away. May an old man inquire how you met this foreign lady?"

"She's as English as you, sir. She was governess to the princess of Zindaria, who is herself an Englishwoman. I met Tibby—Miss Tibthorpe, that is—in Dorset, where she had the neatest wee cottage. It got burned through no fault of hers, and she lost everything. Just a little thing, she is, but with so much courage—" Hearing his voice crack with emotion, Ethan stopped.

For a long time there was only the crackling of the fire in the room, then the vicar spoke. "Mr. Delaney, you've reminded this old man what it is to be young and in love again. It would be an honor and a privilege to assist you in the writing of letters to this fine young woman." He pulled out a handkerchief and blew his nose. "Now, put the chess set back in its place and bring me that writing set. We may as well get started on this letter right away."

Harry rode Sabre up into the hills that overlooked Bath. As soon as rolling fields opened up before them, he let his horse have his head. Sabre leapt forward eagerly, as pent up and in need of release as his master.

Harry crouched low over the horse's neck, urging him faster and faster, glorying in the speed and the sensation of being one with the big powerful beast beneath him. Up here he was free of all the stupid pettifogging rules of society. Up here, thundering over the damp fields, he could think.

Cold, clean air scoured his skin, biting deep into his lungs, making his eyes water and his blood sing. On a horse he felt truly alive. He rode on, oblivious of everything except for the rhythmic pounding of Sabre's hooves on the heavy turf.

With the first burst of excess energy burned off in a mad gallop that sent his heart racing, Harry slowed Sabre to an easy canter along the ridge of the hill. He gazed down at the vista of the town before him. Why would people want to live like that, in rows and rows of squashed-together houses, looking down over rows and rows of other squashed-together houses? Most of them were built with their back to the hills, as if a view of buildings was better than the sight of hills and trees and sky.

He shook his head. He never wanted to live in a town. Bad enough to be cooped up in a small town like Bath; he would hate to be stuck in London.

I'm going to London with Mrs. Beasley. Nothing you can say or do will change my mind.

Harry couldn't understand it. He would have sworn that someone like Nell, someone who loved horses and dogs, would have felt the same way about the city. He recalled the way she'd turned her face up to the rain, to the sky, in the forest that first day, as if it were an act of worship.

And yet she seemed utterly set on living in crowded, dirty London.

I must go to London.

Must? Why? What was so special about London?

Harry sighed. He didn't understand women. He never really had. He'd never pursued a woman like this before— not with so little encouragement. Verbal encouragement, he amended. Nell's lips spoke words of rejection but when he'd kissed her, they told a different story. She wanted him. But she wanted to go to London more.

Why could he not simply accept that? It was undignified to pursue a woman who had refused him. It wasn't as if he was in love, after all . . . Just that she seemed so . . . perfect.

And yet why was she so perfect? In most respects she was nothing like the sort of young woman he'd described to his aunt as his ideal wife.

Was Aunt Maude right after all?

Was he so set on Nell because he wanted to prove he could marry an earl's daughter? Because of what had happened all those years ago with Anthea?

Surely not?

And for the first time in years, Harry found himself thinking—deliberately—about Anthea . . . the woman who'd taught him what it felt like to be in love.

Lady Anthea Quenborough had been one-and-twenty years old, the toast of the *ton*, and the loveliest creature Harry had ever seen in his life. Aged just twenty, he'd fallen headlong in love for the first time in his life—blindly, passionately, besottedly.

Lady Anthea was a few months older than Harry in years, but decades older in experience, though he hadn't realized it then.

He was new to London, and though he knew many young men of the *ton*, it was his first experience with a proper lady. Lady Anthea was a golden beauty, a diamond of the first water, aristocratic, rich, and spoiled; the pampered daughter of a doting father and protective brothers. Some of the most notable men of the *ton* swarmed around her, courting her, vying for her favors.

To Harry's stunned delight, she'd chosen him.

It was a whirlwind romance; within a fortnight she'd admitted him to her bed. She'd been his first.

With his mother's example before him, Harry had treated the local village girls cautiously—he'd flirted and kissed and cuddled a bit, but he'd never let himself lose control enough to compromise them. To compromise a girl meant to marry her in Harry's lexicon, and he wasn't interested in marriage.

And then he met Lady Anthea Quenborough . . . delicate, exquisitely beautiful with golden curls and huge, innocent blue eyes . . .

She'd seduced him at a ball, had led him to a small anteroom, where she'd locked the door, and then proceeded to seduce him on a couch. Dazzled by her beauty, in a haze of lust and love, he never even thought to resist, and they'd done it twice on the sofa and once on the floor.

Foolishly, naively, he'd imagined he was her first, too.

The morning after that ball, he'd proposed marriage. She'd laughed and told him not to be silly. And then she'd seduced him again, this time in her coach.

After a fortnight, he decided—young fool that he was— that he was taking advantage of her and should do the honorable thing. He'd applied to her father, the Earl of Quenborough, dressed in his best clothes and with a collar so tight it felt like it'd choke him. He'd been so nervous . . .

He was right to feel that way, only not for the reasons he'd imagined.

He blurted out to the earl that he loved Lady Anthea and that he believed she loved him, and that they wanted to be married.

"Indeed," Lord Quenborough had said in freezing accents. "We shall see what my daughter has to say about that." He'd rung a bell and sent for his daughter and his two sons. How long it seemed, that silent waiting period, with the cold, proud earl staring at Harry as if he were a beetle.

And finally Anthea had arrived, dressed in white, with a blue ribbon that matched her eyes woven through her tumbled gold curls. Harry had never seen her looking more beautiful.

"Yes, Papa?" she'd said, as innocent as a lamb.

"This crippled bastard wants your hand in marriage," the earl had said. "He says you want him, too."

She'd arched her delicate, dark gold brows. "Marry Harry Morant? Wherever did you get such a ludicrous idea?"

Quenborough jerked his chin at Harry. "From him."

She didn't even look at Harry. She pouted in a manner he'd once thought charming. "This is where kindness gets you. You sit out a dance or two with a cripple and he thinks you're in love with him."

Harry stood frozen with shock. It was true he wasn't much of a dancer. His bad leg made him self-conscious on the dance floor, so he avoided it wherever possible.

But he and Anthea had made love while "sitting out" the dances she spoke of. Tender, beautiful love. Or so he'd believed.

She laughed. "Lord, Papa, when the time comes, I'll choose a gentleman—one with all his working parts, thank you."

The earl had nodded. "I thought as much. Run along, my sweet." She'd left the room without so much as a backward glance.

Harry closed his eyes, trying to drive out the memory of what happened next.

"We'd better teach this presumptuous upstart a lesson, boys," Quenborough had said.

With the aid of a couple of sturdy footmen they'd knocked Harry half senseless and dragged him from the room. They'd taken him to the stables and stripped him roughly, ruining his best clothes. Then Anthea's father and brothers took it in turns to horsewhip him. Thoroughly.

At one stage Harry opened his eyes and saw Anthea peeking around the doorway. For a second he imagined—fool that he was!—that she would run to him and stop the beating, crying out that she loved him, that it was all a mistake.

But she'd stayed silent, watching with bright eyes and a smile he'd never forget . . .

Finally they'd dumped him, half naked and bleeding, on the front steps of his father's Mayfair mansion, then rung the doorbell. It was the middle of the day. People came to stare, but Harry was beyond moving. Quenborough had demanded the Earl of Alverleigh come to the door.

It was the first and only time Harry ever saw his father close up. He'd cracked open one swollen eye and stared. It was like looking in a mirror, only thirty years on. His father was the image of himself and his brother Gabe, only with a harsh, severe countenance.

The Earl of Alverleigh stood on the steps, flanked by

his two oldest sons, Harry's half brothers, Marcus and Nash. Harry and Gabe had known them for a short time at school. Known them and hated them. They stared, Marcus with a cold expression that Harry would remember till his dying day.

"Your bastard, I believe, Alverleigh," Anthea's father had said. "We've had to teach him his place."

Harry's father had taken one long look at Harry, bruised, bleeding, and heartbroken, then said the words Harry would never forget, or forgive. "Glover," he said to his butler, "there is a mess on the front step. Have it removed." He turned and went inside. Marcus and Nash followed without saying a word.

Lady Anthea's father and brothers departed also, leaving Harry to the tender mercies of some footmen who carried him to his father's stables, cleaned him up, and sent him off in a hackney cab to his aunt's house.

Shortly after that, Harry had gone to war, not caring much whether he lived or died. There had been a few close shaves, but somehow his brother Gabe and his friends had looked after Harry until he recovered.

He'd sworn off love and ladies of the *ton* for life.

So why had he proposed to another earl's daughter? It had nothing to do with Lady Anthea, he was certain.

He'd seen her last year. Married now to Freddy Soffington-Greene, she'd turned up at the party for his brother's wedding, poured into a golden dress, falling half out of it.

He hadn't felt the least pang, had even felt mild disgust that he could have fallen so passionately in love with such an obvious woman. Watching her in the company of his brother's friends and relatives Harry realized how very young he'd been all those years ago . . . and what a fool love had made of him.

He'd loved Lady Anthea with all his boyish heart.

Comparing Nell to Lady Anthea was like comparing a dove to a snake.

So whatever he felt for Nell, it wasn't love. It was something more . . . ordinary, and yet . . . better.

He kicked Sabre into a gallop again and rode pell-mell along the ridge of the hills, moving in a semicircle around the town below.

Aunt Maude was wrong about his motives for wanting Nell. It was despite her title, not because of it, that he wanted her.

He was certain of it . . . almost.

A movement below caught his eye. A small figure in a brown hat walked briskly along a path that ran between a dry stone wall and a small coppice. There was something familiar about that hat. Nell had worn one very like it when she'd arrived at the Pump Room. It didn't suit her in the least.

He cantered closer.

"Good afternoon, Lady Helen," he called.

She stopped, then turned and asked bluntly, "Mr. Morant. Are you following me?"

He frowned. "No. I was taking a ride to get a breath of fresh air. I assume you were walking for the same reason."

"I was." She made to move on.

"Can't you stay and talk a moment?"

She hesitated. "I cannot stay, I have only an hour or so free and I'm due back shortly."

"May I walk with you?"

"Yes," she said after some consideration, "but only if you promise not to renew your offer. Or, or do anything else to put me to the blush."

He grinned. "If you mean kiss you again, may I remind you that there is a wall between us."

She blushed. "I know, otherwise I would not have agreed. I will agree to general conversation, and that's all."

"I give you my word." He lifted his leg over the saddle and dropped to the ground. "We shall walk and talk of things general, and Sabre will enjoy what may well be his last taste of fresh grass before winter sets in."

She took a deep breath. "The air is so fresh and clear up here, isn't it?" She took a few more steps and added, "It might be my last fresh air for some time. We leave for London tomorrow."

"Tomorrow?" he said, startled. "I thought you had two more days."

"Mrs. Beasley is bored with Bath. She feels London entertainments will prove more to her tastes."

From her tone, he was sure she felt as he did about the city. He said casually, "Don't you like London?"

She gave him a narrow look, as if to warn him off raising forbidden subjects again, and said, "I remember the London fogs from my season, that's all."

"I hate London," he said. "I don't go there if I can help it. I can't breathe there."

She didn't respond, just leaned over the fence and watched Sabre cropping grass. Harry watched the expressions that passed over her face.

"How I would love just one good gallop over the fields," she said.

"I'll take you if you like."

She pulled a comical face. "Bundled up in front of you like a parcel, or behind you like a piece of baggage? It's a kind thought, but no, thank you."

He promptly offered her the reins. "Then ride him on your own. I'm sure you can."

She laughed. "On that saddle? In this skirt? The amount of leg exposed would be indecent."

His mouth dried at the thought. "You have ridden astride, then?"

"When I was a wild, hoydenish girl," she admitted with a laughing, mock guilty expression. "I had a skirt especially made for it and wore breeches underneath, but Papa was horrified when he found out. He made me promise him I wouldn't ever do it again."

"And you never did?"

"No. I'd promised. Papa knew I didn't break my promises."

There was a slight emphasis on the "my," Harry noticed, as if Papa's promises were something quite different. And he supposed, if the man had gambled everything away, they would be.

"You're still a girl," he reminded her.

She made a wry grimace. "No. No, I'm not. When I was a girl, I was such an innocent, and so naive. I thought everything would go on and on forever, just as it was." She added ruefully, "I lived in a silly dream world, you see; a beautiful, rose-colored bubble."

The bubble had well and truly burst, he saw.

She sighed. "I must get back. Mrs. Beasley went to bed with one of her heads, but she'll be up soon." She broke off with a chuckle. "That's what she calls the headache—'one of my heads'—but every time she says it, I imagine her opening a box and selecting one from a number of severed heads." She gave him a mischievous glance. "Silly, I know."

He shook his head, unable to think of a word to say. When she looked at him like that, her lips primmed with mirth and her eyes dancing, the only thing in his mind was to leap the wall and kiss her senseless.

She looked away. "Sabre is a beautiful creature. May I give him a treat?"

"Yes, of course, but be careful; he's not always a gentleman when it comes to food."

From her skirt pocket she pulled out a slightly browned apple core. She saw his look and explained. "Habit of a lifetime, I'm afraid. I've always saved my apple cores. I keep forgetting I don't have horses anymore." She held out her palm, crooning in a low voice, "Sabre, you handsome brute, look what I have for you?"

At her words Harry felt himself hardening. Thank God there was a wall between them. Sabre responded almost as eagerly, stretching out his head to sniff greedily at the morsel. Harry kept his hand on the halter, just in case, but Sabre lifted the core delicately off her palm.

"Oh, what a slander, not a gentleman indeed. You have beautiful manners, don't you?" she told the horse, rubbing his nose with one hand and reaching up to scratch his ears with the other. "You like that, don't you, darling?"

Harry was tempted to point out he'd like it, too, but he knew she'd walk off on him.

"Those beautiful manners of his are the result of many long hours of training against his own nature. His breed has been encouraged to bite any but their master's hands since time immemorial."

She looked up, her brow furrowed. "His breed? The only horses I've heard of that are still bred to fight are Zindarian warrior horses, and they're supposed to be a myth."

"Then a mythical horse just ate your apple core," he told her.

Her glorious eyes widened. "You mean—" She turned to examine Sabre more thoroughly. "He is different from any other horse I've seen—I remember admiring him that first time in the forest. Is he really a Zindarian warrior horse?"

"Yes, and there are seven more like him in the stables at Firmin Court." Harry couldn't keep the pride out of his voice.

"Seven more?" she exclaimed. "However did you manage that?"

"My brother is married to the princess of Zindaria. Sabre

was their gift to me. My business partner, Ethan Delaney, owns the other seven. He threw himself into the path of a bullet meant for the little crown prince and saved his life. As a reward the prince regent granted Ethan the gift of his choice of seven horses from the Royal Zindar stables for the next seven years."

"But that'll be forty-nine Zindarian horses," she gasped.

"Yes, and nobody has a better eye for horses than Ethan. He'll choose the cream of the crop, and by breeding them with the finest and fleetest English Thoroughbreds, we're hoping to build a stud with a reputation throughout Europe."

"Zindarian warrior horses," she breathed. "I never even believed in them until now. Sabre's very fast, I saw that when you were galloping along the ridge earlier."

"Yes, I'm planning to race him next season." So she'd been watching him, Harry thought, repressing a smile. So much for her accusation of him following her when he'd first ridden up, the minx.

"Oh, how I would love to see all eight of them together."

"You could always come back with m—"

"Please don't!" she said, cutting him off. "You promised you wouldn't ask me again."

"Today. Yes, I'm sorry," he said, not sorry at all. As he thought, she was entranced by the idea of what he and Ethan were trying to do. So what the hell was she doing going to a place like London where all that would be stifled?

"Why are you going to London?"

She gave him a narrow look. "I'm looking for someone."

"A man?"

"No."

"Who?"

"That's my business."

Harry could see she wasn't going to get any more specific. "Are you in love with anyone else?" he found himself asking.

She stopped and turned to frown at him.

"I'm not breaking my promise," he said hurriedly. "Just . . . making conversation."

"Conversation? It feels more like an interrogation."

"Sorry. I'm not very good at conversation," he told her.

She gave him a doubtful look.

"It's true," he assured her. "When I was growing up, Great-aunt Gert used to have my brother Gabe and me in for 'polite conversation' every Sunday afternoon. It was agony. I was a miserable failure at it. Still am."

Her face softened. "Really?"

He nodded ruefully. "My friend Ethan calls me a stump. Mind you, he could talk the leg off an iron pot. He's Irish, and a born storyteller." He smiled reflectively. "On the peninsular Ethan's tales could make men forget their fear and empty bellies . . ."

"Papa had the gift, too," she said after a moment. "So much charm . . . and the stories he could tell . . . He even believed his own stories."

She sighed and walked on. "Tell me more about your friend, Ethan," she said.

"He's older than the rest of us, about forty, an ugly-looking brute with more than a touch of the dandy about him. Ethan's the sort who'd emerge from a battle bleeding from half a dozen wounds and loudly lamenting the ruination of his waistcoat."

She laughed. "He was the man with you in the forest, wasn't he?"

"Yes, that was Ethan." Encouraged by her interest, Harry continued, "In the army he wasn't really one of us; we were officers and he was a sergeant, and officers and men don't mix. But he has a cool head and we were green young fools, and he saved us from making disastrous mistakes a time or two. I always liked Ethan and he's a genius with horses, so after we'd left the army we went into partnership in this horse-breeding enterprise."

"You say he's older. Does he have a family?"

"No. He says he's courting, though I don't know who it can be. I've never even seen him with a woman since the war. As I said, he's no oil painting—not that the señoritas and mademoiselles seemed to mind—but the only woman I've seen him with in England is—" He broke off, frowning. "—Tibby? No, that can't be right."

"Tibby?" she prompted.

"Miss Tibthorpe. She was my sister-in-law's old governess."

"She's old?"

He shook his head. "No. She's a prim little sharp-faced spinster well on the wrong side of thirty, as buttoned up a woman as ever I've seen—" He looked at Nell and added slowly, "But with backbone enough for two. Now I come to think of it, they did spend rather a lot of time together last year. I thought it was because of the boys, but . . ."

"I like the sound of Tibby," she said. "I like the sound of Ethan, too."

"Yes, Tibby's a good little stick, and Ethan's an excellent fellow—and what he can't do with a horse . . . It's uncanny. But no, Tibby's in Zindaria. It can't be her. Ethan's always had the most ravishing mistresses; why would he want to marry an aging spinster with no looks to speak of? She doesn't have a penny to her name, either."

"She sounds a lot like me," Nell said quietly.

"No, you're beautiful," he said absentmindedly. "But Tibby and Ethan . . . I wonder . . ." He walked along, deep in thought.

Nell watched him, a bittersweet taste in her mouth. He'd just called her beautiful, without thought, without calculation, without even realizing . . .

Nobody in the world had ever called Nell beautiful. Except perhaps her mother when she was a baby. And Papa, of course.

"I, I really must go now," she said huskily. "I hope Tibby and Ethan both find happiness."

He turned with an apologetic expression. "I'm sorry, I've been boring on about people you don't even know. I told you I was no good at conversation."

"No, no, it's been fascinating," she said truthfully. "I've loved every minute of it."

Their eyes locked. She was the first to break it.

"I never had a chance with you, did I?" he asked quietly.

"No. I'm sorry, not the way things are now."

He gazed into her face, as if trying to glean a hidden meaning in what she'd said.

Unable to stand the intensity of his gaze she dropped her eyes. "If we'd met a year ago, then perhaps . . ." She made a fatalistic gesture. "But now, I really do have to go. We leave tomorrow morning."

"So this is the last time I'll see you?"

She hesitated. "Yes. Mrs. Beasley requires one more visit to the Pump Room to complete the course of waters her physician prescribed. She'll go first thing in the morning so we can get on the road early."

He nodded gruffly. He had one more day. Less.

"It's been an honor knowing you, Mr. Morant," she said with only the faintest quiver in her voice. She held out her hand to him over the stone wall.

His eyes locked with hers as Harry turned her hand over and placed a kiss in the center of her palm. Her fingers curved around his jaw in a featherlight caress, then she withdrew her hand.

"P-please give my love to everyone at Firmin Court when you return there and—" Her voice cracked and she continued huskily. "T-take good care of them. And of yourself. G-good-bye, Harry Morant." She turned and hurried away down the hill, disappearing in minutes.

Harry mounted Sabre thoughtfully. Everything he'd learned about her in the last hour only confirmed what he'd been thinking for days now. She'd make him the perfect wife.

Not because she was an earl's daughter, but because she was Nell.

Seven

*H*arry found it hard to get to sleep that night. Nell was still set on going to London. It wasn't because of a man; she'd said she wasn't in love with anyone else, and he believed her.

And the Beasley woman had no hold over her, she was just *convenient*.

Harry kicked at the blankets that had become tangled around his legs.

The only reason Nell was going to London was to find someone.

He could find people. He could go to London.

And he wouldn't make her run out in the rain fetching things for him. He would make sure she was warm and dry and comfortable.

She was not indifferent to him, he was sure. Almost sure. Fairly sure.

As sure as a man could be who had been turned down twice.

But she had kissed him back that time in the storeroom. She'd wanted him then.

And he wanted her with a power that almost drove the breath from his body.

More than any woman in his life. Just why she affected him so strongly, he wasn't sure, just that she did. And every instinct he had was telling him to keep her, now that he'd found her again.

His instincts had kept him alive though years of war. He'd learned not to question them.

Harry thumped his pillow decisively. The solution was obvious. He would take Nell to London and help her find whoever it was she had to find. And while they were doing that, he would find out what it was that made her say she couldn't marry him and . . . fix it.

Simple.

As long as he could persuade her to go to London with him.

She hadn't been amazingly persuadable up to now, he reflected. But a man could only try.

And dammit, he would.

They were going to the Pump Room early. What time was early? Dawn, Harry decided. No, before dawn—dawn was around eight, and he had an idea the Pump Room opened before that for ordinary folk. And perhaps for people intending to make an early start to London.

He would get up at five a.m. then, to shave and dress. He wanted to look his best. Every little bit helped.

Third time lucky, they said.

*T*he doors opened at six. Harry entered and sat down beside a column to wait. An amazing collection of invalids passed before him; clearly the times he had come before were the fashionable hours.

He watched people hobbling in, being wheeled and carried and supported in. Poor bastards. They took the waters and left. Harry thanked God for his health and checked his fob watch.

They arrived at half past eight. Mrs. Beasley swept in dressed in a scarlet velvet traveling dress and wearing a hat that bore enough flowers to cover a grave. Nell was in brown again with that ugly little brown hat she always wore. It was the kind of hat that deserved shooting, Harry thought.

He pulled back behind the column a little as La Beasley swept past. Not that she would have noticed. Expecting nobody fashionable, she spared not a glance for anyone else, but imperiously brushed aside anyone in her way.

Nell followed in her wake with a shy smile or a quiet word to the people she passed, and as she paused to let an arthritic old woman hobble to a chair, Harry stepped out from behind his column. She froze for a moment, glanced at Mrs. Beasley, who was oblivious, then shook her head at Harry and hurried after her employer.

As he'd expected, she wasn't intending to speak to him. He waited while she settled Mrs. Beasley in a chair and placed a shawl around her shoulders, then, when she loudly complained that there was a draught, helped her to shift to another chair.

Finally Nell moved toward the pump. Harry stepped into her path. "I must talk to to you," he said.

She glanced back to check her employer hadn't noticed. "No, we've said our good-byes." She filled the glass.

"One final word."

She shook her head and took the glass of hot mineral water to Mrs. Beasley.

Harry moved closer, making it clear to her that he wasn't going to tamely leave. He would speak with her. He folded his arms and waited.

It wasn't long before Mrs. Beasley noticed him, as he'd

known she would. She eyed his body, glanced at Nell, then looked back at Harry to check who he was watching.

Harry inclined his head politely at her but didn't move. The woman preened, fiddled with yet another large jewel resting in her substantial cleavage and gave him a come-hither look.

Harry didn't move.

Nell looked away.

Mrs. Beasley leaned in Nell's direction and said something that Harry couldn't hear. Nell shook her head and seemed to disagree.

Harry tried not to smile. He knew exactly what was happening.

A mutinous expression on her face, Nell marched toward him. "Mrs. Beasley wishes me to convey an invitation to you to join her," she said in a flat voice, and then with a hint of fire, added, "and *I* wish to convey my desire for you to leave."

Harry pulled his fob watch from his pocket and consulted it ostentatiously. Then with a sorrowful expression he hoped was visible from the other side of the room said, "Tell your mistress, I'm desolated to have to disappoint her, but I have an appointment." He smiled and added, "With you in the small room out the back in two minutes."

"No. I won't—"

"Otherwise I will join you both now and tell you exactly what's on my mind."

She narrowed her eyes at him. "That's blackmail."

"Dreadful isn't it?" he agreed. "But effective."

She hesitated, her jaw tightening as she read the determination in his eyes. "Oh, very well, if you must be so unprincipled. But only for a moment."

He inclined his head. "I'll see you there in two minutes' time."

Nell returned to her seat hoping her face didn't show the inner turmoil she was feeling. Wretched man. If she didn't meet him he would make trouble for her.

She didn't want to meet him. What was there to say, after all? She'd said her good-byes, she was ready to leave . . . as much as anyone could be. Oh, why did he have to make it so hard for her?

Stubborn, impossible man. Every man she'd had in her life had let her down in the worst way. Did he think she was going to trust her future and her happiness—and more, her daughter's future happiness and security—to a man she'd met precisely four times?

Even if he was the most appealing man she'd ever met.

Papa was kind and sweet and had bucketloads of charm but he'd ruined Nell's life. As for what he'd done with Torie . . .

And Papa had loved Nell.

Not a single word of love had passed Harry Morant's lips. Not that she would believe it anyway, but still, she was glad of that, at least. The last thing she wanted was a man like him falling in love with her.

How impossible would he be then?

"Well?" Mrs. Beasley said as she returned.

"He said was sorry, but he had an appointment to keep."

"Hmph. I suppose that's why he was here at such a wretchedly unfashionable time. What a pity." She stared across the room at him. "He's such a divine specimen of masculinity."

And an annoying one, Nell thought. Today he was dressed in gleaming top boots, tight buff trousers that molded to his powerful thighs, a dark blue coat and a blue and gray striped waistcoat that contrasted wonderfully with his gray eyes.

He was just too wretchedly handsome for his own good. And he knew it. He must have thought she would take one look at him and fall into his arms.

Well, she had more important things on her mind, and she wasn't falling into anyone's arms, even if they did look like Apollo. With dark brown hair. And gray eyes. And a smile that did strange things to her insides.

The only person Nell had ever been able to rely on was herself. She didn't need her life to be any more complicated. And she didn't give a snap of her fingers for any handsome, lusty, stubborn charmer.

Mrs. Beasley jumped. "What was that for?"

Nell blinked. "What?"

"You snapped your fingers."

"Oh, sorry. I just thought of something."

"Well, don't." Mrs. Beasley sipped the hot mineral water with distaste. "Vile stuff. I can feel it doing me good, but thank God it's the last dose."

They sat in silence for a while. Nell would meet him, all right, she decided. And she'd give him a piece of her mind.

She shifted uncomfortably on her seat. A moment later she wriggled again.

"For heaven's sake, girl, sit still."

"I can't," Nell confessed. "I think I need to visit the necessary. Immediately. The veal olives last night, perhaps . . ."

Mrs. Beasley waved her off distastefully. "Well, run along then. I hope to goodness you're not going to cause any delays on the road, because I'll warn you now, I won't tolerate it."

Nell hurried away toward the back of the room. She slipped through the baize-covered door and let herself quietly into the storeroom. It was empty, then Harry Morant slipped in behind her.

Suddenly the storeroom felt a whole lot smaller.

"I suppose you thought I wouldn't come?" she said. The skin of his jaw had that fresh-shaved look she found so appealing in men. She could smell the faint tang of some cologne.

"I knew you'd come." His eyes crinkled in a faint, triumphant smile.

The smile fanned the flames of her temper. "Only because you'd blackmailed me!" She poked him in the chest with her finger. "How dare you threaten my livelihood?"

"Livelihood!" He snorted. "Working for that witch isn't a livelihood."

She threw her hands up in frustration. "It's not your business. Now, you're wasting my time. We leave for London within the hour." She tried to push past him but he stopped her.

"I'll take you to London."

Nell was dumbfounded. "What?"

"You heard me."

She narrowed her eyes. "But you don't want to go to London. You hate London, you said you can't breathe there."

He made an impatient gesture. "Do you or do you not want to go to London?"

"I do, but—"

"Then I'll take you."

"You can't. It—it wouldn't be proper. If I arrived with you in London, everyone would think I was your—" She broke off.

"My—?" He raised one eyebrow.

"You know very well what," she retorted.

"Perhaps. But it would be quite proper if you came as my wife," he said. "Marry me and I'll take you to London."

Nell started to tremble. *Marry me and I'll take you to London.*

He moved closer. "Look, it's not love's young dream I'm offering you but it makes sense. You and I desire each other—you know that. I need a wife and you need someone to take care of you. And I'll take you to London."

She put out her hands and held him back. He made no attempt to take hold of her, but he didn't move away. His waistcoat was smooth and silken under her fingertips. She could feel the strong, steady thud of his heart beneath her palms. She wanted to pull them back, but she knew he would only move forward again.

"I—I told you I couldn't marry you," she said shakily. "Why won't you listen?"

"Your lips say one thing . . ." He looked at her lips and his voice deepened. "But when I kiss you, they say another."

"It was a stolen kiss," she muttered.

"Perhaps, but you kissed me back. You pulled me closer. You pressed your body against me and ran your fingers through my hair." His voice was deep and intense. "You took my tongue into your mouth."

She made an embarrassed gesture of denial, and he immediately took advantage, moving closer, until he was so close that they stood, breast to chest and thigh to thigh. The heat of his big, hard body burned through her brown stuff traveling gown as if it were the lightest silk.

"You know you want it as much as I do."

She did, God help her.

"You work for that witch because she's going to London. Convenient, you said it was. Marry me and you'll have convenience *and* security. Till death us do part."

Oh God, why did he have to put it like that? Nell thought. As if he knew how much she craved security after twenty-seven years of the shifting uncertainties of life with Papa.

And she did desire him. What red-blooded woman would not? The mystery was why he would desire her, but she didn't question it. She could feel the desire radiating from his big, tense body in the close confines of the store-room.

She swallowed. And now he wanted to take her to London.

The temptation was enormous. If she said yes, she could have everything she wanted . . . almost.

But she would have to lie to get it. Lie by omission.

She turned her head this way and that, trying to escape that intense gray gaze, but it was no use. She was trapped.

He thought her an innocent. He would change his tune if he knew about Torie, she was certain.

He didn't love her. It would take love of an extraordinary degree to take on a wife with an illegitimate child—one she had no intention of giving away or hiding or being ashamed of. What happened was neither Torie's fault, nor hers.

It would take love . . . or perhaps utter indifference. If the latter, then perhaps there was a chance for them . . .

She opened her mouth to explain.

"So this is how you behave!" Mrs. Beasley throbbed from the doorway. "Sneaking off behind my back to fornicate in a storeroom! At nine o'clock in the morning! You little trollop! How long has this been going on?"

"I didn't, it's not what you think—" Nell stammered. "Mrs. Beasley, I promise you—"

"Don't lie to me, strumpet!" *Slap!* Her hand flashed out, leaving a livid mark on Nell's tender cheek.

Enraged, Harry pulled Nell back. "Touch her again, madam, and so help me, though I've never laid a finger on a woman in my life, you'll be the first."

Mrs. Beasley took one look at his white face and glittering eyes and stepped back out of reach. She looked at Nell and said in a loud, spiteful voice, "I always knew you were a trollop! You've been eying off all the men ever since I've taken you on—"

"Silence!" Harry snarled. "Speak to Lady Helen with respect or suffer the consequences."

She flushed angrily and said to Nell. "You know he's a bastard, don't you, Lady Helen? Some lord rutted with his whore of a maidservant and got himself a bast—"

Slap! Nell's hand made a white imprint on Mrs. Beasley's cheek. "How dare you speak about him like that!" Nell flashed.

"You little bitch!" La Beasley surged forward, her arm raised to deliver a back hander.

Harry caught her fleshy arm in mid-swing. "That's enough."

"She's my employee, I can do whatever I like."

"No, madam, she's my affianced wife, and if you touch her, I'll throttle you."

"Get your filthy hands off me, you fornicating bast—"

Nell surged forward to defend him again. Harry dropped Mrs. Beasley's arm and caught Nell around the waist. Trapped between two furious women, he could think of only one thing to do.

He swung Nell over his shoulder and shoved past her gibbering, enraged employer. Ignoring Nell's kicks and demands to be let down, he strode unevenly through the silent, staring Pump Room crowds, his limp very much in evidence.

"Good morning, ladies and gentlemen," he said, as if nothing untoward was taking place. "Just taking my fiancée for a stroll."

"Arr, those waters," one old man said into the hush. "Marvelous what they can do for a body."

Eight

"*P*ut me down," Nell insisted for the twentieth time. She pummeled him with her fists to add force to her demand.

"Not till I've got you safe," Harry stumped on, unperturbed by the stares of strangers on the street. "My aunt's house is around the next corner."

"This is kidnapping."

"So it is." He patted her on the rump and she squeaked with annoyance and thumped him on the back.

Nell subsided as he reached his aunt's house and rang the doorbell. "Good morning, Sprotton," Harry said. "Lovely morning."

"Beautiful, Mr. Harry," the butler responded smoothly, quite as if Mr. Harry didn't have a woman draped over his shoulder.

"My aunt in?"

"No, sir, you've missed her by half an hour or thereabouts."

"Pity. Oh well, when she returns, let her know we have a lady come to stay with us." He bent and placed Nell on her feet, saying, "Lady Helen Freymore, this is Sprotton, my aunt's butler. Sprotton, she'll be staying in the best spare bedroom."

Her hat had fallen off somewhere in the street, her hair was straggling out in all directions, and she was certain she looked like she'd been pulled through a hedge backward, but Nell extended her hand to the butler, saying calmly. "How do you do, Sprotton?"

"Welcome, my lady," Sprotton said and shook her hand with equal dignity.

"Sprotton, Lady Helen's baggage is currently at—" Harry turned to Nell. "Where were you staying again?"

There was no point arguing. She had no future with Mrs. Beasley anymore. Nell gave the butler the address of her lodgings and told him what to fetch. He bowed, issued instructions to two waiting footmen, and sent them off.

"Would you like a cup of tea, Lady Helen?"

"That would be lovely, thank you, Sprotton," Nell said.

"In the withdrawing room?" the butler inquired, indicating the room with a subtle gesture.

"Perfect," Nell said and stalked into the withdrawing room. She was hopping mad.

Harry followed her, his eyes twinkling. She seated herself on a small hard chair and regarded him coolly. "So, as I told you it would, that meeting cost me my job."

"Yes," said Harry. "Sorry."

"You're not sorry at all," she flashed. "You're as pleased as punch about it."

"I know. And once you've calmed down a little, you'll realize you're much better off. I'll take you to London and help you do whatever it is you need to do."

"And what if I don't want to do it with you?"

That wiped the pleased expression from his face. But

only for a second. He shrugged. "Better with me than with that harpy."

"At least with her my personal business would have remained private," she muttered ungraciously.

"And it wouldn't with me?"

"No."

"But you've lived with her for several weeks and you've only met me four times."

"Yes, but even after two weeks with her, she's still a stranger, whereas—" She stopped, aware she was giving too much away. It was frightening how quickly he'd got under her skin.

They sat for a moment in silence. "Thank you for coming to my defense," he said eventually. "I was very touched."

She made an embarrassed gesture.

"It actually doesn't upset me, being called a bastard," he told her. "I've been called one all my life. One becomes inured to such things."

"I could *never* become inured to it," she said vehemently. "I *hate* that word and I won't have it spoken in my house. My presence," she corrected herself belatedly.

He gave her a thoughtful look. "I see."

"No, you don't," she began, but just as she was about to explain, Sprotton entered with the tea tray. To Nell's surprise, as well as the pot of tea, there was a large plate of sandwiches, some ginger cake, and half a dozen jam tarts.

"Surely it's not time for luncheon," she said.

"No, my lady, but Cook thought seeing as Mr. Harry left the house before breakfast he might be glad of a little something before luncheon."

Mr. Harry, whose mouth was already full of ham sandwich, nodded at Sprotton and winked at Nell. When he'd swallowed, he said, "Delicious. Tell Cook she was spot-on as always. I'll pop in myself and thank her later."

He saw Nell's look of surprise and said, "I first met Cook when my brother Gabe and I were growing lads and always hungry. She made it her mission in life to feed us." He took another sandwich and added plaintively, "She still thinks I'm a growing lad."

Sprotton said dryly, "I shall correct her misapprehension, Mr. Harry."

"Do so at your peril, Sprotton," Harry said with a grin and reached for a third sandwich. The butler bowed ironically and glided from the room.

It was the first time Nell had seen Harry Morant in his home environment. She liked the easy way he had with the servants. It made him more appealing than ever.

She drank her tea. She had to tell him.

The door flew open and Lady Gosforth sailed in. "Such a to-do," she declared, removing her hat and handing it to the butler, who'd followed her in. "Another cup, Sprotton. The Pump Room is in uproar, my dears. Such excitement. The whole of Bath is agog." She removed her coat, plumped herself down on the sofa and regarded them with sparkling eyes. "So, we have a wedding to arrange."

"Yes," Harry said.

"No," said Nell.

"Yes," Harry repeated more firmly.

"He's right, my dear," Lady Gosforth told Nell. "There really is no choice after the public scene he made. Did he really carry you bodily from the Pump Room and up the street?"

"Carried her all the way into this house," Sprotton murmured as he filled a cup with tea, added lemon, and passed it to her.

"Wonderful. What a tale! Harry, dear boy, I never thought you had it in you. Will we have the wedding in Bath or in London?"

"There won't be a wedd—" Nell began.

"In London," Harry said. "Nell wants to get to London as soon as possible."

"Excellent. I'll make all the arrangements." Lady

Gosforth drained her teacup and bounced to her feet. "Oh, I do so love a wedding."

"We leave for London this afternoon," Harry told her. "You'll come with us, I hope, Aunt Maude."

Nell almost spilled her tea. *This afternoon?*

"I wouldn't miss it for the world. Besides, someone has to take the poor child shopping—she can't get married in the clothes she has." She bent down and kissed Nell warmly on the cheek. "Welcome to the family, my dear. I've been itching to dress you, just itching!" She sailed from the room, clapping her hands, saying, "Sprotton, call the staff together, we're going to London this afternoon. We must pack."

Nell blinked and caught her breath.

Harry saw her expression and chuckled. "Like a whirlwind when she gets going isn't she?"

Nell nodded, then swallowed. "She's very kind. You all are. But—I can't marry you."

"Nonsen—"

"I'm not *fit* for marriage."

He bent forward in sudden concern. "Are you ill?"

For a second she was tempted to say yes, but she couldn't bring herself to lie to him, not when he'd laid himself so open to her. "Not ill. Morally unfit."

He frowned. "You mean you're not a young innocent?"

"No, I'm not. Not at all."

He shrugged and sat back in his chair. "Which of us are by this age. I'm no pattern card of respectability, myself."

"It's worse than that. I had a baby. A daughter."

He blinked. He was silent a long time, then he said, "Who's the father?"

She shook her head. "It doesn't matter."

"It does."

She set her jaw. "I won't tell you. My daughter has nothing to do with *him*." She almost snarled the word.

Harry frowned. "You mean he doesn't acknowledge it?"

"No." She met his gaze squarely. "You can ask until you're blue in the face but I'll never tell a soul."

"Not even your daughter?"

"Especially not her."

He didn't like that, she could see. Too bad, she wouldn't change her mind.

He had a grim look in his eyes, but his voice was mild enough when he asked, "Where is the baby now?"

"I don't know. I lost her."

"Lost her? You mean—oh, I'm sorry."

"No!" she said quickly, seeing his expression. "Not lost as in—" She couldn't bring herself to say the words. "She's alive, I think—I pray—but she's *lost*. As in I don't know where she is. Papa stole her away from me while I was asleep, and before I could find out where he'd taken her he was dead. I think she's somewhere in London."

He said nothing for some time, looking thoughtful. He was shocked, she knew.

"How long ago did you give birth?"

She stared. It was an odd thing to ask. "Just over two months ago."

He frowned. "Two months? And yet when I first saw you, you were traveling alone, uncared for, on the back of a cart!" He sounded furious. "Dammit, you—someone needs to be taking better care of you than that! Two bloody months!"

"I had no choice in the matter," she said quietly.

He seemed to master his anger. "And now you're starting to look for her?"

"No, of course I didn't wait that long! I went after Papa straight away. But he died on the road. I buried him and then went on to London. I searched everywhere for my daughter. For weeks I walked the streets of London, searching for her, asking everyone I could think of, but finally . . ."

"Finally you gave up."

"No! I'll never give up on her," she said vehemently. "But I ran out of money and I collapsed in the street."

"Dammit! So you fell ill, because nobody was taking care of you." He clenched his fists.

"No, I wasn't eating enough, that was all. I'd been saving every penny for the search for Torie. That's her name, Victoria Elizabeth, after my mother."

He swore again under his breath.

"I realized then I couldn't go on the way I was. I couldn't help my daughter if I was dead in a ditch. That's why I came home, to Firmin Court, to raise some more money to go back and keep searching until I found her."

Harry stared at her. "That's why your feet and skirts were so muddy," he said slowly. "You'd been walking. You walked home. All the way back from London?"

"Oh no," she assured him. "Not all the way. I got several lifts."

"I wouldn't send a mare on a journey like that so soon after giving birth!" He closed his eyes and said something under his breath. "And when you got there, you found your home had been sold."

She nodded. "I was in flat despair at first, not knowing how I could ever get back, but then the vicar saw the advertisement for a companion to accompany a Bristol lady to London. It was the answer to a prayer."

"And you got the harpy from hell."

"No, honestly, I didn't care a rap for the way she carried on. As long as she got me to London to look for Torie, she could call me anything she liked. My only problem with her was the delay she made in Bath to drink the waters."

"Well, there we shall have to disagree, because if she hadn't, I would never have found you again."

She stared at him. "What do you mean?"

"I would have thought it was perfectly obvious."

"You can't still be thinking of marrying me," she told him. "I'm a *fallen woman*!"

"What rubbish, of course you're not. And of course I'm still going to marry you."

"Even though I've had a baby?"

"Yes. I want you to have babies. I want a family."

"But what about Torie?"

"We'll start looking for her as soon as we get to London."

"I won't give her up."

He frowned. "I wouldn't ask you to."

"But she's a—you know—illegitimate. Most men would never even think of taking a child like that into their home."

"I'm not most men. She'll live with us, of course."

She stared at him, unable to think of a thing to say. Her mouth wobbled. Tears slowly filled her eyes and fell, unchecked.

He pulled out a handkerchief and started drying her cheeks. "In my experience it makes no difference if you are or if you aren't illegitimate. My brother Gabe was born in wedlock. His father got some maggot into his head, decided Gabe wasn't his son, and refused to have him in the house. Gabe grew up the spitting image of him. Made no difference. Father never relented. Called him a bastard till the day he died."

"That's terrible," she whispered in a choked voice.

"I was born to the same father, but my mother was a maidservant. As soon as she discovered she was pregnant, he married her off to the the village blacksmith and I was born in wedlock. Legally legitimate. But you know what people call me."

He finished drying her tears and held the handkerchief to her nose. "Blow" he said, and like a small child she blew. She was exhausted.

He put the handkerchief away, then said, "Now that we've got that all cleared up, you'd better go upstairs.

Wash your face and take a nice long nap. I'll wake you for luncheon and we'll leave for London after that."

She stared at him unable to take in such generosity of spirit. "I don't understand; why would you want someone like me when you could have your pick of fresh young girls with no stain on their past?"

"You haven't worked it out yet?"

She shook her head, mystified.

"Because of this," he said and kissed her.

It wasn't the kind of burning kiss of before; it was just a simple kiss, tender and gentle. A promise, an affirmation. And it moved her unbearably.

Harry released her and stepped back. They had their lives to organize. He rang the bell and sent for his aunt's housekeeper to usher Nell upstairs. He hoped she would take his advice about napping. She looked exhausted. He was partially responsible for that but at least now he could ensure she was properly taken care of instead of being run ragged.

Two bloody months!

He forced himself to focus on the task in hand: there was much to do if they were to leave for London today. Normally he would ride, but for this trip he'd hire a post chaise for himself and Nell. He wanted a little privacy. His aunt would follow in her own traveling carriage with her dresser, Bragge. She wouldn't mind.

But first, he had a few letters to write. He fetched a small writing desk from the sideboard and took out a pen, ink, and several sheets of paper.

He trimmed the nib, dipped it in ink, and stared at the blank white paper, his mind filled with questions.

A child. He had to admit it was a shock. He hadn't expected anything like that.

Who the hell was the father? Why wouldn't she say? Did she love him? She sounded as though she hated him, but love very easily turned to hate, he knew. Why hadn't she told the fellow about the baby? He must be married, otherwise he would have married her, surely?

He'd find out, he vowed. The main thing was that he had Nell under his roof. His aunt's roof, he amended, but it was the next best thing. He wasn't going to let her get away from him again.

All he had to do now was find her baby, marry her, and take them both home to Firmin Court. They would be a family. He dipped the pen in the ink and started to write.

He wrote to Rafe and Luke first, asking them to meet him in London. They could help in the search for Nell's baby, instead of racing around the countryside risking their fool necks.

He wrote to Barrow and Mrs. Barrow, telling them he was getting married. The Barrows were the closest thing he had to parents.

Mrs. Barrow would cry, he knew. She always did at weddings, and for Harry's she'd probably weep buckets. She would get a new dress and hat, too. Especially for a fancy London wedding, which it was bound to be with Aunt Maude at the helm. Harry didn't care. He would just as soon do it quickly by special license, but women were different.

Having trapped Nell into marriage, he wanted her to have the wedding she wanted.

He sealed the letter to the Barrows, and then penned a quick note to Ethan, apologizing for leaving things in his hands for so long and explaining that he was getting married. He also asked Ethan to carry out a couple of personal requests.

He smiled as he pictured Ethan's face when he learned that Firmin Court would have a mistress before the month was out and who that mistress was. Harry dusted the letter

with sand and wondered how Ethan's own courtship was
progressing.

*E*than picked up Tibby's latest letter for the third time.
Such fine, elegant script—he could never learn to
write so beautifully, not if he practiced for the rest of his
life. He read it through slowly, his lips moving as he read.

> *I think I told you that when I first came here, my dear
> Kitty-cat was something of a novelty, ginger cats being
> uncommon in Zindaria. I am embarrassed to report that
> they are much more common these days, Kitty-cat hav-
> ing made the acquaintance of several of the palace
> kitchen cats. He also makes up shamelessly to the cook,
> who feeds him tidbits. It is very fine to live in a palace,
> but I must confess that there are days I miss my own
> dear little cottage. But I must not repine. I am a very
> fortunate woman.*
>
> *Callie has been very kind and employed me as her
> private secretary. The job is not very demanding and
> not at all worthy of the substantial salary I am paid, but
> it is interesting. I am now acquainted, through my letter
> writing on her behalf, with half the royalty of Europe,
> and I understand much more these days of the intrica-
> cies of court etiquette.*

Ethan swallowed. Court etiquette—he hadn't even
known what the word meant until he'd asked the vicar. He
was dreaming, hoping a woman who was on letter-writing
terms with half the royalty of Europe would look at a battered Irishman.

> *I am still teaching the boys for some of the time—Jim
> has almost caught up with Nicky. So gratifying to have
> such a quick and able pupil. You would not believe what*

*a little gentleman he has become, though still with that
open, mischievous spirit about him that I so enjoy.*

Aye, Ethan thought gloomily, not like the great thickheaded lummox who'd started his lessons the same time
as Jim.

Tibby's writing was like herself, he thought; small, elegant, firm, and resolute. No fancy flourishes or unneces-
sary curls, every letter precise and crystal clear and not a
blot or a scratching out in sight.

Lord, whatever must she think of his own letters? Even
after getting the vicar to correct his spelling, Ethan made
mistakes on the fair copy he made.

And when he read over his own letters—for he kept the
ones the vicar had written on to check on what he'd told
her and to get the correct spelling of some words—he was
embarrassed at how clumsy they sounded.

But he couldn't stop himself from trying. Ethan dipped
his quill in the ink again and labored on . . .

*I have bort a four room cottage on the western edge of
the estate. Three bedrooms so tis biger than you myte
think. To big for one single man like meself but I have
someone in mynde to joyne me there Im hopeful she will
anyway. I been whitewashing the walls and tidying it up
and its coming up a treat.*

He looked at the letter and sighed. He could describe
the cottage so easy if he was talking; the words were in his
head, fine and bright and shiny. But when it came to writing those same words down and wrestling with pen and ink
and the spelling getting in the way, in the end his words
came out all scratchy and wooden and dead.

There was a pencil in the box with the pens and ink, so
Ethan picked it up. He'd heard people say a picture was
worth a thousand words. He didn't know about that, but it

would take him forever to find words he could spell that would describe the cottage, but he could draw it in a minute.

He'd always been good at drawing, from the time he was a small boy, scratching out a picture in the dirt or with a piece of charcoal. The more he drew, the better he got. In the army he'd been able to draw quick, neat maps and drawings of fortresses and had been promoted as a result. Nobody ever realized he couldn't read. Ethan was very good at finding ways around any reading he had to do.

And nobody dreamed that a man who was so quick with a pencil could be such a dunce with a pen.

With access to paper, pencils, and charcoal he'd done a few drawings of some of his mates and their surroundings. Word spread and Ethan was soon in demand for small sketches to send home to sweethearts or mothers. They even paid him to do it. A picture was better than a letter when folks couldn't read.

And every little bit earned added to Ethan's nest egg. He'd been determined that if he survived the war, he'd make something of himself.

And look where he'd ended up, a partner in a solid horse-breeding enterprise with a fine gentleman like Harry Morant, who was also his friend. And now Ethan had a house of his own.

Pretty good for a man born in a mud-floored hut who'd grown up with hunger gnawing at his belly.

All he needed now was to educate himself to a level where a fine, educated lady like Tibby might consider wedding him, despite his lowly background.

It was like baying at the moon, he sometimes felt. But despite their differences, despite the fact that many in society would disapprove of such an unequal match, Tibby was the lady he'd set his heart on.

He glanced at the sketchbook that sat on the table beside

him. It was open to a full-page sketch of Tibby as he remembered her. He hadn't fallen for her straightaway . . .

He grinned, remembering the way she'd glared at him when he'd been so slow at responding to her silent message that she was being held hostage. What a big stupid he'd sounded like, and how cross she was.

But when he'd snatched her away and galloped off with her . . . thinking she'd go all female and hysterical on him, she'd been thrilled. What was that name she'd called him. Loch-in-something. Scottish, not Irish. Lochinvar, that's who.

And then after he'd carried her to safety, what must she do but come back to help him, armed with a spade.

That's when it had started for him. Such a little bit of a thing she was: her eyes spitting defiance, her cheeks all pink, and her hair coming out of its neat little bun. Ready to defend him—a man twice her size—against the very men who'd held her hostage. A wee lion of a lady. She'd stormed into his heart that day, sure enough, spade and all. And stayed there.

He must find out about that Lochinvar fellow someday. But first he'd finish this sketch.

He quickly drew the cottage he was getting ready for her, with the windows all cleared of ivy and a couple of roses flowering at the door. He hesitated, then with a few quick lines drew the shape of a woman standing looking out, one arm lifted to shade her eyes.

The roses were just sticks now, but come summer, he hoped they'd be blooming. And come summer, he hoped Tibby would be standing there, shading her eyes and waiting for Ethan to come home.

He'd be off to Zindaria in spring to pick out his next seven horses, and he'd pop the question to her then. In the meantime, his letters had to do the courting . . .

He picked up the pen and wrote the final words:

I'm hoping the lady I'm corting wont think it a terible cheek when I ask her but she's so fine and educated she myte not look at a clod like me but a man can only dream.

Respectfuly yours, Ethan Delaney

Nine

Nell was woken by a soft knock on the door. Good heavens, she really had slept. She'd lain on the bed because there was nothing else to do—and besides, she needed to think about all that had happened this morning—and somehow, she'd drifted off.

She stretched, sat up, and called, "Come in."

A young maidservant entered, carrying a can of steaming water. She set it down and bobbed a curtsy. "I'm sorry to disturb you, Lady Helen, but I'm Cooper. Mr. Sprotton and Miss Bragge sent me to assist you. And Mr. Sprotton says to tell you luncheon will be served in half an hour."

"Assist me?"

"Yes, my lady. To dress you and help with your hair and so on, you not having brought your own maid with you."

"Thank you, Cooper, but I don't need a maid," Nell told her as she poured some of the hot water into a bowl. She hadn't had a personal maid for years. Not since her come out.

The girl's face fell. "Oh. Very well, m'lady." She bobbed another curtsy and turned to leave.

Nell frowned thoughtfully. "Cooper," she said as the girl reached the door.

"Yes, m'lady?"

"What are your normal duties?"

"Cleaning, dusting, polishing silver, whatever Mr. Sprotton tells me to do, m'lady."

Nell understood immediately. Her short stint as a paid companion had given her a new understanding of the nuances of life as a servant. Helping Nell, even for a short time, was a step up for Cooper. If she sent the girl back it would reflect negatively on her. "Are you any good with hair?"

Cooper brightened. "Oh yes, m'lady. Me and my sisters, we used to do each other's hair all the time." She glanced at Nell's hair. "I could make you look real pretty, m'lady, honest."

Nell glanced in the mirror and laughed. "Then I'd be delighted if you'd try. It looks a sight at the moment. I knotted it neatly in a bun this morning but I lost my hat, and the bun fell out on the way here."

The girl's face went suddenly blank. "Indeed, m'lady?" she said with careful politeness.

Nell was amused. "Mr. Sprotton instructed you not to mention the way I arrived, didn't he?"

"Yes, m'la—" Cooper clapped her hand over her mouth, horrified. "Sorry, m'lady."

Nell laughed again. "Don't worry, I'm certain the whole of Bath knows by now." She washed her face and hands, dried them on the towel that Cooper passed her, then sat down in front of the dresser.

She pushed back the mop of hair spilling down around her shoulders. "Being tossed over a man's shoulder doesn't do a great deal for one's hairstyle, does it?"

"No, m'lady," Cooper said and began to brush out Nell's hair. "But it's ever so romantic, isn't it?"

"Romantic?" Nell hadn't thought of it like that. She'd been furious at the time. Not to mention uncomfortable.

"Oh yes." Cooper gave a wistful sigh. "Mr. Harry carrying off his lady love in front of all the town, so strong and so handsome, and not caring what anyone thought. Some of the girls below stairs nearly swooned when they heard about it."

"Really?" Nell was bemused. *Mr. Harry carrying off his lady love?* Is that how they saw it?

She recalled Mr. Harry's own words: *it's not love's young dream I'm offering you but it makes sense.*

Cooper smiled mistily into the mirror. "Everyone's just thrilled for you, m'lady. And Lady Gosforth says it will be a big London wedding. And all new clothes for you, m'lady." She sighed again.

Nell sighed, too. She hated shopping for new clothes. She'd been thoroughly miserable in the lead-up to her come out. And during it. The vain attempt to make a silk purse out of a sow's ear.

Her thoughts were miles away as Cooper brushed and combed and pinned and twisted.

"There, m'lady, how do you like that?"

Nell glanced in the looking glass and her brows rose. Cooper had braided Nell's hair around her head and twisted a green and white ribbon through it. A few tendrils had been freed, which softened the effect.

Nell twisted and turned her head, staring at her reflection. The style really suited her and yet it was quite simple and very practical for a long coach journey. "It's amazing. I look like a young girl," she exclaimed.

Cooper beamed at her reflection. "No, m'lady, you look like a bride-to-be."

A bride-to-be. Nell glanced again in the looking glass. Hardly the blushing bride, she decided, but she did look better than she'd looked as a young girl. Papa was in funds at the time of her come out and he'd employed a very intimidating dresser, who came highly recommended. Her taste, and Papa's, ran to ornate and fussy styles: bunches of ringlets, curls, twists, and all kinds of things pinned on her head.

This simple style with a touch of whimsy suited her much better.

"Cooper," she said on impulse. "Would you like to come to London with me?"

Cooper's eyes bulged. "Me, m'lady?"

"Yes, with Lady Gosforth's permission, I'd like you to dress me for my wedding."

"Your wedding, m'lady?" Cooper stared, slack-jawed, then burst into tears.

"But if you don't want to, of course—" Nell began, horrified. "You probably don't want to leave your family—"

"No, no, miss, I mean, m'lady, they'll be right pleased for me, they will." Cooper wiped her face with the corner of her apron. "Sorry for the waterworks, m'lady, 'tis just that it's always been me dream, to work for a fine lady and go to London and I never expected it could happen."

"Lady Gosforth will have to give permission first," Nell warned her.

"She'll give it," Cooper said confidently. "She's that thrilled about you, she'd give you anything you asked for, m'lady. Says you're just what Mr. Harry needs. Oh, wait till the girls below stairs hear about this. They'll be that jealous."

A little dazed at this surprising view of her marriage, Nell went downstairs to luncheon.

As she entered the dining room, Harry jerked to his feet and stood there, staring at her from across the room. His smoky gaze was like a touch. A caress.

She put a hand to her hair self-consciously.

"You look very elegant, my dear," Lady Gosforth said. "No doubt my nephew will seat you in his own good time."

Startled out of his reverie, Harry moved to hold a chair

for Nell to sit down. She thought she felt the brush of fingers at her nape as she sat, but he said nothing and moved to sit opposite her.

A light repast was already laid out on the table. Lady Gosforth said a quick grace, then invited them to eat. "It's very light and plain fare," she told them. "Just the thing for people about to be jolted about in a carriage for hours. Eat up, my dear."

Nell helped herself to some sliced ham, a little chicken, and some bread and butter. She ate very self-consciously. Harry Morant didn't seem to take his eyes off her. It was rather like sitting down to dine with a ravenous wolf, except that he managed to demolish several slices of egg and bacon pie, a venison pasty, and some jam tarts.

"Who did your hair?" Lady Gosforth asked. "It's very good."

"Cooper," Nell told her. "In fact I wondered if you would let her come to London with me. Of course, if you need her here—"

"She'll come," Harry said.

His aunt looked at him with raised eyebrows.

He frowned. "What?" He glanced from his aunt to Nell and back again. "Nell wants her to come," he told his aunt, as if that were a clincher.

Lady Gosforth's brows rose higher. "My nephew has spoken."

Nell was embarrassed. "Not if your aunt needs her," she told him firmly.

Lady Gosforth laughed. "No, no, my dear, it's perfectly all right. You can have the girl as long as you like."

She glanced at Harry, who was crunching through an apple with white, even teeth, then reached out and patted Nell's hand. "I am going to enjoy this."

Shortly after their repast, the carriages trundled up the street. It was rather a cavalcade; Harry had hired a yellow bounder for himself and Nell; a bright yellow post chaise and four, driven by two postilions. Lady Gosforth and Bragge, her dresser, rode in her traveling chaise, and several vehicles followed, transporting a number of other servants and a mound of luggage. Finally a groom on horseback brought up in the rear, leading Harry's horse, Sabre.

"Why do you need a separate carriage, Harry?" his aunt demanded. "There's plenty of room in mine."

"Because I want to travel with my betrothed," he answered.

"It's not proper for the two of you to travel alone and unchaperoned," his aunt insisted.

"What rot, we're going to be married," Harry told her and lifted Nell into the carriage. "And I want to talk to her."

Nell hesitated and was about to jump down—the last thing she wanted to do was to make trouble between Harry and his aunt. Besides, she wasn't sure she wanted to be interrogated by her betrothed when she was stuck in a carriage and couldn't escape.

Lady Gosforth saw her dilemma and said with a twinkle, "Go on, my dear. I can't resist tweaking my nephew's tail from time to time. If he does anything improper, scream." Chuckling, she allowed Harry to help her into her own carriage and in minutes the cavalcade set off.

*T*he postilion gave a shout and the post chaise set off with a jerk. "Alone at last," Harry said.

"Yes." She gave him a bright, nervous smile. She peered with great concentration out of the window. "Such a fascinating sight, Bath, from this angle."

"Fascinating." He sat back, folded his arms, and watched her. He knew better than to rush his fences.

She pointed out interesting sight after interesting sight, never pausing for a moment, leaving no space for any questions he might have. A great many beautiful, interesting, quaint, ugly, or impressive buildings were commented on in detail as the horses labored up steep hill after steep hill. And as buildings gave way to farmland, she rapturized on the beauties of nature.

Harry smiled. She wasn't a natural chatterbox, but she produced a continuous flow of words even his aunt might envy.

But her tactics could only delay matters. She would soon run out of things to exclaim over, Harry thought, crossing his outstretched legs more comfortably and settling back against the padded back. He didn't mind. He could watch her face and listen to that low-pitched, lovely voice for hours and never be bored.

They passed through Bath-Easton, then the village of Box, which she thought very pretty, as was all the countryside in between. He suspected she would have made a fair fist of keeping up the flow of words all the way to Chippenham, except that an edge of desperation had slipped into her voice.

Taking matters into his own hands, he leaned across and kissed her in midsentence. Firmly and possessively. Capturing her mouth with his and stopping the flow of words.

Nell blinked at him as he returned to his seat. "Wh-what was that for?"

"I had to stop you somehow and that seemed as good a way as any."

"Stop me from what?"

She knew perfectly well what. "Putting off the moment. Come on, bite the bullet, sweetheart. You know you're going to have to tell me all about it sometime. It might as well be now, rather than have it hanging over your head. You'll feel better for it, I'm sure."

She sagged against the seat, silently acknowledging he was right. "All right, what do you want to know?"

"Everything you didn't tell me this morning."

"There's not much to tell," she said in a wooden voice. "I fell pregnant. When he found out, Papa took me to a house in another county to give birth in secret so that no one would know and my reputation would not be ruined. Three weeks after my daughter was born, he took her away while I slept, mistakenly believing that was what I wanted. And then he died before I could find out where he took her. That's it." She spread her hands. "End of story."

"Not quite and you know it." There were a lot of gaps in her tale and Harry needed to have them filled.

She tried to stare him down, but failed.

"Who is Torie's father?"

She shrugged. "It doesn't matter."

He smashed his fist against the back of his seat, making her jump. "Of course it damn well matters! Who is the blackguard and where the hell is he? Why didn't he marry you? And why the devil did he leave you to cope with all this on your own?"

She set her jaw and looked away. But not before he saw a glimpse of something in her eyes that made him want to kick himself. Shame. She was ashamed. Of course. And he was riding roughshod over her like a brute.

He forced himself to calm down. He leaned forward and said gently. "You must see that it matters who the father of this child is. I need to know."

"Why?" she challenged him. "You knowing his name can change nothing. It's all in the past and that's where it belongs. Stirring up everything is just . . . upsetting."

"I'm sorry for that, but I can't get him out of my mind," he admitted.

She crossed her arms and stared out of the window for a while. Eventually she said, "Oh, very well, if you must know, he's dead."

Harry frowned. He wasn't sure he believed her. If the swine was dead, why all the secrecy? "Dead? How?"

"He drowned. He went to sea and his ship went down in a storm."

"What was the name of the ship? Where was he going?"

"So this *is* to be an interrogation after all," she flashed.

"No, I'm sorry." He sat back and tried to look relaxed. He wasn't relaxed, not in the slightest. He was wound tense as a spring.

He mastered himself and said more gently, "So, how did you meet him, this—what was his name?"

"He was a friend of Papa's," she told him. "Papa brought him to the house one day and . . . we, we fell in love. And the night before he went away, he . . . we . . . you know. And months later I found out I was increasing, and shortly after that I heard he'd died." She shrugged. "You know the rest."

"A very affecting tale." Harry didn't believe a word of it. She'd recited the tale with too little feeling. She was an emotional creature; she could no more talk unemotionally about the loss of her lover than fly. But he wasn't going to push her any further on the subject just yet. It would only make her pricklier and more defensive.

"Tell me about the place you were kept in."

"I was very lonely," she said, and her voice changed. "Papa left me there with strangers—they didn't know my real name, or his. He paid them to be kind to me."

"And were they kind to you?"

"Oh yes, in their way, I suppose," she said. "But I was miserable. I couldn't even take Aggie, only Freckles, and even so, I wasn't allowed outside, not even to walk Freckles, except after dark."

"Why not?"

"Papa left strict instructions." She shook her head helplessly. "People might have seen me, someone could have recognized me—I don't know. But there wasn't even a proper garden. It felt like I was in prison."

This part of her story was true, he decided. It was all about feelings, not just a recitation of facts. "What did you do?"

"Oh, I read and I sewed—I'd never been interested in sewing before. And I knitted but I wasn't very good at it. Still, it helped to pass the time until m-my baby was born.

My daughter, my little Torie." Her face crumpled. "I loved her. I thought I would keep her, but then I was ill . . . and my father came . . ."

Harry stood it as long as he could, which was about three seconds, then he pulled her into his arms.

"We'll find her, don't worry."

She mumbled something incoherent and tried not to cry. He held her against him, stroking her hair, the nape of her neck, rubbing her back. Dry, silent sobs racked her frame at odd intervals.

He remembered what she'd said, that first day at Firmin Court. *I never weep. There's no point.*

Harry hated hearing women cry. He hated watching Nell fighting these ragged, jerky sobs more. "Go ahead, let it out. Weep," he told her. "You have good cause."

"I won't cry. I don't," she said in a choked voice. "My daughter is alive, I know she is. And I'll find her."

"We'll find her, I promise." He held her tight and wondered what the hell he was doing, making a promise like that when deep down he thought the child was probably dead.

Babies died so easily. Newborn babies taken from their mother had even less chance than most. And if Papa really wanted to get rid of his unwanted illegitimate granddaughter, it wouldn't be too difficult. People did it all the time.

They came to the next post and while they changed postilions and horses, Nell went into the inn and washed her face. She emerged pale and composed.

Harry watched her unhappily. He didn't know the whole story—there were huge gaps that didn't make sense—but she was too emotionally wrung out to go on.

He glanced out of the window. They were nearing Cherrill, he saw.

"Have you seen the famous white horse of Cherrill?" he asked.

"No," she said in a wan voice.

"It's coming up soon," he told her. "A famous landmark hereabouts. You'll see it in a few minutes."

It appeared as promised, around the next bend. Harry remembered the first time he'd seen it as a boy. He'd been thrilled with the sight, a giant figure of a white horse carved out against the green turf.

"They say the tail alone is more than thirty feet long," he told her.

"Amazing," she said dully.

They watched it in silence until it had passed. She shivered.

"Are you cold?" he asked awkwardly.

"A little."

He opened a compartment in the side of the carriage and pulled out a fur rug. He placed it around her. She huddled into it and closed her eyes, shutting him and everything else out.

Damn, damn, damn, Harry thought. So much for not rushing his fences.

*T*hey stopped overnight in Marlborough. Harry had sent a groom on ahead to expedite the changing of the horses at various posts along the way. He'd also arranged accommodation at the Castle Inn, a mansion that only a few years before had been the residence of the Duke of Somerset.

It was dark when they pulled up and the lights of the inn were most welcoming. The groom had obtained a private suite of rooms that contained a sitting room as well as several excellent bedchambers and rooms for the servants as well.

Lady Gosforth, disdaining any food or refreshment, retired straight to her bedchamber, Bragge in close attendance.

"That's it for her for the night," Harry told Nell, seeing her look of concern. "My aunt is always a little unwell after travel. But her maid knows just what to do."

They sat down to dinner. "You were right," Nell told him.

He looked up from carving a capon of veal. "About what?"

"You said it would help to talk, and you were right. I was upset at the time, but since my nap, I've realized I feel a lot better that you know."

He didn't know everything, Harry thought, but now wasn't the time to raise it again.

They were served a delicious meal that included steaming oxtail soup, capons of veal, an excellent steak and kidney pudding and a quince pie with clotted cream. They ate in virtual silence, keeping conversation to the trivial, and at the meal's conclusion agreed to make an early night of it so as to leave first thing in the morning.

Nell examined the door of her bedchamber. "There isn't any lock," she exclaimed.

"No need," Harry told her. "This whole section is private and separate from the rest of the inn."

She looked troubled.

"There's a lock there, on the door that leads to the other part of the inn. It's perfectly secure," Harry assured her.

She bit her lip and looked unhappy, but simply said, "Then I will bid you good night," and retired.

A sound woke Harry in the night. He listened and heard it again, the sound of someone moving softly around the sitting room. Thieves?

He rose and, taking his pistol, quietly inched open the door of his bedchamber. He peered into the darkness, illuminated only by the faint glow from the dying fire. From the corner of his eye he caught sight of an insubstantial ghostly figure. He froze a moment. But then it moved again.

It was no ghost, but Nell in a long white nightgown. He put down the pistol.

"What's the matter?" he asked softly.

She took no notice of him, but padded across the room in bare feet, making for the door.

He followed. "Nell? What is it?"

She muttered something he couldn't make out.

"What did you say?" he whispered. He didn't want to disturb his aunt or the others.

Again she muttered something unintelligible and tugged at the handle of the door.

"It's locked, don't you remember?" he told her, puzzled and disturbed by her strange behavior.

"Got to find her," she muttered. "Find her."

"Find who?"

Again she just rattled at the handle of the door. She said something then turned away and walked swiftly toward the window. She pulled back the curtains. Moonlight flooded in.

And that's when Harry saw her face.

Her eyes were wide open, but they were blank and unseeing. She was asleep, walking and talking, but sound asleep.

"Nell." She tried to unlatch the window. Oh God, she was going to climb out the window.

He caught her by the arm. "Nell," he said more urgently. "Nell, wake up." He was about to shake her awake her when he recollected a story of a man who'd been woken while sleepwalking and dropped dead of shock. He didn't know if the story was true or not, but he didn't want to risk it.

"Got to find her, find her, find Torie," Nell muttered, struggling with the latch on the window.

Oh God. He suddenly understood. He said the first thing that came into his mind. "Torie's safe. She's here."

Instantly Nell turned toward him, her face anxious, her eyes still horribly blank. It was a heartbreaking sight. He lifted her up. She struggled a little, muttering unintelligibly.

"Torie's asleep, she's all right," he soothed her and the

worry slowly smoothed from her face. "Now, go back to bed." Murmuring assurances of her daughter's safety, he carried Nell, docile now, back into her bedchamber and to her bed.

"Torie's asleep and you need to sleep, too," he told her. Trusting as a child she curled up in bed and he pulled the covers over her.

He quietly closed her door and leaned against it with a sigh of relief. Thank God he'd heard her. Lord knows what could have happened if she'd climbed out of the window.

He poured himself a large brandy and sat down in one of the sitting room arm chairs. He'd heard of sleepwalking but he'd never seen anyone do it.

He sipped the brandy and recalled how when she'd first told him about the baby, he'd suspected her, just for a moment, of losing it deliberately. It had only been for a second, and he'd banished the unworthy thought instantly.

Now he felt ashamed for even considering it for a second. He understood the reason for those violet shadows underneath her eyes now. The loss of her daughter was tearing her apart, even while she slept.

He drank the last of the brandy and set the glass down. He hoped to God they found the baby soon. He returned to his bedroom, but just as he pulled his covers back, he heard a door open again.

It was Nell, still asleep, heading for the locked door again. Harry wasn't going to go through all that again.

He reached her in three strides and guided her gently toward his room. "Torie's safe," he murmured. "Now, get into bed," he told her and as before, she climbed into bed. Harry's bed. He slipped in beside her.

"Come here, sweetheart," he murmured. "You're safe with Harry now. Torie's safe. Nell's safe. It's time to sleep." She sighed and relaxed against him. Her feet and hands were frozen. Harry tucked her against him and wrapped his body around her.

He lay there, holding her, feeling her chilled body slowly warm against him. Her feet were like ice. Slowly her breathing eased, and he found himself breathing in time with her. Her nightgown was cotton, old and soft with repeated washing. It was so thin it was almost like holding her naked body. She smelled of clean linen, soap, and woman and his body ached against her, racked with the hot tide of desire.

He ignored it. He had more important things to do. Desire could wait. She was his now, to care for.

And she wouldn't wander the lonely night again if he could help it.

Nell woke to sleepy, gradual awareness. She felt warm, comfortable, safe.

An arm was holding her. Sinewy, hairy, masculine. She felt something else as well, also very masculine.

There was a man in her bed. An aroused man.

Her eyes flew open. With a panicked cry she struck at the man holding her down. Kicking and flailing with her fists she managed to stumble from the bed, dragging most of the bedclothes with her.

She staggered back and stared at the man in her bed.

He sat up, rubbing his chest. His naked chest. She tried not to stare. "Ouch," he said conversationally. "You pack quite a wallop for a lady." He gave her a sleepy grin. "But I forgive you. I trust you slept well. If so, my efforts were well rewarded."

Was he entirely naked? she wondered. What she could see of him was naked. And she didn't want to see any more. "Efforts? What efforts? And what are you doing here?" she demanded.

He just gave her a slow, wicked grin.

"What are you doing in my bed?" she repeated furiously.

He stretched and rubbed his head, looking impossibly handsome. "I'm not in your bed. You're in my bed."

"I am not." She glanced around, and her jaw dropped. She was in his bedchamber. "Wh—How did I get here? Did you—"

"You walked in of your own accord."

"I didn't," she said. She added, less certainly, "I wouldn't." Oh Lord, she thought, she might have . . .

He made no attempt to cover himself, seeming quite unembarrassed by his naked chest and arms. Nell, feeling naked, despite her sturdy cotton nightgown, clutched bedclothes to her.

He leaned back on one elbow and regarded her from the remains of the bedclothes. "I guided you, I confess, but you came very willingly."

"Nonsense," she said defensively. "I don't remember a thing." She would die of embarrassment if he thought she'd come looking for him in the night and just climbed into his bed.

He gave her a searching look. "No, but you know you walk in your sleep. It's happened before, hasn't it? That's why you were worried about there being no lock on the door."

"Yes." She collapsed onto a chair next to the bed, still clutching the bedclothes to her. He understood. Thank goodness. "At Mrs. Beasley's I used to get one of the maids to lock me in at night. And at home, Aggie used to. I should have asked Cooper to sleep with me, but I thought . . . I hoped . . . It seemed . . . I didn't want you to think I didn't trust you."

He asked curiously. "Have you always walked in your sleep?"

She shook her head. "Not since I was a little girl. It started after Mama died, but I grew out of it. It only started again after—" she broke off.

He nodded. "I know. You were searching for Torie."

She put her head in her hands. "What am I going to do?"

"Not you—*we*. And we are going to find her," he said

briskly and swung his legs out of the bed. Nell stared. He wore a pair of white cotton drawers, but they disguised very little about his masculinity.

His very aroused masculinity. She'd felt it earlier, pressing against her.

Her thoughts of Torie were suddenly jerked away by the view of something much more immediately arresting. Her palm tingled with remembrance and blushing, she belatedly turned her head away. "Why didn't you put me in my own bed?" she asked.

"I did."

"What?" She turned. "Then why would I wake in your bed?" Her eyes strayed to his drawers.

"That's not why I put you in my bed," he told her. "The first time you wandered I tucked you back in your bed and thought nothing more about it. Ten minutes later there you were again, trying to climb out of the window. It was fairly apparent that I could either spend the night chasing around after you or take you back to my bed and keep you safe."

"Safe?"

"Safe," he repeated firmly. "And to make sure you slept properly. You did sleep better, didn't you? You look better this morning that you have in the last few days."

She thought about it. She did feel a little less worn than she had for a while. "I suppose I did."

He nodded. "Good. So my plan worked perfectly . . . until you woke up. And started swinging punches."

She gave an apologetic grimace. "I'm sorry. I didn't know it was you."

He frowned. "I know. So who's the blackguard you expected it to be?"

Nell wasn't going to tell him that; not him, not anyone. She jumped up. "It's getting late. The servants will be up and around any moment. I'd better go."

"He raped you, didn't he—the father of your baby?" Gray eyes bored into her.

She froze, her mind a sudden, scrambled blank.

He went on, "That's why you woke in a panic just now."

"No, I—"

"You panicked when you thought there was a man in your bed, but the moment you saw it was me, you calmed right down." His mouth twisted ruefully. "Even though you might have cause for fearing me in my current state."

She bit her lip. He couldn't know; he couldn't. She wasn't going to tell him, wasn't going to tell anyone. And she didn't fear Sir Irwin—she hated him. She'd got a fright, that's all. It had brought the memories back. But she'd rid herself of them before and she would again.

She would not let Sir Irwin play any role in her life. Not even as a vile memory. Or a nightmare.

Harry persisted. "That's why your father took your baby away in the night, thinking he was doing the right thing by you, wasn't it? Making restitution. Releasing you of the burden of raising a rapist's child."

"She's *not* a rapist's child; don't you *ever* say such a filthy thing about my daughter again!" Nell flashed. "She's mine, mine alone, and *nobody* else's. *My* daughter, precious and pure and innocent." And she ran from the room.

S he'd been raped. The words echoed over and over in Harry's head. Of course she had. It all made sense now. Who was the bastard? How had it happened? The questions ate at him.

The memory of their first real meeting suddenly twisted in him like a knife.

Christ! No wonder she hadn't wanted a bar of him in Bath. Why would she want to know the man who, on first acquaintance, had forced a kiss on her? A very carnal kiss. And pressed his aroused body against her.

He closed his eyes and raked his fingers through his hair, and wondered yet again what the hell had possessed him. He'd never done anything remotely like it in his life. He'd always treated women with the utmost respect. And yet he'd behaved like a boor to the most compelling woman he'd ever met.

She'd been violated in the worst way . . .

And then he'd forced her into a situation where she was compelled to marry him.

God, but she must despise him. He swore again and punched the bed.

Ten

"*I* shall ride with Nell in the hired chaise this morning," declared Lady Gosforth at breakfast. "You can ride your horse, Harry. I wish to have private conversation with my niece-to-be."

Nell swallowed. Had Lady Gosforth found out where Nell had spent the night? Was Nell about to get a lecture on morality?

She glanced at Harry. His eyes smoldered with the questions she'd managed to avoid this morning.

On the other hand a lecture on morality might be preferable to an inquisition. She had, after all, done nothing wrong.

"That would be delightful," Nell said briskly. "And I'm sure Harry would enjoy a good gallop. He needs one." She hoped he could take a hint. She didn't look at him but concentrated on buttering a piece of toast she had no desire for. She ate it anyway. It was better than meeting that knife-edged glance across the table.

"Excellent," Lady Gosforth said. "Then we ladies shall have a comfortable coze."

Harry helped first his aunt, then Nell into the hired chaise, giving Nell a be-it-on-your-own-head look as he did. "She never stops talking," he murmured.

Nell didn't mind. It was having to talk about herself that she dreaded. Lady Gosforth was every bit as likely as her nephew to interrogate Nell, and she'd be far less tolerant, Nell was sure.

"My basket!" Lady Gosforth called sharply as Harry was about to close the door. Her dresser, Bragge, passed in a large, covered basket.

Nell stared at the basket, feeling a little sick. It was in just such a basket that Papa had taken Torie away, only without the cover . . .

It was stupid, Nell knew, but for a few moments, she could not breathe.

Lady Gosforth placed the basket on the seat beside her. She undid the catch and flipped open the lid. The basket was lined with blue cotton, not white satin, and contained dozens of skeins of fine white wool.

Nell started to breathe again.

"I knit," Lady Gosforth explained, seeing Nell staring. "Unfashionable, I know, but it's useful and it relaxes me. I can't bear embroidery or all that nonsense. I like to make something that can be used."

Nell nodded, as if she was listening. One more day, she told herself. One more day and they would be in London. Tomorrow morning . . .

The carriage moved off with a lurch and Lady Gosforth pulled out a thick twisted loop of wool. "You don't mind, do you?" she asked Nell, leaning forward.

"Not at all."

"Slip your hands into the center of the skein—see how it's one big loop? Both hands now, hold them apart—that's it. I see you've done this before."

Nell nodded. "Yes, but not for years." She'd wound wool with Aggie when she was a little girl, but when

Aggie's fingers had got stiff she'd stopped knitting.

"Now as soon as I find the end . . . Ah here it is." With brisk movements Lady Gosforth began to wind the fine wool around her fingers, forming the beginning of a little ball. Nell dipped first one hand then the other, releasing the yarn from the loose skein.

For a long time they were silent. They passed out of Marlborough and hit the open road. It was quite pleasant, Nell thought, winding wool and watching the countryside slip by.

"When did you first meet my nephew?" Lady Gosforth asked.

An interrogation after all.

"In a sense, we met in a forest. It was raining, and he was very kind to me," Nell said. She didn't want to explain what had happened in the forest. Something special and magical and private had passed between them that day, and she didn't want to explain it, even if she could. Somehow, she felt it would ruin it if she told. Because in one sense it was nothing, a small, insignificant incident or strangers on a road . . .

"Really, we only met properly when he came to my home—at least, it used to be my home. Firmin Court."

"When Harry bought it?"

"Yes."

"That was the first time you met?" Lady Gosforth looked puzzled.

"Properly, yes. To have a conversation, I mean." The few words he'd uttered in the forest that day couldn't count as conversation.

"And the next time?"

"In the Pump Room in Bath. You were there," Nell reminded her.

Lady Gosforth nearly dropped her ball of wool. "You mean that time in the Pump Room was the second time you'd talked to my nephew? The third occasion you'd met?"

Nell nodded.

"Good God!" She wound wool for a long time, frown-

ing. "I would never have believed it. Three times. He told
me he'd offered you marriage twice before, and you'd rejected him twice."

"That's right."

"You mean he proposed marriage the first time he met
you?"

Nell nodded. "He was just being kind, though. I'd just
lost my home and everything I owned."

Lady Gosforth frowned. "A man who is still unmarried
at the age of nine-and-twenty does not propose to be kind,
young woman. Otherwise he would be married long since.
And the Harry I know does not ask for *anything*. Ever. Let
alone after he's been rejected twice."

"This last time, he didn't exactly ask me," Nell pointed
out dryly.

"Yes and that's even more extraordinary." She regarded
Nell thoughtfully. "I think there's more to this than the two
of you are letting on."

Nell braced herself.

"But no matter, I dare say it's none of my business," Lady
Gosforth said briskly. "I wanted to talk to you about Harry
and also Gabriel. Do you know who I mean?"

"His brother," Nell said.

"His half brother, yes." She fixed a stern gaze on Nell.
"You do know the circumstances of Harry's birth, don't you?"

Nell nodded. "Yes, he was very careful to explain it from
the beginning."

"Good. You know there is a schism in the family?"

"No, I know very little about his family, apart from the
occasional mention of Gabe—and you, of course."

Lady Gosforth nodded. "I thought as much. Did he tell
you that when I first met Harry I wanted nothing to do with
him."

Nell looked at her, surprised.

Lady Gosforth arched her eyebrows. "Well, why would
I? My brother's by-blow?"

Nell stiffened. She clenched her fists inside the skein of wool and said nothing.

Lady Gosforth continued. "Gabriel, too. Naturally I took my brother's side and according to him Gabriel was a cuckoo in his nest, to all intents and purposes a bastard. He was wrong, of course, but my brother was a stubborn and unforgiving man. And certainly someone like Harry—an accident with a maidservant—was far beneath our notice."

"An accident with a maidservant?" Nell said angrily. "What a vile way to speak of anyone."

Harry's aunt gave her a searching look. "It offends you, does it?"

"It does," Nell said, meeting Lady Gosforth's gaze squarely.

Lady Gosforth smiled. "Good for you, my dear. It offends me, too, now, but that's what I thought at the time." Her smile faded. "Let me tell you the whole story—it's a tale I think you should know."

She'd come to a broken thread, so there was a pause while they searched for the new end. Once they'd found it, Lady Gosforth continued. "Gabriel and Harry were brought up by my aunt Gert, a formidable woman who went her own way in all things."

Nell frowned. "But I thought—"

Lady Gosforth nodded. "Harry was initially taken in by Mrs. Barrow, my aunt's cook. His mother had died and he was badly neglected, and there it would have stayed except for the fact that Harry is the living image of his father. The moment my aunt saw the family resemblance she decided to raise both boys as gentlemen—after all it would not do to have a groom who was the living image of the earl. Beside, Aunt Gert had an absurd reverence for Renfrew blood. She said she bred horses and dogs without caring about marriage certificates, and younger sons were no different. And if their father didn't care for them, she would."

Lady Gosforth clucked her tongue over such an outrageous attitude, then continued. "When the time came to send the boys to school, Aunt Gert sent them both to Eton, where Renfrews had always gone—the same school as Marcus and Nash, their two older brothers, attended."

She shook her head. "I don't know what she was thinking—perhaps she thought it would do the boys good to fight it out."

"Fight it out?"

"Yes. It is a peculiarity of the male sex that once they have done their best to beat each other to a pulp, they will often walk away the best of friends. And certainly the stage was set for a fight.

"Marcus and Nash had been taught to look down on and despise Gabriel and Harry, who no doubt resented their older brothers for their privileged position. It made for instant and bitter enmity. Some of it remains to this day, though Nash has managed to create some kind of bridge between them all. A born diplomat, that boy."

She sighed. "To cut a long story short, it got very nasty and Gabriel and Harry were expelled. My aunt was indisposed at the time and asked me look after them. I was horrified. I wanted nothing to do with either boy." She smiled reminiscently and added, "But when I say 'asked' it was an order. Something of a martinet, my aunt Gert, and in my younger days I was too nervous of her to disobey."

It ran in the family, Nell thought dryly.

"Of course, as soon as I saw the two boys I knew my brother was wrong about Gabriel. Both boys have their father's extraordinary good looks—in fact it is an irony that they each look more like their father than the two older boys. Have you met Gabriel?"

"No."

"He and Harry are almost identical, but Gabriel has his mother's blue eyes and her darker hair. Harry's gray eyes, however, come direct from my late brother. Marcus, the current earl, has the same eyes." She shivered. "They can be extremely cold."

They could also burn, thought Nell with a different kind of shiver, and thinking of Harry, not Marcus.

"I remember them arriving on my doorstep, two identical small boys, battered and bruised and stiff and wary. I decided at once that I'd take Gabriel in—he was after all, a legitimate Renfrew, but I had no intention of taking in a maidservant's by-blow, and I said so. I told Gabriel to come in—I had no idea which was which—and said that the other boy could go around the back and the servants would look after him. He could stay as long as he was useful."

Nell put a hand to her mouth to hide her distress. It was cruel, but she knew Lady Gosforth would be regarded by many as keeping up proper standards. Most people would not think twice about it.

She could not bear it if anyone treated Torie that way.

Lady Gosforth said ruefully, "I know, but I never thought of him as having feelings. Harry flung away across the road and stood there, glowering, his arms folded, declaring that he didn't need anyone to look after him.

"Gabriel was furious, of course. He stood on my front step and railed at me and said he wasn't going anywhere without his brother Harry. He told me that like everyone in his family except Great-aunt Gert and Harry, I was ignorant, stupid, and a horrid old snob. And then he stormed across the road and stood there with Harry."

She laughed shakily. "It was raining, did I mention that? They got drenched, but nothing could budge them. Harry wasn't going where he wasn't wanted and Gabriel wasn't going anywhere without his brother. In the end, I was frightened they would get sick and Aunt Gert would blame me so I finally said they could both come in at the front door. Gabriel made me promise that his brother would suffer no further insult. I had to cross the road and invite Harry in personally and then *he* made me promise I would not blame

Gabriel for his loyalty. In the end he came so grudgingly, you wouldn't believe it."

Nell nodded mistily. She could believe it. The stubborn boy had grown into a stubborn man.

Lady Gosforth gave Nell a watery smile. "Aunt Gert knew what she was doing, sending those boys to me. I'd had four babies, you see . . . but none of them lived . . . And when I saw these two stern little half-drowned creatures, looking just as my brother had as a boy . . . two unwanted urchins standing together, side by side against the world, well, my heart cracked wide open."

Lady Gosforth put her wool aside and fished in her reticule for a handkerchief. "The more I got to know them, the more I saw what fine boys they both were." She dabbed at her eyes. "They came to me often then, in the school holidays or when they wanted to visit London. They became the sons I never had. But Harry never forgot that first time. It took him years to finally believe I wanted him and valued him for himself. He's never felt wanted, you see, and he's too proud to ask for anything."

She finished mopping her eyes and blew vigorously into her handkerchief. "And so, my dear, that's why I find it so utterly fascinating that he asked for you twice."

Three times, Nell thought.

"After only three meetings—a girl he barely knows. And when you refused him, he just carried you off and made such a scandal you had no choice. The Harry I know and love would never do anything like that . . . Unless . . ."

Nell waited, but Lady Gosforth said nothing, just went on winding wool.

"Unless what?" Nell asked at last.

Lady Gosforth gave her a troubled look. "Do you love my nephew?"

Nell didn't answer. She didn't know what to say. She wasn't sure yet what she felt about Harry Morant. She was too mixed up to know.

She'd thought she knew what he wanted of her. It had seemed quite straightforward. But since last night, she just wasn't sure of anything.

Lady Gosforth sighed. "Just don't hurt him, my dear. That's all I ask. Don't hurt him."

*A*fter luncheon Lady Gosforth returned to her own carriage, for a nap, she claimed. According to Harry it was her usual custom to nap her way around the country. "Dashed if I know how she does it," he told Nell as he helped her into the yellow bounder. "Carriage lurching and bouncing the whole way. And then the moment she arrives she goes straight to bed." He shook his head.

"You're fond of her, aren't you?" Nell said.

He looked surprised. "I suppose I am, yes." He shrugged. "I don't have much family—just her and the Barrows really. And Gabe, in Zindaria."

No mention of his two other brothers at all, she noticed. "The Barrows?"

"My foster parents. Mrs. Barrow was my great-aunt's cook. She took me in when I was about seven and has mothered me ever since." He grinned. "She still treats me as if I'm seven but she cooks like a dream so I let her."

"Aggie does the same to me."

"And Barrow taught Gabe and me everything we know about horses."

"He must be very knowledgeable," Nell said.

"Yup, he is. So what did you and my aunt talk about?"

"Oh, knitting, things like that," she said vaguely.

"Knitting?" He looked horrified.

"We wound wool."

"Lord. I did warn you." He glanced at her from under his brows. "Did she tell you anything about me?"

"Not much," she fibbed. "She told me how she first met

you and Gabriel, that's all. And how she came to love you like a son."

He looked astonished. "She said that? About me? Like a son?"

"Yes." Nell watched his face. He seemed shocked.

"Are you sure she wasn't talking about my brother Gabe?"

"Of course I'm sure. Why would she be talking to me about your brother?"

He shook his head, still apparently amazed. "What else did she say?"

"She mentioned you and your brother Gabriel are close. Do you miss him a great deal?"

"In a way. We've always done everything together. But it's inevitable that when men grow up they go their different ways. He's in Zindaria with his princess and I have my horse stud to think of now." He looked at her and added, "And you."

For a moment Nell thought he was going to kiss her. Her face heated. His kisses were getting all too addictive. She glanced out of the window. "Oh look," she said, pointing. "Those two gentlemen are having a race across the heath." A little off the road, two young bloods were racing neck and neck, making loud whoops of glee.

Harry looked out and as she'd hoped, he was distracted. The finish line appeared to be a low line of bushes in the distance. Three other young men waited next to it, cheering and whooping as well.

"The bay will win," Nell said. "The chestnut has the better rider, but the bay is the better horse."

Harry watched a moment. She was right. The bay lagged well behind the chestnut, but his pace was long and sure and powerful. He glanced at Nell's intent expression and said, "I'll wager you the chestnut wins."

"I *never* make wagers," she said immediately. There was ice in her voice.

Of course she wouldn't, not with her history. "Not a real wager," he said. "Just for a kiss."

"A what?" Her head jerked around.

"If that chestnut wins, you pay me a kiss."

"Don't be silly."

"What can it hurt? It's just a kiss. Don't you have confidence in your judgment?"

The small pucker between her brows appeared as she tried to ignore his gentle gibe.

"Yep," Harry said softly. "The chestnut's going to win, and you're afraid I'm right."

"Nonsense! Very well, I'll take that wager," Nell declared. "You'll see who's right."

They watched as the two young men hurtled toward the finish line. The bay pulled ahead, eating up the distance in long, powerful strides.

"See, see?" She bounced up and down on the seat. "He's winning, my horse is winning! Come on the bay!"

Harry was winning, too, he thought. With a kiss as the stake, either way, he couldn't lose.

"I won," she crowed. "My horse won."

"Yes," he said feigning regret. "And now I'll have to pay my wager." He leaned forward.

She eyed him nervously. "What are you doing?"

"Paying my wager," he said and before she could say a word he took her mouth in a firm, possessive movement. At the taste of him a quick rush of heat shot through her, and the horses outside, the rattle of the carriage, the world faded away. There was only him, his mouth, his hands, his taste and scent and feel. She melted.

After a moment she realized he was pulling back. She sat up, trying to look as though she hadn't practically climbed on top of him.

"We have an audience," he said with a rueful smile, and she saw they'd come to a small village. People in the street watched them pass. They could see right into the carriage, thanks to the big window at the front. No wonder he'd stopped. She was very glad. Almost.

"That bay was so fast," she murmured, hoping she sounded composed. Wagering for a kiss—it was nearly as dangerous as wagering for money. "I wonder who bred him?"

"He's not as fast as Sabre," he told her. "And Ethan's got a two-year-old Zindarian filly that can already give Sabre a run for his money. We're entering her in the St. Leger Stakes at Doncaster next year."

Nell nodded. "Good idea. Fillies race better at that time of year than in summer. They're less distracted, I think."

He looked at her in astonishment. "That's right."

She laughed at his expression. "Have you forgotten so soon whose grandparents bred racehorses? It was my dream, as well. I have high hopes for Toffee's colt, let me tell you. Did you name him, by the way?"

He smiled. "I called him Firmin's Hope."

"Ohh." It was so unexpectedly touching that for a moment Nell couldn't say anything. She couldn't have picked a better name. It summed everything up; her hopes for the colt, for the estate, and his hopes, too, it seemed. Not to mention the estate workers who would get a percentage of the prize money every time the colt won. "That's a lovely name," she said huskily. "Just perfect."

He stared down at her. "And so are you," he said and drew her into his arms. The village was behind them . . .

The Palace of Zindaria

*M*iss Jane Tibthorpe, known to her friends as Tibby, accepted the dozen or so letters the liveried footman brought her on a silver platter with a quiet thank-you.

She immediately began to sort through them: fancy engraved invitations, correspondence on embossed, linen-weave note paper, letters bearing a royal seal, a personal note from the Duchess of Braganza to Princess Caroline of Zindaria.

"Please take this to the princess," she told the footman. "It is a personal note and should not come to me."

Her fingers froze as she came to a small white letter, written on plain, everyday notepaper. Her heart started thudding under the prim bodice of her plain blue dress.

Tibby knew at once who it was from.

She lived for those letters.

"That will be all, thank you," she told the footman. As soon as he'd gone she swiftly tucked the letter into the bosom of her dress.

Ethan's letters she read in absolute privacy. They were hers and hers alone. As were her sentiments.

She bent quietly to her task, working methodically through the mound of correspondence until her work was done.

By then it was midafternoon. Callie made a practice of observing the English ritual of tea and cakes at this time of day. She did it for Tibby's sake as much as her own, so Tibby had to delay the reading of the letter even longer.

She drank her tea, nibbled on a cake, and attempted to keep up the conversation. Luckily there were guests at the palace and Callie was too busy to notice her friend was distracted. As soon as tea was finished, Tibby excused herself and went out into the garden.

It was a crisp, cold day and she knew where she would be quite alone. There was barely an hour of daylight left— the days were getting so short so quickly—but if she went to her room to read the letters, anyone would know where to find her. She couldn't bear to be interrupted when she was reading one of Ethan's letters.

She headed for the tall hedge maze, walking briskly and unerringly to its center. She sat down on the bench there, took a deep breath and drew out the letter. She broke the seal carefully and opened the letter, smoothing the creases tenderly.

My dear Miss Tibby . . .

The familiar handwriting made her smile, it was so like Ethan: rough-looking, unconventional, and attractive. She glanced quickly at the second sheet, and yes, there was a drawing. She didn't let herself look at it, not yet.

She read the letter slowly, savoring it, hearing in the phrasing and word choice Ethan's own rich deep voice. She loved hearing about the various events of his life, how the horses were coming along, his hopes for a certain filly, his growing friendship with the elderly vicar and the chess games they played so often.

And oh! He'd bought a cottage. A cottage . . . why would he need a cottage? With three bedrooms.

She turned over the sheet of paper and for the first time looked properly at the drawing. It was beautiful, drawn with all Ethan's usual vibrancy and grace. The cottage sprang out of the page, real and vivid, and the roses that arched toward the doorway were so delicate and real one could almost smell them. But the woman . . .

Tibby squinted, trying to make out her features, but it was just an outline, really.

She scanned the rest of the letter quickly and gasped.

. . . the lady I'm corting . . .

Ethan was *courting*! Courting a lady. For a moment Tibby couldn't breathe. It was as though a stone settled in her chest. She stared at the words.

. . . the lady I'm corting she's so fine and educated . . .

Tibby took several deep breaths. She was glad he'd found someone, she told herself, though it was getting a bit hard to breathe. Mr. Delaney—it wasn't proper to be thinking of an engaged man by his first name—was a fine, strong, very attractive man, and with such charm. One of nature's true gentlemen. Nothing was more natural than he'd quickly find himself a lovely young woman to marry and settle down with.

What had she thought? That he'd look twice at a thin stick of a spinster looking down the barrel at her thirty-seventh birthday? Of course not, not a virile man like Ethan. He would have his pick of women. He probably only wrote to Tibby in gratitude for her teaching him his letters.

What a good thing this lovely young woman was educated; she would be able to help Eth—Mr. Delaney with his books.

She was very glad for him, she told herself. Very glad indeed. Thrilled for him, in fact. She would write and tell him so. Immediately.

. . . she myte not look at a clod like me . . .

A clod? How dare this woman—whoever she was—look down on Ethan. If she could not see what a sensitive and intelligent man he was, she didn't deserve to have him.

And Mr. Delaney should not put up with less than the utmost respect from his wife. Tibby would write immediately and remind him. Ethan was sometimes too modest for his own good.

He would probably stop writing to her once he was married.

A drop of rain splattered on the paper. Tibby looked up. It wasn't raining.

She looked at the letter again.

Respectfuly yours, Ethan Delaney.

Respectfully hers . . . Oh, Ethan . . .

Another splat of water landed on the letter, then another and another.

*H*arry woke at dawn. The racket in London always made it hard for him to sleep. It went on till late into the night, and then a man was barely asleep when outside came a rumbling of carriages and wagons and handcarts and the shouts of workmen and pie sellers and God knew who.

It was even more irritating when he was also rock hard and rigid with frustration.

Nell stirred softly in his arms.

They'd arrived late at his aunt's house in Mount Street, made a light supper, and ordered hot baths. They'd gone to bed almost immediately afterward.

Harry had arranged for Nell to have the room opposite his. After she'd gone to bed, he'd waited, leaving his own door ajar.

Sure enough, within an hour he heard her door opening. Nell emerged, glassy-eyed and muttering anxiously, in nightgown and bare feet. She was halfway down the passage before he caught her and gently turned her around. He'd led her back to bed, murmuring reassurances to her about Torie's safety and hoping to hell they were true. He'd coaxed her into the bed and then climbed in with her.

Trustful as a child she'd curled up against his body.

But she was no child and both he and his body knew it. It was agony lying beside her like this. He ached to take her, to make her his. She stirred again and he gently loosened his hold of her, sliding one numb arm out from under her soft, relaxed body.

Resting on one elbow he gazed down at her. She was so lovely in the soft morning light, lying open and unaware, without her usual defenses. The neckline of her nightgown had slipped, revealing one thin, bare shoulder. He bent and softly kissed it.

God, but he hadn't been prepared for this when he'd decided on marriage.

Awake she seemed so independent, so strong, but asleep . . . asleep she was so vulnerable.

She needed someone to care for her.

She needed him.

Harry was glad her father was dead; the man should have been shot for the state in which he'd left his daughter. He'd left her alone, penniless, homeless, and grieving. All that kept her going was the thought of finding her daughter.

What would happen if she never found the child?

God help her. She would need him even more, then.

No one had ever needed him before, not like this. No one had depended on him in such a devastatingly personal way. In the army people had depended on him, but any competent officer would have done just as well. Like chess pieces, they were interchangeable. It was the job that mattered, not the person.

No one had ever really needed Harry at all.

Was this what being in a real family was like? He'd always considered he had a family, of sorts. He had a brother he would die for; Gabe would do the same for him.

But they didn't need each other. Lord, they lived in two different countries, hundreds of miles apart. Gabe might miss him occasionally, but he didn't need him.

Aunt Maude had told Nell she'd come to love him like a son but he knew damn well he wasn't necessary to her in any real way. The Barrows loved him, and he loved them, too, but he'd left them when he was a youngster to follow the drum.

Eight years at war taught a man not to need anyone or anything—even friends you had to steel yourself against depending on, because friends could die in the blink of an eye. Or slowly and painfully. Or be taken away on a cart, to die somewhere else.

Everyone left you in the end.

But if he left Nell—his arms tightened around her at the thought; there was no possible way he could ever leave her, not knowingly . . .

He could kill for her, he could die for her, but leave her? Never.

What if he failed to find her child for her? Would she leave him then?

By the dawn's soft light her hair, spread over the pillow, was caramel and cream. A lock of it straggled in her eyes. He smoothed it back. Her skin was like warm silk.

In sleep she looked less drawn, younger, softer. Her breathing was deep and regular, her lips gently parted. He thought of kissing her awake, quietly, gently, and then deepening it, so . . .

No, not yet. He had to take it slowly with her, let her become used to him, teach her to trust him with her body. She was fragile, vulnerable. God knows what damage that filthy swine had done to her . . .

He would kill for her, all right.

He closed his eyes and tried to make sense of the chaos within him. God, but he hadn't been prepared for these *feelings* when he'd decided on marriage. He wasn't used to feelings.

She was nothing like the confident, well-organized, coolly appropriate middle-class wife he'd planned on. He'd imagined taking a wife would be something like installing a . . . a manager for the house, someone who would attend to all the domestic and societal aspects of life. He'd imagined someone comfortable and biddable who, he hoped, would enjoy the marriage bed.

And whether or not she enjoyed the marriage bed, in the fullness of the time she'd provide him with children and then Harry would have his own family—a real one. All without changing his life too much. And leaving him to get on with the business of breeding champion racehorses.

Nell was about as different from the wife he'd planned on as it was possible to be, but he wouldn't change her for the world.

It was just . . . it took some getting used to.

He wasn't used to having to deal with so many feelings—hers and his. It was unsettling, chaotic.

In the past he knew exactly what he felt and why. He was angry or happy or worried or tired—and there were reasons, always reasons for the way he felt; he was worried because he was facing another battle in the morning, or he was angry because someone had botched the orders, leaving his men ill-equipped or starving.

Feelings used to make sense. Now he didn't know what he felt, and whatever it was, it wasn't comfortable or logical.

She moved and the sweet curve of her behind brushed against him. Harry almost moaned aloud. Some feelings remained logical, if not exactly comfortable.

He held her, aching, desperate to make love to her. In other circumstances he might seduce her now, while she was still all soft and sleepy and warm and trustful in his arms. But he couldn't. It would be breaking her trust.

Her trust was the most precious gift she could give him.

She'd been raped. Harry couldn't even begin to know how that would feel.

The closest he'd come was that terrible beating he'd received from Anthea's father and brothers when he was twenty. Held down, stripped naked and vulnerable, then thrashed till he bled. And Anthea watching, her eyes gleaming with excitement. The most humiliating moment of his life. The worst thing wasn't the blood, or the pain: it was the violation of his sense of self, his complete helplessness in the face of their power.

He remembered it as if it was yesterday, though it had happened nearly ten years ago. For Nell it was not quite a year.

He laid his mouth against her bare shoulder and inhaled the scent of her body. His woman. His to protect and care for.

He didn't know what had happened to her, what that bastard had done, but he knew she would have fought him, as Harry had his attackers. And been held down, powerless and shamed against her will.

After he'd recovered his physical health, he'd picked fights, got into brawl after brawl, always against a group of men, always against the odds, having to prove to himself over and over that he was a man. Finally war had burned the hate and the need for vengeance from him. He was settled and confident in himself as a man, now. Nothing to prove.

What did women do? He didn't know.

But if the two situations were anything alike, she needed to be able to make the choice to give herself if she wanted to. She would need to take control back, instead of having it taken from her.

He would remember that when he finally came to make love to her. It would be soon, he thought. But not today.

He eased his body away from her and slipped from her bed. Failing a dip in an icy cold lake, a hard ride in the cold dawn should do it.

He tiptoed out and crossed the hall to his own room. He'd just pulled on his breeches when he heard Nell's door opening.

In two paces he crossed the room and flung open his door.

"Oh," Nell stood in the passage in her nightgown, but with a shawl clasped around her at least. Her feet were still bare, he noted irritably. Her toes would be frozen. He'd spent a long time warming those toes last night. Like little blocks of ice, they'd been. He felt somewhat proprietal about those toes.

"Oh, good, you're up," she said. "I'll be ready to leave in five minutes."

"Leave?"

"To start looking for Torie."

"It's too early. No orphanage director will be up yet, let alone ready to receive visitors."

"But—"

"We agreed on eight o'clock, remember?" It was the latest he'd been able to get her to agree to. If they hadn't arrived in London in the pitch dark, she would no doubt have gone out looking straightaway.

Her fingers twisted in the fringe of her shawl. "I know, but I can't sleep. I have to start looking."

He was very tempted to tell her that she'd been sleeping perfectly well only a few minutes before, but one look into her agonized eyes and he shut his mouth. It wasn't that she couldn't sleep, it was that she couldn't wait.

"It's been weeks," she said. "But now I'm here and I can't bear to waste another minute. If you don't want to go, that's all right, I'll go by myself." She turned back to her room.

"No, we'll go together," he told her. "I'll meet you downstairs in fifteen minutes."

"Thank you." Her eyes ran over his rough jaw, then his bare chest, and rested briefly on his buckskin breeches. She frowned. "You're not going like that, are you? I mean in riding breeches. And without shaving. It's just, if you dressed more formally, I'm sure they'd be more cooperative."

He raised his brows.

"It's true," she said earnestly, "In my last few days in London, the people I talked to were sometimes quite horridly rude and unhelpful, I think because by then I was looking fairly bedraggled and desperate. So if you were to look . . . I don't know . . . respectable and commanding, it would help."

He was tempted to remind her that in the past she had objected strenuously to his commanding ways, but she was strung tight as a bow, and now was not the time.

"I'll do my best," he said. "And Nell—"

She turned back and he caught her around the waist and drew her against him. "Stop fretting. We *will* find her," he said and kissed her firmly.

Her eyes misted up and she nodded, pressing her lips together as if unable to talk, and vanished into her room.

Harry rang for hot water and ordered a simple breakfast to be ready in fifteen minutes. He shaved—not his best effort, at this rate he might have to think about getting a valet—and dressed swiftly. Luckily whoever had unpacked his clothes had also pressed them and he looked quite respectable. Commanding he could do unshaven and half dressed.

He'd dressed quickly but when he opened his door she was already waiting for him, dancing impatiently on her toes. She was wearing that drab brown dress again. Damn, but he couldn't wait for her to get some decent clothes.

"I don't have a hat!" she said as if it was a major disaster. "You knocked my hat off in Bath, remember, and wouldn't stop to pick it up. And now I don't have a hat! I need to look respectable. They won't be helpful if they don't think I'm respectable. And how can I look respectable if I don't have a hat?"

"We'll get you a hat."

She wrung her hands. "At this hour of the morning? From where?"

He glanced past her and saw her maidservant hurrying along the passageway. "You should've rung for me, m'lady," Cooper began. "I didn't know you'd be up so—"

"Lady Helen needs a hat," Harry told her. "We'll be downstairs having breakfast—"

"I couldn't eat a thing," Nell told him.

Harry tucked Nell's hand into the crook of his arm and said to her maid, "Find her a hat, there's a good girl, and bring it to the breakfast parlor."

"Yes, sir." Cooper bobbed a curtsy and ran off.

"Now, breakfast," he said and led Nell toward the stairs.

"But I don't want any."

"You will eat something or else you won't step a foot out of this house."

"But—"

"Don't argue. Last time you went looking for your daughter you collapsed from hunger. I'm not having that."

She sighed and nodded. "All right. I didn't think . . . It's just that I'm so nervous, I might not be able to keep anything down."

"You will. It's just nerves that make you feel that way. Take it from a seasoned campaigner, you'll feel better with something in your stomach."

They walked down the stairs arm in arm.

"Did you sleep in my bed last night?" she asked abruptly.

"Yes, I did. You started wandering again, so it was easier just to get into your bed and keep you there. And it worked," he added, wondering why the hell he felt so defensive about it. "You slept the whole night through without stirring."

"I wondered if that was it. Thank you."

Harry looked at her in surprise. Thanks were the last thing he'd expected from her.

She explained, "Despite everything, I do feel quite well rested."

It was more than Harry could say. "Breakfast," he said and ushered her into the breakfast parlor. Cook had done them proud on such short notice. She had scrambled eggs, bacon, ham toast, sweet pastries, and a pot of coffee and another of hot chocolate.

Nell opted for a pastry and hot chocolate, Harry for everything else and coffee.

"I made a list last night," he said between mouthfuls. "I've marked the places you went to. We'll start with all the institutions to the northwest of the city first. I assume your father would be most likely to choose a place close to where he was, perhaps an area he was familiar with, rather than riding across town.

Nell nodded. "That makes sense." She hadn't eaten a thing, but at least she was drinking the chocolate. Her fingers shook as she lifted her cup.

He leaned over and caught her hand in his. "Stop worrying, we'll find her. Now eat something."

She nodded. "We will, yes, we will," she said, as if convincing herself. She crumbled the pastry in her fingers, then added in a voice of quiet desperation, "We must."

There was a knock on the door and Cooper came in, with a drab pelisse over one arm and a hat. "I've got a hat for you, m'lady. It's an old one of Lady Gosforth's. I smartened it up with a bit of ribbon and some feathers—"

"Thank you, Cooper." Nell jumped up and jammed it on. She turned to Harry. "Respectable?"

"Very nice," he said. He didn't know much about hats, but he liked this one. It didn't hide her face like so many of the ridiculous things women wore these days.

"Then let's go." Cooper helped Nell into the pelisse. Nell buttoned buttons with feverish, clumsy fingers, saying to Harry, "Aren't you finished yet? We need to leave now."

Harry gave a rueful glance at his half-full plate, drained his coffee cup, and stood.

"Good morning, my dears." Lady Gosforth sailed into the room. She stopped and scanned Nell critically. "Good heavens! Is that my old hat? It looks rather elegant, I must say. There's no need to gape at me like a fish, Harry, I have several times risen at such an uncivilized hour, and with a wedding in three weeks, there's a great deal to be done. Sprotton, some hot chocolate, if you please. I'm drawing up a plan for our shopping expeditions today, my dear. I thought we'd start with a visit to my mantua maker."

"But I can't!" Nell wailed. She turned to Harry, "We have to go."

"Nell won't be free today, Aunt Maude," Harry said. "Pressing business. Tomorrow, perhaps, or some other time," and he marched Nell out the door.

"Good grief, Harry, the girl needs to go shopping. Tell him, my dear—"

But they were gone.

Eleven

"*T*hat was wonderful," Nell gasped as the curricle moved off at a smart trot. "When your aunt came in, I thought we'd never get away."

"I'm wearing my commanding clothes," he said dryly. "Ah, here we are."

To Nell's surprise, Harry pulled up and the groom jumped down to hold the horses. They hadn't even left Mount Street.

"Why are we stopping?"

Harry gestured to a tall building. "The parish workhouse of St. George's, Hanover Square. We might as well start with the closest." He jumped down and lifted her down.

Nell felt suddenly hollow.

The building was large, three stories high, built of brick and good intentions, but grim, nevertheless, with small windows. If there were children inside, you couldn't hear them.

Harry knocked on the door. After a moment, a gaunt woman dressed in gray opened it. She looked at them in surprise. "Can I help you?"

"Harry Morant," Harry said, doffing his hat. "And this is my wife. We wish to speak to whoever's in charge."

Nell barely took in the fact that he'd called her his wife. She was trying to control the shaking that had begun at the words "parish workhouse."

She'd lost count of the number she'd visited before. Had she known this one was so close she would have come last night.

The woman stood back to let them in. "The director isn't in, yet. But I might be able to help."

Inside it smelled of steam and strong lye soap. "Washing day?" Nell blurted and wondered why she'd said it.

The woman gave her a cool look. "Indeed." She turned back to Harry. "How can I help you?"

"My wife's late cousin gave birth to a baby girl several months ago," he said, squeezing Nell's hand so she wouldn't react. "We believe her father might have brought the baby here—tragically, he, too, is dead, which is why it's taken us so long to track down what happened to the child. We wish to raise the child as our own."

The woman escorted them to a small office and took down a heavy blue bound ledger. "When would this have been?"

Harry glanced at Nell.

"Around the nineteenth or twentieth of October," she said. Almost six weeks ago.

The woman turned pages with infuriating slowness. "The nineteenth . . ." she said. "And how old was this child at the time?"

"Five weeks old."

The woman raised her brows. "It's unlikely we'd take an infant of that age," she said. "Was she christened?"

"No."

"But the mother or father was a member of this parish, I presume?"

"Not the mother. I—I'm not sure about the father." She

didn't think Sir Irwin was a member of any parish, but if he was, it wouldn't be a London parish but the church near his home in the country.

"We only take in members of this parish," the woman said. "So if the child is not of this parish . . ." She made to close the heavy book. Harry's hand shot out and slammed on top of the open page.

"Be so good as to check your records anyway," he said in a silky quiet voice that sent a shiver down Nell's spine. His eyes glittered coldly.

"Yes, of course, sir," the woman said hastily. She ran her finger down the list. Nell held her breath.

"The only infants we took in during that week were a boy of two and a girl of ten months who came in with her mother."

Nell's heart sank. From a distance she heard Harry saying, "You said you don't normally take very young babies. Who does?"

"Captain Coram's Foundling Hospital, out in Bloomsbury Fields."

"Then we'll go there next," he said.

Nell was already halfway to the door.

Captain Coram's Foundling Hospital was situated in the more open country of Bloomsbury Fields. An imposing brick edifice, it was built with two substantial wings extending out around a central courtyard.

This time they spoke to the director, a large man in a severe black suit. "Yes, we only take infants under twelve months," he told them, polishing a pair of gold-rimmed pince-nez. "Your cousin's child is illegitimate, I presume?"

Nell could not speak.

"Yes," Harry said.

"The mother's first child?"

"Yes," he said again.

The man placed the glasses on his nose and peered through them at Nell. "And from a mother of good character?"

"Yes," Harry said firmly.

"Then there is a good chance she was admitted here. The nineteenth or twentieth of October, you say." He adjusted the fit of his pince-nez and consulted his records

Nell's hand slipped into Harry's. She waited.

"Several females of that age were admitted in the second to last week of October," he finally said. "What was your late cousin's name?"

Nell stared at him blankly.

"She's not certain what name her uncle might have entered the child under," Harry explained.

"He wanted to hide the scandal," Nell finally got control of her voice. "Her name is Victoria Elizabeth."

The man raised his brows. "Two given names," he said. "I see." He consulted the record and shook his head. "No infant of that name listed."

"What names do you have?" Harry asked.

"I'm afraid I cannot reveal that."

Nell clutched Harry's hand tightly. "Try Freymore."

The man looked through the ledger. "No."

"Denton."

Again that agonizing wait but, "No."

"Firmin."

"No."

"Smith, Jones, Brown."

The man didn't even bother. But his eyes were compassionate, and he rang a small bell. A woman in dark bombazine entered. "Matron, could you please show this lady and her husband the tokens from October of this year? There might be something she recognizes."

"Tokens?" Nell wondered what he meant. She glanced at Harry but he shook his head.

"Come this way, madam," the woman said and bustled

out. The stiff material rustled with every step. She took them
to a small room with a table and a large cupboard. She gestured for Nell and Harry to be seated, then opened the cupboard. It contained row upon row of small boxes, each
bearing a label. She took one down labeled October 1817
and placed it in front of Nell.

"See if there's anything here that rings a bell, madam."
She retired to a corner of the room and waited.

Mystified, Nell opened the box. At first glance it looked
like a pile of rubbish, odds and ends with no seeming relationship or purpose; a key, a small wooden heart with ini-
tials carved into it, an enameled locket, a roll of paper tied
with a grimy bit of ribbon, a piece of rag twisted around a
pin, a button, a broken sixpence, a white silk heart, exquisitely embroidered, a lead fish of the sort fishermen use, a
plaited ring of what looked like human hair. Each item carried a label, tied to it with string.

Curious, Nell picked up the carved heart to read the label. It bore a number and an inscription: *Jimmy Dare his pa
carved this for us both.* Her heart turned over.

"Most of the mothers leave something, a little love token for their baby," the matron explained. "I write some of
the notes. Many of these poor girls can't read or write."

Nell picked up another numbered tag. *God bless and
keep my daughter safe.* Her mouth quivered. With trembling fingers she turned over each label, faster and faster,
praying to find something with Papa's writing on it.

Your da ws a sailor and I lovd im well.

One simply said, *Forgive me.*

The button said, *Tommy Jones from his mam.*

She picked up the embroidered white silk heart. The
card was written in a beautiful copperplate script. *From
your mother who fell from Grace and lost the most precious
Gift God gave her.* Nell's eyes filled with tears.

She examined each and every token and label, hoping
desperately there would be one written in her father's hand.

Finally there remained just the little scroll of paper. With shaking fingers she untied the worn piece of ribbon. She stared at the paper but the harder she stared, the more the writing blurred. All she could see was that it wasn't Papa's writing. And that it was some kind of verse.

"Is it in his hand?" Harry asked.

She shook her head. "But I want to read it anyway."

"Give it here, then." Harry took the paper from her and read in a deep voice:

> *I leave you here my poor wee babe*
> *With tears I do Farewell thee*
> *Though Motherless through life ye'll be*
> *I never will Forget ye.*

Harry carefully tied it up again with the bit of ribbon and Nell wept to see the big hands so gentle with the tiny scrap.

"We use these so mothers can identify their children if need be," the matron said. "Do none of these mean anything to you, madam?"

"No, there's nothing," Nell said in a choked voice. "Nothing." She mopped her eyes with the handkerchief Harry gave her. Had she known Torie was to be taken from her, she would have left something to identify her.

"Not every mother leaves a token," the matron said.

Nell looked up, hopeful. "Can I just see the babies?" she asked. She would recognize Torie, she was sure, even if it was six weeks and one day since she'd seen her.

"Oh, there's no babies here, madam," the woman said. "We send them to wet nurses in the country for the first four or five years, then they come back here to be trained and educated."

"So, where are these wet nurses?" she asked eagerly.

"The director has the details, madam, but without proper identification, he will give you no information, I'm afraid."

"Oh, but—"

"I'll speak to the director," Harry said to Nell. "You stay here."

He emerged from the director's office a short time later with a wintry expression. He tucked her hand into his arm and strode from the building. Nell had to run to keep up with him.

"Well?" she asked breathlessly.

"I have a list of all the wet nurses who were sent a baby girl." He swung her into the curricle. "There are six, but the director does not believe that any of them is Torie."

"But can we check anyway?"

He said in a grim voice, "We can check."

Darkness was falling as they made their way back to London. Nell was glad Harry wasn't much of a talker. She was too tired to make conversation. She was exhausted and dispirited.

They'd visited every wet nurse on the list from the foundling hospital. All of them were in the country, in villages three or four miles out of London. The country was reputed to be healthier for tiny babes than the fog-ridden city with the evil miasma that rose at night from the river, bringing disease with it.

As they'd pulled up at each cottage, Nell had been tense and keyed up. Would this baby be her daughter? Would she drive away from this house with Torie in her arms?

Each time Harry had swung her down from the curricle, he hadn't released her hand. She'd come to depend on that firm silent support. She'd needed it so much.

Because each time her hopes had been crushed.

"It's just the first day," he said abruptly. "There are dozens of workhouses and institutions in London."

"I know."

The light carriage hit a particularly bad pothole and she bounced. In an instant Harry transferred the reins to one hand and pulled her close to him on the seat. He made no move to take his arm away and truth to tell, Nell was glad of it, not just for the added security, but for the warm comfort it gave. He was so big and solid and somehow reassuring.

Nell had never met a man like him before. In the whole of her life, she'd only known talkers. Liars. Dreamers. Takers.

Harry Morant wasn't a talker; he was a doer. A giver.

They'd covered as much territory today as she had in a week on foot. If she'd had the money to hire a curricle or a gig before, she might have found Torie weeks ago. But she had nothing.

Part of her, the angry, desperate, guilty part, kept telling her that if she'd only kept on in those first weeks she would have found Torie.

The other part, the quieter part, reminded her of how helpless she'd felt collapsing in the street, surrounded by strangers. And how terrifying it had been to come to consciousness with strangers pawing through her clothes, touching her body.

That last day she'd collapsed and woken up wet and freezing, her fingers blue with cold. She must have lain unconscious for some time. Her gloves and hat, even her handkerchief was gone. She was lucky the thieves hadn't taken her dress and petticoat. She might have frozen to death, had Freckles not snuggled up along her body, keeping her warm. Nell hadn't been able to stand at first, she was so very weak. She'd realized that night that she could very easily die right there, in the London streets . . . unmissed, unregarded.

She was right to get herself home, to Firmin Court, to get money and help to search properly. She hadn't known everything was gone, and that she'd be just as helpless as before.

She *hated* being helpless.

If she'd come to London with Mrs. Beasley, she would have had no hope of searching these outer villages. She wouldn't even have known to do it.

Before, nobody had told her that all foundling and orphan

babies brought to London workhouses were sent to the country. They'd simply told her they had no babies. And foolish
Nell had taken their word for it.

Why hadn't they told her the babies were sent away? She
wanted to scream with helpless rage. The time that omission had caused her to waste, tramping from workhouse to
workhouse, time she couldn't afford, time Torie couldn't
afford.

If only she'd known Harry Morant back then. Harry
wasn't the sort of man people ignored. Harry pressed for
more information, and when necessary, bribed or intimidated
the information out of them.

They swayed, turning a bend, and Nell leaned in against
him grateful for whatever miracle had brought her to this
man. He didn't talk about what he might do, or would have
done, or could do: he simply did what needed to be done.
Without fuss.

They reached the London road and stopped to light the
carriage lamps. But a mile or so down the road he turned
off in a different direction.

"There's a workhouse at Islington," he explained. "It's
not far off the London road, so your father might conceiv-
ably have gone there. We'll find out where they send their
babies and start searching again first thing in the morning."

She nodded.

He looked down at her and gave her a small squeeze.
"Tired?"

"A little."

He was silent a moment. "I'd like your permission to
take my friends Rafe and Luke into our confidence. We
were in the army together and they're good fellows. They
could visit the various workhouses and find out where the
babies have been sent, and you and I will go there. It's a
more efficient way of searching."

"That's a wonderful idea," she said. Two ex-officers
wouldn't let themselves be fobbed off. If there was news,

they'd get it. As for them knowing, if it was a matter of her reputation or her daughter's recovery, there was no contest.

"I don't mind you telling them at all. I don't care what they think of me, as long as I find my daughter."

He gave her a sharp look. "They'll have nothing but respect for you."

*T*he gas lamps lit the quiet streets of Mayfair. It was late. As they pulled up in Mount Street, Harry descended first, then lifted her down. He paid the groom and they went inside.

They were no sooner in the door when his aunt came bustling out of the drawing room. "My dears, where have you been all this time? Nell, my dear girl, you look exhausted. Harry, your wretched business affairs have—"

Nell braced herself for the interrogation.

"Nell has the headache." Harry cut across his aunt's flow. "You will have to excuse her. She's going to her room to have a bath and lie down." He placed his hand in the small of Nell's back and propelled her firmly up the stairs.

Nell went willingly. "But I don't have a headache," she told him as they reached the first landing.

He paused, his hand warm and strong in the curve of her back. "Which would you rather do—have a bath, take supper in your room, and make an early night of it, or go back downstairs and have my aunt ask you all about your day? Or take you out to the theater or something? You have only to say."

She stared. He'd guessed how she felt about facing his aunt after the day she'd had. "No! No, a bath and a quiet night sounds heavenly. Your aunt is wonderful, but I'm feeling a bit . . . tired." Miserable was a better word, but she wasn't going to give in to it. Tomorrow was a new day.

"What are you going to do?" she asked.

"I'm going to contact Rafe and Luke." He delivered her into the hands of her maidservant and left.

Cooper poured scented oil into the bath and swished it around. "Miss Bragge gave me this bath oil and some special soap for you, m'lady. It's French and smells beautiful, like vanilla and apple blossom and something else."

Nell roused herself to respond. The last thing she wanted to do was to have to chatter on, but Cooper was so determined to prove herself as a lady's maid, Nell didn't have the heart to tell her to be quiet. "I will have to thank Miss Bragge," Nell said. "It's very kind of her."

"She's helping to train me, m'lady. She gave me this and a jar of extract of green turtle oil for your complexion and says you're to rub it in day and night."

"Extract of green turtle oil?" Nell eyed the jar doubtfully.

"It's very expensive," Cooper told her with pride as she helped Nell out of her dress.

"I've never used lotions much," Nell said. The truth was, she never had money for such things.

Cooper tut-tutted. "All complexions need lotions, m'lady. Yours is beautiful now, but you want it to stay that way when you get older, don't you? And keep Mr. Harry looking at you like he wants to eat you up?"

"Eat me up?" Nell looked up in surprise.

Cooper grinned. "Like a half-starved dog lookin' at a juicy bone, m'lady."

"Good heavens," Nell said faintly. She dropped her chemise and stepped into the bath. She was a little self-conscious; she wasn't used to having a personal maid, and she hadn't been naked in front of anyone else since she was a child. She wondered if Cooper would be able to tell from her body that she'd had a baby.

She slid down in the bath. The water was fragrant and beautifully hot and slowly some of the tiredness and tension soaked out of her.

She soaped her washcloth thoughtfully. *A half-starved dog with a juicy bone?*

Of course Cooper had a strong romantic streak, that was obvious. She thought Nell had made a romantic love match, whereas Harry had explained it to Nell in purely practical terms. Her title would be useful and so would she, with his horses. And she knew the estate and the people on it. It did make sense.

But Cooper's observations caused a little prickle of anxiety.

Nell scrubbed herself all over then allowed her maid to scrub her back and wash her hair. She massaged Nell's scalp and neck thoroughly. It was heavenly.

Harry Morant had made it as plain as any man could, right from the start, that he desired Nell. If she closed her eyes, she could feel the exact shape and hardness of him throbbing against her hand.

She closed her eyes and rinsed off the suds with warm water, then wrapped her hair in a towel and stood and dried herself in front of the fire.

Cooper brought her old nightgown to her and slipped it over her head. Nell was a bit embarrassed by the worn and patched garment. She'd never intended another soul to see it. Miss Bragge had probably had some scathing things to say about her wardrobe.

While Cooper supervised the removal of the bath and the water, Nell knelt on the rug in front of the fire, drying her hair. She had memories of doing this with her mother. Mama would towel dry Nell's hair and then comb it through, and she would often tell Nell a story . . .

Nell tried to swallow the lump in her throat. Would she ever get to do that with Torie?

When her hair was almost dry, she moved to the dressing table and sat down. She picked up the jar of green turtle oil, unscrewed the lid, and sniffed. It smelled quite pleasant. She dipped a finger in and applied a dab of lotion carefully to her skin. It felt cool and soothing.

She stared at herself in the looking glass. Her own very ordinary face looked back at her. If only she had taken after Mama instead of Papa in looks. Mama had been a beauty.

She didn't understand what Harry Morant found so desirable about her, but she had to accept it. A delicious shiver ran through her, pooling at the base of her stomach. She had no doubt of his desire.

But it worried her. Because of this desire for her, he'd put everything else aside to bring her to London to search for Torie, a child not his own, who would bring scandal into his life.

His willingness to accept her daughter made her want to weep with gratitude. He'd even planned out the search, like a soldier planning a campaign, she thought with a lump in her throat.

Cooper took up a brush and began to brush Nell's hair.

Nell sat, deep in thought. Because of his desire, Harry Morant would marry Nell, restoring almost everything in her life that she'd lost: a secure future, a respected position, and the home of her heart. She would even have a chance to breed horses as she'd always wanted to.

If—*when* they found Torie, it would be as if all the terrible things of Nell's last year had been wiped away, and only the good would remain. Apart from Papa dying.

And all because of one thing.

Desire.

For a woman who loathed the very idea of sexual congress.

She moistened her lips. It might not be too bad, she thought, not with Harry. Physically, she found him very appealing—beautiful, actually, if you could use that word for a man. And she liked him. More than liked him, a small voice reminded her, even if he didn't want to know . . .

And anyway, it didn't take long. And even when it was

vile, the rewards could be great, she thought, sending up another prayer for Torie.

Mares never seemed to enjoy being covered by a stallion, either. What a mare could endure, Nell could. She just hoped it would be enough for him.

Because what she did have to give him by the bucketful, he didn't want.

Love.

She loved Harry Morant. She wasn't sure when it had happened. Perhaps it was that first day in the forest, when his gray eyes had burned into hers for the longest time. And then he'd reached out and given her his hat . . .

Perhaps it was the first time she'd kissed him. She'd fought the feeling then, denied it, even to herself, when she thought he threatened her search for Torie.

It might have been that moment when he'd said, *She'll live with us, of course.*

Or perhaps it was when she'd realized how he'd held her through the night, keeping her from harm, asking nothing from her even though he badly wanted her.

He'd never asked anything of her.

She suspected he never asked anything of anyone. It was one way to keep yourself safe. Nell had done it herself.

But you couldn't keep yourself safe forever. Nell had felt one flutter beneath her breastbone and then another, and suddenly she was helpless with love for the tiny creature growing inside her.

And that was nothing to what she'd felt when she first held Torie against her heart, inhaling her daughter's scent as she put her to her breast. She would do anything to keep Torie safe. Anything.

But she hadn't kept her safe; she'd slept through the night and let Papa steal her daughter. The thought sent a wave of nausea through her.

There was a knock on the door and Cooper put down the brush to answer it. She came back with a covered tray. "Your supper, m'lady. Mr. Harry had Cook send it up for you."

Nell shook her head. "I don't want anything, thank you. Send it back."

Cooper hesitated, then took the tray back outside.

"W hat are you doing with that, Cooper?" Harry had seen the tray go up, not two minutes before. She couldn't possibly have finished it.

"M'lady said she didn't want any supper, sir."

"Did she eat anything?"

Cooper shook her head.

"Then stop right there," Harry told her and mounted the stairs rapidly. At Nell's door he knocked, opened the door, then took the tray from Cooper's hands. "That will be all, Cooper," he said crisply, stepped into Nell's bedchamber and kicked the door shut behind him.

And froze. Damn. He should have thought of this.

Nell was standing in front of the fire, warming herself. His mouth dried. With the fire dancing behind her that old cotton nightgown of hers was damned near transparent, showing the outline of long, slender legs and lush hips. Her skin was delicately flushed and her hair loose and curling, still slightly damp.

He had thought of it, he admitted.

For the last hour he'd battled against visions of assisting her at her bath, soaping her creamy silken flesh, rinsing her down, then wrapping her in a towel and carrying her flushed and damp to bed.

And now here she was, flushed and silken and damp and smelling like a cake straight from the oven. And wrapped in something a damned sight less substantial than a towel. But he wasn't going to touch her, he reminded himself. And he could handle this.

She eyed the tray suspiciously. "Why did you bring that back? I told Cooper I wasn't hungry."

"I don't care if you're hungry or not," he said, putting down the tray on a small side table. "We went over this at breakfast, so come and eat." He held a chair for her.

He could see the darkness of her nipples through the thin cotton. The first five buttons at the neck were undone, leaving a tempting glimpse of shadowy cleavage. He repressed a groan.

Where had those lush breasts come from? When he first saw her she'd seemed quite flat-chested. Not that it had made a ha'porth of difference to him, then or now.

Every time he came near her, his body responded with such fierce intensity he had to battle to keep it under control.

He shouldn't have come here. He knew how he'd respond. It was stupid, dangling temptation in front of him like this. Bad enough to have to hold her chastely through the night, but now it would be worse, because he would have this vision of her in his mind. In his mind and in his arms.

And in his bed.

Damn good thing there was a table between them. He removed the cover of the tray. He'd ordered a light supper for her: a soft-boiled egg, toast, butter, and marmalade, with a pot of tea.

"I don't want it," she repeated.

"Don't you like eggs?"

"I do normally, but I don't feel like eating tonight."

"You're tired and miserable, that's all. You'll feel better with food in you."

She folded her arms and gave him a mutinous look. He buttered one of the slices of toast, cut it in half, then cut each half into narrow strips. She watched him suspiciously. He neatly cut the head off one of the boiled eggs, sprinkled on salt and a little pepper, then brought the plate with the beheaded egg and the chopped-up toast to her.

She didn't unfold her arms, but Harry didn't care. The pressure pushed her breasts higher and the opening of her nightgown gaped, revealing the lush curves.

He forced himself not to notice. He dipped a strip of toast into the runny yolk of the egg, and held it to her lips.

She pressed them tightly together. He kept it there. "Open the door," he said, as if to a small child.

She tried not to smile.

"Do you know what we used to call these when I was a child?" he asked.

"Toast soldier—mmph," she ended, as he slipped the eggy soldier between her open lips.

She chewed and swallowed. "That was very sneaky—" she began, and he slipped another piece of toast into her mouth. He felt her warm breath on his fingers.

The next time, she tried to dodge him but he was too quick for her and slipped it between her lips anyway. Her eyes danced as she ate it.

By the fifth piece of toast it had become a game; she was laughing and Harry's problem was getting worse and worse. Who would have thought that feeding a woman toast dipped in egg could be an erotic experience?

"I haven't eaten eggs with toast soldiers for years," she told him. "It was always my favorite nursery supper." She moistened her lips, then parted them to receive her next morsel.

Harry repressed a groan. It would be so easy just to lean forward and cover that sweet, rosy mouth with his. But it would be an invitation to madness. She was not yet ready for what he wanted.

He jabbed the soldier into the egg and thrust it forward. A fat drop of yolk fell onto the inner curve of one creamy breast.

"Oh," she said.

Harry said nothing. For a long moment they both stared

at the drop of golden yolk, gleaming and moist against the silken skin. He swallowed, but he could no more resist the temptation than fly.

Slowly, deliberately, he lowered his head and licked the yolk away, laving her skin with his tongue. Her skin was cool and silken smooth. She smelled warm and delicious, like newly baked cakes and autumn apples.

She tasted of woman. All woman.

He inhaled deeply and fought the temptation to bury his face in the fragrant hollow. He grazed the satin skin lightly with his jaw.

"Ohh," she murmured. Her nipples were taut, thrusting against the thin fabric of her nightgown, only inches from his hands, from his mouth. He could feel one brushing against his arm. He moved his arm. She shivered deliciously and her eyes darkened.

At her visible response to him, he felt a primeval surge of triumphant possessiveness. He'd found her, against all the odds he'd found this woman, this one woman like no other, his own personal siren. His woman. His wife.

His wife-*to-be*.

He forced himself to straighten and dip the next piece of toast into the egg, as if nothing momentous had happened. He proffered it, his gaze locked with hers. Her eyes were dark, almost slumbrous with desire. She parted her lips and his fingers brushed against them as he fed the toast to her. He watched hungrily as she slowly chewed and swallowed.

She ate in silence, gazing into his eyes. It felt like she was looking into his soul, but he could not drag his eyes away.

He fed her another toast soldier, then another. All that could be heard in the room was the hiss and crackle of the fire, their breathing, and the soft sounds she made eating. Intimate sounds. Personal. Evocative.

Could she hear his heart pounding? He wondered. He sure as hell could.

He fed her finger after finger of toast until the egg was finished. He was very careful not to let any yolk drip again. He could not trust himself again if it did.

He never lost control. It wasn't going to happen now.

He fetched the pot of marmalade and spread it on the remaining piece of toast, cut it into triangles and handed the plate to her, saying. "Eat."

She gave him a long look, then picked up a piece and crunched into it, starting from one corner and working her way to the end. When she had finished, a tiny bead of jam glistened at the corner of her mouth.

He couldn't take his eyes off it. It was like a beauty spot tempting him. Quivering with each movement of her mouth. He watched as she ate a second triangle and a third. She ate delicately, like a cat, yet that tiny bead of golden jam remained, hovering just above the corner of her mouth.

Her very kissable mouth.

"Tea?" he said and without waiting for her response, poured her a cup, adding milk and a little sugar. Tea would wash it away.

"You remembered how I like it," she commented as he stirred the tea and handed it to her.

Of course he remembered. He remembered everything she'd ever said or done in his presence.

She took a sip and grimaced. "Cold." She put the cup down, saying softly, "We took too long over that egg." It didn't sound as though she regretted it in the least.

Not that he cared. She'd had her chance. That bead of marmalade was still in the corner of her mouth and he could not leave it there a moment longer.

Gazing into the dark golden depths of her eyes, Harry leaned forward until his mouth was a bare few inches from hers.

She swayed against him, lifting her face to his, offering

herself silently to him. With a low groan he licked the tiny drop of marmalade from the corner of her mouth.

"Sweet," he murmured, "yet tangy." He licked her mouth again, though there was no jam left. "Delicious."

He teased lightly along the seam of her lips with his lips and tongue, and she sighed and opened for him. A low growl of satisfaction curled up from deep within him as he drew her against him and kissed her deeply, sealing her mouth with his, learning the taste and texture of her.

Her taste entered his blood like a firestorm and he pulled her closer, feeling the gentle give of her softness against his hardness. He kissed her deeply, stroking the inside of her mouth and feeling her arch and shudder against him with each movement. She was flame to his tinder, the headiest wine.

She murmured something and rubbed the palms of her hands along his jawline, sliding her fingers into his hair.

His kisses deepened as she caught the rhythm that was burning him alive, racking his body in a fierce primeval thundering that swamped his senses.

Nell kissed him back, blindly, passionately, following his movements and her instincts. He tasted salty, spicy, darkly masculine, and he kissed her with a fierce hunger that melted her bones.

It awakened a hunger deep within her, one she'd never before experienced, one that had nothing to do with food.

She loved the feel of him, the taste, the delicious friction where his bristles rasped against her skin. She clung to him, her body pushing against him over and over in a rhythm she dimly recognized.

And then she felt a hard thrusting at her belly that she definitely recognized. Suddenly she realized the meaning of the rhythm.

A thread of blind panic quenched the heat in her blood. Shocked at herself, at what she'd been about to do, *at what she had been craving*, she jerked her head back and stared at him. "No," she whispered. "I can't."

He paused, his mouth still hot upon her, and she braced herself to shove him away. She was not ready, it was too soon, too unsettling. She had to *think*. And she couldn't while he was here.

But before she could move or say a word, he released her and stepped back, his chest heaving.

"You're right." His voice was deep and ragged. He straightened his clothes and ran a hand through his thick, dark hair. "I should never have let that happen. Not yet. Not until we're married, until you're ready. Your virtue is safe with me, I promise. Good night." He cupped her cheek gently and walked stiffly toward the door.

Nell blinked, her mind reeling at his response. She'd said no. And he'd listened. He'd stepped back at once, uttering words that sliced through every defense she had, cutting right to the heart.

Your virtue is safe with me, I promise.

She had no virtue left to protect, he *knew* that. And yet he'd promised to protect hers anyway. And with such quiet sincerity, as if there was no question or doubt in his mind.

Giving her back her honor.

He paused at the door. "Are you all right, now?"

"Y-yes, perfectly all right, thank you," she managed.

"Good, I thought you'd feel better with some food inside you. Sleep well."

She stared at the closed door, wanting to go after him, knowing she could not. What she felt had nothing at all to do with food, and everything to do with Harry Morant.

Sleep well, he'd told her. Harry hoped she would, but he put no faith in it. For an hour at most he'd managed to distract her, stop her fretting about her lost baby.

He'd succeeded in distracting himself more. He groaned. Whatever had possessed him to feed her?

He wasn't going to do it again. Not until they were safely married.

From now until their marriage, if she wanted to starve herself, he would let her. Probably. It was only a few weeks away. She wouldn't do herself that much damage. Probably.

He crossed the hall to his bedchamber and rummaged around in the drawer till he found what he was looking for. He'd noticed it last time he was here, a small bell with a handle. He tied it to a loop of string, tiptoed back across the hall and attached it to her door handle.

If she opened the door, the bell would wake him up.

He knew he ought to just cross the hall and get into bed with her, chastely, as he had the past two nights. She slept better if he did. The lilac shadows around her eyes had faded considerably since he'd started to share her bed.

Harry, on the other hand, wasn't well rested at all.

And when he was short on sleep, his self-control wasn't as reliable. And after the last hour, his self-control was considerably challenged.

He wasn't sure it was possible for him to share a bed with her any longer. Not without making love to her. And she wasn't ready for that.

He needed physical relief. Desperately.

He was fairly certain much more holding her without making love to her would kill him. He would explode.

It had taken every shred of strength he had to pull away from her and stride coolly from the room.

But she'd said no, even though he knew that she wanted him. And Lord, how the thought of her wanting him fired his blood anew.

But no was no. In Harry's code that was that.

Who was the bastard who'd raped her? The question ate

at him. He wasn't going to get off scot-free, not if Harry had anything to do with it.

No man who forced a woman deserved the title of man.

And a man who would force someone like Nell . . . such a man didn't deserve to live.

Twelve

*E*than squinted over the letter that had arrived that day
from Tibby. It was not her usual neat hand. She must
have written it in a hurry. And in the rain, for the paper was
crinkled in spots, and some words were blotchy where the
ink had run.

> *My dear Mr. Delaney,*
>
> *I must confess to some concern as to the tone of your
> last letter, particularly when you were talking about this
> woman you are courting. Far be it from me to criticize a
> woman I've never met*

Ethan frowned. Never met? Who the hell did she think
he was courting?

> *but it seems to me that she does not value you as she
> ought. You are a fine, decent, honorable, intelligent man,
> Mr. Delaney, and the equal of any one in the land.*

Ethan read that part again, savoring the sound of the words: fine, decent, honorable, *and* intelligent. He didn't know another living soul who'd describe him in those terms. Someone might describe him as fine. Or decent. And possibly honorable. But never all three at once and never with the word "intelligent" attached.

Never accept inferior treatment, and do not look down on your background for the things that cannot be changed, and for which you cannot be blamed. What is important is what you have done with your life, and the skills you have learned, and most of all your heart. If this woman does not value this about you, my dear Mr. Delaney, she is not worthy of you.

Here the writing got very blotchy indeed. The rain must have set in, he thought. That would explain the odd way she'd ended it.

I say this as your former teacher, to whom your welfare and future happiness is important.

Yours most sincerely, Miss Jane Tibthorpe

Ethan grinned as he carefully folded her letter and put it in the box with all her letters.

So Tibby didn't like the sound of this woman he was courting, eh? A touch of the green-eyed monster perhaps? "I hope so, darlin'. I hope so indeed," he said as he closed the lid of the box.

"She might yet entertain feelings for me after all, Freckles, so what do you think of that?" The dog thumped her tail on the floor.

"Aye, and she reckons I'm intelligent, too. Not bad for a formerly illiterate Irish clod, eh?" And with a jaunty step he headed off to the vicarage.

* * *

"Now, Vicar, what can you tell me about some fellow called Lochinvar?" Ethan moved his only remaining knight. "Checkmate," he declared and sat back.

The vicar frowned over the board, then shook his head. "Bless my soul, I never saw that one coming. Excellent, my boy, excellent."

Ethan repressed a grin. He was looking down the barrel of forty years, but the old man still called him "my boy." "Do you know who I mean?"

"Lochinvar? Yes, I know," the vicar said. "This is to do with your lady love, I suppose."

"Yes, I'd never heard of him, but she knows all about him, it seems."

"Then your Miss Tibby has a soft spot for a romantic hero."

"Oh." Ethan frowned. He wasn't a romantic sort himself, and certainly no hero. Romantic sorts were handsome and dashing. He was just a battered old tomcat, looking to settle down with a woman he had no business to love. He was banking on Tibby's fondness for taking in strays.

The vicar quoted, " 'So faithful in love, and so dauntless in war; There never was knight like the young Lochinvar'!"

Ethan sat forward. "A fighter, was he? She told me once that when we first met she'd thought me a young Lochinvar."

The vicar's brows rose. "Good heavens. What did you do?"

"She was bein' held hostage by some villains who were after a princess and her son."

"A princess?"

"The princess was Tibby's former pupil and she was comin' to Tibby in secret, or so they thought. But the villains had got wind of it and got there before the princess. I knocked at the door for directions and there was Tibby, white as a ghost, scared to death, and furious with it." He grinned reminiscently. "A brave little thing, she is. She slipped me a note tellin' about the men who were holding her prisoner, but I never even looked at it. She gave me such a look for being a big stupid—she didn't know then I couldn't read."

"So what did you do?" the vicar asked, as eager as a boy.

"I snatched her from the hold of the blackguards, tossed her on me horse, and galloped off with her to safety."

"Wonderful, wonderful! What an adventure," the old man exclaimed. "No wonder she calls you young Lochinvar. It's Sir Walter Scott, from *Marmion*, which was all the rage twenty years ago. A long poem," the vicar explained, seeing Ethan's blank expression. He quoted, "'Oh, young Lochinvar is come out of the west! Through all the wide border his steed was the best.'"

Ethan brightened. "That's like me. I reckon I've got the best horses in the county."

"'And, save his good broadsword, he weapon had none; He rode all unarmed, and he rode all alone!'"

Ethan sat back. "Nope, the man's a fool. If you're riding alone, you need to be better armed than that. A knife in your boot, at least."

The vicar smiled. He fetched a bound volume from the bookshelves, found the page, and handed it to Ethan. "Read it."

Ethan read it slowly through, stumbling over an unfamiliar word or two, and then sat back, thoughtful. "So, he kidnapped Fair Ellen from her wedding . . ."

The vicar sighed. "Yes. I've never understood the fair sex's fondness for young Lochinvar. I would have thought it would make for a shocking scandal, not to mention a difficult legal problem—getting the first marriage annulled—particularly difficult, I would have thought, when all the bride and groom's relatives were out to kill young Lochinvar. The Scots, you know, take their feuds very seriously. The whole thing was extremely ill-judged. But there is no accounting for female fancies."

Ethan agreed. "If it was me, I'd've grabbed the woman the first time around, right after her pa told me no, instead of waiting till the last minute, then riding in and upsetting the wedding. Women hate that. It's their big day. I bet Fair Ellen gave him an earful about it every day for the rest of his life, poor divil."

*T*he bell jangled on the door handle of Nell's bedchamber sometime after midnight. Harry stumbled from his bed in his smalls and hurried down the hallway after her.

She was half running, muttering in an anguished voice, "Where is she? Where? Must find her, find her, find her."

As always the sight of her distress in her sleep moved him deeply. He caught up with her at the top of the stairs and turned her around, catching her in the circle of his arm. "Hush, sweetheart," he murmured. "Torie is here. She is safe."

This time she struggled with him. "No, no, not her. Not Torie. Not my Torie," she muttered vehemently, pushing his hands away desperately, trying to shove her way past him. She was surprisingly strong.

"Come to bed," he said, and when she continued to fight him, he scooped her off her cold, bare feet and held her against his chest.

She stared past him with blank, heartbreaking eyes. "Is she dead, is she? My Torie?" Tears slid down her cheeks.

Her silent, blind grief tore him apart. He carried her back down the hallway and to bed. He held her against him, her face resting on his chest, wet with tears. He kissed them away, tasting the salt and wishing he could take away the pain.

He told himself that in the morning she would remember none of this.

It didn't help. He held her against him, rocking her,

murmuring reassurance and comforting lies, soothing her with words and hands until the storm of midnight grief had passed. Finally she lay limp and exhausted in his arms, her breathing slowed, and she slept the sleep of the weary. And Harry, exhausted, slept, too.

In the morning he took her riding in the park, to blow the cobwebs away. Riding helped when you were tense. And Nell was so tense she could snap.

The search had been going on too long.

*M*asculine voices sounded in the hall as Nell emerged from her bedchamber, washed and changed after her ride in the park. The exercise had done her good.

Curious to see Harry's friends, she came quietly halfway down the stairs and paused.

What would they think of their friend marrying a fallen woman? she wondered. Not that she cared what they thought, as long as they found Torie. But it might matter to Harry.

One was Rafe Ramsey and the other Luke Ripton, but which was which?

The taller of the two men was extremely elegant, with a superbly cut dark blue coat, highly starched shirt points, an intricately tied neck cloth, buff breeches, and gleaming boots. His attire bore all the hallmarks of a dandy. What distinguished him from that fraternity, she thought, was his broad shoulders, not the result of tailor's padding, and his strongly muscled horseman's thighs.

He must be Rafe. She'd got the impression from Harry that Rafe was coolheaded and deceptively indolent. Nonchalant was a word he'd used and this man certainly gave that impression.

Harry had called Luke their "fallen angel" and when she saw his face, she understood why. He was darkly beautiful and somehow tragic-looking, with dark eyes and cheekbones a woman would weep for. His thick dark hair was tousled, and he wore his neck cloth carelessly knotted. He seemed full of restless energy, for he moved the whole time, snapping his whip against his boots, pacing back and forth as they talked, and punctuating his sentences with lively gestures.

The clock chimed in the hall for quarter to eight. Nell took a breath and continued her way down the stairs.

She knew to the second when Harry caught sight of her. Their eyes met and she warmed under his gaze. She was aware of his friends looking but she didn't care. She felt pretty when Harry looked at her like that. Cooper had braided her hair again and this time she'd woven a primrose yellow ribbon through it.

Harry came forward and took her hand as she descended the last few steps. "These are my friends, Nell: Rafe Ramsey and Luke Ripton. Gentlemen, my betrothed, Lady Helen Freymore."

"How do you do, Mr. Ramsey, Mr. Ripton." Nell curtsied, pleased that she'd guessed correctly.

"Delighted to meet you, Lady Helen," Rafe Ramsey said. He had curiously heavy-lidded eyes of a piercing pale blue. They rested on her coolly. Uncomfortable eyes, she thought as he raised her hand to his lips. She wasn't sure she liked Mr. Ramsey.

"Harry told us about your problem," Luke said bowing over her hand. He looked at her with intense, dark eyes. "We'll do our best to find your baby, I promise."

Without warning Nell found herself tearing up. She gave him a wobbly smile, nodded, and squeezed his hand.

Harry stepped forward and put an arm around her waist.

"Let us go into the breakfast room," Rafe suggested. "Harry promised if we got here at this impossible hour, he'd feed us, Lady Helen."

They all went in to the breakfast parlor. Harry's friends

seemed to know their way around his aunt's house, she thought, watching them head straight for the array of covered dishes on the sideboard. They seemed very much at home.

"We've known Harry and Gabe since school," Rafe explained. Those uncanny eyes must have noted her surprise. "We've run tame in Lady Gosforth's various homes since we were raw striplings."

"I thought you were in the army together," she said.

"We were," Luke told her. "We all joined up together."

"Couldn't get rid of them," Harry grumbled as he held a chair for Nell to be seated. "Gabe and I tried but they followed us."

"Followed? Interesting word," Rafe drawled. "My father bought me my colors, and then you and Gabe talked Great-aunt Gert into buying yours and then if I recall Luke decided he might as well come, too."

"Mmm, yes, well, someone had to come to keep you lot out of trouble," Luke said, piling a plate with sliced ham, sausages, and eggs. The other two men laughed.

"Drag us into it, more like," Harry said. "Looks like an angel, but he's a demon for trouble, my dear, I warn you." He placed a plate in front of Nell. "Apple fritters. Cook thought you might enjoy them, but if you'd prefer a more standard breakfast . . ."

"No, thank you, these look delicious." And they did, with crisp lacy edges, oozing with apple and sprinkled with sugar and cinnamon. For once she felt hungry.

Satisfied, Harry heaped his own plate and sat down.

"So, Lady Helen," Rafe said, "My felicitations on your approaching marriage. Though perhaps felicitations is the wrong word. Sympathy, perhaps. It's about time someone came along and civilized this brute."

Nell gave him a sharp look, unsure of whether there was some hidden edge to what he was saying.

"I don't think he needs civilizing at all," she said and took a mouthful of apple fritter. "I am very well satisfied with him the way he is."

Luke fell back with an expression of feigned shock. "Good Lord, a woman who doesn't want to reform a man," he exclaimed. "Do you know how rare you are?"

Rafe Ramsey gave her a long look. "Lady Helen, you can't possibly wed Harry."

She eyed him guardedly and said nothing.

"You must marry me instead," he said.

Nell blinked, unsure of where this was leading. The pale blue eyes regarded her blandly, but she thought she saw a lazy twinkle in them.

"Are you trying to steal my betrothed from me?" Harry said and poured Nell some more hot chocolate, apparently unconcerned.

"Naturally," Rafe responded. "Who wouldn't? A charming lady who has no intention of reforming a husband after marriage? What man wouldn't want to snap her up?"

"Ah, but if I married you," Nell told him seriously, "I'm certain I'd have to change my mind about that."

There was sudden silence, then a roar of masculine laughter. Rafe tried to look affronted, but he soon succumbed to laughter as well. He gave Nell a wink and she smiled shyly back. It seemed Harry's friends had accepted her.

"I'd know that sound anywhere," declared Lady Gosforth, bustling in. "Rafe, my dear boy, and Luke, it's been too long."

They leapt to their feet and made beautiful, elegant bows that Lady Gosforth ignored, kissing them each fondly on the cheek. She waved them back to their seats, firing questions at them about their various relatives and at the same time issuing instructions to Sprotton.

Nell listened quietly, enjoying the exchanges. It was clear this was a routine event. Lady Gosforth treated Harry's friends as if they were her own relatives and they were obviously fond of her, too. For a girl who'd spent so many years

without family or the company of people her own age, it was
heartwarming to watch.

But as the laughter and the exchanges about people she
didn't know continued, Nell's mind wandered. With Rafe
and Luke combing the various parish workhouses, they
had a better chance of finding Torie. She sneaked a glance
at the clock on the overmantel. It was getting late.

She saw a movement outside the door. It was Cooper,
bringing Nell's pelisse and bonnet down, as requested, for
an eight o'clock departure.

Harry must have seen her, too. He set his cutlery together, drained his coffee, put his napkin to one side, and
said, "It's time we were off."

Immediately his two friends did likewise. It was obvious they'd been soldiers, she thought. Immediate attention
to the matter in hand.

Lady Gosforth watched in dismay as Nell stood as well.

"You're not taking this girl out all day again today, are
you?" she said to Harry. "She has a trousseau to prepare."

"The shopping must wait," Harry said. "There are legal
and business matters we must complete first. To do with the
estate," he added, when it looked as though his aunt would
question him further.

His aunt made a scornful noise. "As if Nell would be in-
terested in that. The girl needs clothes, for heaven's sake.
You two boys must agree with me, I'm sure." She looked at
Luke and Rafe for support.

Rafe carefully picked a piece of invisible fluff off his
immaculate coat, frowning with extreme concentration.
Luke had produced a small book from his pocket and consulted it earnestly. Neither appeared to hear her question.

Lady Gosforth snorted. "You boys stick together, as
usual, I see. Well, my dear, it's up to us women—"

Nell said urgently, "I'm sorry, Lady Gosforth, but I really must go with him."

"Very loyal of you, my dear," Lady Gosforth said, rolling her eyes. She turned back to Harry with a look that made it clear who she blamed for the ruination of her plans—and it wasn't Nell. "How on earth can I get this girl's trousseau and wedding dress prepared in time if you keep dragging her off all day? The wedding is in less than three weeks!" She gave her nephew a militant look. "I don't care what you say Harry, I've made appointments for Nell with my mantua maker, my milliner, the boot maker—"

Nell sent Harry a look of desperate entreaty. He could see she was on the verge of blurting everything out. She'd wanted to tell his aunt what they were doing. It was only right if they were going to be bringing Torie into Lady Gosforth's home, she said. She might object.

She might indeed, Harry thought, remembering his own first experience with his aunt. Few people would condone illegitimacy. Aunt Maude had made an exception for a blood relative then, but he was well aware that it was Gabe who'd forced her hand. Nell's baby was no relation to her.

He gave Nell a tiny shake of the head and told his aunt, "Very well, you can have Nell for two hours today from one o'clock onward."

"Two hours?" His aunt gave a disapproving huff. "You expect me to arrange a trousseau in two hours?"

"No, but you can get have your mantua maker here at one o'clock when we return for luncheon and she can take all Nell's measurements. That will give you something to start on."

"But Nell will want to choose, you foolish boy. The whole point of new clothes is the pleasure of deciding, isn't it, my dear?"

Nell stared at her, wanting to scream with frustration. Lady Gosforth was being very kind but Nell just wanted to leave and look for her daughter. Now! She didn't care about clothes.

But generosity had been thin on the ground in Nell's life recently, and she couldn't reject Lady Gosforth's kindness, especially when she'd put everything aside for Nell's benefit. Torn, she looked at Harry, not knowing what to say or do.

He stepped forward. "Her maid can do it," he said. "She can shop for Nell."

Cooper, standing quietly in the doorway, gasped. Her hand flew to her mouth in shock.

Nell, too, was stunned, but it was a brilliant solution. Nell had limited interest in clothes at the best of times and none at all at the moment, but Cooper . . . Cooper would love it.

"Her *maid*?" exclaimed Lady Gosforth, appalled. "Harry, don't be ridiculous!"

Nell raised her brows at Cooper.

"Why not?" Harry continued. "You said yourself she was talented. She'll know what Nell needs."

Cooper, incredulous but eager, nervously nodded back at Nell.

"But you can't. A maid is all very well," declared Lady Gosforth, "but she simply can't—"

"It's the perfect solution," Nell interrupted. "I truly don't have the time at present to go shopping, but Cooper does know what I need, and she has excellent taste. I'm sure she will also benefit from your advice, and that of Miss Bragge," she added tactfully. "You don't mind, do you, Cooper?" Nell asked, waving her in.

Cooper's eyes shone with excitement. "Oh no, m'lady. You won't be sorry, trusting me in this, m'lady, I promise you."

"Excellent," Harry said briskly, as if the impatience to go was all his. "Now I'm sorry but we really have to leave."

"But I was looking forward to taking Nell shopping," said Lady Gosforth, disgruntled.

Nell pulled her arm from Harry's grip and ran back and

gave the elderly lady a hug. "And I would love to go shopping with you, too, dear Lady Gosforth," she told her. "But this truly is urgent business. I'm sorry, but we will have a lifetime in which to go shopping, won't we?"

"Yes, my dear, I suppose so. It's just, your trousseau—"

"Will be a beautiful surprise."

Lady Gosforth considered the thought and brightened a little.

"We'll see you at one, Aunt Maude," Harry said and escorted Nell to the waiting curricle.

His friends each had a curricle and pair, she saw. Their grooms had been walking them up and down to keep the horses from getting cold. "What splendid horses," she commented as Harry lifted her up. She swiveled in her seat and eyed the two pairs critically as he climbed in after her.

Rafe and Luke, who were waiting for their curricles to be brought up, stared. "Good God," Luke exclaimed. "Don't tell me she likes horses as well? She *is* the perfect woman."

"I know," growled Harry, wrapping an arm around her and hauling her along the seat to his side. "But she's mine. See you at one."

Nell gave him a sideways glance and a shy smile. *The perfect woman?* She knew it was just part of the banter he had with his friends, but his gruff possessiveness warmed her. As did the hard band of muscle clamping her to his side. It stayed there long after his friends had disappeared.

As they continued their search for her daughter, Nell vowed that next time she woke to find him in her bed she would not be such a coward.

"So, who was Torie's father?" Harry asked out of the blue. The question had been eating at him ever since he'd understood what had happened to her.

Beside him, Nell stiffened. They'd just left one of the

cottages in which an abandoned baby girl had been placed with a wet nurse. Yet another baby girl who wasn't Torie.

"You don't need to tell me any details," he said quickly. "Just who he was."

"No one," she told him.

"Nell."

"You don't need to know. There's no point."

No point? Of course there was a point. He kept his voice calm. "Why do you say that?"

"My father tried to call him out after—you know. He used the pretext of cheating at cards—it would have made a scandal if it had been over me. Papa wanted above all to protect my reputation."

It would have been a damn sight more to the point if Papa had protected his daughter in the first place, Harry thought with quiet fury.

"But Sir—he—the man—refused to fight Papa. He called him a poor loser, but he knew what it was about."

"So he knows about the bab—"

"He knows nothing," she said vehemently. "He doesn't even know I fell pregnant in the first place. Papa challenged him months before I realized my . . . my condition."

"I see."

She gave him a square look. "And if I gave you a name, you'd probably want to do the same as Papa, wouldn't you?"

Not quite, Harry thought. He wouldn't challenge a piece of scum like that to a gentleman's duel on some pretext and then give up when the scoundrel declined to fight. He would just beat the bastard to a pulp.

She must have read the truth in his eyes, for she nodded. "Only two people know who fathered my child and Papa was one of them. He—the man knows nothing about it and that's the way I want it to stay. It's better for everyone, Torie especially."

Harry could see that. She wouldn't want her daughter to know she was the child of rape. Who would?

But the question still gnawed at Harry. Who the hell was the swine?

*T*hey returned to Mount Street at one o'clock. As well as luncheon Harry had arranged to rendezvous with Rafe and Luke to see what they'd learned.

Nell was feeling disheartened and gloomy. The list of places to search that Harry had made when they'd first begun their search was getting shorter. They'd covered so much ground and still there was no sign of Torie.

And she was upset and angry with Harry. "How can you tell it's not Torie?" he'd asked at the last place. Adding, "All babies look alike to me."

All babies were not alike, and she was furious with him for suggesting it. She'd flared up at him and snapped his head off for the remark and they'd come home the rest of the way in silence.

But with silence had come reflection, and with reflection a terrible realization.

His comment was innocent enough; she knew he hadn't meant anything by it. The problem was it had ripped off a scab, one she'd been trying to ignore. And underneath, the fears and doubts were festering.

Would she, in fact, recognize her own child? Her heart told her she would, but the more cribs, the more tiny chubby faces she saw with fuzzy domes and solemn expressions and rosebud mouths, the more the doubts started to creep in . . .

Babies changed so much in six weeks.

*A*fter luncheon, which was eaten in an atmosphere of quiet tension, Nell was whisked off by Lady Gosforth to be measured for her trousseau.

She liked pretty clothes as much as the next person, but

now, the whole process chafed at her. They measured every imaginable part of her, the thin, ferociously stylish mantua maker wielding a tape measure and rapping out numbers in French to her assistant. Then her feet and calves were measured and a template drawn. And then her head likewise, and a number of hats commissioned, including one for riding.

Nell endured it all in relative silence, trying to be as polite and cooperative as she could but wholly unable to enter into the spirit of things. She left most of the decisions to Lady Gosforth, Cooper, and Bragge.

She felt sick at heart. What if Torie was one of those babies they'd seen and her own mother hadn't recognized her?

The mantua maker, the boot maker, the tailor—for her habit—and the milliner's assistant noticed nothing amiss, but Lady Gosforth did.

The moment they'd finished, Lady Gosforth dismissed them all. As soon as they were alone she pushed Nell onto the settee and plumped down beside her. "What's the matter?" she demanded, fixing her with a gimlet stare.

"Matter?" Nell began.

"Don't try any of that nonsense on me, young lady. Do you think just because I use spectacles for reading that I cannot see what's as plain as the nose on my face? Whatever it is that's been taking you and my nephew out all day every day, it's got nothing to do with Harry's legal business or the estate. It's all about you. I can see it in his eyes."

Nell bit her lip.

Lady Gosforth continued, "Last night you came home looking as sick as a parrot, and now both of you have returned with faces as long as a wet week. And you, my girl, have approached the purchase of some beautiful clothes— clothes that any other young woman your age would give her eyeteeth for—as if it were a . . . a visit to the dentist. So . . ." She waited.

Nell didn't know where to start. She'd wanted to explain to Lady Gosforth about her daughter; it hadn't felt right not to tell her. She was relieved now that the moment had come, but it was all so huge, she didn't know how to begin.

Lady Gosforth leaned forward and took her hand. "Listen, my dear," she began in a much softer tone, "I never did have a daughter, though it was the dearest wish of my life, and you don't seem to have a mother, so—"

Nell burst into tears.

By the time Harry came to fetch Nell, wondering what had held her up, Nell had sobbed out most of her story on Lady Gosforth's large and comforting bosom.

As soon as he entered, Nell jumped to her feet, saying, "Is it time to leave now?"

Harry's gaze shot straight to her red-rimmed eyes.

"It's all right, Harry," Lady Gosforth said. "Nell has told me everything and we've both had a good cry, which has done both of us a power of good, though you wouldn't think so to look at us, I know. Now off you go and find that baby."

They walked together to the front door, where the curricle was waiting. Lady Gosforth gave Nell a quick hug. "You will know her when you see her, my dear, I am certain, so don't worry."

Harry gave Nell a shocked look. "Was that what upset you before?" he asked as they drove off. "The fear that you wouldn't recognize Torie?"

She nodded miserably. He put his arm around her, saying nothing.

*T*hey returned late again that night after another long and fruitless day. Harry tried to boost Nell's spirits all through supper, but a small stone of doubt had settled in her heart.

If her daughter was lost forever, Nell didn't know how she could ever live with the knowledge. If she'd only slept that night with Torie in her arms, instead of leaving her in the basket . . . It would haunt her forever. She could never forgive herself.

Harry sat beside her, talking with quiet resolution of what tomorrow might bring and passing her dishes he hoped would tempt her appetite. Though her fears had driven away all appetite, Nell ate to please him and because she knew she should.

She might be plagued with doubts and fears and riddled with guilt, but she would never give up on her daughter. While there was breath in her body, she would search.

Thirteen

The following morning, Nell awoke to the soft sound of rain pattering against her bedroom windows.

It was too wet to go riding in the park. She would copulate with him this morning, she decided. She owed him that, at the very least.

Harry lay on his side, one arm sprawled protectively across the pillow above her head, the other curved around her waist, his hand loosely splayed across her midriff, just beneath her breasts. Nell lay curled against him, his relaxed, brawny body a source of warmth and comfort. Her feet were tucked between his calves. She felt safe, protected.

She turned her head so that her cheek lay against his arm and breathed in his clean, masculine scent, now so familiar to her, and so dear.

With Harry sleeping beside her she didn't feel so alone, so lonely. Amazing how in such a short time she'd grown accustomed to sleeping with a man in her bed.

Or rather awakening to one. Every night she went to bed

alone and each morning woke up, well rested in his arms. Presumably she was still walking in her sleep.

His breathing was steady and regular. His arousal pressed into her bottom, as always. It intrigued her. She knew about how horses reproduced, and dogs, and it seemed people were much the same. Except, she wasn't in season, so why would he be aroused?

The why didn't matter, she told herself. He was ready for her and this morning they would . . . what was the correct word? Mate? Copulate?

He stirred, moving sleepily. His legs brushed against the skin of her thighs, and the sensation shivered through her, not unpleasantly. His arousal pressed insistently against her.

It was time.

She took a deep breath and turned over to face him. He was awake and watching her.

"Morning," he said in a deep, slightly hoarse voice. He smoothed a curl of hair out of her eyes and tucked it gently behind her ear. "Did you sleep well?"

"Yes. Thank you." His hot flesh brushed against her stomach and she blinked.

"I'm disturbing you," he said instantly. "I'll leave." He made to move away.

"No, s-stay." Her voice came out as a thread.

Harry frowned. She looked and sounded scared stiff. He glanced around the room, but all was still and silent. "What's the matter?"

"Nothing." She swallowed. "I want to c-copulate with you."

Harry scrutinized her face. "No, you don't," he said after a moment. She was strung tight as a bowstring. So was he, though in a different way.

"I do, I really do. You've been so kind to me, so good." Her eyes were wide and clear and anxious. "I want to thank you, and I know you want me, so . . ." She swallowed again.

She was *grateful*. Harry tried not to let his feelings

show. He was angry, not with her, but with himself, for not seeing this coming.

She wanted to thank him—dammit!—by making the ultimate sacrifice.

He wanted her body, yes, but not like this, as some kind of payment. And he sure as hell didn't want her *gratitude*.

"You don't want me, and you don't need to thank me. I'm away to my morning ride. I'll see you at breakfast." He leaned forward and kissed her briefly on the mouth. Her lips were cold and trembling. He flung back the covers to get out.

"No," she said and made a grab for him. He was pretty sure she'd been aiming to catch him by the waist. Or the thigh. The hem of his drawers, perhaps . . .

It wasn't what she ended up holding. Through the cotton of his drawers she held him. His body responded instantly.

She gripped him more firmly. He tried not to arch against the pressure. He clamped his jaw tight. He must have made some sort of noise because her eyes widened in concern.

"Did I hurt you?" she asked. The hand gripping him loosened, but didn't let go.

"No," he managed. "What the hell do you think you're doing?"

"I want to copulate with you. Today. Now."

Yes, to pay off her debt, he thought bitterly. "And what if I don't want to copulate?"

"You do," she said with flat certainty. "I might be ignorant of many things but I've watched enough stallions covering mares to know you're ready to mate. With me. Now."

Shudders rippled through him. God, yes, he was ready to mate with her now. He had been since the moment he'd clapped eyes on her. But he wasn't an animal and he could control his desires. He could.

Her hand tightened around him. He gritted his teeth and waited. There was a long silence.

He ought to pull away now. She was shaking like a leaf. But he couldn't make himself move. He'd wanted her too long. He wasn't in control at all he realized. Only part of him was, the part that refused to leave. He couldn't help giving in to it. To her.

"I don't know what to do next," she said in frustration. Her eyes were bright with unshed tears. "Tell me what to do."

He was tempted to just take over and do what he'd been dying to do ever since he first saw her: take over, make love to every inch of her.

But then he remembered what had been done to her. If he gave free rein to his lustful instincts, she'd be even more terrified than she was already.

It was probably going to kill him, but if he didn't want to bed a sacrificial lamb—and he sure as hell didn't—he had to let her feel her own way into this.

Feel being the operative word.

"Do whatever you want," he grated. Bad enough that his body was racked with the effort of restraining every instinct, now she wanted instructions?

She gave him a frustrated look and he recalled that she might be a mother but she was virtually inexperienced. He swore silently.

"Look, touch, taste," he explained. "Do whatever you want to me, I won't mind." He gave a rueful smile. "I'll love it whatever you do. You're right, I want you, badly. But I'll never do anything you don't want me to. I'm putty in your hands."

"Putty?" she said with a glint of humor. "This doesn't feel like putty to me." She squeezed.

He gave a small choke of laughter. It lightened the moment, eased the tension. He felt her relax a little.

He watched her thinking it over, still holding firmly to his cock through his drawers.

"I'm usually naked," he said.

Her eyes went to the buttons on the waistband, then she slowly let him go. He wanted to tell her to take it back, but he gritted his teeth and waited. It was going to be hell, but if he could only be patient and keep himself under control, heaven could be just around the corner.

Heaven was here in a thin white cotton nightgown, frowning and blushing as she undid the buttons of his drawers. There were only three. She had them undone in a trice.

She glanced at him. "You really did mean naked?"

"Yes," he ground out. She seemed surprised. So the bastard had been dressed, Harry surmised. Good. The more differences between them the better.

She pulled his drawers slowly down, past his belly button and pausing at the place where the arrow of dark hair down his belly thickened. Without taking his eyes off her, he lifted his backside off the bed to enable her to pull his drawers off. She took a deep breath and dragged them down past his knees. Her eyes widened as his cock sprang free.

He kicked his drawers off the rest of the way and tried to look relaxed as she examined him. She was blushing furiously, but her jaw was set at a determined angle. She was going to go through with it.

So was he. The thought gave him a spurt of wry amusement. Which of them was the sacrificial lamb? He was starting to wonder.

Her lips were parted; her breaths came in soft puffs. She was aroused, Harry saw. Not as much as he was, but it was a hopeful sign.

Her hand hovered indecisively over his cock. Harry held his breath, but she moved to his chest. She smoothed soft, cool palms over him, exploring the difference between them. The friction of skin on skin.

She leaned over him, her breasts swaying behind their white cotton shroud. He followed the sharp peaks of her nipples with hungry eyes. She explored his body, running her hands across his shoulders, down his arms, her brow furrowed in concentration. Learning him. Her lips were parted and he caught the scent of her. He craved the taste of her in his mouth.

But if he moved, if he touched her, started kissing her, he might not be able to stop. She lightly brushed against his nipples and he arched involuntarily. Make that would not be able to stop.

He closed his eyes, thinking that might make it easier. It didn't. With each caress, each stroke, his body thrummed to the call of male to female. And the scent of warm female intensified. Every particle of his body strained and ached and throbbed to join with her.

Harry clenched the bedsheets in determined fists. If it killed him, he would endure this. For her. It didn't matter that every shred of control he had would be stretched to the limit.

Because that's what she needed from him.

She was a coward, Nell thought, avoiding his . . . thing. She didn't have a word for it. A horse's was called a pizzle, but it didn't seem right somehow, to use the same word for a man.

It had felt hot through the cotton before. But it had grown bigger since she'd stripped him naked, and she was a bit hesitant to touch it again, yet. She would, of course, in the end.

She tried not to think about the end. This was different. This was fascinating. To have this big, magnificent male animal naked under her touch, lying there like a big lion, tense, but so willing to be petted . . .

His desire for her was palpable. She felt warmed by it. More than warmed. Scorched. And yet she didn't fear it.

His skin was so smooth and resilient, nicked and scarred in a number of places. Years at war, he'd said once.

"Where did you get this?" She traced a jagged white scar with her finger.

"A French bayonet," he told her. He didn't take his eyes off her.

She placed a finger in a puckered hollow of skin. "And this?"

He frowned. "A ball, I think. Or maybe some shrapnel."

"You don't know?"

He gave a faint smile. "I believe I was insensible at the time the surgeon dug it out. I got this at the same time." He turned his head and she saw a scar running behind his ear and up into his scalp.

She arrowed her fingers through his hair, cupping the scar, massaging his head lightly. "You might have died," she said softly.

He gave an indifferent shrug, as if he didn't care. Nell was shocked. But she supposed it was how men at war had to think, otherwise they'd be paralyzed with fear.

As she almost was. She had to get on, on to the part she both dreaded and longed for, the part where they joined. She'd distracted herself with his scars, but he must be getting impatient. Not to mention cold.

"Are you cold?"

He gave her a slow smile. "Do I feel cold?"

She ran her palms across his shoulders and down his arms, then smoothed them across his chest and slowly down his stomach. No, he didn't feel cold. Nor did she for that matter.

There was not an ounce of fat on the man; he was all hard muscle, sinew, and bone.

Power. She remembered how small and light and helpless she'd felt as he'd tossed her over his shoulder that time. She recalled how he'd throbbed against her palm in that darkened stable.

He could have taken her at any time.

She brushed her fingers across his small, hard nipples, and he arched a little and made a soft sound deep in his throat. He liked it. Did it feel like when she touched her own nipples? When she'd been pregnant, they were so sensitive . . . She could feel them now, brushing against the cotton of her nightgown.

She circled the small male nipples, around and around, feeling his involuntary response. She scratched her nails lightly across them. He inhaled sharply and the gray gaze darkened.

He didn't try to control her. He just lay there, watching her with smoky gray eyes, letting her touch him as she willed.

She could feel her own heartbeat. It was racing and she panted, as though she'd been running a race.

Nerves, she told herself. The more she dallied in this pleasurable exploration of his body, the more the thing she had to do was delayed. Get it over with. Get it done.

She took a deep breath and let her hand continue its exploratory path down the hard ridges of his stomach, following the line of dark hair that led toward his . . . shaft. The word came to her at last. His shaft.

With one finger she stroked it from the base to the tip, then ran the tip of her finger around the head. His breath hitched in, and she took a quick glance at his face. His eyes were heavy-lidded and dark. Keeping her eyes on his face she ran her finger around the head of his shaft again, and again he gave a ragged gasp and clenched his jaw. The muscles of his arms and legs were corded. His heels dug into the mattress and he clenched the sheets in his fists, as if anchoring himself to the bed.

"It's not pain you're feeling, is it?" she asked, stroking him as she spoke. The skin of his shaft was velvety soft. Beneath it he was hard and hot.

He shook his head and gritted his teeth.

"You like this, don't you?"

His eyes burned into her in silent, potent confirmation, and she felt a small feminine thrill. She was doing this to him. She gripped his shaft at the base with her whole hand

and ran it very slowly to the knob at the end. He groaned and flung his head back. She ran her hand up and down again, squeezing firmly and again he moaned and clenched his body as if in pain. There was a bead of moisture at the tip and she ran the hollow of her palm over it, around and around, and he shuddered violently.

"No more," he grated, his jaw clenched and his head flung back.

She let go of him instantly. "What is is?"

He opened his eyes and gave her a flat look. "I'm ready to mate with you and one more touch like that and I'll ejaculate."

She understood at once. Stallions did it, too.

She went cold. He was giving her a way out. Letting her know she didn't have to go through with it.

But she did, she did. She had to get it over with. She would not live her life in fear of this, she would not.

The time had come. She pulled up her nightgown to halfway up her thighs and said, "Then come on, mate with me. Now."

He didn't move for a moment, so she reached out and grasped him again. He needed no second urging. He surged on top of her, spread her legs, and touched her there. She stiffened as she felt his fingers parting her flesh. He stroked her lightly and she started to relax, but then he touched something and a sudden convulsion arced through her. Before she had time to think, his hand moved again, and again a hot spear of sensation roiled through her.

He made a deep masculine sound in his throat and she felt him enter her. He thrust once, twice.

And she went blank.

Harry felt it at once, felt her stiffen, her body freeze. He was sure it wasn't hurting her. She was ready for him, she was warm and wet and slippery, and she'd been so sweetly responsive.

He stopped moving at once. "Nell, what is it? What's the matter?"

She didn't respond. She was stiff, but her whole body shook. And not in a good way.

"Nell? Sweetheart?"

Her eyes were closed, her face set in a grimace.

Harry knew immediately what he'd done. He'd effectively pinned her down so she couldn't move. He cursed himself silently. There was only one thing he could think of to do.

Still deep inside her, he rolled over, taking her with him. Then, though it was just about killing him, he watched her face and waited.

It felt like forever before her stiffness drained away and her eyes cautiously opened. Confused, she stared down at him. "What are you doing? Finish it."

He shook his head. "You finish it. Or not. Your choice."

She stared down at him. "But you're the man."

"And you're the woman," he answered softly. "It takes two."

Her brow furrowed. "How?"

"You can ride, can't you?" He placed his hands on her hips and moved her a little, to give her the idea. "This way you control everything."

Not quite believing him, she moved experimentally and he saw as well as felt her response. Scowling in concentration, she moved again. He groaned and slipped his hand between them. She started as she felt him stroke the tiny nub, then gasped. He felt her body clench around him in response.

It was going to be all right, he thought dazedly as the last of his ragged control dissolved and he surged upward, into her. She gasped and gripped him inside and out, with thighs and inner muscles. He bucked and thrust and she rode him as masterfully as any horse, faster and faster, gasping with each movement even as she urged him on.

At the last moment, when he knew he was about to come, he called her name. "Nell, Nell!" Assertively, needing her to respond.

Her eyes flew open and she stared at him, dazed, preoccupied, riding him furiously.

"Look. At. Me," Harry grated, and her eyes locked with his, and in that moment, joined in mind and body, they arched in a long, shuddering climax. He heard a faint high cry join with his hoarse shout of triumph, then everything splintered around them.

*A*fter some time, Harry became aware that she was lying on his naked chest, weeping silently.

Something in his chest clenched. There was nothing a man could do when a woman wept, except to hold her. He'd learned that from Barrow, when he was a young boy and was shocked to see Mrs. Barrow, the strongest woman he'd even known, weeping in Barrow's arms.

"Men chop wood, or punch things," Barrow had told him afterward. "Women weep. There's naught to do, lad, except to hold them and love them until it passes."

So Harry held Nell, soothing her with his hands, stroking her hair, holding her against him, loving her silently.

Loving her?

Oh God. He hadn't expected that. He pushed the thought away. He wasn't ready to think about anything like that.

He eased her down beside him, murmuring meaningless comforting phrases. "There, there . . . it's all right . . ." Not having the least idea of what they meant.

Damp tendrils of hair clung to her cheeks and forehead, and as he smoothed them away, without quite thinking about it, he planted small kisses where each tendril had lain: her cheekbones, her temples, kissing her eyelids and tasting salt.

She looked up at him with tear-drenched eyes and he

kissed the corners of her eyes, then down along her jawline to the sensitive spot beneath her ear. She curled against his mouth like a cat. Desire flared again as he tasted, kissed, comforted. And aroused.

This time, he resolved, it would be all about pleasuring her. Not copulation. Making love.

That word again. Love.

He closed his eyes and returned to kissing her.

"No," she said suddenly and pushed him away.

He froze. What had he done?

"Didn't you hear the clock chime just now?" She sat up. "It's quarter to eight. Rafe and Luke will be here any minute. We need to get dressed and get ready to leave." She slipped out of his arms and out of bed.

Harry sighed and pulled a sheet around him.

Another fruitless day of searching. It had grown very cold, and Nell was huddled into a fur rug. Because of the rain this morning, Harry had hired a chaise, which had come with a driver. The closed chaise provided more privacy as well as protection from the elements. Nell sat beside Harry on the seat with her feet tucked up, leaning against him, tucked into the curve of his arm with her cheek snuggled against his shoulder.

However awkward and fraught with tension this morning's lovemaking had been, the result had been a new physical easiness with each other. Harry was glad of it.

Nell had been silent for most of the last hour.

They couldn't see much; the drizzle fogged up the windows, but the smoother ride told him they were back on main roads again and nearing London. The carriage lamps had been lit a short while before. Their blurry golden glow swung rhythmically in time with the horses' hooves.

"Papa brought him to Firmin Court," she said, as if continuing a conversation. "He'd been playing cards with him at some house party and he invited him home. For me, I suppose. Papa wanted me to get married, and Firmin Court was a tempting dowry."

She was tempting enough as she was, Harry thought, but he didn't interrupt. He'd known at once who she was talking about. He didn't know what had prompted her to talk about it now—perhaps the intimacy of the closed carriage with the rain falling outside, the swish of the wheels, and the clip-clop of the horses' hooves.

"I disliked him on sight," she said. "You know how sometimes you meet someone for whom you have an instant, unreasonable antipathy?"

"Yes."

"It wasn't that I knew the kind of man he was," she qualified. "I just disliked him. He was good-looking, I suppose, but his eyes were too close-set and he had a mean mouth. He smiled too hard at me and gave me all sorts of compliments but he never actually looked at me. All the time he was looking around the house, summing up its value." She paused. "I could see he was disappointed. Papa always did put things in the best possible light. I was a beauty and the estate rich and full of priceless treasures."

"You are a beauty," Harry said. "And the estate will become rich, just you wait and see."

She smiled. "Sir—he couldn't see it."

Damn, she'd almost let the name slip. Harry was determined to learn it.

She was silent for a while, then said, "He was the sort of man who chased the housemaids. Even when they're not willing." Her fingers tightened around his arm. "Especially when they're not willing. Our housemaids were good girls. Both were betrothed to men on the estate. He didn't care."

"What happened?" Harry prompted.

"I caught him trying to rape one of them. I hit him over the head with a wet mop. He was furious. The mop was a bit smelly, but I didn't care. I was furious, too. I berated him in front of her and all the other servants. I ripped into him, calling him all manner of unflattering epithets." She grimaced.

"I made an enemy of him at that moment. It was too late for him to leave that night, but I told him he was to leave in the morning."

She took a shaky breath and continued, "I didn't trust him. I posted two footmen at the foot of the stairs to the maids' quarters." She shuddered. "It never occurred to me that he would come after me—a gentleman's daughter in her own home."

Harry hugged her tight, saying nothing.

"B-but he did," she finished shakily. "And I brought it on myself."

"Nonsense," he growled fiercely. "It was not your fault in the least. You protected those girls and it was the right thing to do. Your father should have thrown him out then and there."

She sighed. "Papa had lost the game, he was drunk, insensible. Besides, he never would have suspected a gentleman would . . . do that."

The way she always defended her father irritated him. The man was useless. He'd let her down in every possible way, and yet she loved him still. "He should have done it to protect his servants. It was his responsibility as their employer."

"Y-yes, but it was I who humiliated him—"

"By stopping his nasty habits?"

"By insulting him in front of the servants."

He snorted. "You heaped insults on my head at the top of your voice in front of the whole of Bath and it didn't bother me in the least."

She frowned at him and said slowly, "Yes, but you're different."

"Exactly. I'm not a filthy rapist who preys on women. I'm a man."

She stared at him for a moment, her lips trembling. "Yes,

you are a man—a wonderful man." And she flung her arms around him and hugged him convulsively.

He gathered her against him. "It was not your fault, not in the least."

"No, no, it wasn't," she mumbled into his neck. Slowly he felt the tension drain out of her.

After a long silence she sighed and rubbed her cheek against the fabric of his coat. "I feel so much better now that we've talked about it," she told him. "There's just one more thing I need to tell you, and then it's done and I will never have to speak of it again."

Harry tensed. His name. He wanted the bastard's name. He'd sworn to avenge her.

"It was over very quickly," she told him. "I was asleep and it was half done before I knew it." She shivered. "So that's it. Now you know everything."

"Not quite everything."

"I won't tell you his name," she said firmly. "He knows nothing about Torie and I want it to stay that way. A father has rights over a child, you know. He could take her from me and the law would allow it."

"Nonsense. You'll be married to me," Harry told her. "And I would never allow such a thing to happen."

She shook her head. "No, I won't risk it." And that was her final word.

*H*arry brooded over the story that night, as he waited for her to undress. She was still too shy to let him help her disrobe and he wasn't going to push it. He would sleep with her tonight and not wait for her to start sleep-walking.

He fetched a sheet of paper, a pen, and ink and sat down to write to Ethan. Someone at Firmin Court would know who that bastard was. That old woman, Aggie—she'd know. A few discreet questions would be all it took.

Ethan knew how to be discreet. He didn't need to know any details, just find out who the visitor was who'd gone sniffing around the housemaids and been told off by Lady Nell.

When he'd finished the letter, sealed it, and sent it off to be posted, he knocked on Nell's door.

"Come in." She was sitting bolt upright in bed, that blasted nightgown buttoned to her chin.

"There's not much point in starting the night separate," he told her. "We both know where we'll end up, so with your permission . . ." He waited for her assent.

She thought for a moment, then nodded and blushing rosily, flipped the covers back in a wordless invitation.

Harry stripped quickly and slid into bed beside her. "Now kiss me," he murmured. She needed no further encouragement.

Fourteen

It was the most important letter Ethan had ever written, or was likely to write again. His whole future happiness hung on it. It was also the most difficult. This was one letter he wasn't going to let the vicar read and correct.

Tibby was in England. Just a few miles away. The message had come the previous day. She'd come with Gabe and the princess and the two little boys. They were all staying at Alverleigh, the home of Harry's despised half brother, the earl.

Harry wouldn't like that, Ethan knew. But Ethan didn't care. Tibby wasn't over the sea in Zindaria; she was less than a day's ride away.

My dear Miss Tibby . . .

No. He scratched it out.

My darlin Miss Tibby . . . No. He scratched out *Miss*.

My darlin Tibby . . . Would she think it was presumptuous? She was very proper, his Tibby. He groaned. She wasn't his Tibby, that was the problem.

He put down the pen and wiped his palms for the fortieth time. He was sweating. In December.

He'd made a draft and corrected it as best he could without help. This was the final copy. He kept wasting paper trying to decide how to start. "Bite the bullet and get on with it, Delaney," he told himself.

He picked up the pen and started again:

My dear Miss Tibby,

I have taken your words in your last letter to hart and I take leave to tell you that I will call on you at Alverly next Wednesday in the afternoon. I hope it is convenient.

Yours truely, Ethan Delaney

There. It was done. He blotted it carefully, then folded it and sealed it with a blob of red sealing wax. Red for danger. Red for blood. Red for love. In an old habit he'd thought long forgotten he crossed himself, kissed the letter, and whispered, "Godspeed."

Then he pocketed the letter and headed outside. If he didn't post it now, he'd get cold feet again.

*I*t was the seventh day of their search. The weak winter sun was sinking in the west and Nell and Harry were heading back to London. Nell sat hunched in the corner of the curricle, staring out at the passing scenery, silent and withdrawn.

They'd crossed off the last address on their list.

Between the four of them, they'd visited every parish workhouse, the foundling hospital, the asylum for female orphans in Westminster, every charitable institution who cared for orphans and unwanted children, and every wet nurse connected with every charity in and around London.

There was no sign of Torie at any of them.

In one last desperate effort, they'd decided to reenact Nell's father's journey from the house where she'd given birth to Torie, through the village where he'd died, and thence to London.

They'd spent some time in the village where he'd died questioning people. They established that no, he hadn't had any basket or any child with him when he'd collapsed. And no, nobody in the area had suddenly acquired a baby.

Yes, it was certain he'd been seen coming toward the village from the direction of London.

Nell had laid flowers on Papa's grave and they'd continued on their way, stopping at each hamlet and village and inquiring. It was hopeless, Harry thought. It was seven weeks ago now.

He just hoped the asking would help Nell to accept the loss of her daughter. His fear was that she never would.

They slowed to pass through a flock of geese being herded through a tiny hamlet that consisted of a lone church, surrounded by farms and scattered cottages.

As they passed the church, Nell sat up suddenly. "Stop!" she shouted. "Stop here. Stop!"

Harry pulled up the horses, but she'd already scrambled down from the curricle and was racing back toward the church.

"Here, hold the horses," he said to a goose herder and tossed him the reins. "There's a shilling in it for you." And he hurried after Nell.

She stood in the entry porch of the church, staring at a basket of vegetables sitting there.

"What is it?" Harry asked her.

She turned a glowing face to him. "It's a basket."

He frowned and shook his head, mystified.

"People leave things on church doorways in baskets," she said excitedly. "Babies. They leave babies. How many times have you heard of babies being left on the steps of a church?"

Practically never, Harry thought. It was fairly common in Spain, he knew, but they were convents, and nuns took children in. English vicars seemed less likely to do so in his opinion.

"We never thought to check the actual churches."

Harry's heart sank. Another recipe for slow heartbreak, he thought. It had been agonizing enough to watch her slowly killing herself with worry and to know there was nothing he could do to stop it.

"And this is St. Stephen's," she said feverishly.

He gave her a blank look.

"Papa's middle name was Stephen. It might be an omen. He believed in omens. We have to ask," she said and headed around the side toward the vicarage at the rear.

Harry followed. She was clutching at straws.

It was a small house, with a neat, well-kept garden, bare now in the cold season. The brass bellpull gleamed with elbow wax and polish. Nell pulled on it, dancing impatiently from toe to toe as the musical jangle echoed within.

A middle-aged woman with iron gray hair answered. "Yes?"

"Did anyone leave a baby here?" Nell blurted without preamble. "Seven weeks ago, a baby in a basket?"

The woman frowned. "Was it seven weeks? I thought it wasn't near as long ago as that."

Nell paled and staggered. She clutched the woman's arms in a convulsive grip. "You mean there *was* a baby?"

The woman nodded, clearly rather taken aback by Nell's wild-eyed intensity. "A little girl, poor wee thing."

"Where is she now?" Nell demanded, panting.

The woman pointed and, almost without looking, Harry knew where.

"Where? Which house?" Nell stood on tiptoe, peering eagerly at the houses in the distance.

Harry took her arm. "In the churchyard, Nell," he said quietly.

She frowned, puzzled, not understanding. "The church-yard. Who lives in the churchyard?" And then she knew. "Noooo," she wailed, turning back to the woman. "It can't be. She's alive, tell me she's alive."

The woman's eyes filled with sympathetic tears. "I'm sorry lass. Nobody knew she was there, see? The vicar had gone off to London for the night and I was at my sister's, so there was nobody to hear the poor little creature crying."

Nell gave a choked sob.

The woman went on, "It was a bitter night and the frost killed the last of my flowers. The babe, too. She was dead when we found her in the morning. So pretty she looked, like a little frozen angel in her satin-lined basket."

"S-satin-lined . . ." Nell fainted. Harry caught her before she fell. Refusing all offers of help from the woman, he carried Nell back to the curricle. She wasn't ill, just bro-kenhearted.

She sobbed most of the way home, not normal weeping, but terrible wracking sobs that seemed torn from her body.

Harry held her hard against his heart. Each convulsive sob that juddered through her was like a cut to his body. If only he could have made it end differently. He held her and rocked her gently, hating being so damned helpless. He was furious. He needed to punch someone.

He'd come back. He'd do something about the grave, but for now, all he wanted to do was kill. He'd never known such anger.

Vengeance is mine, saith the Lord, but Harry burned to avenge the wrong done to her. He had nobody to punch. Yet. And when he did find the swine, it would be a damned sight more than a punch.

In the meantime, he had a precious, distraught woman to care for.

He took her home, gently undressed her down to her chemise, put her to bed. "I want to stay with you," he told her and waited. He wouldn't force himself on her.

"Stay," she said in a thready whisper.

Thank God. He didn't know how he would have left her if she had wanted to be alone. He quickly stripped and climbed into bed with her. She was shivering. She reached for him immediately and pressed herself against him as if she couldn't get close enough. "Don't leave me," she whispered.

Something cracked deep within him. "Never," he croaked. In her grief she had turned to him. She needed him. He was no damned use to her, but she still wanted him.

For a long time they lay together silently. Eventually she stopped shivering. He thought she'd fallen asleep when suddenly she said, "I keep thinking of her, crying, and nobody to hear. Such a horrible, painful way to d—"

"No." He cut her off. "It wouldn't have been painful at all."

She pulled back. Swollen amber eyes fixed on him with painful intensity. "How could you know?"

He knew about all sorts of deaths. Soldiers did. But he didn't tell her that. "In the war, in the Pyrenees one time, there was an unexpected blizzard. Later, we found some bodies. Soldiers. They'd fallen into a narrow gully and frozen to death."

She shuddered. He pulled her close again and continued in a low voice. "They'd fallen on top of each other. The man on the bottom of the pile was alive, though he was half frozen. He told me later that in all that snow, they'd slowly fallen asleep. Nobody cried out. There was no pain at all, he said. In fact, the most painful thing, he told me, was his body coming back to life. Excruciating was the word he used. But slowly freezing in the snow was peaceful and quiet."

She gave a long, jagged sigh and subsided against his chest. He felt her tears on his skin, but she made no sound. He wrapped her in his arms and cradled her against him until she finally slept.

She didn't move a muscle all night. The sleepwalking had ended. The search was over.

N ell spent the next day in bed, in a darkened room, grieving. She'd sent Harry away in the morning, pleading a migraine. She couldn't face the world. Not yet. The pain of losing Torie was too intense.

That night she made bitter, silent love with Harry and fell asleep almost immediately afterward.

Next morning she feigned sleep until Harry left. How was she ever going to face the rest of her life? she thought despairingly and pulled the covers over her head.

The answer came to her from Aggie, from the terrible time after Mama had died. "Take it one day at a time, lovie. One step at a time if you have to. The living owe it to the dead to live; you owe it to your mam to live. You know she'd want it that way."

The memory of those words had given Nell strength before, after Papa died and when she'd searched for Torie the first time. And later, when she'd walked, defeated and exhausted from London to Firmin Court. One step at a time. And later, when she'd found Papa had lost everything and she had no home, no money, and no family, she managed to keep going then, one day at a time.

No more. She couldn't face another day. She couldn't bear to go on. It was all too painful.

She rolled over and buried her face in the pillow. And smelled Harry's dear, familiar smell. She lay there for a while, breathing it in, thinking about everything he was to her, everything he'd given her, everything he was that made her life still worth living. Gathering her strength again to go on.

She didn't just owe it to the dead to keep living, she owed it to the living. To Harry. Because she loved him.

She rang for Cooper and pulled open the curtains, letting the cold light of day stream into the room.

She had promises to keep.

A s she went downstairs she heard the sounds of an argument coming from the drawing room.

"We are damned well not having it there!" Harry growled as Nell reached the door.

"If you weren't so stubborn you would see at once why it is the perfect pl—" Lady Gosforth broke off as Nell entered the room. Lady Gosforth hastened to embrace her. "My dearest girl, I am so glad you've decided to join us. I'm so, so sorry to hear about your little one. How are you feeling?"

"Are you all right?" Harry hovered protectively.

She smiled and nodded. "What were you arguing about?"

"Nothing," Harry said immediately.

She raised her brow at him, then turned to his aunt.

"About where to have the wedding," Lady Gosforth said. "But perhaps you want to delay it."

Nell shook her head. "No. There's no point in delaying. What was your disagreement about?"

Lady Gosforth waved her hand. "Oh, I had everything organized, and now he wants to overturn all my arrangements."

"Why?" Nell asked.

"Because we're not getting married at Alverleigh," Harry growled, glaring at his aunt.

"What is Alverleigh?" Nell looked at Harry.

"The family seat," Lady Gosforth answered.

"My half brother's lair," Harry said at the same time.

Lady Gosforth glanced at Nell. "Please don't take this the wrong way, my dear, but you must acknowledge that there will be talk, if only from the way Harry kidnapped you in Bath. If you are married from Alverleigh, it gives a clear signal to the world that both you and Harry have the support of the Earl of Alverleigh and the rest of the family. Then if any whiff of scandal surfaces later, it will not signify."

"It's the Renfrew family seat," Harry said. "Not my family at all. I'm a Morant, remember?"

Lady Gosforth gave an airy wave. "Pooh, just because your mother married a Morant, it doesn't make you one. With that face, you're a Renfrew through and through."

Harry scowled at her and she added, "Besides, I hope you're not going to deny Gabriel as a relative."

"Of course not."

"Well, Gabriel's spending Christmas at Alverleigh with his wife, Princess Caroline."

"What?" He looked astounded. "The whole of Christmas? I thought he'd be having it with us."

"He is. We're all invited. The whole family," his aunt stressed the word "whole."

Harry didn't look too pleased. "When was this arranged?"

Lady Gosforth waved a vague hand. "Ages ago. I believe Nash arranged it when he was in Austria. He popped over to Zindaria and to all intents and purposes got on famously with everyone there." She gave Harry a beady look. "But then Nash has charming manners."

He grunted. "Nash is a diplomat. Being charming is his trade."

"Mules being yours," his loving aunt said sweetly.

His lips twitched. "I can put up with sharing a table with Nash if I have to, but not Marcus."

"Marcus?" Nell asked.

"The Earl of Alverleigh, the head of the family and Harry's oldest brother," Lady Gosforth explained.

"Half brother," Harry snapped. "And he doesn't acknowledge me."

"He does now," Lady Gosforth retorted. "He has ever since he came into the title. It's you who don't acknowledge him." She snorted delicately. "That stiff neck of yours is pure Renfrew, too."

"He's a coldhearted bullyboy, like his father."

"His father," Nell noted, not "our father."

"He's soon to be Nell's brother-in-law. I'm sure at this time it will be a comfort to Nell to know she has a whole family ready and willing to welcome her into their hearts," Lady Gosforth added pointedly.

Harry gave her an arrested look. "How do you know they want to welcome her?" he asked in a milder voice.

"Because Marcus told me so when he offered to have the wedding there in the Alverleigh family chapel."

Harry frowned. "Why there? Why not in London?"

"Because despite her colors, Nell is still in mourning for her father, and now, of course, for little Torie."

Nell's eyes flooded. She turned away, pressing her quivering lips together until she had control of them again. Harry put his arm around her in instant support. Nell nodded her thanks then stepped away. She had to learn to manage on her own. She could not be forever falling in a heap on him.

"So it would not be appropriate for her to be married in St. George's, Hanover Square," Lady Gosforth continued more quietly.

"Her own village church would be appropriate," Harry said firmly.

For a moment, Nell was so tempted. To go home to Firmin Court and be married in the church she was baptized in . . . To see the church pews filled with all the dear familiar village faces she'd grown up with—they'd all come to see her wed, she knew.

But she'd planned to have Torie baptized there, at the ancient stone font where Nell had been baptized, and Nell's mother, and her grandmother, and who knows how many generations before her had been baptized. Somehow, she couldn't yet face that font, not after having lost Torie.

Lady Gosforth was clearly trying to broker some sort of

reconciliation between the estranged half brothers. Harry was defensive and hostile about the two older brothers. Nell didn't understand why, and she didn't want to interfere.

But she knew what it was like to have no family at all.

"I would like to be married at Alverleigh if you don't mind," she told Harry.

"Why would you want to go there?" Harry demanded. "You don't know any of them."

"No, but I would like to," she said simply. "I don't have any family and I would like to meet yours. But not if you don't want them to meet me, of course."

Harry stared at her. "Nothing of the sort. They would be privileged to meet you. It's not that, it's just—oh, hang it, Nell, do you really want to go there?"

"Not if you don't want to." She waited.

He threw up his hands. "Then we'll get married at Alverleigh, but don't blame me if you hate it there." He looked at his aunt, whose eyes were gleaming with amusement. "And don't blame me if I punch Marcus in the face."

"No, dear boy, we won't; we'll probably be delighted if you do," Lady Gosforth said.

"What?" Nell and Harry both said in surprise.

She shrugged. "Men always start out punching each other and then end up the best of friends. Nell, the day Harry and Gabriel met, they were just little boys and yet according to my aunt they tried to tried to kill each other— and from then on they were inseparable."

She smiled at Harry, "So if you pick a fight with Marcus, we'll know that in your peculiar masculine way you're just trying to make friends with him, won't we, Nell, dear?"

Harry looked so appalled by this view of things that Nell was forced to fold her lips and look at the floor for fear of smiling. She didn't trust herself to meet Lady Gosforth's eye.

Lady Gosforth continued, "Now, run along Harry, now

that Nell's up, I want to talk to her about her trousseau. You do something about yours."

Harry gave his aunt a narrow look. He was well aware of his aunt's tactics, Nell decided.

Lady Gosforth added, "And mind you have something decent to wear instead of that old coat. Take Rafael with you. That boy is elegant to the fingertips; he can advise you. And hire a valet while you're about it; heaven knows you need one."

"Yes, General Gosforth," Harry said dryly. He turned to Nell. "She's a designing old harpy, so don't let her wear you out."

"What do you mean old?" his aunt said indignantly.

Harry winked at Nell. "You don't have to do this, you know," he said in a low voice.

She gave him a misty smile. "I know, but I want to." And to her surprise, she did.

The moment Harry left the room, Lady Gosforth embraced Nell. "I am so proud of you, my dear."

Nell was puzzled. "For what?"

She gestured Nell to sit with her on the sofa. "For the way you handled Harry just now. It was perfect. And I'm enormously grateful. He needs his family, but he'd deny it to his last breath. My brother's actions wrought emotional havoc among his sons, and now he's gone, it is my dearest wish to see the family whole and at peace again. Your wedding could be the beginning of that process."

"Then I'm glad of it."

The older woman hugged her again and said in a different voice, "And I'm proud of you for getting up and going on, though I know how hard it is for you, my dear."

Nell looked away as her eyes filled with tears again. "Do you?" she said dully.

"I bore four living babies in my youth, four beautiful

boys," Lady Gosforth said in a quiet voice. "Not one of them lived to his first birthday."

Oh God. Nell turned back, tears spilling down. "They all died?" She couldn't imagine it. "I'm so sorry."

Lady Gosforth nodded, her own eyes wet. "My tiny darlings. To this day I cannot hear a baby cry without thinking of them."

"How did you ever go on?"

The old lady gestured in a poignant echo of her usual airiness. "One keeps busy, as you and I will do in the next few days. Thank God for shopping, eh, my dear? And fittings and visits and anything else you can do. Keep busy. It's all one can do. One must not give in to despair." She rose from the sofa.

Suddenly Nell understood so much more about Lady Gosforth's relationship with Harry and his brothers. And even his friends. No wonder she wanted the four brothers to be reconciled and be a family again. Her family.

"Now, I know you're not in love with my nephew—"

"But I am," Nell interrupted.

"What?"

"I love him very much. With all my heart," Nell told her. "I have from the beginning, I think, only it all happened so fast I wasn't sure." She made a helpless gesture. "I don't see how anyone could help loving him."

Lady Gosforth sat down again with a thump. "Oh, my dear, you cannot know how glad that makes me. He doesn't know, of course."

"He must." She'd shown it to him as clearly as she could.

Lady Gosforth shook her head. "Harry doesn't believe he's worthy of love. Never has. And now he's failed you—"

Nell stared. "Failed me? How can he think that after all he's done?"

Lady Gosforth shrugged. "It's what he thinks. As to why? He's a man. They think differently to us."

Nell thought about it. She'd never told him she loved

him, but there were reasons for that. "He said right at the beginning that he doesn't want that sort of thing from me." And she'd used it as an excuse for not saying it ever since, she realized.

Lady Gosforth snorted. "A thickheaded Renfrew to the core. What he means is that he's not going to let anyone close enough in case they reject him or abandon him."

"I see," Nell said slowly. Yes, of course. She'd been so lost in her own misery and loneliness for such a long time, she couldn't see his. She hugged Lady Gosforth tightly.

"What was that for, my dear?"

"Harry is so lucky to have you, Lady Gosforth," Nell said. "They all are. *We* all are."

"Oh, pish, tush, my dear," she said, clearly delighted. With a resumption of her usual manner, she added crisply, "And it's high time you started calling me Aunt Maude. Now let's get on with this trousseau."

Nell was almost tempted to call her General Gosforth, as Harry had, but all she said was, "Yes, Aunt Maude."

*T*he next few days passed in a frenzy of shopping. Nell had very little time to herself, and though grief was always a part of her, like a huge, gaping hole in her center, she was grateful for the distraction.

Lady Gosforth was right. Keeping busy did help.

They visited so many shops her head was in a whirl; milliners, glove makers, haberdashers, jewelers, and perfumers. Nell became familiar with places such as Bond Street and the Pantheon Bazaar where she was almost tempted into buying a colorful parrot, as well as a lovely green shawl.

And all the time she learned things about herself she'd never known before.

Lady Gosforth had put it very bluntly: "Ladies like you and I, Nell, will never be pretty, but we can be elegant, which is a great deal more useful. Prettiness fades after a few years, but elegance only increases with age."

Nell was struck by her wisdom. It was true. Lady Gosforth, with her long face and Roman nose, wasn't what people called pretty, but she was immensely elegant and, despite her age, still very striking.

And the best thing about it was that unlike the features you were born with, elegance was something you could control. She resolved to become elegant.

At the mantua maker's Nell learned that simple lines and soft colors became her best. She was amazed at the difference to her looks some colors made. All these years she'd worn dark brown for practical reasons and it made her look sallow. But a light gold, or peach shade made her look quite different, and soft greens really suited her.

She learned to be bold. After the disaster of her coming out, where her own quiet tastes had been scorned and she'd been dressed in fussy, frilly dresses in white or bright "girlish" colors, she'd lost all confidence.

This time her clothes had also been chosen by someone other than Nell, but oh, what a difference. Cooper had done her proud, she realized, as had Bragge and Lady Gosforth. There was nothing she didn't like—not one thing! And some clothes she really loved.

As she donned dress after dress for fittings, she slowly realized that she'd been right, back then; that simple styles did suit her better, that the soft colors she preferred did suit her.

At the milliner's, trying on dozens of hats, Nell learned from Lady Gosforth, Bragge, Cooper, and the milliner that she had a good face for wearing hats. She'd never known that before.

They went to the tailor where two riding habits had been commissioned. The first had been made in camel-colored fabric with blue and gold trimmings. It was beautiful and fitted her perfectly. The second one Lady Gosforth had left for Nell to choose the fabric. She looked at all the selections, her eyes automatically going to the browns and dark-colored lengths. And then she saw a length of purple fabric and her breath caught.

Be bold, she thought. "I'll have it in that," she said.

There was a short silence. The tailor, Lady Gosforth, and Bragge exchanged glances.

Cooper, frowning thoughtfully, lifted the fabric and draped it around Nell. "What do you think?"

Her audience stared. "Excellent choice," Lady Gosforth said after a moment. "I never would have thought of that color for you, but it's perfect. You will set a fashion. Cream facings I think—"

"Palest primrose," Cooper interrupted, then paled at her own temerity.

Lady Gosforth narrowed her eyes. "Palest primrose, yes. The bold choice again. And a hat to match with a pale yellow feather." She stared at Cooper down her long nose and gave a nod. "You have a flair for this, girl. Well done. Between us we'll have my niece becoming a byword for style."

Cooper blushed and tried not to beam with pleasure.

Lady Gosforth's words warmed Nell, too. Not just the amazing idea of her becoming a byword for style, but the even more precious words, *my niece.*

It was another step forward, a small stake in the future.

One day, one step at a time she was managing. She was coping. By day—most of the time—she was all right; night was the problem.

They made love every night now. She craved the ecstasy, the intimacy, and the temporary oblivion of it. She usually fell asleep straightaway.

It was the bleak hours before dawn that haunted her, when she lay wakeful in Harry's arms while he slept.

She would think about the day to come or the one that had passed, about riding in the park with Harry and Rafe and Luke, or about the parrots and the monkeys in the Pantheon Bazaar, or how she'd learned to tilt a hat just so for the best effect, and then suddenly the hole inside her would wrench open again, as she remembered that she'd never get to do any of these things with her daughter, with Torie.

Then she would weep, silently in the dark, so as not to wake Harry.

One day, one night at a time.

Fifteen

*E*ach night as she made love with Harry, Nell thought about what Lady Gosforth—she still found it hard to think of her as Aunt Maude—had told her: *Harry doesn't believe he's worthy of love. Never has.*

If he didn't know by now that she loved him, there was only one thing for it: she would have to tell him. The trouble was she was such a coward about doing it.

What if Lady Gosforth was wrong? What if he'd meant exactly what he said when he'd told her he didn't want love from her?

What if she bared her heart to him and he was embarrassed by the whole thing? She would die of mortification.

Or what if he looked at her uncomfortably and then, as men did, changed the subject?

The worst and the most likely possibility was that he'd be kind about it. She couldn't bear it if he was kind and understanding, as if she'd made a complete fool of herself but he didn't mind. Because he was kind.

Each night she nerved herself to tell him and each night she took the cowardly way out, saying nothing.

Harry glanced over his letter to Ethan. He reminded Ethan to find out the name of that visitor who'd bothered the maids. He still hadn't heard back. He told Ethan that his wedding had been moved to Alverleigh and that Gabe and the princess, Tibby and the boys were there already and that if—when Ethan discovered the name, he should now send the letter to Alverleigh. He underlined it.

There was also a considerable list of things to be done. Ethan would probably want to shoot him when he read the list. He'd bargained for horses, not all this.

But a man only got married once.

He added a postscript reminding Ethan they would be off to Alverleigh in two more days.

He also wrote to the Barrows, inviting them to come to Alverleigh for his wedding. And if the earl didn't like that he could lump it. Mr. and Mrs. Barrow were more family to Harry than any coldblooded, blue-blooded earl.

In the morning they were leaving for Alverleigh.

Tonight had to be the night, Nell told herself. There wouldn't be another opportunity like this. Who knew how it might be at Alverleigh? She might hardly see him. She had to screw her courage to the sticking point and tell him. And show him as well. In more ways than one.

She'd never removed her nightgown before, and he'd never asked. He'd caressed her through it and slipped it up as far as her hips, but she'd been shy about being completely naked with him, and—again—had taken the coward's way out.

Tonight she stopped being a coward. Tonight she would bare herself to Harry Morant—body and soul.

After dinner she ordered a bath to be set in front of the fire in her bedchamber. While footmen lugged cans of hot water up the back stairs and Cooper swished a generous splash of oil of roses into the water, Nell placed candles around the room. She sent a footman to fetch a screen and placed it in front of the bath.

When the footmen had all left, Cooper helped Nell to disrobe.

"Thank you, Cooper," she said as she stepped into the bath. "Please extinguish the lamps before you leave, and then tell Mr. Harry I would like to speak to him."

Cooper's eyes widened but she'd been very well trained and made no outward sign. She knew, of course, that Harry slept with Nell each night—Nell imagined the whole household did, but everyone pretended not to notice. There was, after all, to be a wedding in less than a week.

Nell sank into the hot water and waited.

Harry knocked on Nell's bedchamber door and, hearing her respond, went in. There was no sign of Nell. He frowned at the dim room, lit by just perhaps a dozen candles. Were her lamps not working? Was that the problem? Then why send for him and not a footman?

Then he heard a splash of water and noticed the screen. His mouth dried. That fantasy he'd had of attending her in her bath leapt back as if it had never faded. He forced it again from his mind. She was a very modest woman. Such an idea would no doubt shock her.

"Nell? Did you want something?" What was that smell? Roses? In December?

"Yes." More swishing of water. "Could you come here a moment, please?"

Harry's heart started thudding. He stepped around the screen and stopped still. Every coherent thought drained from his mind. He could only stare. She was so damned beautiful.

In a semicircle of candlelight she sat in her bath, blushing, naked, all peach and gold and soft, wet skin. Her hair was knotted high, damp tendrils clinging to her temples and neck. Full, creamy breasts were not quite submerged, rosy dark nipples soft in the warm water. Under his gaze they stiffened to firm, ripe berries.

Her legs were long, her knees floating islands in the fragrant bathwater. Through the rippling water he could see the dark gold vee where her thighs met at the base of her belly.

With some difficulty he managed to say, "What did you want?" It came out in a croak. All he could think of was what he wanted.

She pulled a sponge from the water and slowly soaped it. He watched mesmerized as her breasts swayed with each movement. She held the sponge out to him and he put a hand out blindly, but at the last moment she pulled it back.

"Perhaps you should take off your coat," she suggested.

He dragged it off quickly and tossed it on a nearby chair.

She gave him a speculative look. "And perhaps your shirt, too. You wouldn't want to get it all wet, would you?" Her eyes gleamed.

And his brains started working again. His modest little Nell was going all out to seduce him, like a siren of old. Every male drop of blood in him seized the challenge: Who would seduce whom?

He gave her a slow smile. "A wet shirt? Perish the thought." He unknotted his neck cloth, tossed it on top of his coat, and pulled his shirt off over his head.

The sherry-colored eyes surveyed him with deep feminine approval.

"Now, give me that sponge." Taking it, he stepped behind her. Lord, she was even beautiful from the back. He squatted down and started with her back, rubbing it with firm, circular movements, then up and down the length of her spine.

"Soap." She passed it back to him and he soaped up his hands and massaged her neck and shoulders until she was almost purring and arching against him like a cat.

"Lift up your arms," he murmured, his mouth just inches from her ear, and when she did, he slid his hands slowly around her ribs and soaped her stomach. His chest pressed against her back. Her breath hitched each time his forearms and the sides of his hands brushed against her breasts but he made no move to touch them. At first.

He waited until she was panting and writhing subtly against him, and when he finally took the hard, thrusting nipples between his fingertips, she moaned and jerked in an instant climax.

She tried to get out then, but he pressed her back into the water.

"Not yet."

He moved around to the front of the bath, facing her.

"Give me your foot," he said.

"But I want to—"

"Foot." He held out his hand.

A touch sulkily she stuck her foot out of the water, splashing him deliberately. "Sorry," she said unrepentantly as she surveyed the damp patch at his crotch. She grinned and splashed him again. "Oops."

Her smile vanished when he lifted her foot to his mouth. "Harry, what on earth are—ohhh," she gasped as he sucked on her toes. They curled against his tongue and he sucked harder, running his tongue along the seam between each toe. She tasted of roses.

He nibbled and sucked and at the same time began to soap her legs, running his hands down between her thighs. They quivered and fell apart and his fingers sank into her soft cleft, caressing her deeply and again, she climaxed in moments.

He lifted her out of the bath, wrapped a towel around her, and carried her to the bed, where he dried her carefully and then proceeded to make love to her again. She was more than ready for him and as the climax built and the ecstasy roared through him, she came with him as they crested, shattered, and plunged into oblivion.

He wasn't sure how much later it was when he became aware of her stirring sleepily against him. "It wasn't supposed to be that way," she muttered. "I was going to seduce you."

"But you did seduce me," he said.

"No, you took over." She sighed against his chest. "But I love you anyway."

Harry froze. "What did you say?" he said after a minute.

But she was asleep. He tried to tell himself he'd imagined it or misheard it. But he'd heard it clear as day.

She didn't mean it the way he thought she did, though, he was sure. It was the sort of thing people sometimes said.

It was just that nobody had ever said it to him before.

Could she really mean it, or was it simply gratitude? He didn't want gratitude.

He didn't deserve gratitude—he hadn't managed to save her baby. He hadn't even avenged the great wrong done her.

He had no right to love.

Yet.

*H*e awoke to busy fingers and the sensation of a soft, luscious body smelling of roses and sweet, aroused woman . . . She climbed on top of him and his eyes flew open. And fastened on creamy, silken breasts.

"Are you awake, Harry Morant?" She said to him in an oddly determined voice.

He wrenched his eyes off her breasts and looked into the sweet face. "I'm awake."

She lifted herself over him and slowly took him into her

body. "Are you listening to me, Harry Morant?" She said undulating her body in a way that drove him wild.

He groaned at the sensation. She tweaked his nipples and his eyes flew open again.

"I said, are you listening?"

"I'm listening," he managed. "Though it would be a damned sight easier to concentrate if you stopped doing th—aahhh."

"Stop talking and listen. I love you, Harry Morant."

His eyes flew to hers.

"I love you," she said again, deliberately. Her body began to move in a slow rhythm and each time she moved, she said it again: "I love you, I love you, I love you."

Still moving, she bent and planted kisses across his chest, murmuring, "I love you," between each one.

His chest felt like it had a burning rock lodged in it. He couldn't say a word.

"I love you." She wrapped her arms around him, and suddenly heaved to the side. They rolled, still joined, and he was on top. "I love you," she repeated, and his body started to pump, harder and harder, and with each thrust she said it again, her clear sherry eyes never wavering from his. "I love you, Harry. I love you."

The dark, consuming wave of passion took him higher and higher, denial pounding furiously through him, and still he heard it. "I love you."

And as he roared and the world splintered into rapture, he heard them again, the words he could not get enough of, but did not deserve: "I love you, Harry Morant."

*H*arry had made an appointment to ride in the park with Rafe and Luke before breakfast. He wished he hadn't now. His heart was so full. *I love you, Harry Morant.* What did a man say to that? He'd done nothing to deserve it. She probably wanted the words back, but he could not say them.

Yet.

He slid out of bed reluctantly and drew the covers over her small, silken body. He padded from the room and changed quickly into his riding clothes.

Rafe and Luke were waiting in the hall. "Sorry I'm late," Harry said, snatching his hat and coat.

Rafe sniffed and frowned. "Is that roses I smell? In December?"

Luke sniffed and shook his head. "Can't smell anything."

Rafe leaned toward Harry, sniffed again, and arched his brow. "Changed your cologne, dear boy?"

"Nope." Harry shrugged into his coat, still trying to deal with the jumble of confused emotions. One thought stood above them all. Nell *loved* him.

He felt so unworthy of her gift. But he would earn the right to it, he swore. Somehow.

Rafe gave him a thoughtful look. "I see."

"What time are you leaving for Alverleigh?" Luke asked.

"The general has arranged the cavalcade to leave at ten," Harry said. "Are you sure I can't persuade you two to come with us?"

"Into a den of Renfrews with brotherly love so thick on the ground? Not likely," Luke told him frankly.

"Yes," drawled Rafe. "Spare me the delights of your family reunion, dear boy. I've been to war, remember, and though it had its moments, I've had enough of it for the present."

"You'll come to the wedding," Harry reminded them.

"Of course. Wouldn't miss it for the world," Rafe said.

"Oh, you're still here," said a voice from the stairs. "I'm so glad I didn't miss you."

Harry turned as Nell came skipping down the stairs. A lump formed in his throat. She was so beautiful. So precious. He strode toward her and managed not to snatch her up and twirl her around. He took her hand and, looking deeply into her glorious eyes, kissed the hollow of her palm.

Her clear amber eyes glowed with love. "I love you, Harry Morant," she whispered.

"You look beautiful," he said, his voice hoarse with emotion.

"Yes, my new habit. Isn't it smart?" She twirled. "I have another one being made—wait till you see that."

"I liked what you wore last night better."

She blushed rosily and turned to greet his friends.

"Now I can smell roses," Luke said.

"My bath oil," she confessed. "Isn't it delicious?"

Rafe gave Harry a knowing look. "Delicious."

Harry tried not to smile.

Later in the park, he watched Nell put her horse through its paces. "She's a magnificent horsewoman, don't you think?" he said to Rafe.

"Magnificent," Rafe agreed, adding, "You're a lucky man, Harry Morant. You and Gabe, both."

Harry gave him a quizzical look.

"You've both found the most extraordinary women. I can see it in your eyes—first Gabe and now you. You both have the look of men who love and are loved."

Harry was taken aback by the comment. Rafe was always the cool one; nothing affected him. He never talked about such things as feelings, let alone love.

Neither did Harry. Yet. His eyes returned to where Nell was edging from a decorous canter to a wholly improper gallop. "You'll find out one day," was all he could say.

Rafe shook his head. "Won't happen. My fate is about to be sealed. My brother's picked out the perfect brood mare for me, some ghastly heiress with excellent antecedents."

Harry gave him a sympathetic look. Rafe's elder brother, Lord Axebridge, and his wife were childless, so it was now Rafe's duty to marry and provide an heir. Lord Axebridge

had thrown himself into the task of finding the heir's
mother with enthusiasm, bringing his fascination for breeding livestock together with his passion for increasing the
family coffers.

"She can't be that bad, surely?"

"Oh, she looks all right, I grant you," Rafe said gloomily.
"But she laughs like a braying donkey."

"Can't you get out of it?"

Rafe shook his head. "I've had a year to come up with
someone as suitable and failed. There's a house party at
Axebridge in the new year. Unless something happens to
prevent it—lightning striking me perhaps—the betrothal
will be announced at its conclusion. I tell you, Harry, there
are times when I want to chuck my duty to the family and
flee to the ends of the earth."

"W ho will I meet at Alverleigh?" Nell asked Harry.
They were traveling in another yellow bounder and
Nell was realizing how hard it was to keep busy while sitting in a carriage for hour after hour. At every church they
passed, her thoughts turned to Torie . . .

"As far as I'm concerned, the most important person is
my brother Gabe. He's the best of good fellows. You'll like
Callie, his wife, too—Princess Caroline of Zindaria," he
added as an afterthought.

"I've never met a princess."

Harry squeezed her hand. "She'll tell you to call her Callie, like the rest of us do. Then there's the boys, Nicky—
Prince Nikolai—and Jim, an orphaned fisher boy they took
in as a companion for Nicky. And Tibby, Miss Tibthorpe
who used to be Callie's governess. You remember her—
she's the one I suspected Ethan was sweet on."

"Oh yes. Who else?"

"My half brother Nash, he's the diplomat. You'll probably

like him. He has a way of charming people," Harry said darkly, in a voice that implied "charming people" was akin to robbing them blind.

Nell repressed a smile. It was clear to her that Harry actually liked Nash, but wished he didn't. "And I know about Marcus, the earl," she said. "Why do you dislike him so much?"

"Because he's one of those cold, superior types who hold the rest of the world in contempt," he said without hesitation. "He made life a misery for Gabe and me during the short time we were at the same school. He's a ruthless bastard." He gave a mirthless laugh. "He and his friends hounded us out of that school." .

"I thought you were expelled for fighting."

His head snapped around. "How did you know that?"

"Your aunt told me."

He grunted. "It's true enough. It was Marcus we fought. Him and Nash and the rest of their bullyboy snob friends. You'll see what he's like when you meet him. You could pick him out of a crowd—he's got the coldest eyes in the world."

"Then why would he offer to host our wedding?"

Gabe snorted. "My bet is that he was press-ganged into it by our mutual aunt. Once that woman gets an idea in her head she's like a cavalry charge, sweeping all before her."

"Yes," Nell said, smiling. "And you're all too fond of her to object."

He snorted, but he didn't deny it.

She watched the passing scenery and thought about what Harry had told her. It seemed Nash had been more or less forgiven for their schoolboy enmity, but Marcus hadn't. Why?

And if Harry was still so resentful of the earl, then why had Gabe agreed to stay at Alverleigh? The two brothers were very close. She knew enough to know that if Gabe wasn't already at Alverleigh, wild horses wouldn't have dragged Harry there.

Finally they passed through the ornate wrought iron gates and headed up the long, curving drive. Alverleigh House took her breath away. It was huge, four stories high, with a central section and two sweeping wings. Twelve Palladian columns supported the curved front entrance, which was reached by a very grand set of wide marble steps. The raked gravel driveway curved around a magnificent formal garden in the center. In the sweeping lawn to the left of the building stood a large clipped maze. On the right stretched a magnificent informal garden in the style of Capability Brown. Its focal point was a wide lake with an island featuring a picturesque ruin of a Greek temple.

Nell's nervousness grew in the face of all this grandeur. "You didn't tell me it was this big," she said, straightening her clothes and hair.

"I didn't know. I've never been here before," he said, surprising her. "It's Gabe's first visit, too—and he's a legitimate son."

No wonder he was bitter. But there was no time to discuss anything further, for the horses were slowing and servants came running to assist them to alight and take their baggage.

A tall gentleman came hurtling down the steps, three at a time. There was no need for Nell to ask who he was; he was the spitting image of Harry, except his hair was darker.

The two men embraced, thumping and hugging each other joyfully in a violent masculine fashion.

"Uncle Harry," a high little voice shrieked and Nell turned to see two small boys hurtling at breakneck speed down the steps, the smaller of the two making no concession to an ungainly limp that was an uncanny echo of Harry's.

"Nicky!" Harry picked the limping boy up and whirled him around, laughing. "And Jim. How you've both grown." He grabbed the other little boy and slung a boy over each shoulder where they dangled, upside down, shouting in mock indignation and giggling.

He would make a wonderful father, she thought wistfully. She could just imagine him with a little girl . . .

Nell saw she was being observed by an upside-down prince and forced herself to smile. "I know exactly how that feels," she told him.

Laughing, Harry put the boys down and introduced her.

"So, my new sister, delighted to meet you," Gabriel Renfrew said with a warm smile. He kissed her on the cheek. He had very blue eyes, otherwise the resemblance was amazing.

To Nell's enchantment, both little boys received their introduction with beautiful formality, clicking their heels in unison and bowing stiffly in the Prussian manner. Then they rushed off to look at Sabre, who'd been brought by a groom.

"Young savages," Gabriel Renfrew laughed, and linked his arm with Nell's. "Come and meet Callie, she's been dying to meet you."

"But the boys need to watch out for Sabre—" Nell began.

"They're Zindarian boys—or Jim's as good as," Gabe told her. "They're used to the ways of Zindarian horses. Sabre is a pussycat compared to some in the royal stables. Ah, here's my Callie now." His voice warmed.

At the top of the steps stood a woman with dark curly hair and a sweet expression. The princess. She was small and round. Very round.

Nell faltered, staring up at her. The princess smiled down at Nell. Harry hurried up the steps ahead of Nell to greet the princess with a hug and a kiss.

Nell didn't move. There was a reason why the princess was so round. She was pregnant. Ripely, gloriously pregnant.

"Are you all right?" Harry's brother said beside her.

"Yes, just recovering from the jolting of the carriage," Nell said brightly, and with a deep breath she climbed the steps to meet her pregnant future sister-in-law. One step at a time.

"I'm so happy to meet you," the princess said, giving Nell a warm hug. "Welcome to the family. I've always wanted a sister."

It was such a warmhearted and generous greeting that Nell forgot her nerves. She smiled. "Me, too."

The princess turned, saying, "Where is Tibby? I'd thought she'd followed me out."

"The post arrived fifteen minutes ago," an elegant, loose-limbed man said from behind her. "There was a letter for her. Marcus gave it to her in the hall just now."

Since he was not Marcus, he must be Nash, Nell thought. He was clearly a Renfrew.

Nash shook Harry's hand warmly and kissed Nell's hand in a gallant manner. "Welcome to the family, Lady Helen," he said with a dazzling smile. "I hear you're an outstanding horsewoman. I hope you'll come out riding with me one morning."

"That would be lovely, thank you," Nell told him. Charm was right.

As they turned to go in, a tall, serious-looking man with a grave, unsmiling face came out of the house. The earl.

He bowed formally to Harry and bowed over Nell's hand in the correct manner. "Welcome to Alverleigh, Lady Helen, Harry," he said. "My butler will escort you to your rooms."

Nell met his gaze and caught her breath. There was a clear family resemblance between all the brothers, but where Gabriel and Nash both had very blue eyes, the earl's eyes were gray: cold, smoky gray. He had Harry's eyes. It was uncanny.

The earl continued. "Tea will be served in the green sitting room in half an hour. Someone will come to show you the way." He gave her a clipped nod, then turned away.

The coldest eyes in the world, Harry had called them. She'd thought the same about Harry when she first looked into his eyes. And then he'd given her his hat.

Nell, still trying to take everything in, was grateful when Harry took her arm and steered her in the wake of the butler.

She'd expected to be put in different wings for the sake of propriety, but the butler conducted her and Harry along the same corridor, which made her hopeful. The size of the place was a little intimidating. One could easily get lost.

The butler opened a door. "Your bedchamber, Lady Helen."

"What a lovely room," Nell exclaimed. "And look at the view."

"Lady Gosforth requested this room especially for you m'lady," the butler told them. "And Mr. Morant, if you would step this way, please?" Harry disappeared.

Nell explored her room. It was even more luxurious than Lady Gosforth's London town house. There was a door set into the side in the wall, and out of curiosity, she opened it.

It led to another bedchamber—Harry's. He sat on the bed reading a letter.

"Oh, you're in here," she said.

He jumped about a foot and thrust the letter in his pocket.

"What's that?" Nell asked him.

"Nothing. Just a letter from Ethan. About nothing. Horses, bills, the usual thing. Nice rooms, aren't they? Aunt Maude requested this one especially for me, the butler said. Adjoining rooms. I told you she knew."

Nell had to agree. Up to that point Nell had been certain that Lady Gosforth had no idea that she and Harry had anticipated their wedding vows.

But she didn't care about that in the least at present. Something had changed. There was an air of tension about him, different from the way he'd been when they first arrived.

"Are you sure that's all the letter was about?"

"Yes." There was a grim look in his face as he told her, "It just confirmed something I thought all along."

"What?"

He shook his head. "It's to do with business. Nothing to do with you."

Nell frowned. "Even if it's horrid news, I'd rather know."

"It's not horrid news. I'm very pleased to get it." He kissed her, a brief decisive kiss. "But it's men's business."

She stamped her foot. "No, I hate this. I want to know." He wasn't telling her the truth. Years of experience with her father loomed.

He gave her a stern look. "Don't argue with me about this, Nell. This is men's business. Now, wash your face and hands and we'll go downstairs."

"And this is my dear friend Miss Tibthorpe," said Princess Caroline, who was presiding over the tea tray. "Tibby, this is Harry's bride-to-be, Lady Helen Freymore."

The woman called Tibby didn't move. A small, thin, sharp-featured woman in her middle thirties, she stood with her hand pressed to her bosom, staring out of the window.

"Tibby?" the princess said.

Tibby started and looked around. "Oh, please forgive me," she said hurriedly. "I was miles away. Lady Helen, how do you do?"

"Is anything the matter, Tibby? Not bad news, is it?"

Tibby looked at her blankly. "No." She flushed. "I mean, I don't know. I haven't read it yet. Please excuse me, I need to . . ." And she ran out of the room.

"Do forgive her," the princess said. "She does this every now and then when a letter from a certain person arrives. She's always a little agitated afterward."

Nell knew how she felt. What had Ethan said in the letter

that had caused that grim look in Harry's eyes? It was very unsettling. If she didn't know better, she'd think . . .

The princess picked up the teapot. "But look at me, rattling on about Tibby when you've only just met her. Let us pour the tea. Lady Gosforth has retired to her bedchamber to lie down until dinner and the men and boys have gone off to the odious stables to look at some horrid horse, so we won't wait for them. Don't you just loathe horses?"

"No," Nell said. "I adore them. I'm planning to breed them."

The princess laughed. "Then you're marrying into the right family. Every single member of it is horse obsessed. Except me. Now, do you take milk or lemon? Neither? Good." She passed Nell a cup of tea. "And now you shall tell me how you met Harry."

Nell smiled and took a sip of tea. "I'm not sure where to start, Princess Carolin—"

The princess held up her hand. "Please, you must call me Callie, as the others do. We are going to become sisters. I've never had a sister and I always longed for one."

"I'm the same," Nell said.

Callie lifted her cup to drink and suddenly gasped. A faraway look came into her eyes.

After a moment, she blushed and looked shyly at Nell. "My baby moved. I'm sorry, I know it is indelicate of me to mention such a thing, especially in front of an unmarried girl, but this baby is so precious to me."

Nell shook her head, her eyes prickling with tears. "I don't think it's indelicate at all, and you need not mind me."

Callie laid her hand on her swollen belly. "For nine years after Nicky's birth I thought I was barren and, oh—" She broke off again.

Nell smiled at the look of rapture in the princess's lovely green eyes and remembered how she'd first felt the miracle of Torie moving inside her. She said softly, "It's the most wonderful feeling in the world, isn't it? Feeling that tiny flutter beneath your heart and knowing that there's a tiny babe growing inside you. And feeling such intense love . . ."

She stopped suddenly, aware she'd said too much.

The princess stared at her wide-eyed.

Nell bit her lip. She hadn't meant to tell anyone, but it had just slipped out. And now it had, she didn't regret it. It it was right for Harry's family to know. They'd welcomed her as one of them. Her secret would come out eventually— look at how easily it had slipped out with the princess. And Aunt Maude. And if they found out later rather than sooner, well, that would feel like a betrayal of their trust. She wanted their acceptance, but not under false pretenses. She wanted them to know the truth. She took a deep breath and began.

By the time the men arrived from the stables the tea was cold and Nell had told the whole story to Callie. The only part she left out was Sir Irwin. She was determined to bury that part of her life completely.

In the telling, both women had wept and embraced and Nell had found a friend. A sister.

Harry took one look at the swollen eyes of the two women and guessed what they'd been talking about. He sent the boys to the kitchen and was about to hustle his brothers away when Nell interrupted him. "No, please, everyone, come in. There is something I have to tell you all. It has been weighing on my conscience—"

"You don't have to explain anything to them," Harry snapped.

"No, Harry. If I am to become part of your family, they should know the truth. I would feel like an impostor other-wise."

"What rot. You are to be my wife. No impostor about it."

"He's right." Gabriel crossed the room and put his arm

around his wife. "You don't have to tell us a single thing. You are to be Harry's wife, and that's enough for any of us."

"I agree." Callie took Nell's hand and squeezed it in a silent show of support.

Neither Nash nor the earl said anything.

Nell looked at Harry. "If you ask me to, I will say nothing."

He gave her a goaded look. "It's not me I'm worried about, you foolish woman. Tell them whatever you like, it makes no difference to me." He came and stood beside her, arms folded, like a protector.

"Then I want to explain," she said. "I would rather my story didn't leave this room, but—"

"Rest assured, it won't." Nash crossed the room and sat down. The earl remained standing stiffly beside the doorway.

Quickly and simply Nell told her story. In a calm voice born of emotional exhaustion, she told them everything, from discovering she was pregnant to seeing the basket of vegetables on the church steps.

She didn't tell them how she had come to be pregnant in the first place. That was nobody's business but hers.

"And so," she finished, "now you know."

Callie jumped up and hugged her wordlessly. None of the men moved. They were all looking at the earl.

There was a long silence. Then the earl cleared his throat. "I have a question."

Everyone stiffened. Nell tensed as beside her Harry clenched his fists.

Nell straightened, as if about to face sentence. "Yes?"

"Your father is dead."

Nell blinked. "Yes."

"And you have no male relatives in this country?"

"That is correct," she said with a quick glance at Harry. He shook his head, as mystified as any of them as to what the earl was getting at.

The earl cleared his throat again and looked at her with Harry's eyes. "Then may I offer my services to give the bride away?"

"*I* still don't trust him," Harry growled in bed that night. "One gallant gesture doesn't wipe out the things he's done in the past."

"But didn't Nash do them, too? You seem to have forgiven him."

"Yes, but he was younger than Marcus. Marcus was always the leader. And besides, Nash apologized last year. And he helped Gabe and Callie a great deal."

"Maybe Marcus will apologize, too."

He snorted. "Pigs might fly. He's too stiff-necked to apologize about anything. And some things can't be cured with words."

He'd been very badly hurt, she saw. "What did he do to you?" she asked softly.

He gave her a flat look. "You're going to keep on about this, aren't you?"

"It's just that I don't understand. I'll always take your side anyway, you know that. But I would like to understand."

He sighed. "Very well. But get comfortable, it's a long story and not very interesting, so you'll probably fall asleep."

She snuggled in. And he told her the story of his first love, Anthea, who'd betrayed him in the worst way and watched secretly as he was thrashed to within an inch of his life.

Nell was horrified and angry and hugged him convulsively as if somehow she could comfort his youthful self.

And somehow he did feel comforted.

"And then they took me, half naked and bleeding and worse, and dumped me at the foot of the steps of my father's London house—Alverleigh House, in the heart of

Mayfair. And of course my father, the Earl of Alverleigh, had to be in," he said bitterly. "My first meeting with my real father and I was half naked and bleeding and unable to stand."

"Why did they take you there, if you didn't know him?"

He shrugged. "No doubt Lord Quenborough took the view that my father should take responsibility for his bastard."

"And did he?"

"He took one look at me and said to the butler, 'Glover, there is a mess on the front step. Have it removed.' I'll never forget those words."

Nell gasped. "So heartless."

"And then my brother Marcus came down the steps and stared at me, those pitiless eyes of his taking in every detail. He didn't say a word to me. Just stared and then followed his father back inside. Like father, like son."

"I understand now," she said, her arms around him. "It would be very hard to forgive such cruelty. And I'm sorry for bringing it all up, stirring up old hurts and opening old wounds."

Harry kissed her, feeling comforted. He'd never told anyone that tale, only Gabe. And then not in such detail.

He didn't feel stirred up, though, or as if old wounds had reopened. Instead he felt . . . healed.

Telling her, lying entwined with her like this, talking in quiet voices into the night, made him realize how young he'd been. It wasn't love he'd felt for Anthea, he suddenly realized. It was infatuation, calf-love, his first serious boyhood crush.

It wasn't love at all.

It was nothing like love.

"Oh Harry," Nell whispered. "I love you so much . . ."

She looked at him with eyes full of love and expectation.

Harry stared down at her. He couldn't speak the words she wanted to hear. They were stuck in his throat. They would remain there, he knew, until he did something, until he was able to give her more than words.

They made love again, and it was slow and tender and bittersweet. The unspoken words hung silent and heavy in the room.

Sixteen

C ooper put the last touches to Nell's coiffure. She'd
tried something different again, plaiting in sections of
hair in a continuous circle around the crown of Nell's head,
like a coronet.

Nell regarded her reflection with amazement. Who was
that elegant young woman? Certainly not Nell, the hoyden
who'd grown up in the stables with her skirts hitched up to
stop them dragging in the mud and her hair falling down
around her ears.

Lady Helen, perhaps? No, she'd never felt like a Lady
Helen. Lady Nell now . . .

"You're glowing, m'lady," Cooper told her. "You look
wonderful."

"Thank you, Cooper, you've worked miracles."

"I can only do so much, m'lady. 'Tis love does the rest,
I reckon."

Nell blushed. He'd made love to her last night with a
tender sweetness that had melted her completely.

And very early this morning they'd made love again

with a fierce passion that had burned her last inhibitions up in glorious conflagration. She was still a little stiff from it. She didn't mind at all.

He still hadn't told her he loved her. Physically, she felt well loved, but she craved to hear the words from him. More and more she recalled his words back when he had first proposed. *It's not love's young dream I'm offering you.*

It wasn't love's young dream she wanted. Just love. Harry's love.

There was a knock on the door.

"Come in," she called.

A footman entered and bowed. "I've been sent to show you to the breakfast parlor, m'lady."

"Oh, thank you. Can you just call Mr. Morant, please?"

The footman frowned. "But he's already left, m'lady."

"For breakfast?" She frowned. It seemed unlike him.

"No, m'lady, he had his breakfast an hour ago. He left for London straight afterward."

"What?" Her jaw dropped.

"Yes, m'lady."

Why go to London without even telling her? She could only think of one reason—that letter. Nell flung open the connecting door and hurried through. She searched but there was no sign of the letter. Nor was there a note from Harry explaining why he'd gone off without telling her.

An ominous feeling grew inside her.

She turned to the footman. "Take me to Mr. Gabriel Renfrew immediately."

"He's in the—"

"Please, just take me. And hurry." She didn't know the layout of the big house yet.

They passed along the corridor, down the stairs, through several twists and turns until finally the man knocked, then threw open a door. "The breakfast parlor, m'lady."

Gabriel was about to sit down at the table, a plate of roast beef in his hand. His brothers, Nash and Marcus, had already started. At her entrance, they rose to their feet, as usual. She tried to catch her breath.

"Lady Helen, what is it?" the earl asked.

Nell looked at him, not quite sure how to begin. The preposterous idea in her head just kept growing.

"Harry has gone to London," she said.

The earl nodded. "Yes, on business," he said.

She looked at Gabriel. "I don't think so. I think—I think he might have gone to kill a man," Nell said. It sounded so dramatic when she said it aloud. But every instinct she had told her he'd gone after Sir Irwin.

"Why on earth would you think such a thing?" Gabriel asked her. "Here come and sit down. Have a cup of tea."

She allowed him to seat her and accepted the tea, but she didn't drink it. "He's been after this man for some time. He—he's very angry with him."

"Yes, but you don't go around killing people because you're angry with them."

"No, but I think he might challenge this man to a duel."

There was a short silence. "A duel?" Gabriel's gaze sharpened. "For what reason?"

Nell swallowed. "Me." She forced herself to meet their eyes. "It's the man who—who—r-rap—"

"We understand," Nash said, cutting her off compassionately.

"But if you're right," Gabriel said, "why didn't he challenge this man before. Why wait till now?"

"He didn't know the man's name until now. I refused to tell him. But I believe the information was in the letter he got yesterday. It would explain his tension afterward."

The men exchanged glances. "You might be right," Gabe said. "I've never known him to challenge anyone to a duel, but over this, any man would."

"I don't want him to fight Sir Irwin," Nell said. "Please, you must go after him and stop him."

"We will," Gabriel said. "But if it did come to a duel,

he's a very fine shot and a master with a sword. I'd back Harry against almost anyone in the country."

"There are laws against dueling," the earl said. "I'm a magistrate."

"Exactly!" She wrung her hands in distress. "What happens if Harry kills Sir Irwin? I don't want him to be hanged or transported or to have to flee the country as a fugitive from justice." She loved him. She wanted to marry him and live at Firmin Court and breed horses and have babies with him.

"We'll take care of him, don't worry," Gabriel assured her. "What's this villain's name?"

"Sir Irwin Clendinning."

"And where does he live?"

She looked at him blankly. "Oh no!" she wailed. "I don't know where he lives."

There was a short silence while they mulled over the problem.

"*Sir* Irwin?" Nash said suddenly. "He's a baronet."

She shook her head. "Yes, or a knight, what does it matter?"

"Debrett's," Nash said. "He'll be listed." They raced to the library.

The book lay open on a table. "Here it is," the earl said. "Open at his entry. Harry must have looked him up, too." He jotted down the address. "Right, let's go."

"You?" Gabriel said in surprise.

The earl gave him a cold look. "Yes. Why not?"

"Oh please, just hurry," Nell beseeched them, and they forgot their differences and went.

Sir Irwin Clendinning's house lay on the outskirts of London on the busy Great North Road. Wagons, coaches, and vehicles of all sorts rumbled nonstop past the house. Harry wondered how anyone could live in such a place. The din was frightful. But this was the address he'd been given.

Harry rode in through the open gate. A chaise waited in the short driveway at the front of a slightly run-down house. A large, nattily dressed, sandy-haired man was about to climb into it: Sir Irwin?

He edged Sabre in, ignoring the man's oath of annoyance as he pushed the big horse between man and coach.

"What the devil do you think you're doing, sir?" Unlike his house, the man was very carefully maintained. The big bastard was something of a dandy. Harry imagined the man holding down Nell's small body and cold rage roiled in him. But he couldn't allow it to boil over. Not yet.

"Sir Irwin Clendinning?" One needed to check that the swine was indeed the swine.

"Indeed, and the owner of this property. Who the hell are you?"

Harry swung down off Sabre. "Harry Morant."

Sir Irwin took in Harry's dusty clothes and sniffed his disdain. "I don't believe I've had the pleasure," he said dismissively and made to step around Harry. "Kindly get that creature off my property."

"Oh, it won't be a pleasure," Harry said with silky menace.

"What the devil—"

But that was all he had time for before Harry grabbed him by his very elegant coat. Practically lifting him from his feet.

"Get off me, you—!"

For answer Harry swung him around and smashed him against the door of the carriage. The coachman reacted, struggling to pull out an ancient rifle. Reluctantly Harry let go of Sir Irwin and dragged the man down. He went sprawling. A boot mid-rifle and the weapon was rendered useless.

"This is a private matter between me and your master,"

Harry growled to the coachman. "Get out and stay out if you value your life."

The horses plunged restlessly as the coachman hauled himself to his feet, took one fearful look at Harry's face, and disappeared fast.

Sir Irwin had the same idea. With savage invective he launched himself at Harry, trying to shove him aside and go the same way as his coachman.

For answer Harry grabbed him by the neck and jammed him hard against the carriage. Sir Irwin struggled, kicking and shoving, but he was hanging like a man in manacles. They were much of a size, but Sir Irwin was no match for a man who'd spent years at war.

"Help! Murder! Mohocks!" Sir Irwin yelled, but his voice was drowned by the sound of the traffic on the Great North Road.

"I don't think murder is on the agenda today. Just a gelding," Harry said pleasantly and thumped him against the coach again.

Sir Irwin turned a ghastly color. "G-geld—what do you mean?" His eyes flickered past Harry's shoulder. "Get him!" he yelled.

Two of the servants had come creeping up behind Harry. He dropped Sir Irwin, swinging a punch as he turned. He smashed his fist into the first man's jaw and almost in the same movement sank another punch into the second one's solar plexus.

The first man staggered back, the other sank to his knees on the driveway, gasping for breath. Harry picked him up by the scruff of the neck and threw him on the lawn. Several other servants had gathered in the open doorway. He raised his fists invitingly. "Anyone else for a taste of home brewed?"

They backed away as one. Obviously there were things that needed doing inside. Urgently. Domestic stuff.

The door slammed closed. Sir Irwin was alone.

A faint flash of light gave Harry warning. He swiveled, just in time to catch Sir Irwin's arm as it started its murderous descent. A knife, thin and deadly . . .

Harry grabbed the man's arm and wrested the knife from him. Sir Irwin was fighting harder now, terror lending him strength, but years of campaigning had Harry's muscles honed and ready. Sir Irwin's life of indolence meant he could never come close to winning.

"Knife in the back, eh?" Harry growled, twisting his arm and thrusting him backward with revulsion. "Swine. But I might find a use for it later." He flung the knife down behind him so it stabbed deep into the lawn.

"Rush him, you cowards, he's not armed," Sir Irwin yelled toward the closed door of the house. The door didn't open. Only curtains twitching in the window embrasures said they were still observed.

Enough. Harry grabbed him by his lapels, feeling revulsion gut deep. "Speaking of cowards," he growled. "Where were we? Oh yes, let's talk about women . . ."

Sir Irwin's eye narrowed. "Women? If some little whore has come running to you with her tales, she's lying," he blustered. "Happens all the time, some slut trying to trap me into marriage. I'm a man of substance."

"I'm talking about a lady."

Sir Irwin looked taken aback for a moment, then rallied. He tried to push Harry back. "Then you have the wrong man. I use sluts, the ones who are asking for it."

"Funny, I heard some of them fight."

Sir Irwin's lip curled. "Some women like it rough. They just don't like to admit it. Makes them embarrassed," he said with a sneer.

His teeth were very even. Like rats' teeth, Harry thought. The man made him want to vomit.

"Mutual pleasure. Can't blame a man for that."

"And do you like it rough, too?" Harry asked silkily.

"Sometimes," he said warily. His knee jerked upward as he tried to knee Harry in the balls.

Harry blocked the action with his hip. "You like it when they fight, don't you?"

For answer, Sir Irwin spat at him. As Harry's head jerked back, Sir Irwin tried to gouge Harry's eyes.

Knocking the clawing fingers aside, Harry slammed a fist into Sir Irwin's mouth. "So you do enjoy a fight," he said softly. "Then let's enjoy ourselves."

Like a pig on a spit the man struggled, spitting out a tooth and swearing horribly.

"But you said you liked it rough. Changed your mind?"

"Stop," Sir Irwin wheezed. "Whoever she was, I'll pay."

"Nonsense, this is for free." Harry's fist slammed into him again. "You told me you like it when they fight. Well, I'm fighting. It's fun, isn't it? Mutual pleasure. I'm certainly enjoying this." He gripped him around the throat. "And now for the gelding . . . where's that knife of yours?"

Sir Irwin snarled and bucked. His thick fingers scrabbled at Harry's wrists.

"Stop, you fool, you can't kill him!"

For a moment Harry didn't register who it was. His rage was all but overpowering him. Dammit, he almost felt capable of going ahead and gelding, not just threatening. To let this lowlife live . . .

But it was Gabe, sweeping in the gate like a madman, shouting at the top of his lungs. The carriage horses reared and backed. Before Harry could respond he'd leapt from his horse and hauled Harry off Sir Irwin. Sir Irwin fell to his knees, gasping for breath, and Gabe hauled Harry away.

"Get off me you idiot," Harry snapped. "He's not dead."

"Not yet, but—"

More people poured in at the gate. Nash jumped off his horse, and grabbed Harry, too. And then—Harry blinked—of all people, Marcus.

"What the hell?" He flung off his brothers' restraining hands. "What the hell are you all doing here?" There were horses everywhere, servants opening the door again, passersby peering in at the gate. Sir Irwin, gasping for breath on the ground.

"Saving you from yourself," Gabe told him.

Sir Irwin hauled himself to his feet, scrabbling toward the carriage door. Harry lunged toward him but Gabe held him back. "Let him be."

"Much as you'd like to—much as he deserves it—you can't kill him," Nash added.

Harry stared at Nash as if he'd grown two heads. "I wasn't planning to."

Nash gestured to Harry's coat, which he now saw was covered with blood. "You're giving a damned good impression of it."

Harry made a disgusted noise. "Diplomats! It's just a little blood. I'm giving the swine the thrashing he deserves. And then I thought I'd geld him."

"Ware behind!" The shout from an unknown voice came from the steps.

Harry and Gabe, acting on instincts honed by years at war, ducked and whirled at the same time. A ball whizzed past Harry's ear. He heard an equine scream. Sabre reared and plunged. There was a thin line of blood on his horse's flank.

Sir Irwin had a pistol in each hand. He dropped the one he'd fired and transferred the other to his right hand.

"Where the hell did he get those?" Nash demanded, trying—to Harry's disgust—to shove Harry behind him.

"The carriage." Marcus was already moving toward Sir Irwin as he pointed the pistol at Harry. "Put it down," he commanded.

Sir Irwin raised the second pistol and pointed it at Harry. "You've ruined my teeth, you bastard. I'm going to kill you for that."

"You'll swing if you do," Marcus told him.

Sir Irwin's eyes flickered. "I was attacked for no reason. I have witnesses."

"I am the Earl of Alverleigh and a magistrate," Marcus said. "If you pull that trigger, I promise you, you'll swing."

"And before you swing, my brothers will geld you," Harry said.

The pistol wavered. "B-brothers?" Looking wildly from one to the other, Sir Irwin began to back away. "You won't get me, you won't. Stay back, stay back all of you." With the pistol trained on them he stumbled backward.

"I'm not letting him get away," Harry snarled and made a dive in his direction. Sir Irwin cursed and the pistol went off.

"Harry!" Gabe yelled.

Harry shook himself. "The bastard missed."

Sir Irwin shot out into the road. Harry raced after him.

There was a loud noise and an almighty scream.

"What the hell?" Harry skidded to a halt. A heavy coach was skewed across the road, the horses plunging and rearing. Harry dived for the leaders' heads, dragging them down, uttering soothing noises.

Gabe joined him in a flash and between them they managed to calm the horses. "What the hell happened?" he asked the coachman as soon as the horses were under control.

"It weren't my fault, sir," the coachman explained. "I never seen him coming. He just run out into the road. Is he dead?"

They looked. Sir Irwin lay still and glassy-eyed in the road, the lower half of his body a crushed mess. Dead indeed.

And gelded to boot. Poetic justice, thought Harry as he surveyed the mangled mess. He hadn't planned for the man to die but now he had . . . Nell would never have to risk running into the bastard again.

"Get his body off the road," Marcus ordered, marshaling the servants who had come to look.

While they were doing that, another servant, a man in a neat black suit came diffidently forward. He was leading Sabre. "Captain Morant?"

Harry turned. "Yes?"

"That's the fellow who shouted 'ware behind,'" Nash said.

Harry looked at the man with new interest. "Are you indeed? I have you to thank for my life then."

The man, who was about Harry's age, said, "No thanks necessary, sir. I don't hold with men shooting other men in the back. Especially when one is a brave officer and the other a . . ."

"Slug?"

The man grimaced. "He was that, sir, and more. I don't hold with the way he went on and the things he done."

"To women?"

"Yes, and to his own flesh and blood."

Harry frowned. "What do you mean, his own flesh and blood?"

"An old man come here once, with a baby, reckoning that Sir Irwin was the father—"

A baby? Harry was suddenly intent. He gripped the man's arm. "When was this? What happened to the baby?"

The man looked surprised. "My first week, sir. middle of October. He made me take the baby to this place—the kind of place I wouldn't keep a dog in, let alone your own flesh and blood! Made me sick to my stomach, it did, sir. I would've given me notice only jobs for old soldiers ain't too easy to come by."

"You have a new job as of now," Harry told him. "You're going to show me where you took that baby. Can you ride?"

He nodded eagerly. "That I can sir, as long as someone lends me a horse."

"Gabe, lend this fellow your horse," Harry said. Gabe whistled and his horse came trotting up.

"What's your name?" Harry asked.

"Evans, sir." He saluted.

Harry's brow rose. "What regiment were you in?"

Evans grinned. "Yours, sir. I was batman to Major Edwardes, until he was killed."

Harry clapped him on the shoulder. "Good man. Deal with all this, can you?" Harry said to Gabe, gesturing to the chaos. "Evans, here, who was poor Johnny Edwardes's batman, says an old man brought a baby here to Sir Irwin in October."

Gabe's face lit with understanding.

Harry shook his head, warning. "Whatever you do, don't tell Nell what I'm doing. It will kill her if it turns out to be another false hope."

"Go on," Gabe said. "We'll manage here. If a magistrate and a diplomat can't sort out this mess, I don't know who can."

"And what'll you do?" Harry asked as he mounted.

"Supervise the troops, what else? Now go, and good luck."

"*A* Mr. Ethan Delaney," the Alverleigh butler, Tymms, announced. Nell looked up with interest. This was Harry's friend and business partner.

A man of medium height, broad-shouldered, tough-looking, and with an attractively battered face entered the room. He was dressed with elegance, with a boldly embroidered waistcoat and gleaming high boots.

He bowed to Callie, saying in a soft Irish voice, "Princess Caroline." His gaze dropped to her waistline and the formality dropped as his dark face split in a broad grin. "Now, isn't that a fine sight to behold? Congratulations, ma'am, I'm sure Captain Gabe is as proud as punch."

Callie, smiling, came forward and gave Ethan her hand. "Mr. Delaney, and indeed I'm very pleased to see you, too."

He glanced around the room, saw Lady Gosforth and

bowed. "Lady Gosforth," he said with a smile. "I would ask how you were keeping, but I can see for meself you're looking splendid."

Lady Gosforth blushed slightly. She said in a caustic tone that fooled no one, "Mr. Delaney, I see you haven't given up your shocking propensity to flirt with old women."

"Now how would you know that when there's not an old woman in sight?" he responded promptly.

She sniffed, but her lips twitched.

Callie introduced Nell. The Irishman bowed. His eyes narrowed and then suddenly he smiled. "The lass from the cart." He recalled his surroundings and said with a smile, "If I'd realized Lady Helen and the lass from the cart were one and the same, I'd have understood everything a lot earlier."

To Nell's surprise, instead of merely shaking her hand, he kissed it with a simplicity than moved her. "I've been working at Firmin Court nigh on six weeks, m'lady, and have heard nothing but praise for Lady Nell from everyone on the estate. They're all waitin' for you to come home, where you belong."

Nell's eyes prickled. "Thank you, Mr. Delaney. I can't wait to go home and see them all, too."

His face crinkled in a smile. "As a matter of fact, at Harry's request, I've brought someone with me that you might be glad to see."

Nell gave him a puzzled look.

"She's tied to the banister outside," Ethan said.

Curious, Nell looked out of the door. A sudden commotion sounded in the hall: a dog yipping excitedly and scrabbling to be free.

"Freckles!" Nell cried and ran to greet her beloved dog.

Ethan glanced around the room a third time, as if expecting to see someone else.

"Will you take a seat, Mr. Delaney?" the princess asked.

Ethan hesitated. "I was hoping . . ."

"All the gentlemen have gone to London," Lady Gosforth told him.

"Indeed? A pity to have missed them," he said, still looking.

"She's in the maze, Mr. Delaney," Callie told him softly.

Ethan smiled. "You're a princess indeed, ma'am," he murmured and swiftly left the room.

*E*than stood facing the high wall of greenery, his heart beating as if he'd run a race. "Miss Tibby, are you in there?" he called.

There was no answer but he thought he heard a sound. "Tibby?"

"E-Ethan? Is that you, Ethan?"

"It is indeed."

"D-don't come in. I can't see you." She sounded slightly panicky.

He entered the maze, noting the direction of her voice. "But I've come all this way to see you. Don't you want to talk to me, Tibby?"

"No—y-yes, but not just now. I-I'm not ready," she wailed. "You're early."

Ethan smiled. "Only by a day." He hadn't been able to wait until Wednesday. He twisted and turned and doubled back. The fates were on his side. He found very few dead ends.

"You're not going to make me wait another day, are you, Tibby?"

"Oh. Oh no. I look a sight! Oh dear."

He turned a corner and there she was, sitting on a bench in the center of the maze, clutching a handful of letters to her breast. Her eyes were wet, and her hair was a mess. She hastily wiped her cheeks and straightened herself. She tried to hide the letters under her skirts.

Ethan recognized them. They were letters he'd written her. She'd been reading his letters and weeping over them.

"Why are you crying, Tibby?" he asked softly. "Is it me bad spelling? I've been working hard and my reading is as good as anyone's now, but spelling, well, spelling is a tricky thing indeed."

"No, of course not, Ethan," she said on a hiccup. "They're beautiful letters. All your letters are beautiful."

"So what's upsetting you?" he asked and sat down beside her and took her dainty little hand in his big, rough paw.

"Nothing, nothing at all," she said, scrubbing at her cheeks and trying to gather her composure. "In fact I-I am delighted at your news."

"Me news?"

She stared at him with large, drowned brown eyes. "You're getting married, aren't you? That's what you've come here for, isn't it? To invite me to the wedding."

"It is indeed," he said solemnly. "So, will you come?"

Her face quivered but she mastered herself and said firmly, "I would be honored. Wh-who is the bride?"

"Well, as to that, I haven't actually asked her, yet."

Tibby frowned. "Ethan, why are you hesitating? Because if it's some absurd notion of inferiority—"

Ethan sat beside her on the bench. "The thing is, Miss Tibby, I know I'm bog Irish by birth and I've led a rough life, and she's such a fine lady—"

"If you dare run yourself down again in my presence, Ethan Delaney, I—I'll—" As she looked up to give him what for, she broke off, realizing how very close he was.

Ethan didn't give her time to get anxious and send him away. He kissed her. Her mouth was soft and she tasted sweet, and flustered and female.

He drew her against him and kept kissing her. Her hands fluttered helplessly, then settled against his chest, and after a moment she started kissing him back, clumsily and with a total lack of expertise that just about melted his heart.

"That's it, me darlin'," he murmured. "Come to Ethan."

She pulled back. "Oh, Ethan, we mustn't. You're getting married."

"Yes, but only if you'll have me," he told her.

It took a moment for his words to sink in.

"You mean me?" she gasped. "You want to marry *me*?"

"Aye. 'Tis the dearest wish of me heart and has been for some time now."

"Me?"

He smiled. "If you'll have me."

"You know I'm thirty-six."

"And I'm nearly forty and this lovely thirty-six-year-old is the sum of all me dreams." He smoothed back her hair.

Her face crumpled. "Oh, I've never been called lovely in my life."

"You've been talking to the wrong people, then," he said simply. "Or maybe they've never looked into those beautiful brown eyes of yours. Or listened to you readin' a story by candlelight, and seen you when you look up and smile without thinkin'." He smoothed back her hair and kissed her again.

Tears spilled down her cheeks. "Oh, Ethan, you have such a gift with words." She straightened, trying to be sensible. "But what if I'm too old to have children."

He kissed her again. "Whether we have little ones or not is in the hands of God. Now, will you put me out of my misery and tell me yes or no."

She stared at him. "Of course it's yes!" she said. "A thousand times yes. Oh, Ethan, I never dreamed—" And she hurled herself into his arms and kissed him as if her life depended on it. Ethan's battered old heart nearly burst with love and pride.

By the time the kiss was finished, they were both breathing heavily and Tibby was seated on his lap.

"I can't wait to show you the cottage," he told her. "I've fixed it all up nice, like the one you had that burned down, but it's waiting for you to make it a home."

She nodded. "I'm a good housekeeper."

He gave her a quizzical look. "I'm not talkin' about housekeeping, darlin'. I'm talkin about a place a man can come home to and sit by the fire, with you readin' to me, or sewin', and then the two of us goin' up to bed and makin' the sort of love that'll melt your bones."

She sighed and hugged him harder.

"Some of the happiest evenings of me whole life were those ones we spent together last year, when young Nicky and Jim had gone to bed, and you'd be teachin' me and readin' to me from your books, and I'd sit there and watch your sweet face and dream you were mine."

"Oh, Ethan."

"The only part I didn't like was when I went to me own bed and you went to yours. I love you, Tibby, with all me heart."

Her eyes filled with tears. "Oh, Ethan, I never knew. Why didn't you say?"

"I had nothing to offer you then," he told her. "But now I have a cottage and I'm full partner with Harry—those Zindarian horses I'll be gettin' every year have made a big difference. So, now I'm in a position to ask you."

"I would have married you with nothing." And she kissed him again.

Ethan kissed her until they were both almost mindless with it and caressed her breasts through her dress. He ran his big, rough-skinned hands gently over her body and she shivered with pleasure. Still kissing her, he slid one hand slowly up between her silky soft thighs. She squeaked and gasped and wriggled a bit, but made no effort to stop him. She trembled and clung to him, kissing him feverishly.

And on a hard bench in the middle of a maze in December, Ethan brought Miss Tibby to her first-ever climax.

Afterward he held her on his lap, her small, delicate body curled into his.

"That was extraordinary," she said at last. "I never knew . . . I had no idea."

"The next time had better be in our marriage bed," he told her. "Otherwise I'm liable to lose me head and take you. And when I take you, Tibby, I want it to be in our own bed, in our own home."

"Oh yes, please, Ethan," she said. "I love you so much. I just never dreamed . . ."

Ethan kissed her again.

Seventeen

*E*vans led Harry into a part of London he'd never been to, down near the docks. The streets were narrow, full of ragged children, beggars, prostitutes, and filth. The buildings were old and crooked, as if grown like fungus instead of built by man; they were dingy and squalid and mean.

Harry had always hated cities and this seamy quarter was the best reason he'd seen yet for staying out of them. Dear Lord, how could people live like this?

And how could anyone bring a baby into this?

"Nasty place to live, it is, sir," Evans said, as if reading his mind. "My mam lives in Wales or I would have taken the little one to them. Fond of babes, is Mam. She had eight of us, you know."

He led them further into a network of intersecting streets and finally pointed down a narrow alleyway. "Down there," Evans said.

It was too narrow to accommodate a horse. "Wait here and mind the horses," Harry told him. "Which house?"

"The last one at the end, you can't go no further. Go in

and climb the stairs all the way to the top, and it's the green door." He gave Harry an ironic look. "Ask for 'Mother.'"

*T*he house stank. Trying not to breathe too deeply, he climbed the rickety stairs and knocked on the green door.

It opened a crack and an eye peered out at him. A voice said, "S'a gen'lman, mum."

"Lemme see."

A second eye replaced the first, then the door cracked open a foot. A gross, dirty woman in a low-cut dress looked him up and down. She tugged her bodice lower and eyed him knowingly. "And what can I do for you, me handsome?" She reeked of gin.

Harry's stomach churned. He said coldly, "I'm here to speak to 'Mother' about a baby."

The woman cackled. "Well, you've come to the right place, dearie. I'm Muvver. No shortage of babbies here." She stood back and waved him in.

The floor was covered in containers of all sorts: fish boxes, egg boxes, a lidless trunk, even a broken old drawer or two—anything that could be turned to use as a bed for a baby. The boxes were lined with straw. In every box lay an infant, sometimes two, laid head to tail.

Harry harnessed his rage. He was here for just one baby—Torie—but later, he would do something about this place.

"Which do you want, dearie? These ones is taken—their mas are out workin'." She made a ragged sweep with her arm.

No mother would choose to leave a child in these conditions unless they were desperate, Harry thought.

"Mother" pointed. "The orphans are through there. Take your pick."

Dear God, they were for sale?

He said stiffly, "I am looking for a baby girl brought here at the end of October. She was in a basket lined with white satin."

"Oh yes, I remember that basket. We don't have it no more."

A coldness ran down his spine. "You mean she died?"

The gross woman cackled as if he'd made a fine joke. "Lor' love you, sir. No, we sold the basket and 'er pretty clothes. The babby's through there." She pointed to the orphan section. "Tilda, show the gen'lman your little pet."

A young woman, a simpleton, led Harry to the other room. There were three boxes in the room.

"Them two's boys, and this one's me little pet," the girl said, and pointed.

She lay quietly in an egg box, wrapped in rags. All he could see in the gloom was her eyes watching him. He couldn't see what color they were, but Harry was suddenly sure what color those eyes would be—a clear sherry, just like her mother's.

Torie, at long last.

"She's me little pet, she is," the girl said. "Want a feed, lovie?" She gently scooped the infant from her nest of stinking straw, opened her bodice, and presented a swollen breast to the infant. She was none too clean and Harry's first thought was to stop her, but then he realized that this simple girl might be the reason Torie had survived these conditions.

Tilda rocked and crooned as Torie fed. "My own babby died, she did, but then this one come in, all clean and pretty. Me little pet, aren't you, lovie?"

Harry's gaze wandered to the other two boxes. Where had those two little scraps of unwanted humanity come from?

There but for the grace of God lay himself. Had Barrow not been unable to bear the sight of a small boy, neglected and abused, and taken him in, God only knew what might have become of him.

Harry waited until Torie drunk her fill. "I'll be taking her, now," he told the girl as she jiggled the baby against her shoulder. She looked distressed. "She'll be all right, I'm taking her back to her mother. But thank you for taking such good care of her."

He glanced at the two little figures in the other two boxes. "I'll give you five shillings now if you feed those two like you fed your little pet. And someone will come in a few weeks and give you a guinea if they're still alive. Can you do that for me, Tilda?"

She nodded and snatched the coins, looking furtively over her shoulder to the other room.

"Now wrap her up warmly for me, I'm taking her home."

Tilda nodded and wrapped Torie in some grimy rags. "She'll need her little dolly."

Harry frowned. "What little dolly?"

The girl pulled a small cloth doll from the baby's box. "It's hers, my little pet's."

"Very well." He shoved it in his pocket. "Now, give her to me." He carried her gingerly through to the other room. He'd never carried a baby before.

"You've got her, then," the woman called Mother said. She held out a grimy claw. "That'll be twenty quid."

"What?"

She shrugged and said like a horse dealer, "She's healthy and she's a good little thing, 'ardly ever cries, 'ardly ever have to give her a dose."

Harry frowned. "A dose?"

In answer the woman reached down beside her chair and lifted a blue bottle. "Blue ruin," she said with a grin of rotting stumps. "Better'n muvver's milk for keepin' a baby quiet." She uncorked the bottle. "Good for baby and good for me." She took a long swig, smacked her lips, and offered it to Harry.

He declined it with a shudder. He'd drunk blue ruin often enough in the back room at Jackson's boxing saloon.

He looked at the woman and shuddered again. Giving it to babies—ye gods!

He knew it was done. Some of the camp followers fed their babies a little gin or rum in the war to keep them quiet. But what people did in war was one thing. This was quite another.

"I'm not paying you a penny," he told the woman. "This child was stolen from her rightful mother and you were paid by a villain to take her. We're leaving."

Ignoring her indignant screech and the torrent of abuse that followed him down the stairs, he took Torie out into the cold December streets. He handed her to Evans, mounted Sabre and took her back. It was cold, too cold for a baby dressed in nothing but rags. He opened his coat and tucked Torie inside, carrying her in the crook of his arm.

"Come on, sweetheart, let's get you cleaned up."

It was too late to get back to Alverleigh tonight. Too late and too cold. "The nearest respectable inn," he told Evans.

*T*hey found an inn and Harry ordered a meal for himself and Evans to be served in an hour, and in the meantime for a small bath and warm water to be brought up to his room.

It was dark, but he sent Evans off to try to purchase clothes for a baby and anything else he thought Torie might need. Thank goodness for Mrs. Evans and her large brood.

He carefully laid Torie on the bed and began the process of unraveling the noisome rags she was wrapped in. The last few were stuck to her little body and when he tried to peel them off her, she cried. And cried. And cried.

It was a heartbreaking sound. Harry was frantic. He had no idea what to do. He picked her up carefully; without the bundled rags she was so tiny and fragile he was afraid of damaging her.

He scooped her up with one hand behind her neck, supporting her head, and held her against his shoulder the way he'd seen women do it. She howled miserably.

"There, there," he murmured, "it won't be so bad once you're all cleaned up and nice."

She continued howling. Harry paced up and down, feeling increasingly frantic.

A maidservant arrived with a small tin bath and a can of hot water. "Thank God," Harry greeted her with relief. He held the baby toward her. "She's crying. What do I do?"

The girl shrank back. "I don't know," she said. "I don't know nothing about babies." She dumped the bath in front of the fire, half filled it with water, and put the can beside it "She's probably just hungry."

"Hungry?" Harry said. "But she had a feed a couple of hours ago."

The girl gave him a pitying look. "She's a *baby*."

Harry felt like an idiot. Of course. Tiny growing creatures fed all the time. He knew that about puppies and foals, why hadn't he thought of that for Torie? "Milk," he told the girl. "Fetch some milk for her, immediately."

She gave a smirk and left.

Harry rubbed Torie's back soothingly. She kept yelling. "Dinner's coming now," he told her. "Won't be long."

The girl brought the milk back in a peculiar-shaped china receptacle, with a hole in one side and a nipple-shaped spout at the end with perforations in the end. It was warm.

"You're lucky Cook had this bottle," the maid said. "Somebody left it behind a few weeks ago."

He took it and carefully tried to apply the nipple to Torie's lips.

Nothing. She roared louder than ever.

"It's best if you're sitting," the girl advised.

He sat on the bed and cradled her in his arms, rocking and murmuring. He placed the china nipple against her mouth. She sobbed bitterly.

"Tip it up a bit," said the maid.

He tipped it so some of the milk splashed into her mouth. She kept crying, but the little mouth took in some of the milk. The rest dribbled down her chin. He gave her the bottle again, but she wagged her head, avoiding it, and sobbed.

"Used to the breast, I expect," the girl said. She was enjoying watching him flounder.

"I thought you didn't know anything about babies," Harry said accusingly.

"I don't," she said firmly and left.

He struggled on, holding her, rocking her, nudging her lips with the nipple, trying to coax her to drink, and finally persistence paid off. Torie's howls died a sudden death and she began to drink.

Relief swamped him. She drank a good amount of the milk in the container and when she subsided, he put it away.

"Now for your bath," he told her, and the moment he spoke, she started to wail again. He tried the milk, in case she was still hungry but she howled. He picked her up and started rubbing her back, to soothe her.

A violent burp erupted from the tiny body, and a trickle of sour milk ran down his coat. She stopped, and Harry held his breath, but then she looked at him and kept crying, though not so desperately.

Maybe the bath would help. Harry put his hand in the water. It was no longer hot, just a bit warmer than lukewarm. He was tempted to call the girl back and get some hot water, but Torie's sobs were killing him, so holding her carefully, he lowered her into the bath.

The howling abruptly stopped on a hiccup. Her eyes widened as if she were concentrating intensely on the sensation.

"Not used to water, are you?" he said.

She gave a little shuddery breath and moved her hands. Her tiny fingers opened and closed as if trying to grasp the water.

Harry chuckled and immediately she looked up at him. "You like water, don't you? Let's see if you like this." He swished her gently back and forth in the water and felt the tense little body relax.

She looked at him solemnly, a small angel, who'd never yelled blue murder in her life.

"I expect butter wouldn't melt in your mouth, either," Harry told her.

The water turned a dirty gray. Slowly the rags wrapped around her little hindquarters softened and he was able to peel them off her one by one. Her delicate skin was red where they'd stuck.

"You need some salve on that, you poor little mite." Harry wished Mrs. Barrow was here. She'd know what to do about that redness. He lifted her out of the dirty water, laid her on a towel, bolstered her with a couple of pillows, and rang for someone to remove the dirty water and rags.

He ordered a second bath and sent a message to the cook for a handful of salt and some almond or olive oil or goose grease.

He bathed Torie again in warm water with a little salt and she screwed up her face at first. He suspected it might sting a little so he swished her back and forth in the water to distract her. She loved it, kicking her little legs and gurgling with pleasure. He chuckled at the sound and again, she stared at him as if fascinated.

He washed her thoroughly, lifted her out, dried her, and lightly stroked almond oil over her skin. "That should help soothe you," he told her.

She watched his face intently. She had her mother's eyes. She was all Nell, he thought. Her mother's daughter, wholly and completely.

Evans wasn't back yet, so he wrapped her in a clean, dry towel, then slipped her into a pillow slip.

"Now, go to sleep, sweetheart," he told her and left her

to it. She took a deep breath, her face turned red and—
"Don't start again," he begged her. She looked at him with troubled eyes, her lips trembling.

"That's blackmail," Harry said severely.

She opened her mouth. He sighed and picked her up. She calmed immediately.

"That appalling woman told me you were a well-behaved young lady," he told her. "Of course, those weren't her exact words, but it's what she meant. How am I going to explain to your mother that you've picked up bad habits while you've been away?"

She sighed and watched him with big eyes. Nell's eyes.

He rocked her against his chest. "Your mother is going to be overjoyed to see you. She's been breaking her heart over you, young Torie, and I can see why. So it's going to be a big day tomorrow and you need plenty of sleep."

He placed her back on the bed in the nest of pillows. She immediately wailed. He picked her up and she stopped.

"All right, I'll hold you till you fall asleep." She fitted perfectly in the crook of his arm. "Sleep, do you understand, young lady? That's an order."

She watched him with wise little eyes and batted her small fist around. He'd never realized what a miracle a baby's hand could be; five little fingers, each with perfect miniscule fingernails. Her closed fist was like a little fern, ready to unfurl. He stroked it with his index finger, marveling at how big and coarse his hand looked by comparison.

Her tiny fist unfurled and five impossibly small fingers closed around his index finger and clung tightly. She gave a little sigh, the long lashes fluttered and she fell asleep, still clutching his finger.

Harry's chest felt thick and full.

The little scrap of humanity clung to his finger, claiming him. And Harry's heart was lost to her. Torie was his. Or rather, he was Torie's. For life.

Just like that, he had a daughter.

Evans returned forty-five minutes later and found Harry sitting on the bed. "I'm sorry, sir, I was only able to get some cloths—for the wetness, you know."

"Didn't you get any clothing? She's got none. I threw out the rags she was washed in. They need to be burned."

"I'll work out something, sir," Evans said. "And perhaps while I'm at it you'd like me to wash your shirt. And I'll take your coat. It's ruined, of course, but you'll need something to wear home, so I'll see if I can get it looking a bit more respectable."

Harry stared at him. "Evans, what did you do for Sir Irwin?"

"I was his valet, sir."

Harry grinned. "Excellent. In that case you may take my shirt and coat with my goodwill, and see what you can do with them. I've needed a valet for some time."

"Thank you, sir. You won't be sorry, sir."

"I'm no dandy," Harry warned him.

Evans tried to hide a smile. "Oh, I realize that, sir."

"Hmm," he said. "In the meantime, there's a pie there getting cold."

"Thank you, sir." Evans lifted the lid and saw that none of the food had been touched.

"Not hungry, sir?"

Harry shook his head. "Starved. But I can't move."

"Can't move, sir?" Evans looked concerned. "Did you hurt yourself?"

Harry looked sheepish. "No, but I've been captured," he admitted. He glanced down at the infant sleeping in the crook of one arm, still clutching a finger of the other. "I'm terrified she might wake up and set to howling the place down again. My daughter has a powerful set of lungs on her."

"*Your* daughter, sir? But I thought she was—"

"No," Harry said firmly. "She's mine. Her mother and I have been searching for her for weeks."

Evans's face cleared. "Then it was all a terrible mistake, sir?"

"That's right, Evans. A terrible mistake." There was no need for anyone to know any different. Harry looked down at the tiny scrap holding on so tenaciously. "But she's back where she belongs now, or she will be once she's in her mother's arms."

*H*e hired a chaise for the trip home; horseback would jolt Torie too much. Evans rode behind, leading Sabre.

He'd considered going shopping to buy a carry basket and baby clothes, but neither he nor Evans knew where such things could be purchased—in Evans's experience women made them—and in the end Harry decided it was more important to get Torie back to Nell. The most important things were napkins and milk, and Harry had stocked up on both.

So Torie came home to her mother dressed in several towels and a pillow case and she rode in Harry's arms. She seemed to like it there very well, gazing around her with bright, interested eyes, fingering the buttons on his coat and clinging firmly to his finger whenever he presented it.

When they turned into the drive at Alverleigh, she was sound asleep, tucked snug inside his coat. He'd stopped a few miles away and fed her and burped her and changed her napkin so she would be clean and content and ready to meet her mother. For a tiny scrap of perfection, she was able to make the most horrendous sounds and smells. The carriage pulled up and Harry climbed carefully down so as not to waken her.

Tymms opened the door and before he could say anything Harry shushed him with his finger. "Don't say anything to the others, just inform Lady Nell—discreetly—that a visitor—no, two visitors await her in the blue salon."

Tymms gave an impassive bow, dying of curiosity but too dignified to show it, and glided away.

Nell sat in the drawing room, trying her best not to fidget or pace. She fondled Freckles's ears absently. Harry had sent her Freckles. Why? Because he thought she would need comforting? She was pleased to have her dog, of course, but she hated being kept in the dark. She was worried sick about Harry. His brothers had all returned, and all that they would tell her was that Harry was all right and that he had business in London and would be back in time for the wedding.

They told her Sir Irwin had been crushed by a passing coach, and that she did not believe. It was a ridiculous tale.

They told her Harry was perfectly all right, but they'd brought Sabre home and he'd been grazed by a ball.

A *ball*. So there had been shooting.

They were telling her lies for her own sake. And it drove her mad. As if Harry, knowing how worried she was about him, would go off to London on business.

"Nell, dear, wouldn't you like to learn how to do this?" Aunt Maude said to her. She was teaching Callie and Tibby how to knit. "I know you're worried, my dear, but it helps to keep busy."

Nell shook her head. "I'm terrible at knitting." Knitting only served as a reminder.

Aunt Maude nodded and left her be.

Tymms silently entered the room and to Nell's surprise, came right up to her, bowed and said discreetly in her ear, "There are two visitors for you, m'lady, waiting in the blue salon."

"Two?" Nell jumped up and hurried out. Was it men come to tell her Harry was hurt, or worse? That sort always traveled in twos.

She pushed open the door to the blue salon. It was

Harry, standing with his back to the door, looking out the window.

"Harry." She flew across the room.

He turned and she skidded to a halt, seeing what he held in his arms.

"Shhh," he said softly. "Not so loud. You'll wake the baby." He smiled.

She stared, rooted to the spot. Stock-still. What was he doing with a baby? Where had he got it? And why?

A cold, sick feeling stole though her. Did he think that he could bring her a substitute for Torie? Did he understand so little how she felt?

She forced herself to speak. "I don't . . . I don't need . . ." She pointed at the baby, her hand shaking.

"It's Torie."

The words tore her fragile composure apart.

She shook her head. "Torie is dead. She died—"

"No," he said gently. "This is Torie. Your father took her to Sir Irwin."

She stared, trying to work out why he would say such a thing.

"I don't believe it. Why would he do such a thing?" she whispered.

"Because the law is that a baby belongs to its father. It's the same reason that Lord Quenborough dumped me on my father's steps that time—because I was his responsibility. This truly is Torie, your Torie."

Nell took a ragged inward breath. Her hand flew to her mouth. She started trembling. She couldn't take her eyes off the bundle in his arms. She didn't believe it, but oh . . . how she wanted to.

She couldn't bear to look, to experience again the pain she knew would come when she saw that this baby, like all the others, wasn't her daughter.

She couldn't bear not to.

She edged forward, one shaking hand outstretched, the

other clutched fearfully to her breast. It wasn't Torie, Torie was dead, she tried to tell herself, protect herself, to stifle the hope burgeoning within her.

Hope was the cruelest emotion.

The baby in Harry's arms stirred and yawned mightily. She opened her eyes and looked at her mother.

And Nell saw her own mother's remembered eyes, saw her father's brow, saw—

"Oh God, it's Torie," she sobbed and lifted her daughter from Harry's arms. She laid her face against Torie's soft little neck and breathed her in. Her baby, her daughter, her Torie.

"Torie, oh, Torie." Trembling violently, she sank down on the sofa cradling her precious burden, rocking her, weeping.

She smoothed shaking fingers over Torie's face, remembering the delicate whorls of her ears, the soft golden fuzz.

Something dropped out of the fold of the towel. A small rag doll.

Nell stared. "Oh my God. What is that?"

Harry bent and picked it up. "Just a doll the girl gave me. She said it was Torie's, but it's noth—"

"Turn it upside down," Nell whispered.

Harry turned the little rag doll upside down and as the skirt fell down, another head appeared. "Very curious," he said.

"It's a Cinderella doll. I made it for her before she was born," she whispered. "Just like the one Mama made for me. I'd forgotten all about it. Papa must have taken it, too. She truly is my very own Torie." She buried her face in her baby again.

Torie clutched Nell's hair and pulled. "Look how strong you've grown, my darling," Nell said, laughing and sobbing at the same time.

Harry carefully untangled the little fingers from Nell's hair and sat down, his arm around Nell, around both of them. It felt so right, so perfect.

She looked up at him, trying to find words for something for which there were no words, and saw that his eyes were wet, too. It would take a lifetime.

He held her, watching silently as she examined every inch of Torie, marveling at the changes and trying to cope with the floods of emotion. So many weeks of aching and grieving and now Torie was back in her arms.

"Isn't she beautiful, Harry?" she sobbed. "I told you she was beautiful."

"Of course she's beautiful," he told her, his voice hoarse with emotion. "She takes after her mother."

*T*he door opened and Aunt Maude looked in. "Nell, are you all—" She broke off. "Oh . . . oh, my dear . . ."

"I have my Torie back, Aunt Maude," Nell said mistily. "Harry found her for me. He promised he would and he did."

Aunt Maude tiptoed over and gazed at the baby. And gooed, and cooed. And then frowned. "Have you dressed my great-niece in a pillowcase, Harry Morant?"

Harry shrugged. "She hasn't got any clothes," he confessed. "But she doesn't mind, do you, sweetheart? She likes wearing towels and a pillowcase." He tickled Torie, who scrabbled happily at his hands.

"Towels and a pillowcase?" his aunt exclaimed in quiet horror. "You've dressed that poor infant in towels and a pillowcase? Wait here." Aunt Maude swept from the room.

She returned a few minutes later carrying a large basket. Nell recognized it from the journey from Bath. She dumped it on a table and ordered, "Bring that child over here."

Nell brought her and watched, astounded, as Lady Gosforth brought out tiny white garment after tiny white garment. There were dresses, vests, bootees, caps, tiny mittens, shawls, and blankets, all exquisitely made. Some were even lined with silk. "Where did you get all these from?" Nell asked, half knowing the answer already.

"I told you I had to keep busy," Lady Gosforth told her quietly, with a look. "I knew there would be a use for them one day, and now, here is Torie to make it all worthwhile." She caressed the soft little cheek gently. "Now let's get her into some pretty clothes and take her to meet the rest of her family."

*A*fter supper Harry found his brother Marcus standing staring down at Torie in the cradle he'd had fetched from the attic.

Harry squared his shoulders. He'd come to swallow his pride and thank his brother. Within two hours of Torie's arrival at Alverleigh, Marcus had found a wet nurse, a healthy, sweet-tempered young woman of the estate who had a babe of her own and milk to spare.

As Harry entered the room, Marcus looked up with a sheepish expression. Harry soon saw why. Torie was staring up at the earl with her wise little eyes, gripping his finger in a hold Harry knew well.

Her other fist waved aimlessly in the air. Harry caught it and went to tuck it back under the blankets, but Torie grabbed a finger and held on. She had them both, now.

"Got a grip on her like a little wrestler," Marcus said softly.

"I know," Harry said.

"Every time I try to pull away from her, she screws up her little face and gets ready to cry," Marcus told him.

"I know," Harry said.

The two men stood on either side of the cradle, caught by two tiny hands. For a long moment neither of them spoke. Then Marcus said, "I'm sorry about the way we treated you at school."

Harry said nothing.

"And I'm sorry for what happened that time on the steps of Alverleigh house," Marcus continued. "Father was wrong to treat you like that. Nash and I argued with him about it inside. But he was adamant."

Harry swallowed.

"He was a hard man, our father," Marcus told Harry. "I'm sorry."

And with those few, simple, unambiguous words the animosity of years began to drain from Harry's heart.

"Thank you for arranging the wet nurse," he said. And Marcus knew what he meant. They were both men of few words. They were brothers, after all.

Eighteen

The wedding was held on Christmas Eve and, as promised, it was small, private, and very beautiful.

The ancient Alverleigh family chapel was filled with flowers grown in the estate greenhouses: amaryllis, white narcissi, hellebores, and bright poinsettias.

An organ played quietly as the guests seated themselves on oak pews polished to silk by age and beeswax.

It was a family wedding, but the Renfrews were a large family. The church was full of well-wishers. Aunt Maude sat in the front row, a wisp of lace held at the ready. Tibby and Ethan sat together, holding hands in secret. Tibby's eyes were glowing. Nash sat with Aunt Maude, and Rafe and Luke with Harry's beloved foster parents, Barrow and Mrs. Barrow. Mrs. Barrow and Nell's old nurse, Aggie, were cooing over Torie while her wet nurse waited by. Freckles sat by the church door, freshly brushed by a prince of Zindaria and wearing a festive red ribbon around her neck.

Harry stood at the altar with his brother Gabe.

The music swelled into the bridal march and Nell walked down the aisle on Marcus's arm. She was dressed in an exquisite cream silk-and-velvet dress trimmed with peach and green. She carried a huge bouquet of creamy orchids and wore a single orchid in her hair.

Harry felt his heart swell.

Princess Callie attended her, glowing in a gown of emerald green velvet and wearing her mother's tiara. She was escorted by two small, solemn boys wearing Royal Zindarian uniforms.

Nell had eyes only for Harry as she walked slowly down the aisle. She took his hand, smiling mistily, and turned to face the minister.

"Reverend Pigeon," she gasped. It was her own parish vicar, the dear, gentle old man who'd baptized her and seen her through so many trials. Tears rolled down her face but she didn't care.

Neither did Harry; she was his bride, his lady, his madonna, and she glowed like a pearl against the dark beauty of the ancient church.

*A*s they walked back from the chapel to the house, Barrow came up beside Harry. "If you don't mind, lad, me and the missus won't stay for Christmas."

"Is there a problem?" Harry asked.

"No, no, everyone has been very kind. No, it's them little lads. Not Nicky and Jim, I mean the two wee babes you mentioned when you told us how you got young Torie back. It's affected the missus powerful bad. She was up half the night frettin' about them. So we thought, if you don't mind, we'd borrow young Evans and go to London and fetch them."

"Fetch them?"

"Aye," Barrow said. "About time we had some young life around the Grange again. What with you and Mr. Gabe all grown up, and then Nicky and young Jim livin' away in Zindaria, the place has been powerful quiet. Got on her nerves, it has. Moping around the place with nothing to do."

Harry repressed a smile. As if keeping house for her husband and a dozen grooms was nothing to do.

"But with a couple of little 'uns to raise, now, that's the kind of thing that perks Mrs. B. right up," Barrow finished.

Harry nodded. Mrs. Barrow's capacious bosom overflowed with maternal love. Harry had benefited from it himself, as had Gabe and, for a while, young Nicky and Jim. The idea of her fretting over the two orphan baby boys he'd mentioned didn't surprise him at all.

"Yes, of course you can take Evans. And Rafe and Luke are going back to London for Christmas—take them with you. And I'll give you some money for the girl called Tilda."

"Actually, Mrs. B had an idea about that lass, too."

"Who, Tilda?"

Barrow nodded. "A lass like that, with only a few candles in her brainbox, is easily led astray, but under my good lady's wing, well, she'd learn how to live right. We'd protect her from them who prey on simple young women. She could give Mrs. B. a hand with the young 'uns, if you have no objection, that is."

Harry grinned. "No objection at all. That girl saved Torie's life."

"We'll be off tomorrow then," Barrow said.

"Godspeed." Harry embraced his foster father. "And for heaven's sake don't let Mrs. Barrow go inside that house . . . not unless you want to see her swing for murder."

"Rafael, my dear boy," Lady Gosforth said as the wedding party sat down to dine. "I've seated you with a friend of mine, Lady Cleeve. Look after her, will you? She doesn't know many people."

Rafe looked across at Lady Cleeve, an elderly lady with

white hair. He masked his disappointment and bowed gracefully. "I'd be delighted, Lady Gosforth."

She laid a hand on his arm to detain him a moment. "You're a good boy, Rafe," she said. "Ask my friend about her long-lost granddaughter. I think you'll find it an interesting tale . . ."

*T*he wedding celebrations had been going on for some time when suddenly there was a commotion on the terrace outside. Shod hoofs rang on the paving stones. The guests turned curiously toward the windows.

Showing no sign of alarm the Earl of Alverleigh signaled servants to draw back the curtains. Three large dark horsemen stood silhouetted against the gray afternoon sky. To everyone's surprise, the earl ordered the French windows opened, despite the cold.

There was a buzz of surprise among the crowd: the horsemen wore black masks to conceal their faces. Apparently unworried the earl stepped forward. "Who are you and what do you want here?"

The masked man in the center replied. "I am Not-So-Young O'Lochinvar, and I've come for Fair Tibby."

A ripple of amusement and speculation passed through the spectators as Tibby slipped through the crowd and stared up in amazement at the horseman. "Who did you say you were?"

"Not-So-Young O'Lochinvar," he answered in soft Irish burr. "Fair Tibby, will you come away wi' me?"

Her eyes widened. "Now?" She glanced down at her soft wool dress. It had been snowing earlier.

"Aye, now," he said, and as if at a signal his two tall companions dismounted. He passed one a bundle, and the man shook it out. It was a long, crimson, fur-lined cloak. He wrapped it around Tibby's shoulders.

" 'Tis only rabbit, but ye'll not be cold," O'Lochinvar told her. "So will you come, Fair Tibby?"

She looked up at him, her heart so full she was unable to speak, and nodded.

Without another word the two men lifted Tibby up in front of O'Lochinvar. He had a cushion tied to his saddle. "It won't be as uncomfortable as last time," he murmured, wrapping his strong arm around her. Tibby didn't care. She would have gone anywhere with him.

"Fare thee well," O'Lochinvar addressed the watching party. "And fear not," he added, looking straight at Princess Callie. "Fair Tibby is safe with me. You're all invited to the weddin'." And he galloped away with her to the west.

"Oh, Ethan," Tibby said when she could finally speak. "That was wonderful."

"You don't want to go back?"

She shook her head. A few flakes of snow floated down.

"I've bespoken two rooms at the inn in the next town," Ethan told her. "If you want, I can hire a maid to play propriety."

She turned her head and looked up at him. "No maid," she said firmly.

He smiled and tightened his grip. They rode on into the darkening night.

"Ethan, are you a rich man?" Tibby asked him after a few minutes.

His white teeth flashed and he said in an easy voice, "No, darlin', I'm not. Does it matter?"

"Yes," she said. "It does matter. Very much."

He looked down at her in faint consternation. "It does?"

She nodded solemnly. "If you're not a rich man, it changes everything."

"What? But you knew—"

Tibby continued, "We cannot afford to waste good money on a second room. One should do us both nicely."

* * *

*I*t was Christmas Eve. Nell woke in the night and found Harry awake, propped on his elbow, watching her.

"What's the matter?" she asked, sitting up. "Is it Torie?"

"No, no, she's sound asleep in her cradle, there," he said soothingly. Nell wasn't yet able to let Torie out of her sight.

"It's nothing. Go back to sleep." He lay down again. His arm slipped around her, drawing her against him in that beloved, familiar way, and she closed her eyes and thought no more of it.

But an hour later she woke again, and found him still awake and staring down at her.

"What is it, Harry?" she whispered.

He didn't say a word. The tendrils of sleep were trying to drag her back, but the expression in his eyes caught her and held her fast. She sat up on her elbow and put a hand to his cheek. "You look so grim. What is it?"

He didn't answer.

Her anxiety grew. "Has something happened, Harry? Tell me. Whatever it is, we will weather it."

"Nothing's wrong."

She scanned his face worriedly. "Something must be bothering you, otherwise why can't you sleep?"

He stared down at her for a long, intense moment, then gave a low, deep groan. "I love you," he said.

She sat up. "What did you say?" she asked breathlessly.

"I love you, Nell." He wrapped his arms around her and pulled her hard against him, clutching her so tightly the breath was almost squeezed from her lungs. "I love you so much."

"I thought—" she began.

"I think I fell in love with you that first day in the forest, but I didn't believe . . . didn't think . . ." His embrace tightened. "I couldn't tell you then; you would have thought me insane."

"No, I—"

"And then I kidnapped you and trapped you into marriage." He shook his head. "I was so arrogant, so certain I could do what I promised . . ."

He fell silent. She wasn't sure what he was thinking, but she didn't interrupt.

"And then we didn't find her," he said. "And I'd trapped you with false promises."

"No, I—"

"But then I did find Torie, and I made it right, so now I can tell you."

"Tell me what?" She knew, but she'd ached to hear it for so long and needed to hear him say it again.

"That I love you. That you are my heart, my life." He wrapped his arms around and pulled her hard against him, clutching her so tightly the breath was almost squeezed from her lungs. "I love you, Nell Morant. Don't ever leave me."

"Never," she whispered. "Never, my love. I love you, Harry Morant. First you captured my body, then you stole my heart. I am yours forever, body and soul."

Author Note

I have taken a few liberties with the details of the foundling hospital process. They had stopped accepting tokens from mothers more than fifty years before my story starts, and the items were stored in envelopes, not in a box with tags. But I was so moved by the tokens when I saw them in the Foundling Museum that I couldn't resist using them in my story. I suspect it was also easier for my characters to get information from the director than it probably would have been; however, I ascribe that to Harry's commanding ways. Exceptions are often made to rules.

If you are visiting London, the Foundling Museum is well worth a visit, and very easy to get to by the Tube. There is also more information on my website: www.annegracie.com.

"What a remarkable writer [Anne Gracie] is. I can't think of another writer who seamlessly combines quite as she does the most sparkling comedy with such heartbreaking emotion."
—Anna Campbell, author of *Untouched*

Look for the next book in the Devil Rider's series by Anne Gracie.

Coming Fall 2009 from Berkley Sensation!

Enter the rich world of historical romance with Berkley Books.

Lynn Kurland

Patricia Potter

Betina Krahn

Jodi Thomas

Anne Gracie

Love is timeless.
penguin.com

M9G0907

Discover Romance

berkleyjoveauthors.com
See what's coming
up next from your
favorite romance
authors and
explore all
the latest
Berkley,
Jove, and
Sensation
selections.

Fall in love

- See what's new
- Find author appearances
- Win fantastic prizes
- Get reading recommendations
- Chat with authors and other fans
- Read interviews with authors you love

berkleyjoveauthors.com

M1G0907